Subjects of Affection

Rethinking the Early Modern

Series Editors

Marcus Keller

Ellen McClure

Feisal Mohamed

Subjects of Affection

Rights of Resistance on the Early Modern French Stage

Anna Rosensweig

Northwestern University Press
Evanston, Illinois

Northwestern University Press
www.nupress.northwestern.edu

Printed in the United States of America

10 9 8 7 6 5 4 3 2 1

ISBN 978-0-8101-4446-0 (cloth)
ISBN 978-0-8101-4445-3 (paper)
ISBN 978-0-8101-4447-7 (e-book)

Cataloging-in-Publication data are available from the Library of Congress.

CONTENTS

Acknowledgments vii

Note on Translations xi

Introduction
The Right of Resistance 3

Chapter One
Affective Evidence 21

Chapter Two
The Mourner 55

Chapter Three
The Rebel 91

Chapter Four
The Hero 123

Chapter Five
The Savior 159

Conclusion
The Subject of Rights 185

Notes 191

Bibliography 217

Index 227

ACKNOWLEDGMENTS

A central argument of this book is that what often seems to be an individual endeavor is, in fact, collective. This book simply would not exist were it not for the contributions of others. My first thanks go to Juliette Cherbuliez, whose graduate seminar on early modern tragedy at the University of Minnesota introduced me to the period and the genre. The seminar paper I wrote for that class contained the initial idea for what eventually became my dissertation and has now become this book. Conversations with Juliette have shaped my thinking in countless ways. I am so grateful for her advice and friendship, her intellectual rigor and generosity, and her provocations to write—and rewrite.

I am grateful to the members of my dissertation committee at the University of Minnesota: Daniel Brewer, Mária Brewer, Nancy Luxon, J. B. Shank, and Margaret Werry. Individually and collectively, they have offered much guidance and support. Work on my dissertation was greatly facilitated by a doctoral dissertation fellowship from the University of Minnesota and a Charlotte W. Newcombe Fellowship from the Woodrow Wilson Foundation.

During my graduate studies, I had the good fortune to attend Bonnie Honig's seminar, "Antigone in Contexts: Humanism and the Challenges of Democratic Theory," at the Cornell School of Criticism and Theory, which helped me begin to articulate the interdisciplinary stakes of my project. I am grateful to Bonnie for her work and her example, as well as for fostering such a lively community. I am also grateful to colleagues from that seminar, especially Glenn Mackin and Stephanie Youngblood, for all their insight and good cheer.

I conducted much of the research for chapter 1 of this book as a Provost's Postdoctoral Scholar at the University of Southern California (USC). Natania Meeker and Antónia Szabari welcomed me to the Department of French and Italian at USC, helped me navigate Los Angeles, read drafts of my work, and shared ideas over innumerable cups of coffee. I am honored to have been their colleague. I am also thankful to have been part of a writing group with Carrie Hyde and Anna Krakus, which began during those years in Los Angeles. And I thank Jessica Rosenberg and Matthew Goldmark for being excellent travel companions and for their general camaraderie.

At the University of Rochester, I thank the faculty, staff, and students in the Department of Modern Languages and Cultures, the Graduate Program in Visual and Cultural Studies, and the Susan B. Anthony Institute for Gender, Sexuality, and Women's Studies for all their support and encouragement. Special thanks to Hsin-Yun Cheng, Carrie Heusinkveld, June Hwang, Ryan Prendergast, and Chenchen Yan, who read drafts of chapters and patiently talked through ideas. A semester-long fellowship at the University of Rochester's Humanities Center provided space and time to think and write. I thank Joanie Rubin for championing these fellowships for junior faculty at Rochester. I am also thankful to Joanie for facilitating a manuscript workshop that allowed me to get timely and concentrated feedback from senior scholars in my field. Katherine Ibbett, Ellen McClure, and Phillip John Usher made time in their very full schedules to read my manuscript, travel to Rochester, and spend two days offering their insight and advice. I thank them for being so generous with their time and ideas, and for their many other acts of collegiality and kindness.

One of the best parts of studying early modern France is the vibrant intellectual community at SE17, the North American Society for Seventeenth-Century French Literature (NASSCFL), and beyond. I am especially grateful to Faith Beasley, Hélène Bilis, Elizabeth Black, Jean-Vincent Blanchard, Hall Bjørnstad, Alison Calhoun, Andrea Frisch, Claire Goldstein, Sylvaine Guyot, Larry Kritzman, Michael Meere, Jennifer Row, Christophe Schuwey, Jennifer Tamas, Anne Theobald, Ellen Welch, Toby Wikström, and Kathleen Wine for being such wonderful friends, mentors, and collaborators. Special thanks to Kathrina LaPorta and Ashley Williard for reading chapters and providing feedback at crucial moments.

Joy Palacios has read countless pages of my writing over the past few years. I am so grateful for her keen observations throughout our writing exchanges, as well as for her friendship.

Kelly Condit-Shrestha, writing partner par excellence since graduate school, has witnessed much of this long journey.

Josh Boydston and Danielle Genevro helped immensely with copyediting and formatting and Lia Swoope Mitchell provided invaluable assistance with translations. I thank them for the great care they put into their work.

Many thanks to Ellen McClure, Elissa Park, Trevor Perri, Maia Rigas, Patrick Samuel, Anne Strother, and everyone at Northwestern University Press. I am also grateful to the two anonymous reviewers whose thoughtful reading of the manuscript helped me to strengthen its arguments. I thank *Renaissance Drama* for permission to reprint in revised form sections of chapter 4, which initially appeared in my article "Closed Heart, Open Secret: Exposing Private Liberty in Pierre Corneille's Last Tragedy," *Renaissance Drama* 46, no. 2 (2018): 231–52.

Friends and family have helped this book become a thing in the world. I thank my parents and siblings for all of their love and support.

Hélène Brown and Randi Browning have been exemplary teachers and confidantes. I cannot thank them enough.

My Minneapolis people, Greta Bliss, Laura Burch, Rachel Gibson, Rebecca Halat, Anaïs Nony, Mira Reinberg, Adair Rounthwaite, and Tracy Rutler. In many ways my heart belongs to our time together in that city.

Joel Burges, Lisa Cerami, Josh Dubler, Kristin Doughty, Rachel Haidu, and Kate Mariner are the best friends and colleagues a person could wish for. I thank them for everything.

Athene Goldstein welcomed me to Rochester and helped make it home.

My therapists, Carol and Sheila, helped me work through periods when writing felt impossible.

And finally, I thank John Komdat, whose daily acts of love have sustained this project, and Sadie, whose imminent arrival helped me finish it up. This book is dedicated to them.

NOTE ON TRANSLATIONS

Primary sources are cited in French and accompanied by an English translation. When selecting translations, I endeavored to balance accessibility with a desire to retain the source's polyvalence and ambiguity. I have in a few cases modified published translations or provided my own. When citing early modern texts, I have largely preserved the original spelling, punctuation, syntax, and capitalization. Throughout the book there is some variation in the spelling of character names. I have retained French spelling in direct quotations (Athalie, Cornélie, Pompée), but use English spelling for characters drawn from history who appear in multiple sources (Athaliah, Cornelia, Pompey).

Subjects of Affection

INTRODUCTION

The Right of Resistance

In August 1572, French Huguenots traveled to Paris for the wedding of Marguerite de Valois and Henri de Navarre. A marriage of political design, the union between Marguerite and Henri was supposed to bind together two royal families: Marguerite was the sister of the young French king Charles IX, and Henri had recently succeeded his mother to the throne of Navarre. As the wedding approached, the royal family and their allies also claimed that the marriage would promote peace between factions of Roman Catholics and Huguenots, whose conflicts had since 1562 caused widespread death and destruction. The Valois-Navarre union was promoted as an event that would encourage affection, if not necessarily between the bride and groom, then between the royal family and the Huguenots, and thus throughout France as a whole.[1]

Instead of fostering affection between Catholics and Huguenots, the Valois-Navarre marriage set the stage for one of the most violent events of the French religious wars: the St. Bartholomew's Day Massacre. On August 21, 1572, an assassination attempt against the Huguenots' most prominent leader, the Admiral Gaspard de Coligny, heightened tensions between Catholic and Huguenot factions in Paris. Two nights later, on the eve of the feast of St. Bartholomew, violence engulfed the city, as Huguenot leaders and followers alike were targeted and killed. The conflict quickly spread from the capital to other French cities, leading to the death of thousands of Huguenots and reigniting war.[2]

The historical record remains unclear about exactly who or what caused the St. Bartholomew's Day Massacre. Although Charles IX initially denied any involvement in Coligny's death, the king quickly reversed course, stating that he had in fact ordered the assassination because the admiral had been plotting a seditious coup. Many contemporaneous reports blame Charles IX for ordering the death of Protestant leaders. However, Charles IX had a reputation for being inconstant and suggestible, which led many to speculate about which players in the king's inner circle might have pushed the young king to make such an order. Some blamed his mother, the powerful Catherine de Medici. Others blamed members of the Guise family, prominent Catholic nobles known to exercise formidable influence at court. Contemporaneous accounts also raised the possibility that the massacre was not caused by royal directive. Perhaps, they suggested, Catherine de Medici or one of the Guise organized the massacre without the king's blessing. Or perhaps the violence originated with the people of Paris, as a result of heightened tensions in the capital.[3] Together, these competing accounts create an "epistemic murk" that surrounds the massacre's origins.[4]

At the heart of the epistemic murk surrounding the St. Bartholomew's Day massacre is the question of political affection. Although the royal family had claimed to love their Huguenot subjects, many doubted whether those claims had been sincere. Some sixteenth-century accounts argued that the marriage of Henri and Marguerite was not designed to foster affection between the royal family and the Huguenots, or between Catholic and Huguenot factions, but was instead a trap designed to lure Huguenots to Paris and, ultimately, to their deaths. Those attempting to come to terms with the massacre had to confront the particular difficulty of judging royal intent through royal expressions or assurances of emotion. The king may say he loves you and mean something else entirely.[5]

This book argues that the promise of affection between the royal family and their subjects is crucial to understanding the theories of resistance that were elaborated in the massacre's aftermath. Theologians and political philosophers from the Catholic and Protestant sides of the confessional divide had considered when and how subjects might legitimately resist their king since the outbreak of religious tensions in France well before the St. Bartholomew's Day Massacre.[6] In the wake of this event, however, this question of legitimate resistance became increasingly urgent. As I will explain in more detail below, the *droit de résistance*, or right of resistance, is largely thought to have disappeared from French political thought in the aftermath of the religious wars, as an absolutist theory of monarchical power gained prominence, making claims of tyranny more difficult to advance.[7] I contend, however, that the conceptual framework of the droit de résistance endured throughout the seventeenth century. I suggest further that recognizing the endurance of the droit de résistance makes this early modern concept available to more recent discussions about the modern subject of rights and contemporary political subjectivity more broadly.

This study demonstrates how the droit de résistance persists during the seventeenth century by broadening our understanding of this concept's relationship to literary form. Intellectual historians have tended to locate the droit de résistance in political treatises.[8] These texts are an important part of the story, but only a part. I argue that tragic drama provides a robust consideration of the droit de résistance during the religious wars and sustains the conceptual framework of this right during the wars' long aftermath. As I will show, French tragedy vividly depicts the embodied, affective qualities of early modern political subjectivity, qualities that are crucial to understanding early modern resistance theory. While attending to the specificities of resistance treatises and tragedies as forms of political writing, I also explore how reading these forms together brings into sharper focus their political implications. In the introductory pages that follow, I provide an overview of the droit de résistance and its attendant questions as theorized in treatises during the religious wars. I then canvas how tragic drama from the sixteenth and seventeenth centuries takes up this concept, often reimagining its limits and possibilities.

Theories of Resistance

During the sixteenth-century religious wars, theories of resistance proliferated as the conflicts strained notions of France as a unified spiritual and political community. Theorizing resistance was primarily a Huguenot endeavor during the first decade of the religious wars, becoming especially urgent after the St. Bartholomew's Day Massacre in 1572. Shifts in the political landscape during the 1580s then led some Catholic factions to advance many of these tenets of resistance. Ideas that Catholics had previously deemed heretical and seditious began to appear in texts concerned with Catholic survival when staunchly anti-Huguenot factions were frustrated with what they perceived as the more conciliatory approach of the Valois monarchy and the moderate Catholic factions.[9] In addition, Catholic theories of resistance became more salient as the Valois monarchy failed to produce an heir and as the idea that the Protestant Henri de Navarre might succeed Henri III to the throne seemed more and more possible.

The most well-known Huguenot resistance treatises—François Hotman's *Francogallia* (1573), Théodore de Bèze's *Du droit des magistrats sur leurs subjets* (1574), and the anonymously published *Vindiciae contra tyrannos* (1579; hereafter *Vindiciae*)—largely avoid making explicit reference to the events of the religious wars. Instead, these texts take a more theoretical tack, drawing their justifications for resistance from ancient and biblical sources rather than current events.[10] In so doing, the treatises present their ideas about legitimate resistance as universally acknowledged rather than as polemical, even though they clearly carry a partisan charge. This rhetorical strategy allows the treatises to link common ideas about monarchical power and good government during this period with a radical justification of resistance.

During the sixteenth century, royal power was not thought to be absolute. Kings, like all humans, were considered fallible and thus susceptible to falling sway to the excesses of passions such as anger or greed. Good kings were those able to resist these excesses and thus to rule on behalf of the common good, rather than in their own interest. Kings who succumbed to their passions, however, could be labeled tyrants. The distinction between kings and tyrants was crucial, because, while subjects had a duty to obey their king, many held that they also had a right to resist a tyrant. Whereas this right was widely recognized, its limits and possibilities were subjects of much contention. Questions such as "Can anyone recognize tyranny?" and "What means of resistance are legitimate?" preoccupied those on both sides of the confessional divide.

The *Francogallia*, *Du droit des magistrats sur leurs subjets*, and the *Vindiciae* approached these questions by grounding their theory of resistance in two key concepts: liberty of conscience and popular sovereignty. Liberty of conscience had become an especially important idea during the first half of the sixteenth century, as the Reformation spread through France and as Protestants began to grapple with how they might maintain their faith while living under Catholic rule. Following Martin Luther and John Calvin, many Protestants figured their hearts and minds as spaces of private liberty that were to remain free from monarchical rule. Liberty of conscience served not only as a shelter of faith but also as the means through which subjects could identify tyranny. A king who attempted to impose his will on a subject's heart, mind, or spirit was not a true king but a tyrant.[11]

Huguenot resistance treatises held that all subjects could recognize tyranny, but they drew a distinction between those who could actively resist a tyrant and those who could not. Private subjects, or *particuliers*, could recognize tyranny, but only those who had a public function, or *personnes publiques*, could organize active resistance to tyranny. When faced with tyranny, particuliers had three options: they could flee, suffer in silence, or appeal to a personne publique. Who counted as a personne publique varied among (and within) resistance treatises. In general, personnes publiques were nobles, legislators, magistrates, and others with some representative role.

When organizing resistance, personnes publiques acted on behalf of the people as a whole in defense of popular sovereignty. Resistance treatises stipulated that God had vested political authority in the people rather than in the king. The primary political relationship was thus not between God and the king, as theories of absolutism would later maintain, but rather between God and the people.[12] Drawing from ancient and biblical sources, the treatises argued that power flowed from God to the people, who then appointed or elected a king to govern them. *Du droit des magistrats*, for example, notes how the biblical King David, recognizing that power passed from God to the people and from the people to kings, did not take power until he had received divine and popular approval: "Il ne fait pas un pas pour approcher du throne Roial, que Dieu ne l'y pousse, & que le consentement du peuple ne l'appelle" (he did not even stir a foot to seize the royal palace except in so far as God Himself caused him to advance and he was called by the unanimous consent of the people).[13] In this scenario, the king's power depends on the force of God and the will of people.

Huguenot resistance treatises relied on the principle of popular sovereignty to make a coherent case for legitimate opposition to monarchical power, but these treatises were not democratic. By drawing a distinction between particuliers and personnes publiques, these treatises distributed power differentially rather than equally among all subjects. In so doing, the treatises participated in a wider aristocratic ethos of sixteenth-century France that placed a high value on nobility. Noble status not only conferred on an individual a relatively privileged position within the social order, but this status also carried certain responsibilities, such as that of protecting the public good from tyranny.[14]

While acknowledging the emphasis placed on nobility within sixteenth-century resistance theory, I argue that the personne publique was a much more capacious figure than it initially seems. As I will detail in chapter 1, a subject's legitimacy as a personne publique rested most explicitly on social status. And yet, a closer reading of Huguenot resistance treatises reveals that social status alone was not sufficient for a personne publique to act on the people's behalf. A personne publique also had to have an emotional bond with the people. Within these texts, expressions of public pleasure or pain function as what I call "affective evidence" of a personne publique's legitimacy. Absent this affective evidence, the personne publique had no authority. The importance of affective evidence, I argue, led Huguenot resistance treatises to introduce a number of exceptions to the idea that a personne publique had to have a preexisting public role to serve the people. If those with a preexisting public role remained unmoved by the people's pain or failed to secure the people's pleasure, then a private person could become a personne publique.

A note on terminology: in detailing the political work that affect performs within resistance treatises, my language varies between a historical and a theoretical idiom. Acknowledging that words like "passions," "emotions," "feelings," and "affects" have distinct genealogies, I use them interchangeably in order to emphasize what they have in common. My objective throughout this book is to show how passions, emotions, feelings, and affects are not pre- or extrapolitical, but are instead crucial to the work of political legitimation. My ability to accomplish this objective is indebted to insights of scholars from two distinct but related fields: the history of emotions and affect theory. History of emotions scholars, such as William Reddy and Barbara Rosenwein, have brought into focus how communities share emotional repertoires, as well as how social and political pressures shape the ways in which emotions become intelligible to particular groups at particular times.[15] Affect theorists, such as Sara Ahmed, Lauren Berlant, Teresa Brennan, Ann Cvetkovich, and Rei Terada, have interrogated how affections, passions, emotions, or feelings (as they are variously defined according to different historical and theoretical idioms) move among individuals and collectives, and have examined the social and political implications these movements carry.[16] In my study of resistance theory, affective evidence denotes both an attribute of the personne publique and the transmission of feeling between the personne publique and the people. "Affective" is my adjective of choice in part because it emphasizes how feelings exceed the bounds of any one individual, and also because "affective" resonates with the uses of the word "affection" in early modern France, which encompass both feeling and physical movement. The entry "affection" in *Le dictionnaire de l'Académie française* (1694) begins, "*Affection.* s.f. Inclination, passion qui fait qu'on veut du bien à quelqu'un, ou qu'on se plaist à quelque chose" (Affection. s.f. Inclination, passion that makes one wish the best for someone, or that makes one feel pleased about something).[17] Affection promotes emotional and physical proximity. One moves, or rather, is moved by, the object of one's desire. Affective evidence is evidence of this kind of movement toward or desire for proximity. This form of evidence helps us to understand how the people's feelings about a personne publique constitutes a kind of political inclination, leaning, or proclivity.

Affective evidence allows the category of the personne publique to stretch beyond what resistance treatises most explicitly endorsed. Huguenot resistance treatises reserved the possibility that a private person could become a personne publique under exceptional circumstances when those traditionally recognized as public persons proved unresponsive to public feeling (I will say more on this in chapter 1). But the reception history of these treatises, and most particularly of the *Vindiciae*, indicates that for many readers the exception defined the rule. Those rumored to be associated with the anonymously published treatise were celebrated by some and condemned by others for justifying the resistance to tyranny of any private person. This interpretation of Huguenot resistance theory was adopted by those who wished to portray it as seditious. For example, the Catholic cleric Jean Baricave published a lengthy refutation of the *Vindiciae* in 1614, in which he argued that the *Vindiciae* was directly responsible for the assassination of Henri IV, writing that the treatise's "infernal doctrine had placed in the hand of that monster Ravaillac the cunning dagger with which he pierced the heart of the invincible Henri IV."[18] For Baricave, the *Vindiciae* moves its readers to regicide. Members of the Catholic league also adopted this interpretation of the *Vindiciae*, recognizing its political potential and wishing to use it for their own ends, namely resistance to Henri III (whom they deemed insufficiently committed to preserving the Catholicism of France) and resistance to Henri IV (who could not legitimately reign, they argued, because he was at heart a Protestant, despite his conversion to Catholicism).

While at first glance the category of the personne publique seems to be limited in Huguenot resistance treatises to those with officially recognized public positions, such as magistrates, nobles, and electors, the category quickly becomes much broader once we take affective evidence into account as a necessary condition for a given person to occupy the role. This category expands still further when readers and critics follow these treatises to their logical—if radical—conclusion. I argue that, although the capaciousness of this category contributed to the decline of resistance theory within French political writing as the conflictual sixteenth century gave way to a supposedly well-regulated seventeenth century, this capaciousness has also made the category available to other genres and other historical moments, from the seventeenth century to today. In the following sections I first outline the historical narrative that led to the decline of both resistance theory and its central figure, the personne publique. Then, building on recent scholarship that has called elements of this narrative into question, I explain how the constellation of concepts that made resistance theory possible—liberty of conscience, collective authority, affective evidence, and the personne publique—persisted in tragic drama throughout the seventeenth century. This dramatic persistence, I argue, makes the relational form of political subjectivity imagined by resistance theory available to current debates about the liberal subject of rights, a concept that also finds its roots in the early modern period, and which has long dominated debates about political subjectivity in the European tradition.[19]

Absolutism and the End of War

Theories of legitimate resistance proliferated during the religious wars, binding liberty of conscience with collective authority through the personne publique. At the same time, however, the religious wars threw into crisis both the subjective and collective elements of the droit de résistance. The wars raised concerns about the consequences of subjective freedom, given that members of both Protestant and Catholic factions argued that the other side's freedom of belief was dangerous to the public good and disastrous for the possibility of communal salvation. Indeed, the wars called into question the very possibility of a unified community, or a "whole people," that could exercise its sovereignty and authorize resistance to a tyrant.[20]

If the religious wars stretched the subjective and collective elements of the droit de résistance to their limits, the official declaration of the end of war made this right theoretically inoperable. When Henri IV declared an end to the religious wars with the Edict of Nantes in 1598, he did so in a way that shored up monarchical authority against both the charge of tyranny and the possibility of claims to a legitimate right of resistance. The edict famously declared that the wars should be expunged from public memory. The events of the wars should be considered "comme de chose non advenue" (as though they had never happened), and French subjects were barred from renewing the memory of the wars and from quarreling with their fellow subjects on religious grounds.[21] The edict restored Catholicism as the official religion of France but also made provisions for the toleration of Protestant communities. Protestants were explicitly allowed to worship privately in their own homes and to congregate for worship in designated towns where they were concentrated.

In addition to making allowances for Protestant life and worship, the Edict of Nantes also contributed to a shift in the relationship between religious belief and public life. Whereas religious belief had been an integral part of public positions and actions during the sixteenth century, the edict effectively declared that one's religious belief should be kept distinct from one's public life.[22] The separation of private belief and public life ordered by the edict became an integral part of the theory of absolutist monarchy. Absolutism gained prominence during this period in part because it offered a political solution to the problems raised by the religious wars by conceiving of the state as what Reinhart Koselleck has called a "supra-religious" source of power that would adjudicate religious disputes.[23]

The theoretical framework of absolutism that developed in the aftermath of the religious wars maintained that the king was uniquely privy to divine will and was thus the only individual truly capable of knowing what was good, right, and virtuous. The king's unique access to divine will meant that subjects theoretically could no longer make legitimate charges of tyranny or claims of resistance.[24] Under absolutism, individual subjects retained their liberty of conscience—as a leftover from the era of the religious wars—but this liberty was now relegated to the private sphere.[25] The subjective perception of justice that had allowed personnes publiques to resist the monarch on the people's behalf could no longer legitimately be mobilized.

The monarchy also took direct aim at the category of the personne publique itself. As absolutist doctrines gained prominence, those who would previously have been considered public representatives were denied this role. According to a royal decree from 1631, for example, the king was the only true personne publique.[26] In this political climate, nobles, magistrates, and legislators were left with few options. Some turned their energies toward gaining the king's favor and cultivating a high social standing. Others attempted to assert their right to critique the king and his advisers, citing their position as public representatives. On several occasions, for example, members of the parlements reiterated their long-standing right to review and consent to legal decrees. These claims, however, were rejected by the monarchy.[27] Without a recognized public office or role, those who would challenge the king had no recognized basis on which to do so.

The Limits of Absolutism

It is important to acknowledge not only how absolutism reconfigured political thought in the wake of the religious wars but also the limits of the absolutist project. The absolutist monarchy's declarations of its own power—such as the Edict of Nantes or the 1631 declaration that the king was the only true personne publique—have cast a long shadow over the historiography surrounding the end of the religious wars, as well as the extent of monarchical control throughout the seventeenth century. During the nineteenth century and most of the twentieth, historians and literary critics alike tended to take absolutist doctrine at its word and thus worked with the assumption that this political ideology had become so dominant that it prevented the articulation of any viable alternatives. Nannerl Keohane, for example, has argued that the seventeenth century enjoyed "no coherent theory of opposition" to monarchical power. She writes, "During the first half of the seventeenth century, rebellion was common in France and theories of rebellion almost unknown. Even during the Fronde, in the 1650s, little that deserves the name of theory appeared to justify what was being done."[28] Although we might productively interrogate Keohane's distinction between theory and practice, it helpfully underscores how the perception of absolutism's hegemony within seventeenth-century political thought has marked the study of this time period. Much scholarly attention has been devoted to understanding the cultural and artistic mechanisms through which the monarchy asserted its authority.[29]

More recently, historians and literary critics have questioned the extent to which the absolutist monarchy was as ever as total and complete as it declared. To name just a few examples, William Beik and Susan Kettering have demonstrated how the monarchy struggled to assert itself over competing systems of patronage and provincial authority.[30] Sarah Hanley and Arlette Jouanna have traced the slow development of absolutist ceremonial practices and absolutist efforts to reshape the political lexicon to justify notions of divine right and reason of the state.[31] Juliette Cherbuliez has illustrated how the literary practices of those exiled from the court fostered collaborations that decentered the king.[32] And Claire Goldstein has exposed the extent to which the architecture and landscaping at Versailles are indebted to their decidedly less absolutist counterparts at Nicolas Fouquet's Vaux-le-Vicomte.[33] Together, these studies (among others) indicate how the absolutist monarchy's reach was often shorter than its rhetoric claimed. They make it possible to take seriously the historical changes engendered by the rise of absolutist doctrine, while at the same time acknowledging the forms of political, religious, and aesthetic heterodoxy that persisted throughout the seventeenth century.

Scholars have most recently turned to affect to critique traditional accounts of absolutist power. Whereas traditional accounts recognize how the monarchy sought to overwhelm its subjects through all-encompassing spectacle, Katherine Ibbett and Chloé Hogg have identified ways in which the monarchy worked to engage its subjects in forms of emotional connection.[34] Ibbett demonstrates how in the wake of Louis XIV's Revocation of the Edict of Nantes in 1685 that the monarchy mobilized "a language of nonconsensual compassion" to interpolate Protestants as marginal subjects, but subjects nonetheless.[35] For her part, Hogg argues that novel forms of news circulation contributed to the formation of "absolutist attachment" between the king and his subjects. Unlike absolutism's subjectively overwhelming spectacles, forms of absolutist attachment allowed the monarchy emotionally to engage its subjects in the machinations of power. This emotionally charged absolutism solicited subjective participation by those it sought to rule.[36] *Subjects of Affection* builds on this recent revalorization of affect's role in French political life to show how tragedy imagines affective attachments that exceed the monarch's grasp.

The Tragic Stage

Subjects of Affection joins efforts to rethink absolutism's reach by offering an account of the droit de résistance's persistence in seventeenth-century tragic theater. As I have noted, theories of absolutism delegitimized the droit de résistance by pulling apart this right's subjective and collective elements and thus rendering inoperable the political force of the personne publique. However, even as these dimensions were estranged in the realm of political discourse, tragedy held them together. *Subjects of Affection* tells the story of how tragedy, during the religious wars and throughout the seventeenth century, maintained and reworked the ties that bound liberty of conscience and public authority. I demonstrate how the conceptual structure of the droit de résistance can be found in tragedies by Robert Garnier, Jean de Rotrou, Pierre Corneille, and Jean Racine, some of which were contemporaneous with the sixteenth-century resistance treatises and others of which appeared long after the official end of the religious wars.

Tragedy might seem to be a particularly unlikely cultural site from which to locate a survival, or afterlife, for the droit de résistance. In French literary history, the genre has long been read as one that was ultimately concerned with the exercise of sovereign power and with absolutism in particular. For example, scholars have examined how Louis XIII's chief minister, Cardinal Richelieu, sought control over dramatic production and printing to secure the theater as a site that reinforced the king's strength.[37] Others have emphasized how tragedy participated in the elaboration of the king's royal body as a unique source of political authority.[38] When viewed as a genre with close ties to the historical king, tragedy seems to support a theory of absolute monarchy whether it stages strong or weak sovereigns and whether it offers portraits of good kings or bad tyrants. Tragedies that feature strong, just kings are thought to reflect the historical monarch's glory. Tragedies that feature weak kings or bad tyrants serve as contrastive examples that underscore the historical monarch's glory. Within this tradition, if tragedy raises the possibility of resistance, it is only to depict its inevitable "containment" or reabsorption into monarchical order.[39]

Recent scholarship on seventeenth-century tragedy, however, has called into question the close connection between tragedy and absolutist power. This scholarship has focused less on the monarchy's involvement in tragedy's production and reception and more on the ways that tragedy exposes the fissures and contradictions of absolutism. Ellen McClure's analysis of diplomatic figures in the works of Corneille and Racine, for example, has added nuance to absolutist conceptions of the king as a singular source of power. She demonstrates that, although the ideal ambassador acts as a transparent conduit of royal power, ambassadors on the tragic stage often prove themselves to be less than ideal and end up accruing some power of their own.[40]

Other scholars have questioned tragedy's long-standing association with absolutism by exploring the genre's relationship to other forms of political thought and action. Hélène E. Bilis has demonstrated how tragedy's examination of the king in his capacity as judge evinces the "double bind of tragic royal representation," that is, "how to navigate between the increasing emphasis on safeguarding the dignity of the royal function while also placing a monarchical character at the heart of tragic drama."[41] Bilis's account shows how the relationship between the historical king and tragic representations of kingship remained a subject of uncertainty and experimentation. Katherine Ibbett's work on Corneille's tragic drama highlights its preoccupation with questions of governance and the maintenance of power, questions more often associated with Machiavellian political thought than with absolutism.[42] Individually and collectively, these studies broaden our understanding of tragedy's politics by illustrating how the genre calls monarchical power into question.

Subjects of Affection seeks to further this broader understanding of tragedy's politics by examining how the genre offers a meditation on resistance that exceeds the absolutist framework. Tragedy's mediation on resistance becomes intelligible, I argue, only when we interrogate the genre's historiography. Historical narratives of French tragedy often privilege the genre's "neoclassical" period, beginning with Corneille's *Le Cid* (1637; first performed, 1636) and concluding with Racine's *Phèdre* (1677). These two plays make convenient bookends, with the controversy surrounding *Le Cid* marking the rise of Richelieu's theatrical influence—which was exercised in part through the newly founded Académie française and its articulation of what we now refer to as the "rules" of neoclassical drama—and *Phèdre* marking the pinnacle of neoclassical expression during Louis XIV's personal rule, the historical moment at which absolutism was arguably at its strongest.[43] In addition to limiting how we view these two plays (as well as those situated chronologically between them), taking *Le Cid* and *Phèdre* as the beginning and end of French tragedy obscures what these seventeenth-century tragedies share with their sixteenth-century counterparts and thus reinforces the sense that tragedy serves as a literary handmaiden to absolutism.

French tragedy emerged as a genre long before *Le Cid*, stretching back to the 1530s rather than the 1630s. Vernacular tragedy developed in France during the 1530s and 1540s, when dramas by Euripides, Seneca, and Sophocles began to be translated into French along with editions of Aristotle's *Poetics*. Translations of ancient models led to original compositions, which often reworked Greek and Roman subjects and sources. During this period, many asserted that this ancient genre was particularly well suited to the moral character of France itself.[44] Greek and Roman tragedies communicated the grandeur of these ancient civilizations. Translating, adapting, and reconfiguring these works was in part a means of claiming the ancients' past for France's present.

As the conflicts between Catholic and Protestant factions intensified during the sixteenth century, leading eventually to civil war, tragedy's relationship to the character of France took on another dimension. Greek and Roman tragedies not only attested to their respective civilizations' grandeur but also warned of civil war as a threat to their grandeur by chronicling how civil war devastates populations and engenders crises of authority. For French dramatists, tragedy offered an ideal poetic space from which to lament their own nation's condition of civil war and to call attention to its disastrous consequences. During this period, tragedy was seen as the genre most suitable for making sense of France's present condition, and the events of the civil wars were seen as material suitable for tragedy.[45] The dramatist Jean de La Taille, for example, drew strong connections between the internecine conflicts of antiquity and the bloody clashes that were ravaging France in his *De l'art de la tragédie* (1572), which argued that to write a tragedy one had only to look at "les pitieux desastres advenues nagueres en la France par nos Guerres civiles" (the horrible disasters recently brought upon France by our civil wars).[46]

As Gillian Jondorf has noted, although seventeenth-century tragedies share much with their sixteenth-century predecessors in terms of form as well as content, these commonalities typically go unrecognized. Seventeenth-century dramatists and dramatic theorists often cite ancient inspirations but rarely acknowledge their literary debt to the work of such sixteenth-century dramatists as Étienne Jodelle, La Taille, and Garnier.[47] This lack of acknowledgement can be explained in part by changing aesthetic tastes. Sixteenth-century dramatists often drew from a Senecan model of tragedy, which relied heavily on long speeches in which characters extolled a particular principle or virtue. This model largely fell out of favor during the seventeenth century, as dramatic theorists critiqued its lack of action and verisimilitude.[48] Aesthetic tastes also shifted in terms of staged violence. While staged violence occurred frequently in sixteenth-century tragedy, particularly in the tradition that Christian Biet has termed "theater of cruelty," offstage violence became the norm during the seventeenth century, with characters reporting on stage the violence they had witnessed elsewhere.[49] During and after the seventeenth century, shifts in tragic construction such as these have often been understood less as the evidence of poetic preferences as they change over time and more as the realization of a universal ideal.[50]

Working against this tendency to celebrate seventeenth-century tragedy as a universal—and thus depoliticized—poetic ideal, Andrea Frisch has emphasized how the aesthetic imperatives of the genre are part of a specific, historically situated political agenda. Whereas, as we have seen, tragedy during the sixteenth century was thought to be the ideal genre for reckoning with the religious wars, Frisch argues that during the seventeenth century tragedy participated in the political imperative to leave the religious wars behind.[51] The difference in these two political contexts—during and after the wars—helps us understand why the genre's history has been so thoroughly split in two and why it has been difficult to track the continuities that persist across the seemingly rigid divide demanded by the official end of war.

Frisch is careful to note that, despite tragedy's participation in the absolutist imperative of "oubliance," the genre never manages fully to forget the religious wars. She maintains instead that seventeenth-century tragedy carries with it the sublimated concerns about religious difference and the limits of community that persisted in the wars' aftermath.[52] As a result, rather than reducing tragedy to a mere weapon in the absolutist arsenal, Frisch's study instead acknowledges the real historical and aesthetic shifts brought about by the end of war without making this end as definitive as absolutist doctrine declared.

In the chapters that follow, I focus less on the imperative to forget and more on what tragedy remembers despite this imperative. As Michel de Certeau has so powerfully written, the process of separating one historical period from another is at its core a process of separating "what can be *understood* and what must be *forgotten*."[53] In addition to forgetting the wars as such, seventeenth-century tragedy was also compelled to forget the possibility of legitimate resistance. And yet, Certeau continues, "whatever this new understanding of the past holds to be irrelevant—shards created by the selection of materials, remainders left aside by an explication—comes back, despite everything, on the edges of discourse or in its rifts and crannies: 'resistances,' 'survivals,' or delays discreetly perturb the pretty order of a line of 'progress' or a system of interpretation."[54] *Subjects of Affection* brings into relief the shards of resistance theory as they remained in tragic drama. To do so, I read tragic drama as "between poetry and performance," to borrow W. B. Worthen's formulation.[55] This means that I attend both to the poetic structure of dramatic text and to the ways in which these structures make possible certain configurations of bodies and feelings.

Throughout *Subjects of Affection* I demonstrate how the political potential of a dramatic text often coalesces around a gesture or set of gestures, such as the raised arm of protest or the tender grip of love. Together, these gestures form what I call a repertoire of resistance. In the field of performance studies, Diana Taylor's distinction of repertoire from the archive has become a useful—if contested—heuristic. For Taylor, whereas the archive represents authority and statis, the repertoire is a site of opposition and fluidity. Although the archive contains the written word, the repertoire transmits embodied practices. Taylor advanced this distinction in the context of Spanish conquest of the Americas, during which forms of written documentation suppressed and supplanted forms of embodied transmission.[56] Others have subsequently worked to excavate cultural and political repertoires, such as performance practices or oral traditions in other contexts where these repertoires have been similarly suppressed and "forgotten," to return to Certeau's formulation.[57] As politically urgent as Taylor's recognition of the repertoire remains, scholars such as Rebecca Schneider and Worthen, however, have argued that Taylor's distinction between the archive and the repertoire itself obscures how texts themselves transmit modes of embodiment and corporeality. Put another way, texts contain repertoires, or corporeal traces, that trouble the seemingly static, sovereign archive from within.[58] By understanding gestures that appear in French dramatic texts as part of a repertoire of resistance, my aim is to show how these texts exceed their historical assignment to the archive of absolutism.

As mentioned above, in the wake of the wars, absolutist doctrine positioned the king as the only legitimate personne publique. This claim held affective implications. If the king was the only personne publique, then he was the only acceptable public object of the people's affection. Tragic drama, however, demonstrates that affective evidence does not always line up in the king's favor. In other words, tragedy explores what happens when the people's affection and approval attach to someone who is not the king. In so doing, tragedy indicates that affective evidence remains a powerful indication of political legitimacy—above and beyond any royal decree. Tragic drama continues to push the boundaries of the category of the personne publique by casting a variety of figures as public representatives.

In chapter 1 I detail how affective evidence secures the personne publique's legitimacy in sixteenth-century resistance treatises such as *Francogallia, Du droit des magistrats*, and the *Vindiciae*, and I situate this process of political legitimation within the wider context of sixteenth- and seventeenth-century theories of the passions in politics as well as on the stage. Chapters 2 through 5 explore how tragedy sustains and reworks the ties that bind liberty of conscience and collective authority through its staging of affective evidence in its myriad forms. Readers familiar with French tragedy will notice that the plays I spend the most time with are not the most canonical. As part of the ongoing effort to pluralize conceptions of this genre, I have selected plays that are less often cited as exemplars of French tragedy. The plays discussed in these chapters help us to see French tragedy differently. In focusing on how these relatively noncanonical plays reanimate the right of resistance, I also suggest how more well-known plays, such as *Le Cid* and *Phèdre*, participate in this political work. Throughout these chapters I historicize French tragedy by attending to how specific plays intersect with historical moments such as the religious wars (1562–98), the Fronde (1648–53), and the Revocation of the Edict of Nantes (1685), while also opening up questions about how the genre's political potential exceeds this historical frame.

Chapter 2 examines how sixteenth- and seventeenth-century tragedy uses affective evidence as an index of political legitimacy in a way that expands the category of the public representative. Whereas the public representatives of sixteenth-century resistance treatises were typically men of high social standing, tragedy suggests that women can also fill this role. The chapter focuses on two tragedies about the resistance to tyranny organized by Cornelia, the widow of the Roman general Pompey: Garnier's *Cornélie* (1574) and Corneille's *La mort de Pompée* (1644). These tragedies emphasize the specificity of their shared heroine's objections to Caesar's tyrannical rule. However, the tragedies also reveal that Cornelia's specific claims are ratified by the communal laments of the Roman people.

Chapter 3 casts the tragic figure of Antigone as a public representative. In Garnier's *Antigone, ou La piéte* (1580) and Rotrou's *Antigone* (1639; first performed, 1637), she speaks the language of subjective freedom while remaining physically and affectively gripped by her family and city. A tension between speech and gesture in these dramas illustrates how declarations of independence depend on specific, and often troubling, forms of attachment. These attachments raise questions about whether Antigone's rebellion is virtuous or seditious, which can only be settled by popular approval.

Chapter 4 explores the implications of resistance theory for our understanding of heroism in Corneille's drama. Through readings of *Nicomède* (1651) and *Suréna* (1674; first performed, 1675), I argue that Cornelian heroism is communally constituted rather than uniquely vested in the heroic figure. By tracing the affective relationships between staged characters and the unseen body politic, I show how the hero functions as a locus of collective resistance.

Chapter 5 examines how the structure of the droit de résistance similarly alters our perception of the figure of the savior in Jean Racine's biblical tragedies. *Esther* (1689) and *Athalie* (1691) feature characters who are positioned to secure the future of their people through the revelation of their true identities. Both tragedies position the savior's exceptional purity and innocence as potent weapons against an oppressive tyrant. As we will see, however, it is the communal reception of the savior's singular virtue that poses the real threat to sovereign power.

By reading these tragic figures—the mourner, the rebel, the hero, and the savior—as public representatives, I explore not only how tragedy sustains the political subjectivity associated with the right of resistance but also how this political subjectivity offers an alternative to the liberal model of individual rights. When absolutism reconfigured the landscape of political thought in a way that pulled apart the subjective and collective dimensions of the droit de résistance, it also set the stage for the emergence of the modern individualist model of rights. While the individualist model of rights was explicitly developed in opposition to absolutism, it nonetheless followed a path laid out by absolutism in its conception of the individual as a discrete and autonomous entity. Whereas the individual subject of sixteenth-century political thought had a profoundly communitarian constitution, in following the path laid out by absolutism, the modern rights paradigm lost sight of how the political power of the individual depends on his or her relationships, such as familial ties, romantic desires, and religious affiliations.

In recent decades, the ostensibly autonomous subject put forward by liberalism has been powerfully critiqued by poststructuralists of many theoretical stripes. A challenge in the wake of these critiques has been to recuperate a sense of individual agency without falling back on an untethered sense of the self.[59] Early modern tragedy helps us to meet this challenge by offering us a model of subjectivity that privileges individual liberty without denying attachment.

Early modern tragedy invites us to reach back to a form of political subjectivity that predates both absolutism and the emergence of liberal political philosophy. Many of the tragic figures in this study have been put forward as early modern blueprints of the modern individual. They possess great personal strength; they are valiant and self-reliant. And yet, despite their individual strength and virtue, these figures' political power derives from their connection to others—from staged characters and choruses to unseen collectives. The physical and emotional interactions among bodies—onstage and offstage—show us how communal attachments undergird personal claims and capacities.

Chapter One

Affective Evidence

The *Vindiciae contra tyrannos* (hereafter *Vindiciae*), which was first published in Latin in 1579 and then in French in 1581, was one of the most widely circulated treatises on resistance during the religious wars in France. Addressed to an audience of "christian princes," the *Vindiciae* opens with a critique of Niccolò Machiavelli that anticipates the treatise's polemical reception: "Je savoy bien Messeigneurs, qu'en publiant ces questions d'Estiene Junius Brutus, touchant le vray droit et la puissance du Prince sur le peuple, et du peuple sur le Prince: il se trouveroit des gens qui m'en sauroyent mauvais gré" (I was not unaware, princes, that when I published these investigations of Stephanus Junius Brutus into the true right and power of a prince over the people and of the people over the prince, there would be some who would rebuke me).[1] The preface explains that the ideas put forward by Brutus, the pseudonymous author of the *Vindiciae*, run counter to what he sees as a disturbing trend in French political life: an appreciation for Machiavellian ideas. The preface does little to explicate Machiavelli's philosophy. Instead, the author assumes his readers' familiarity with its tenets and argues that this philosophy is to blame for the ongoing civil conflicts in France. Machiavelli and his followers have nurtured a love of tyranny, diminished concern for the public good, and sowed general discord. The *Vindiciae* offers a corrective to these ills, outlining how to reject tyranny, foster civic virtue, and restore harmony. With nothing less at stake than the survival of France, the preface affirms the author's commitment to publishing the *Vindiciae*. Although the vehemence with which the Machiavellians are sure to express their displeasure causes the author fear, love encourages him to publish: "Mais la ferme amitié et singuliere affection que je porte au bien public, à quoy je pense continuellement, m'ont arraché ceste peur" (But my constant love for the commonwealth, and the unalterable disposition which I always bear toward it, have shaken this fear from me).[2] Love has conquered fear.

The prefatory framing of the *Vindiciae* as an anti-Machiavellian tract implicates the treatise in a wider debate about the role of the passions in political life.[3] During the Renaissance, the passions were broadly understood as forces that, if properly channeled, could benefit the public good. Princes, jurists, and other public figures were trained in the skills of classical oratory and eloquence so that they might effectively deploy their powers of persuasion in ways that promoted the general welfare. It was likewise broadly understood that, if the passions were not properly channeled, they could become forces of destruction and division. A king too susceptible to the passions could become a tyrant. A people too susceptible to the passions could become a mob. The use of the passions in public life had to be carefully calibrated to prevent such abuses.[4]

Machiavelli's ideas seemed dangerous during this period in part because they departed from conventional wisdom about the relationship between political virtue and the passions. Particularly troubling for Machiavelli's French readers was his claim that political virtue depended not on a leader's innate goodness or on his ability to harness the passions in service of the public good, but instead on shows of strength and political savvy. For Machiavelli, in other words, the question of how to be a good king or prince was one of effective action rather than of right thinking and feeling. Whereas a people's love for a ruler had long been taken as a sign of his virtue—and their hatred a sign of his wickedness or tyranny—Machiavellianism brought such correspondences into question.[5]

In the context of sixteenth-century France, to accept Machiavelli's vision of politics would be to renounce the possibility of a shared perception of justice, order, and harmony at a moment when this possibility had already been diminished by civil war. By framing the *Vindiciae* as a critique of Machiavelli, the preface maintains that a shared sense of right and wrong was still possible in France. This is why the preface can so confidently divide the *Vindiciae*'s readers into two camps: those who share the author's affection for France and recognize the treatise's virtue and those whose lack of affection for France corresponds to their failure to recognize the treatise's truth.

In this chapter I argue that certainty about the enduring correspondence between affection and virtue served not only as the stated motivation behind the *Vindiciae*'s publication but also as the structuring principle of its theory of resistance. The *Vindiciae*, as well as other sixteenth-century resistance treatises such as François Hotman's *Francogallia*—also known as *La gaule francoise* (Latin 1573; French 1574)—and Théodore de Bèze's *Du droit des magistrats sur leurs subjets* (1574) use affection as an index of political legitimacy. Affection enabled these treatises to affirm what Machiavelli's thought had called into question: the distinction between good kings and tyrants. A good king loves his people and they love him. By contrast, a tyrant loves only himself and, in acting on behalf of his personal interests rather than the public good, provokes the people's ire. As I will show, affection was a concept that allowed resistance treatises to determine who might legitimately resist a king who had become a tyrant. Resistance treatises understood affection between a people and a political leader as a sign of that leader's virtue. In so doing, they made affection a condition of virtue's legibility, its ability to be recognized. In other words, resistance treatises figured expressions of affection as what I call "affective evidence" of political legitimacy.

Attending to how affective evidence secures legitimacy in *Francogallia*, *Du droit des magistrats*, and the *Vindiciae* allows us to better understand the political stakes of French resistance theory. As I will explain in more detail below, resistance theory rests on the conjunction of subjective liberty and popular sovereignty. When intellectual historians and legal scholars have discussed these treatises, they have tended to address these concepts separately. As a result, they have identified both elements of sixteenth-century resistance theory as precursors to ideas at the heart of modern political thought without taking into account how resistance treatises position subjective liberty and popular sovereignty in relation to each other.[6] In sixteenth-century resistance treatises, it is affective evidence that binds together subjective liberty and popular sovereignty. Following the trail of affective evidence allows us on the one hand to appreciate the differences between this early modern rights paradigm and its modern counterpart. On the other hand affective evidence helps us to recognize the enduring political potential of this paradigm.

Although *Francogallia*, *Du droit des magistrats*, and the *Vindiciae* were all written from a Huguenot perspective, these texts position themselves above the partisan fray and internecine violence that marked the French Wars of Religion (1562–98). Huguenot resistance treatises are primarily theoretical texts, drawing most frequently on ancient, biblical, and medieval sources to make their points, rather than on current events in war-torn France.[7] For example, while the *Vindiciae*'s preface addresses the religious wars directly as we have seen, the treatise itself refers to them only obliquely. Explicitly disavowing partisan politics, the *Vindiciae* and other Huguenot resistance treatises claim their goal is to preserve the Christian unity of France that the religious wars threatened to destroy.[8] *Francogallia*, *Du droit des magistrats*, and the *Vindiciae* each depict the natural state of France as one, cohesive spiritual and political unity. This unified, Christian France reads as what Barbara Rosenwein would call an "emotional community." Emotional communities, Rosenwein explains, are groups "that have their own particular values, modes of feeling, and ways to express those feelings."[9] Emotional communities are normative. They define themselves through shared modes of feeling and against those who do not share these modes. As the *Vindiciae*'s anti-Machiavellian preface illustrates, members of the emotional community imagined by Huguenot resistance treatises would all share an understanding of what constitutes virtue, goodness, and affection, as well as share a conviction of these categories' stability and legibility.

Francogallia, *Du droit des magistrats*, and the *Vindiciae* claimed to be nonpartisan defenders of Christian unity, but they were often read otherwise. Indeed, many readers of these Huguenot treatises, especially Catholic theologians and political philosophers, maintained that these were radical texts whose authors were bent on destroying the very community that they purported to defend. This discrepancy indicates that the unified emotional community of Christians the Huguenot resistance treatises championed simply did not exist. By the 1570s, when these treatises were first published, members of Protestant and Catholic factions held divergent ideas about who the Christian community included. Members on both sides of the confessional divide appealed to the righteousness of "true Christians," but this appellation meant something different for each side. This historical disagreement tells us that, when Huguenot resistance treatises delimit a Christian community based on invariable, uncontroversial ideas of virtue, goodness, and affection, their gesture is performative. In other words, Huguenot treatises do not describe a preexisting emotional community, but instead rhetorically produce the very community to which they refer.[10]

The performative nature of the emotional community in Huguenot resistance treatises has important consequences for the notion of affective evidence. The treatises put forward the idea that affection between a community and its political representative serves as a sign of that representative's legitimacy. If, however, virtue, goodness, and affection are variable qualities that are subject to change depending on one's political perspective, how can these qualities reliably determine which representative might legitimately resist tyranny on the people's behalf? These questions lurk throughout *Francogallia*, *Du droit des magistrats*, and the *Vindiciae*, even as the treatises refuse to recognize them. In the following sections I explore how affective evidence is at once straightforward and slippery in these treatises, a duality that makes the question of legitimate representation more complicated than it may initially seem.

The King's Love and the People's Consent

Published in the wake of the St. Bartholomew's Day Massacre, Hotman's *Francogallia*, Bèze's *Du droit des magistrats*, and the *Vindiciae* appeared at a particularly fraught political moment during the religious wars in France. As I noted in the introduction to this book, the royal family's involvement in the massacre has been the subject of much historical debate. Whether Charles IX or his mother, Catherine de Medici, ordered the assassination of Admiral Gaspard de Coligny and the widespread violence that followed remain open questions. What is clear, however, is that the massacre changed the monarchy's affective orientation to the people of France as a whole. Denis Crouzet has argued that during the first decade of religious conflict the monarchy's primary objective was to preserve the integrity of the body politic. This task could be accomplished by promoting Renaissance ideals of love, harmony, and order. The monarch's abiding love for his subjects would foster and sustain a well-ordered, harmonious society in which divisions could be peacefully reconciled. The St. Bartholomew's Day Massacre brought an end to this aspirational stance. The extent and intensity of its violence made clear what Crouzet calls "l'idéal d'un règne d'amour" (the ideal of a reign of love) could not be sustained. Catholics saw Protestants as a threat to their spiritual salvation, and Protestants saw Catholics as a threat to their survival.[11] These divisions meant that, as Hélène Merlin-Kajman has noted, the spiritual body of France, its *corps mystique*, was no longer coterminous with its political body, its *corps politique*.[12] Royal love simply could not bridge this gap. Following the massacre, the monarchy's political strategy was more aligned with the interests of Catholic factions and less conciliatory toward Protestants.[13]

Francogallia, Du droit des magistrats, and the *Vindiciae* base their theory of resistance on the idea that a king's love for his people evinces his political legitimacy, the very idea that the St. Bartholomew's Day Massacre had brought fatally into question. Good kings, the *Vindiciae* tells us, are like good husbands and fathers (I will return to the gendered nature of this comparison later) in that they rule by "charité & singuliere affection" (charity and singular affection) rather than by pride or mere desire to dominate.[14] While it is tempting to read the treatises' emphasis on royal love as either a failure to understand shifts in the political landscape or an attempt to mitigate these shifts, I instead heed Paul-Alexis Mellet's warning against imposing too narrow an interpretive frame on the treatises. Resisting what he calls the "Saint-Bartholomew's Day trauma thesis," which position the treatises' critique of tyranny as a reaction to the horrors of the massacre, Mellet underscores that many of the ideas contained in these treatises predate the event itself. In other words, while the treatises were published in the wake of the massacre, and while the massacre may have contributed to the spread of resistance theory, it did not give rise to this set of ideas.[15] Broadening our interpretive frame allows us to better appreciate not only how the treatises use affect as an index of legitimacy but also these texts' enduring political potential.

Huguenot resistance treatises echo the more widely held Renaissance ideal that a king's love for his people is a part of a well-ordered, harmonious society. The treatises draw on the Platonic trope of musical harmony to depict this ideal society. Hotman's *Francogallia* states, for example:

> [I]l faut, que ceux, qui jouent des instrumens de Musique, ou qui chantent à plusieurs parties, tienent une mesure, et sonnent un chant harmonieux, meslé de divers sons, ou de diverses voix amassées et accordées ensemble, lesquelles, si elles viennent à s'esclater tant soit peu, et à sortir hors de ton, font mal aux oreilles de ceux qui s'entendent en l'art de la Musique: et cependant cette harmonie ne vient d'ailleurs, que de la consonance parfaite, et bien accordée de voix differentes: ainsi en matière de gouvernement d'une chose publique, qui est composée de personnes de haute, de moyene et basse qualité, quand les parties differentes s'unissent, lient et incorporent ensemble, il n'y a harmonie si musicale, de melodie mieux accordée qu'est celle de la concorde, qui procède de l'union, charité et meslange des citoyens d'une mesme ville, qui est comme une chaine forte et roide, pour assurer et retenir l'estat d'une chose publique, qui ne peut en sorte quelconques durer longtemps sans justice.[16]

> With lyres and flutes, and also with voices raised in song, a certain harmony should emerge from the individual sounds, but a trained ear cannot endure an altered or discordant note. This harmonious and agreeable concord is produced, however, from the regular arrangement of dissimilar sounds. In the same way a commonwealth which is regulated by reason produces harmony through the consent of dissimilar elements, drawn, like from the sounds, from the highest and the middling orders, from the lowest and the intermediate estates. What is called harmony in song by musicians, is called concord in a commonwealth. In such a state concord provides the narrowest and best assurance of security, which no general agreement can embody unless it is accompanied by justice.[17]

Just as the different sounds of instruments and voices join together to make musical harmony, the different parts of the body politic join together to produce a stable society. To sixteenth-century readers this emphasis on harmony and order would have carried an emotional or affective valence. As I will discuss in more detail later in this chapter, whereas sadness and pain were the affective states that accompanied civil unrest, happiness and joy accompanied stability and good governance. Central to the affective undertones at work in Hotman's comparison of musical and political harmony is the term "charité." Derived from the Latin *charitas*, in sixteenth-century France charité was used as a synonym of love or affection. We have already seen the conjunction of these terms in the *Vindiciae*, with the dyad "charité & singuliere affection" used to describe a good king's emotional orientation to his subjects.[18] But the connection between these terms long preceded Huguenot resistance treatises. Robert Estienne records the affinity between these terms in the entry for "Charitas" for his *Dictionarium latinogallicum* (1552), offering examples such as "Charité et amour entre les hommes" (Charity and love between men) and "L'amour que les meres et peres portent à leurs enfants" (The love that mothers and fathers have for their children).[19] In both the familial and political realms, charité indicated the proper emotional stance—love—that one should have toward those in one's care.[20]

In Hotman's ideal of political harmony, parts of the body politic join together through a kind of shared affiliation. It is important to note that this vision is neither egalitarian nor democratic. It is not a meeting of equals that Hotman promotes, but instead the perfect arrangement, or "consonance parfaite" of a predetermined hierarchical order. For Hotman, political order brings together members from different social ranks.[21] This emphasis on hierarchy, order, and harmony is crucial not just for Hotman but also for Bèze in *Du droit des magistrats* and for the *Vindiciae*. All three treatises are careful to distinguish their prescriptions for legitimate resistance to tyranny from illegitimate forms of conspiration and sedition. Bèze, for example, disassociates his ideas from "ces enragez Anabaptistes ou autres seditieux et mutins" (the fanatical Anabaptists or other factious and mutinous men).[22] Whereas legitimate resistance is driven by and should inspire "Pieté & Charité" (Piety and Charity),[23] conspirators and mutineers are "dignes de la haine de tout le reste des hommes, & de tresgrieves peines pour leurs demerites" (most worthy of the hatred of all their fellowmen, and even of the severest punishments).[24] Much like the *Vindiciae*'s preface excludes those in favor of Machiavellian politics from the emotional community of its virtuous readers, *Du droit des magistrats* excludes Anabaptists and their ilk from those deserving love and affection.

Unlike conspirators and those promoting sedition who foster disorder and unrest, those engaged in legitimate resistance seek to maintain the established order so as to secure "la tranquilité publique" (the public peace).[25]

Given Hotman, Bèze, and the *Vindiciae*'s concern with maintaining a harmonious hierarchical order, it is perhaps unsurprising that they approach the question of whether and how legitimately to resist the king through a carefully elaborated structure of social rank and political stature. What may surprise modern readers, however, is the way that these treatises position the king and the people. As I noted in this book's introduction, whereas theories of divine-right monarchy that we have come to associate with the "absolute" monarchs of the seventeenth century held that power flowed from God to the king, who then rules over his subjects, in sixteenth-century resistance treatises, God vests political power in the people as a whole, corporate body that elects or appoints a king to manage or administer governmental affairs. According to this arrangement, the people's primary fidelity is to God. Their fidelity to the king is secondary, binding them to his authority only insofar as he proves himself to be worthy of God and the people.[26]

Resistance treatises describe these layered relationships of fidelity between God, the people, and the king as affective covenants or contracts. The *Vindiciae* is most explicit on this count, often using the words "contrat" (or its verbal form "contracter") and "alliance" in tandem. To cite but two examples, in detailing the honor that God bestows on kings who uphold his precepts, the *Vindiciae* writes of "l'alliance qui se contractoit entre Dieu & le Roy" (the [alliance] which is . . . made between God and the king),[27] and in relating God's reassurance to the biblical King Solomon, the son of King David, the treatise notes, "le Seigneur dit, Si tu gardes ma Loy, je confermeray avec toy l'alliance que j'ay contractee avec David" ("If you observe My law," says the Lord, "I will confirm with you the [alliance] which I [contracted] with David").[28] At times "alliance" appears by itself to name the ties that bind God, the people, and the king: "Quant aussi l'alliance se passe entre Dieu & le Roy, c'est à condition que le peuple soit & demeure toujours peuple de Dieu" (When the [alliance] is ratified between God and the king, it is done on this condition: that the people should be and should remain forever the people of God).[29] Much like "charité," the term "alliance" carried an affective charge during this period. In addition to marriage pacts and agreements between political entities, "alliance" was also used more generally to indicate affinity or affection. In the *Dictionarium latinogallicum*, Robert Estienne frequently uses the dyad "alliance et amitié" when glossing Latin words. His entry for "Cognatio" (family, relationship, or affinity) reads in part, "Alliance et amitié que deux personnages ont ensemble pour avoir versé en mesme science" (Alliance and love that two people share because of their facility with the same knowledge).[30] And Jean Nicot writes in his *Thresor de la language francoyse tant ancienne que moderne* (1606), "L'amitié et l'alliance qu'on a l'un avec l'autre, à cause d'estre d'un païs" (The love and alliance that one has with another, which arises from having common origins).[31] The term "alliance" signals that individuals and groups are bound together as part of the same emotional community that could be forged through shared knowledge or political fidelity.

Affect serves not only as a kind of material, or substance that binds together God, the people, and the king, but also as the evidence, or proof, of how they are functioning. As Bèze notes in *Du droit des magistrats*, joy and pleasure result when these relationships are working properly: "les Rois s'enjouisent de leur peuples & les peuples de leurs Rois, & Dieu prenne plaisir en tous les deux" (the kings may rejoice in their peoples and the people in their kings and God in both).[32] On this point, the treatises often refer to the common Renaissance distinction between good kings and tyrants: good kings govern in accordance with their love for the people, but tyrants rule in ways that maximize their own pleasure or desire. By neglecting the public good, Hotman notes in *Francogallia*, tyrants provoke the people's anger and must employ foreign guards or mercenaries to ensure their personal safety and position. Good kings would have no need to take such precautions: "Car ils se faisoient tant aimer, qu'ils se tenoyent plus asseurez de la bien veillance, l'affection, la bonne grace et amour de leurs sujets, que s'ils eussent eu toutes les gardes du monde" (Because they were so loved, the good will and affection and the good grace and love of their subjects protected them more surely than all the guards in the world).[33] A king loved by his subjects has no need of guards. The people's love protects him. To the often-posed question in sixteenth-century France of whether it was better for a king to be loved or feared (also known as the clemency-rigor debate), Huguenot resistance treatises answered unequivocally in favor of love.

Since the people's contract or alliance with God precedes their alliance with the king, a king who loves himself more than God or the people could legitimately be opposed. Huguenot resistance treatises ground this rationale for legitimate resistance in biblical verse, a favorite being the injunction from Acts that one should obey God rather than men.[34] In addition to biblical justifications such as this, resistance treatises bolster their claims that the people can legitimately oppose—and even depose—a king through historical precedent. *Francogallia* deals most thoroughly with the historical roots of the people's authority, claiming that the people's right to resist tyrannical kings can be evidenced by their role in electing kings. Although it was commonplace in sixteenth century to think of kingship as fundamentally linked to the idea of dynastic succession, Hotman argues that it was not always so. The ancient Franks elected their kings: "Quand ils elisoyent des Roys, il ne les elevoyent pas là pour estre des tyrans, ou des bourreaux mais pour estre leurs Governeurs, leurs tuteurs gardiens et defenseurs de leur libérté (When they appointed kings for themselves, they were not appointing tyrants and butchers, but rather guardians, governors and tutors for their liberty).[35] Hotman underscores the practice of election—and the conception of kingship as administrative rather than absolute—to reconcile the Franks' reputation as fierce defenders of their liberty who nonetheless accepted monarchical rule.

Hotman's account of these ancient elections alerts us to their affective and embodied qualities. For example, on the election of Childeric, the event that united the Franks and the Gauls, he writes:

> Mais apres le decès de Merovee, toutes les deux nations se joignirent en un corps de Republique, et elurent pour leur Roy Childeric son fils d'un commun accord: et l'ayant mis sur un pavois, à la manière accoustumée, et porté sur leurs espaules trois fois tout à l'entour de l'assemblée du peuple, avec grand batement de mains, et acclamations de joyee, le saluèrent Roy de France et de Gaule.[36]

> By the time of his death a single [Republican body] had been created by the two peoples, the Gauls and the Franks, and with a common mind they all elected Childeric, the son of Merovech, as king. They placed him on a shield according to their custom, bore him thrice upon their shoulders round the assembly, and saluted him as king of Francogallia with enthusiastic applause and the greatest rejoicing of all present.[37]

This example reframes what is often cited as a foundational moment for dynastic monarchy in the territory that would become France, as a key point in a long genealogy of royal election. As King Merovech's son, Childeric would come to be known as the first in the Merovingian line, but Hotman emphasizes that neither royal blood nor any other hereditary benefit makes him king. Instead, the people who elevate him to this position make him king through their "common accord." As Hotman describes, this gesture of elevation is literal. Following an already established custom, members of the public place Childeric on a shield, hoist him onto their shoulders, and parade him around three times for all the assembled people to see. Collective expressions of joy ratify this physical gesture, marking the unification of the Franks and Gauls as one people under Childeric. The people of this newly formed, singular "corps de Republique" display enthusiasm for their appointed king with claps and shouts. This act of elevation not only celebrates the king while but also affirms the people's authority. Their physical and emotional approval supports and sustains Childeric's power. In other words, the people's physical and emotional approval offers proof of the king's legitimacy.[38]

Accounts of ancient election ceremonies in *Francogallia* (as well as in other Huguenot resistance treatises) not only establish a long precedent for popular sovereignty in the French tradition but also teach us how to recognize the people's authority through what I call affective evidence. When describing the election of Clovis II, Hotman notes that the people applauded "avec batemens de mains and cris de joye, le haussèrent sur un bouclier et l'establirent Roy sur eux" (with both clapping and shouting, and, lifting him upon a shield, made him king over them).[39] The same elements we saw in Childeric's ceremony are present here as well: the shield on which to raise the king, the people's applause, and their cries of joy. These claps and cries are embodied, emotional signs of the people's approval. In other words, these collective expressions of pleasure offer affective evidence of the people's consent to be governed. Indeed, just as in the case of Childeric, Hotman insists that royal elevation depends on popular approval rather than royal lineage. (Clovis III, like Childeric, succeeded his father to the throne.) Hotman writes: "Les Rois de France estoyent ancienment etablis plustost par le consentement et la volonté du peuple, que par droit de succession" (The kings of Francogallia were constituted by the authoritative [consent and will] of the people).[40] The terms "consentement" and "volonté" both reinforce how the people express affectively their ultimate authority over the king. The emotional resonances of volonté are more clearly legible to modern readers than those of consentement as volonté continues to communicate desire and inclination in addition to its association with the more rational faculty of the will.[41] Consentement requires a bit more explication. Derived from the French verb *consentir* and its Latin precedent *consentio*, which literally join "to feel" (*sentio*) and "with" (*cum*), consentement denotes agreement and concord between two or more parties. During the sixteenth century, consentement was used in a range of contexts, from music and architecture, to politics, religion, marriage, and other domestic affairs in order to express harmony, affinity, affection, or pleasure. To cite but one example, Michel de Montaigne, uses the term consentement when discussing women who object to the bonds of marriage. It is perfectly understandable, he writes, that women would disagree with social norms that were imposed on them by men. As a result, "Il y a naturellement de la brigue et riotte entre elles et nous; le plus estoit consentment que nous [les hommes] ayons avec elles, encores est-il tumultuaire et tempesteux" (There is naturally strife and wrangling between them and us: the closest communion [consentement] we have with them is still tumultuous and tempestuous).[42] In other words, any sympathy or fellow feeling established between men and women is necessarily tenuous given their respective social positions. Montaigne's example helps us to understand the emotional overtones of consentement, as well as this concept's fragility. As in Hotman's account of Clovis III's election, Huguenot resistance treatises repeatedly remind us that kings require the people's consent to rule legitimately and alert us to the many royal missteps that would lead the people to withdraw their consent.

Affective evidence remained a sign of popular sovereignty even after the people stopped assembling to elect their king. Resistance treatises argue that while the days of the people placing a king on his shield and hoisting him onto their shoulders may have been long over by the sixteenth century, the political force of this practice nevertheless persisted. The *Vindiciae* warns kings not to forget their ongoing debt to the people and reminds kings that they are "de mesme paste et condition que les autres, eslevez de terre par les voix et comme sur les espaules du peuple jusques en leur throne " ([of] the same [material and conditions] as other men, and that they are elevated from the ground to their position [on the throne] by the votes and, as it were, on the shoulders of the people).[43] The treatise metaphorizes the embodied, emotional gestures of ancient elections without losing sight of their material origins; kings are made of the same substance as all others. The treatises support their claims of popular sovereignty's endurance by pointing to contemporary political practices such as the coronation ceremony. The *Vindiciae* states:

> Quand le Roy de France est sacré et couronné, les Evesques de Laon et de Beauvais, Paris Ecclesiastiques, demandent au peuple là present, s'il desire et commande que celui qui assiste lors, soit Roy? Et le formulaire du sacre porte qu'il est lors esleu par le peuple. Le peuple ayant donné signe de consentir à cela, le Roy jure, qu'il conservera tous les droits, privileges et loix de France universellement, qu'il n'alienera point le Domaine. . . . Aussi n'est-il pas ceint de l'espee, ni oinct, ni couronné des Pairs, qui portent lors des chapeaux de fleurs sur leurs testes, et ne reçoit le sceptre et la verge de justice ni n'est proclamé Roy que premierement le peuple ne l'ait commandé.[44]

> When the king of France is inaugurated, the bishops of Laon and Beauvais—as ecclesiastical peers—first ask the whole people, which is there, whether it desires and orders that he should be king? For this reason it is even said in the formula of inauguration that he is elected by the people at that point. When the people is seen to have consented, he swears that he will protect the laws and privileges of France and all rights in their entirety; that he will not alienate the domain, and so on . . . Indeed, he is neither girded with the sword, anointed, nor crowned by the peers (who are themselves adorned with coronets); nor does he receive the sceptre and rod of justice; nor is he proclaimed king, until the people has ordered it.[45]

Although the inauguration of French kings in many ways represented a celebration of dynastic succession (the treatises must confront this historical problem at every turn), the coronation ceremony also confirmed the people's ultimate authority. Much like the biblical king David had refused to approach the throne until called by the people (an example I discuss in this book's introduction), French kings are not anointed or crowned until those assembled express their "desire et commande" that these actions take place. The *Vindiciae*'s formulation, which closely follows that of the ceremony itself, underscores that the people's collective affect, their desire, not only shapes the people' political authority but also makes this authority legible. As in the ancient election ceremonies, these coronations require evidence of the people's approval.[46] The king only swears his oath once the people have expressed their consent (le peuple ayant donné signe de consentir à cela). The *Vindiciae*, however, does not detail how those assembled would indicate their consent, leaving us to wonder what the ceremonial vestiges of ancient claps and shouts might look and feel like.

If the *Vindiciae* and other Huguenot resistance treatises do not enumerate the people's signs of consent in contemporary coronation ceremonies, the treatises do suggest how the people communicate their approval of a king more generally. What emerges throughout these texts is that the presence of popular consent may best be understood as the absence of dissent. Put another way, affective evidence of the people's approval registers less as a specific expression of emotion, and more as a general sense of peace and order. On this point we might remember Hotman's valorization of musical harmony as a fitting analogy for political harmony.[47] For its part, the *Vindiciae* insists that the people's consent to be governed by kings is in keeping with their natural inclination toward liberty, since good kings promote peace and prosperity.[48] But in Bèze's *Du droit des magistrats*, we find a particularly powerful example of how the absence of discord indicates the presence of consent. Bèze writes effusively about the happy state of England under the reign of Elizabeth I: "Quant au Royaume d'Angleterre le plus heureux qui soit aujourdhui au monde, & que Dieu vueille maintenir en sa tranquilité" (As regards the kingdom of England, the most blessed of all, as many as may be seen today in the whole world—would that it may long continue in that blessedness).[49] Associating England's happiness with its tranquility, Bèze goes on to compare England's affective state with that of other countries:

> Et certainement l'heureux repos duquel il [le royaume d'Angleterre] jouit il y a desja plusieurs annees, sous le tresdoux et benin gouvernmenet de leur serenissime Roine Elizabeth, estant comparé avec le paouvre & miserable estat de tant d'autres pais, montre par experience combien est heureuse et profitable une telle moderation de la puisance Royalle pourvue qu'elle soit bien practiquee, et que les Rois craignans Dieu, & aimans leur peuples, souffrent d'en estre non pas gouvernez comme pupilles (ainsi que parlent les flatteurs de cour, mangeans le pain pestri aux larmes du pauvre peuple) mais addressez & avertis avec l'obeissance & la reverence qui appartient à leur majesté.[50]

> And certainly, if we wish to compare that blessed tranquility which they have been enjoying for many years now under the kindest and most peaceful reign of her most serene Majesty Elizabeth with the wretched and unhappy condition of so many other parts, we shall learn from experience as such how beneficial and blessed that moderation of royal power is, if only it be rightly employed and if the very kings, Godfearing men and lovers of their people, allowed themselves, not to be swayed by it as (if they were) wards (in need of guardians)—as flatterers at court who stuff themselves with bread kneaded with the tears of the wretched commons are wont to say—but to be directed and advised by it, yet with that respect and obedience which befits their majesty and is due to it.[51]

To happiness and tranquility, Bèze adds "repos," a term that, as Domna Stanton notes, indicated during the early modern period an ideal state of peace and contemplation, be it personal or collective.[52] For Bèze, Elizabeth provides her people with this enviable state of repos, which offers his readers a model of what the relationship between a monarch and her rulers should feel like. As we have seen in previous examples, good rulers should love their people. They should heed divine wisdom rather than the counsel of flatterers who promote personal gain rather than the public good and in so doing encourage the monarch to cause the people pain and sadness. To follow Elizabeth's example is to foster a general sense of welfare and happiness. By emphasizing tranquility and repos as the correlatives of happiness, *Du droit des magistrats* suggests that the opposite state of discord and unrest would indicate the people's displeasure with their monarch and a withdrawal of their consent to be governed.

Public Representatives

If the people's consent authorizes a king's rule, then the people's lack of consent authorizes resistance. The people's divinely conferred sovereignty permits it to oppose a king who takes power unjustly or who becomes a tyrant after taking the throne. The *Vindiciae* imagines that some might object to this people's right to resist a tyrant on the grounds that the exercise of such a right would lead to disorder and confusion: "Quoy, direz-vous? faudra-il que tout une populasse, ceste beste qui porte un million de testes, se mutine et accoure en desordre pour donner ordre à ce que dessus? Quelle addresse y a-il en une multitude desbridee? Quel conseil et quelle prudence pour pourvoir aux affaires?" ("What?," you may ask; "Ought a whole multitude—that monster, I say, with countless heads—to rush headlong in raging fury at this problem, as if it were in battle formation? What order can there be in such a mob, what counsel, what manner of dealing with affairs?").[53] To these objections of its imagined interlocutor, the *Vindiciae* explains that while it is the people as a whole, corporate body that confers or withdraws its consent on kings, only select representatives of the people may organize resistance to a tyrant: "Quand nous parlons de tout le peuple, nous entendons par ce mot ceux qui ont en main l'autorité de par le peuple, asavoir les Magistrats qui sont inferieurs au Roy, et que le peuple a deleguez, ou establis en quelque sorte que ce soit" (When we speak of the whole people, we mean those who have received authority from the people—the magistrats, clearly, who are inferior to the king and chosen by the people, or constituted in some other way).[54] The treatise claims to resolve the problem of disorder by distinguishing between the people and its representatives. The people rendered here as the disorderly *populace* run the risk of promoting discord and disunity. The representatives, however, can be trusted to discharge the people's political authority in an orderly manner. As I will explain, much like we can locate the people's approval of their monarch through their collective expressions of emotion, we can identify the people's approval of their representatives through similar forms of affective evidence.

Who are these representatives whom the people have authorized and who may resist a tyrant on the people's behalf? Huguenot resistance treatises explicitly state that only certain subjects may legitimately serve as the people's representatives. As I note in this book's introduction, the treatises distinguish between particuliers, or private persons, and personnes publiques, or public representatives.

Whereas particuliers have little recourse against tyrannical kings other than to flee or pray for the situation to improve, personnes publique may undertake and organize active resistance to tyranny. At first glance, the type of person who may serve as a legitimate public representative seems relatively straightforward. The treatises clearly state that magistrates, members of legislative bodies, and members of the nobility may represent the people. For example, when Hotman asserts that throughout the history of Francogallia the people's consent authorizes kings, he makes clear that he speaks specifically about how the authority of the people is discharged through the orders and estates: "la souveraine et prinicpale administration du Royaume des Francsgaulois appartenoit à la generale et solennelle assemblée de toute la nation qu'on a appellé depuis l'assemblée des trois estats" (the highest administrative authority in the kingdom of Francogallia lay in the formal public council of the nation, which in later times was called the assembly of the three estates).[55] *Francogallia* rhetorically replaces the people as such with the orders, or estates. In this formulation, representatives officially take the place of the people. The part takes the place of the whole.

The *Vindiciae* performs a similar rhetorical operation when explaining how people's superiority over the king allows them to depose him should he display signs of tyranny, but the treatise also introduces an element of ambiguity into the question of who may serve as a public representative:

> Davantage, nous avons prouvé que tous Rois reçoivent leur dignité Royale de la main du peuple: que tout le peuple consideré en un corps est par dessus et plus grand que le Roy: qu'iceluy Roy est tant seulement premier et souverain gouverneur et serviteur du Royaume, qui n'a pour maistre et vray Seigneur que le peuple. Il s'ensuit donc que le tyran offensant le peuple commet felonnie contre le Seigneur du fief, blesse la sacree Majesté du Royaume, est rebelle: et pourtant merite la punition ordonnee par les loix, voire encores plus grande. Pourtant, ce dit Bartole, il pourra estre deposé par le Seigneur souverain, ou justement puni suivant la loy Julia

> condamnant ceux qui font violence au public. Le souverain c'est tout le peuple, *ou ceux qui le representent*, comme ceux que nous appellons Electeurs, Palatins, Pairs, Estats et autres.[56]

> We have proved, then, that all kings receive their royal dignity from the people; that the whole people is more powerful than, and superior to, the king; that the king is only the supreme minister and agent of the kingdom or empire, but the people truly lord. It follows, therefore, that a tyrant commits a felony against a people as lord of the fief; that he is guilty of high treason against the kingdom or empire, and is a rebel; and consequently that he has infringed the same laws and deserves far heavier punishments. Thus, says Bartolus, he could be deposed by a superior, or most justly punished according to the Julian law on public force. For the superior is the whole people, *or those who represent it*—the electors, palatines, patricians, the assembly of the estates, and the rest.[57]

The passage makes clear that the people as a corporate body, "le peuple consideré en un corps," is superior to the king. Precisely who speaks and acts on behalf of this body is a more complicated matter. The *Vindiciae* indicates that it is "tout le peuple, ou ceux qui le representent" who possess sovereign authority. The list of recognized representatives, "Electeurs, Palatins, Pairs, and Estats" is followed by "et autres," suggesting both that the kinds of possible representatives are too many to fully enumerate and, more radically, that the category might conceivably stretch to include representatives for which the *Vindiciae* does not account.

Although the ability to serve as a representative is most explicitly based on place or position, on one's role within established social and political structures, what quickly becomes clear in these treatises is that one's public office itself is not sufficient to secure one's legitimacy. What is required in addition to such an office is the people's approval. In *Du droit des magistrats*, Bèze describes a chain of influence whereby particuliers must appeal to their lower magistrates, who must then appeal to members of the Estates general, who must then appeal to the king to rein in tyranny:

> Les particuliers . . . puissent avoir recours à leurs Magistrats subalternes, les sommans de leur devoir, par lesquels estant emploiez ou par la plus saine partie d'iceux, j'ai deja dit ce qu'ils doivent à Dieu & à leur patrie. Et quant aux Magistrats inferieurs, c'est à eux de se joindre ensemble, & de presser l'assemblee des Estats se conservans cependant autant que faire se peut et doit contre une tyrannie manifeste.[58]

> [Private persons should] betake themselves to the intermediate magistrates and take them to task concerning their duty . . . It is assuredly the duty of the subordinate magistrates at once unanimously to insist on an assembly of the Estates and meanwhile as far as they can and may to defend and protect themselves against undisguised tyranny.

In outlining this chain of influence, Bèze indicates that particuliers have not only the authority but also the duty to summon and compel their magistrates to act on their behalf to address manifest tyranny. He also suggests that lower magistrates and members of the Estates have the duty to take seriously the people's concerns. A good public representative, *Du droit des magistrats* implies, will register the people's discontent and take appropriate action.

What are particuliers to do if their established public representatives fail to register their displeasure with a tyrannical king? Resistance treatises offer a few different modes of recourse, which range in the extent of legitimate activity that they afford to particuliers. The paradoxes that arise from this—at times contradictory—range of options help us to better understand the ambiguity that surrounds the treatises' political implications. This range of options differs depending on the type of tyrant at hand. If the tyrant has come to power through usurpation, and the people do not consent to his rule, then private persons may legitimately resist—even if their public representatives do not. If, however, the tyrant has come to power through usurpation, and the people *do* initially consent to his rule, or if a previously just, legitimate king begins to act tyrannically, then private persons legitimately cannot resist if their public representatives do not. Instead, particuliers whose public officials are unmoved by public outcry about a tyrannical monarch must either flee the tyrant's territory or remain and quietly endure the tyrant's rule. In other words, the treatises seem to suggest that private persons who find themselves in this situation have no recourse against an unresponsive public other than to leave or to suffer patiently.[59]

Yet, while resistance treatises at times encourage particuliers to flee or suffer patiently, these texts also suggest that, if established public representatives fail to register the people's displeasure with a tyrannical king, these representatives may be ignored and replaced by those who are more responsive to the people's concerns. Throughout their examinations of just and unjust resistance, these texts often rhetorically equate kings and other public representatives, using phrases such as "des Rois et autres Magistrates" and emphasizing that, much like other magistrates, kings are mere mortals, made of the same substance or *masse* and subject to the same passions as other members of the community.[60] The treatises use the king's status as a mere mortal and magistrate to justify how he might be legitimately removed and replaced if he began to show signs of tyranny. If the king's status as a magistrate allows resistance treatises to argue for legitimate opposition to a tyrannical king, then readers may reasonably assume that other magistrates, such as the "magistrats subalterns" and "magistrats inferieurs" may also legitimately be opposed. At other moments the *Vindiciae* is more direct about the people's ability to remove and replace their public representatives. Noting that public officials have a duty to preserve the "salut et la liberté du peuple," the *Vindiciae* writes that, if these officials fail to do so, "la loi permet [le peuple] de choisir un autre avocat, et de nouveau poursuivre son droit" (the law allows [the people] to elect another patron and pursue their right anew).[61] Passages like this one indicate that, although resistance treatises do at several points explicitly restrict particuliers to private suffering or exodus if their public representatives are unmoved by their concerns, these texts also leave open the possibility for particuliers to seek different representatives if they find themselves in such a situation.

The *Vindiciae*'s rhetorical invocation of a stable, coherent emotional community strengthens the idea that public representatives must be responsive to the people's complaints to maintain their legitimacy. Much like the *Vindiciae*'s preface distinguishes between virtuous readers and their vicious Machiavellian counterparts by way of their imagined affective responses to the treatise's argument, the treatise itself uses affect as a means to distinguish between good and bad public representatives. "Une conjuration est bonne ou mauvaise, selon que la fin où elle vise est bonne ou mauvaise, et selon aussi que sont affectionnez ceux qui la font" (A league is good or bad, as its purpose is good or bad, [and according also to how those who undertake it are loved]).[62] One can determine whether a political plot is legitimate or seditious based not only on its expressed ends but also on the objects of its participants' affections. With this statement, the *Vindiciae* performatively presumes an emotional community that is in agreement about what is good and what is bad, as well as between worthy and unworthy objects of affection. The treatise repeatedly reaffirms the existence of this unified, stable emotional community through its appeals to divine and natural law. For example, when discussing whether foreign leaders should step in to help a population suffering under tyranny (a subject I will take up in more detail later), the *Vindiciae* appeals to the idea that members of the Christian church are bound together as one body. Members of this body necessarily feel each other's pain and respond to each other's suffering. As a result, the text argues, "quiconque n'est esmeu de la douleur, de l'embrasement, et de l'agistation de l'Eglise, ne peut estre du corps d'icelle" (one who is not roused by the church's pain, its conflagration, or its being tossed to and fro, is not of that body).[63] Linking together the ideas of physical and affective pain, of being moved physically and emotionally, the *Vindiciae* makes an individual's failure to properly sense and respond to suffering grounds for exclusion from the Christian community. Assertions such as these help us understand how a public representative, to maintain his legitimacy, would need to demonstrate his sensitivity to the people's suffering.

The *Vindiciae* offers two alternative kinds of representatives that might act on the people's behalf when their existing public officials—nobles, magistrates, members of the estates—fail to respond to the people's complaints: the extraordinary liberator and the foreign prince. An extraordinary liberator is a private person whom God appoints to act on the people's behalf. The treatise explains the special status of this potential liberator: "si on les considere en eux-mesmes, on les pourroit nommer particuliers, dautant qu'ils n'avoyent point de vocation ordinare" (Certainly if you consider them all in themselves, you can say that they were private individuals, because they were not constituted ordinarily).[64] Extraordinary liberators have no position or social role that qualifies them to resist tyranny. Their divine appointment, however, allows them to transcend their particularity and take up arms against the tyrant. "Mais puis que nous savons qu'ils ont esté extraordinairement appellez, & que Dieu luy mesme leur a (s'il faut ainsi parler) mis son espee en la main, tant s'en faut que nous les estimions particuliers ou personnes privees, que mesmes nous les esleverons beaucoup plus que les Magistrats ordinaires en quelque degré qu'ils puissent estre" (But since we know that they were called extraordinarily, and that, as it were, God manifestly girded them with His sword, not only do we not consider them private individuals, but we deem them to be more powerful than any ordinary magistrate).[65] God's appointment not only authorizes these private persons to act as public officials but also elevates them over any "magistrats ordinaires." In other words, the extraordinary liberator's legitimacy exceeds that of previously acknowledged representatives, whose authority derives from their public position or rank.

If the *Vindiciae* puts forward the divine appointment of an extraordinary liberator as a hopeful possibility for people suffering under a tyrant, it also cautions that this kind of exceptional representative raises a problem of authenticity. How are people to determine whether an extraordinary liberator is truly appointed by God, or merely believes or pretends himself to be so appointed? The treatise names biblical figures, such as Moses, Deborah, Jehu, and Ehud as examples of extraordinary liberators.[66] In these cases, biblical authority confirms that these figures from the past were indeed divinely appointed. Absent such confirmation, and without the benefit of hindsight, how can the people be sure of the extraordinary liberator's legitimacy? In other words, on what basis can extraordinary liberators of the *Vindiciae*'s present and future be determined? The treatise clarifies that the problem of a potential liberator's authenticity is solved if the people hear God appoint an extraordinary liberator himself or through his prophets. It is when God's voice cannot be heard that the people must be wary: "Mais dautant que Dieu ne parle point de sa bouche, ni extraordinairement par des Prophetes, c'est en ceci que nous devons estre bien retenus & sur nos gardes" (But when God has neither spoken with his own mouth nor, extraordinarily, through the prophets, we should be especially sober and circumspect in this matter).[67] In this situation, the treatise counsels those who believe they have been authorized to resist tyranny to conduct a thorough examination of themselves: "si quelqu'un pensant estre inspiré du sainct Esprit, s'attribue l'autorité susmentionnee, je le prie de se bien sonder & voir s'il n'est point enflé d'arrogance, prendre garde qu'il ne soit Dieu à soy-mesme, & ne concevoir de sa teste telle opinion de soy. Qu'il ne conçoive donc point de vanité, s'il ne veut enfanter mensonge" (For if anyone lays claim to that authority for himself, as though he were inspired by the divine spirit, he should certainly make sure that he is not puffed up with pride, that he is not God to himself . . . and that he does not, therefore, conceive a vanity and beget a lie).[68] Self-conceived liberators must search themselves for vanity and arrogance as the presence of these qualities signal that they have made a mistake. If this vanity and arrogance are present then the would-be liberator is not an agent of God but merely a god unto himself. The *Vindiciae* effectively charges presumptive extraordinary liberators with examining themselves for affective evidence of their authenticity—or its lack—and then acting accordingly, either proceeding with their divinely authorized campaign or recognizing that they are driven by human feeling and standing down.

The *Vindiciae* also charges the people with making the distinction between a divinely appointed liberator and a merely ambitious pretender. If the people are not able to make such a distinction, they risk fighting under the sign of heresy, while mistaking it for the sign of Christ.[69] If the people cannot see or hear God directly, as was the case with the miraculous examples recounted in the Bible, then the people must determine whether the liberator exhibits the attributes of divine direction through their emotional response to the liberator's speech and actions: "il faut pour le moins que par les effects nous sentions que Dieu besonge miraculeusement en nos coeurs: c'est que nous ayons un esprit vuide de toute ambition, un vray & ardent zele, droite science & conscience, de peur qu'estans guidez d'erreur ou d'ambition, nous ne servions aux idoles ou à nous-mesmes plustost qu'au vray Dieu" (it is necessary that we should at least [feel that God works miraculously in our hearts by its effects]: a mind empty of all ambition, authentic and earnest zeal, and finally conscience and knowledge, so as to prevent him being led on by error to foreign gods, or becoming over-excited by the frenzy of ambition to serve himself rather than the true God).[70] The people must examine their responses to the potential extraordinary liberator in a way that parallels the liberator's own task of self-examination. These parallel examinations produce a bond between the people and the liberator that hinges on affective evidence. The liberator's divine appointment—and thus his political legitimacy as a public representative—is confirmed not only by his own assessment of his virtue and modesty but also by the people's capacity to perceive, to feel these qualities.

In addition to the extraordinary liberator, affective evidence also secures the legitimacy of foreign princes in the *Vindiciae*. As I briefly alluded to earlier in this chapter, the treatise argues that private persons may appeal to a foreign prince for defense against a tyrannical king in cases when their traditional public representatives remain unresponsive. The *Vindiciae* initially argues that particuliers may appeal to a foreign prince given the unity of Christendom: "il y a une seule Eglise, de laquelle Jesus Christ est le chef, et dont les membres sont tellement unis et conjoints que le plus petit entre eux ne peut estre offensé, que les autres n'en sentent le coup et la douleur" (the church is one, of which Christ is the head, and the members of which are so united and harmonious that none of them—not even the least—can suffer violence or harm, without the others being injured and feeling pain).[71] The church forms one body, of which Christ is the head, and each member of this body feels the pain of all others. In this formulation, the *Vindiciae* preserves the idea of a well-ordered, stratified society in which each member has a specific place, while also insisting that the members of this society feel each other's pain. By binding all Christendom through the possibility of shared pain, the treatise authorizes alliance between particuliers, or "le plus petit" of one kingdom and the rulers of another. This shared sensibility crosses national borders, serving as the affective evidence that authorizes intervention in cases of tyranny when the people's usual representatives remain unmoved.

Affective evidence does not merely provide a justification for foreign intervention, but also mandates it. The *Vindiciae* states that if a tyrannical king harms his subjects in one part of Christendom, then the leaders of all other parts have a duty to protect them. The treatise arrives at this conclusion by noting how various Christian kingdoms have formed alliances to protect each other from the Turks: "que veulent dire tant d'alliances et tant de croisades contre les Turcs, s'il n'a point esté loisible aux Princes Chrestiens, voire aux plus eslognez de retirer l'Eglise de Dieu de la main des tyrans, et les Chrestiens captifs hors du jong de servitude?" (why so many allied campaigns against the Turks, and so many crusading proclamations against them, if it was not lawful for any Christian prince, even the most distant, to free God's church from tyranny and captive Christians from the yoke of servitude?).[72] By posing a series of questions such as this, the treatise argues that, if Christian Princes may legitimately come to each other's aide to protect against an external enemy, then these same princes also may act to protect against an internal enemy: a Christian king who acts tyrannically and thus heretically against his people. Moreover, Christian Princes who deliver their religious brethren from a tyrannical Christian king are just as heroic, if not more than those who protect their brethren from Turks: "Brief, si l'on a estimé actes heroiques d'afranchir les Chrestiens de servitude corporelle (car quant aux consciences les Turcs ne contraignent personne) est-ce pas chose encores plus louable d'afranchir et remettre en liberté les ames captives?" (If, in short, it was pious to free Christians from bodily slavery (for the Turks coerce no-one [in conscience]), is it not much more so to manumit the souls of the wretched, and restore them to liberty?).[73] The Turks imprison the physical bodies of their Christian captives without making demands on their souls. The tyrannical Christian king, however, violates the freedom of his subjects' souls by prescribing how they must pray and in what manner they must display their love of God. Since the tyrant's violation of his subjects' souls, their inner liberties, is more egregious than any physical captivity, the *Vindiciae* suggests that resistance to this violation is just as legitimate—if not more—than resistance to the Turks. When confronted with a Christian tyrant's infringement on his subjects' souls, rulers from throughout Christendom have a duty to intervene.[74]

According to the *Vindiciae*, piety, justice, and charity together move foreign princes to act against tyranny. The treatise states: "La pieté commande qu'on maintiene la Loy & l'Eglise de Dieu: la justice veut qu'on lie les mains aux tyrans ruineurs du droit et de toute bonne police: la charité requiert que l'on tende la main & qu'on releve ceux qui sont accablez" (Piety commands us to keep the law of God and to protect the church; justice bids us to check tyrants and overthrowers of right and the commonwealth; and charity to succour and lend a helping hand to the oppressed).[75]

The triumvirate of piety, justice, and charity that should motivate foreign princes to intervene echoes Hotman's emphasis in *Francogallia* on the people's "consentement et volonté" during ancient election ceremonies, and the *Vindiciae*'s own emphasis on how representatives express the peoples "desire et commande" during contemporary coronation ceremonies. In these accounts of how the people elect and approve their kings, as in the *Vindiciae*'s descriptions of how foreign princes must lend a hand against tyranny, no attempt is made to separate political will, reason, and emotion, or to valorize one over the others—as we moderns are often tempted to do. Instead, throughout the resistance treatises, these forces are inseparable. Piety, charity, and justice all animate each other.

Much like affective evidence justifies a foreign prince's intervention, it also provides the basis on which those suffering under tyranny may evaluate the foreign princes' motives. The *Vindiciae* warns that some foreign princes may invoke piety, justice, and charity as pretexts for intervention when their real motivation is not the defense against tyranny but instead the expansion of their own power and territory.[76] How are the people to distinguish between a foreign prince who sincerely desires to help his suffering neighbors and a foreign prince who merely intervenes out of self-interest? As in the discussion about the legitimacy of extraordinary liberators, the *Vindiciae* turns to past examples for clarity. When recounting several of these past examples, the *Vindiciae* notes that sincere princes enjoyed the collective approval of those whom they saved from tyranny: "Tandis que l'Empire Romain demeura libre, on l'appella la sauvegarde de tout le monde contre la violence des tyrans, pource que le Senat estoit le port et refuge des Rois, peuples et nations" (Thus as long as the Roman empire remained free, it was often called protection of the lands of the world against the plundering of tyrants, because the senate was the haven and refuge of kings, peoples, and nations).[77] This example casts the Roman senate as a sincere foreign liberator, noting that it was viewed favorably by the kings, people, and nations to whom it provided safe harbor. The treatise continues: "Semblablement, Constantin, appellé par les Romains contre Maxentius, eut Dieu pour general de son armee, et toute l'Eglise celebra merveilleusement ce voyage" (So when Constantine was summoned by the Romans against tyrant Maxentius, he had God as leader of the army, and his expedition was extolled with wonderful acclamations by the whole church).[78] This second example notes how Constantine was "merveilleusement" celebrated for his righteous campaign against tyranny. In both cases, there is evidence of general approval for the foreign power's intervention among those delivered from tyranny. These examples demonstrate how collective expressions of joy, comfort, or relief previously legitimized foreign princes as representatives of the people and suggest that one may use similar signs of affection to determine the legitimacy of a present or future intervention.

The *Vindiciae* underscores the importance of affective evidence as a means of determining a foreign prince's legitimacy through its appeals to readers' ability to consult their conscience. Whereas in the case of extraordinary liberators, as we saw above, the treatise encourages members of *le peuple* to let both "droite science & conscience" be their guides, when it comes to foreign princes the treatise privileges the former over the latter. To address this question, the *Vindiciae* argues, "il faut aporter plus de conscience que de science" (conscience [*conscientia*] is more necessary than knowledge [*scientia*]).[79] Both these terms appeal to readers' knowledge, but the use of *conscience* in this context foregrounds a kind of knowledge that binds the individual subject to the collective. In other words, the knowledge that *conscience* provides is both deeply felt within oneself and shared with others. We begin to see the particularity of *conscience* by looking at the 1579 Latin edition of the *Vindiciae*, which distinguishes between *scientia* and *conscientia*.[80] While the term *scientia* alone designates knowledge as such, be it general or specific, the addition of the prefix "con-" emphasizes shared knowledge or perception, "a knowing along with others."[81] During the sixteenth century *conscientia* and its French counterpart *conscience* principally indicated the shared knowledge of morality, or a common sense of right and wrong. Individuals could examine their sentiments, speech, and actions to assess how they measured up to these shared moral standards. Robert Estienne's *Dictionarium latinogallicum* and Jean Nicot's *Thresor de la language francoyse tant ancienne que moderne* both emphasize this sense of self-examination or reflection with phrases such as "Tesmoignage en son esprit d'avoir bien vescu" (Testimony in his mind of having lived rightly), "La conscience est le tesmoignage ou recordation qu'il a en son esprit d'avoir mal fait, le remors" (Conscience is the testimony or record that he has in his mind of having done ill, remorse),[82] "Examiner sa conscience" (To examine one's conscience), and "Estre seur de sa conscience" (To be sure of one's conscience).[83] By emphasizing how the people need to draw on *conscience* when assessing the legitimacy of a foreign prince's intervention, the *Vindiciae* binds each person's interior sense of right and wrong to the common moral perception shared across the emotional community invoked by the treatise itself.

Although the *Vindiciae* rhetorically positions itself above the fray of religious division, it is important to situate its appeals to conscience, as well as to the emotional community these appeals performatively sustain, through a Calvinist idiom. Indeed, both the *Vindiciae* and Bèze's *Du droit des magistrats* draw on Calvin's understanding of conscience.[84] Calvin's mobilization of the term is consistent with the term's more general sixteenth-century use in that it binds individual and collective perceptions of right and wrong. What is specific to Calvin's use of *conscience* is how it configures divine and monarchical power. For Calvin, a person's conscience must be kept free from monarchical interference because it is bound only to God. A monarch who attempts to force religious beliefs on his subjects becomes a tyrant because he violates the bounds of his temporal jurisdiction. Citing an example of such a violation, Calvin writes in the *Institutes*, "But since it is clear that the law has been imposed by men, I say that it is both a tyrannous law and one promulgated in contempt of God, who, binding consciences to his Word, would have them loosed from the power of men."[85] Calvin's liberty of conscience is thus not a freedom *to* believe whatever one wishes (as modern usages of the term would often have it), but rather a freedom *from* monarchical meddling.[86] Calvin argued that the conscience had to be politically free because it was only truly bound to God's law alone. To consult the working of one's conscience was to attune oneself to God's judgment and direction. In so doing, one would effectively attune oneself to a community of believers who were similarly bound.[87] While individual subjects are born with a knowledge of God's demands, they must nonetheless cultivate their ability to perceive the workings of their conscience because this ability can be dulled by sin and human desire. As Darren Walhof has observed, for Calvin, adhering to one's conscience requires a particular form of knowledge, one that is both intellectual and embodied. Calvin "employs terms such as *sensus*, which suggests some type of sensation or feeling, though it is perhaps best rendered as 'awareness,' and *persuasio*, which is variously translated as 'belief,' 'conviction,' or 'persuasion.' Other terms that Calvin uses to describe this innate sense of God's existence include 'impression' (*impressio*), 'presumption' (*praesumptio*), and 'notion' (*notio*)."[88] All these terms demonstrate that conscience involves affective rather than purely intellectual or "theoretical" faculties.[89] Conscience impresses on and moves individual subjects to follow God's precepts. One feels the demands of conscience individually, but in so doing adheres to a community of believers who are similarly moved.

Given this Calvinist context, when the *Vindiciae* appeals to conscience as the means through which the people will determine a foreign prince's legitimacy, the treatise is referring in large part to the people's shared ability to know God's judgment through a kind of sense perception or feeling. The intervention of a sincere foreign prince may look the same as that of an opportunist looking to expand his territory. The treatise implies, however, that these two different kinds of intervention will not feel the same by distinguishing between true "pieté" and the "voile de pieté" (cloak of piety).[90] True piety and fellow feeling are not self-interested and care only for the good of the other: "la pieté, soigneuse du bien d'autry" (piety . . . seeks the good of another).[91] This distinction indicates that a foreign prince's words and actions are not enough to determine his legitimacy. Legitimacy must be felt. The treatise concludes this section by arguing that those foreign princes who act out of self-interest when responding or failing to respond to those suffering under tyranny seek to destroy the affective bonds that unite the Christian community: "Ceux qui ne tienent conte de telles choses, veulent chasser la pieté, la justice, & la charité, voire les abolir tellement qu'il n'en soit plus parlé au monde" (Those who destroy these things, wish to destroy and annihilate piety, justice, and charity entirely from our midst).[92] As a result, the treatise reinforces the importance of these affective bonds, those frequent companions "la pieté, la justice, & la charité," as the forces that serve as arbiters of political virtue.

If a people suffering under tyranny must use affective evidence to determine a foreign prince's sincerity, so must foreign princes use this kind of evidence to clarify their own motives. The *Vindiciae* notes that some foreign princes have declined to protect their neighbors from tyranny—when such action would have been justified—for fear that they would be perceived as opportunists seeking to augment their territory. To those foreign princes who are worried about being perceived as opportunistic and infringing on the just rule of a king over his people, the treatise writes: "Vous direz, je crain qu'un secourant l'un je ne face tort à l'autre: et je vous respon que vous voulez couvrir vostre lacheté du manteau de justice: et si vous mettez la main sur la conscience, vous confesserez que c'est toute autre chose que justice ce qui vous destourne de vostre devoir" (You will say: "I fear that in fending off wrong from the former, I am doing it to the latter." But, on the contrary, you want a cloak of justice to conceal your injustice. If you consult [your conscience], it is not justice, but rather some other cause which moves you to desert your office).[93] In the Calvinist lexicon of the *Vindiciae*, to place one's hand on one's conscience would be to examine one's inner, innate perception of God's judgment and direction. The required gesture here is metaphorical, much like the treatise's reminder to kings that their authority derives from the people relied upon the metaphorized gesture of the people raising up their king. And like that "gestural echo," to borrow a phrase from Joy Palacios, the hand on one's conscience retains some of its corporeal valence.[94] The equivalent phase in the Latin version of the *Vindiciae* reads, "si te ipse consulas," which could be rendered in English as "if you consult your very self" or "if you really look inside yourself," reinforcing the notion of inner perception so important to Calvin's understanding of the conscience.[95] In his translation of the *Vindiciae* from the Latin, George Garnett emphasizes the corporeal location of this self-examination by rendering the phrase, "If you consult your own heart."[96] Although, as we have seen, the French text does not explicitly indicate in this passage that to put one's hand on one's conscience is to put it one's heart, the treatise at times uses the terms *cœur* (heart) and *conscience* (conscience) synonymously. Public representatives, for example, are sometimes described as having a good or bad heart and sometimes as having a good or bad conscience.[97] The overlap between these terms is also consistent with Calvin's *Institutes*, where he frequently refers to the heart as a metaphorical place where one's inner perception meets God's judgment. In one of many passages affirming that good works are not sufficient for salvation, Calvin writes, "Therefore, as works have regard to men, so conscience refers to God. A good conscience, then, is nothing but inward integrity of heart."[98] To place one's hand on one's conscience is thus quite likely to place one's hand on one's heart, a figural place that harbors a person's inner liberty and piety and that nonetheless can be located on the body. The gesture of placing one's hand on one's conscience then connotes the ability to feel one's true motives, both physically and emotionally. As such, when the *Vindiciae* instructs, princes to examine their consciences, it effectively instructs them to search themselves for affective evidence of their virtue and thus of their political legitimacy.

The *Vindiciae* positions the foreign prince and the extraordinary liberators as exceptional figures who may step in when the usual channels of resistance fail, but the treatise's emphasis on the affective relationship between a suffering people and these exceptional figures is consistent with the role of affect in resistance theory more broadly, throughout the *Vindiciae*, as well as in *Francogallia* and *Du droit des magistrats*. Attending to the importance of affective evidence in these treatises allows us to understand the structure of resistance theory with its emphasis on order, harmony, and social stratification. The people authorize kings and public representatives alike through their expressions of affection, whether loud rounds of applause or the quiet peace of consent. Affective evidence also helps the people identify alternative public representatives, when those who occupy official positions fail to respond to the people's pain and suffering. However, while affective evidence allows us to appreciate these carefully elaborated structures, it also complicates these structures in ways that have powerful implications for resistance theory's reception both during and after the religious wars.

Affective Ambiguities

Resistance treatises mobilize affective evidence as a way to *solve* problems of political legitimacy. A good king fosters happiness, pleasure, and peace, whereas a tyrant foments complaint, pain, and unrest. Yet, as we have seen, affective evidence also raises questions of political legitimacy. The *Vindiciae* warns, for example, that appearances can be deceiving and maintains that any king, magistrate, extraordinary liberator, or foreign prince who claims to act in the people's interest may merely be playing a role. The treatise suggests the difference between a true public representative and someone who simply looks like one can be discerned through affect. In other words, authenticity can be felt. But the *Vindiciae* does not address the possibility that the feeling of authenticity may itself be manufactured. As a result, the treatise valorizes affective evidence without taking fully into account its particular challenges, such as the danger of confusing felt emotion from performed emotion, and the difficulty of verifying the sincerity of others' emotions. The particular challenges of affective evidence contribute to anxiety about resistance and representation as more radical interpretations of the *Vindiciae* circulated during the 1580s.

As the religious wars continued, many found in the *Vindiciae* (and by extension Huguenot resistance theory in general) a justification for any private individual to take up arms against the king. This interpretation stems in part from the *Vindiciae*'s discussion of foreign princes. During this discussion, the *Vindiciae* opens the possibility for the further expansion of who might legitimately serve as the people's representatives against tyranny, which, like the other expansions of this category, rests on affective ties. After establishing that any Christian prince had the right and the duty to oppose tyranny of another Christian prince, the treatise argues that this right and duty also extends beyond the bounds of Christendom.[99] The foreign prince likewise has a secular duty to intervene, which is based not in the body of Christ but rather in the "natural obligation of every man to his fellow man."[100] This natural obligation encourages private individuals to come to their neighbor's aid—and to take a maximalist view of who counts as their neighbor. "Le Juif n'est pas seulement prochain au Juif, mais aussi au Samaritain & à tout autre homme, dit Jesus Christ" (Christ says that a Jew is not only the neighbour of a Jew, but also of a Samaritan and of any other man).[101] If individuals must conceive of all others as their neighbors, the treatise argues, then so must foreign princes see all other peoples as deserving of their care and assistance. The treatise states: "Nous devons aimer notre prochain comme nous-mesmes . . . Et personne ne disputera s'il est loisible de secourir un autre . . . attendu que ce qui se fait par pure charité est plus juste & louable que ce que l'on execute par colere" ([We] should love a neighbour as ourselves. . . . Nor will anyone who judges it just to protect himself dispute whether it is lawful to defend another . . . since what [one does through] pure charity is considered more just than what [one does through] anger).[102] The love and charity that compels private individuals to protect his neighbor similarly compels princes to protect neighboring peoples. Love and charity also serve as indications that private individuals and princes are both motivated by care for their neighbor rather than by self-interest.

By rhetorically equating the obligation of private individuals and foreign princes on the basis of a common, shared humanity that can be validated by expressions of love and charity, the *Vindiciae* minimizes the distinction between the rights of private persons and public representatives that it had previously taken care to establish. As George Garnett writes, "If the basis for a neighboring prince's duty to intervene in a case of secular tyranny is the natural obligation of every man to his fellow man, then it is difficult to see why any individual may not act for the same reasons."[103] Through its analysis of the foreign prince, the *Vindiciae* comes to stand at odds within itself, as well as with *Francogallia* and *Du droit des magistrates*. In general, the treatises distinguish between tyranny of usurpation and tyranny of exercise when detailing the legitimate powers of particuliers. As noted above, in cases of usurpation, *all* subjects are permitted actively to oppose the tyrant, even particuliers. But in cases of tyranny of exercise, which occur when a previously just king begins to act like a tyrant, *Francogallia* and *Du droit des magistrats*, along with much of the *Vindiciae*, place "restraints" on the ability of particuliers to act against tyranny. When faced with tyranny of exercise, particuliers must instead act through their intermediaries, their sanctioned public representatives. In contrast, the *Vindiciae*'s discussion of foreign princes seems to obviate the need for this kind of mediation and representation. As Garnett notes, in this passage, "The only difference [between private persons and princes] is the greater power and therefore greater responsibility of the prince."[104] This final section of the *Vindiciae* suggests that the difference between private persons and princes is one of degree rather than kind. In so doing, the *Vindiciae* eliminates the distinction not only between how particuliers should respond to tyranny of exercise and tyranny of usurpation, but also, and more importantly for my purposes here, the treatise collapses the distinction between particuliers and private representatives.

What is striking about the *Vindiciae*'s confusion of its own categories is that both the categories and their confusion stem from readings of affective evidence. On the one hand, affective evidence subtends the treatise's careful analysis of legitimate resistance. Only those public representatives who sincerely register and respond to a people's affective orientation to their king may legitimately resist on that people's behalf. On the other hand, the treatise uses affective evidence to support its point that all persons are bound together through their common humanity. The idea that piety, charity, and justice should move all private persons to assist their neighbors (broadly defined) competes with the idea that private persons must wait while affect moves through the appropriate structures of resistance.

During the 1580s the carefully elaborated structures of resistance based on social order and harmony receded into the background as the notion that private persons could resist tyranny directly made its way to the foreground. This radical interpretation of Huguenot resistance theory was adopted by those who wished to portray it as seditious. For example, the Catholic cleric Jean Baricave published a lengthy refutation of the *Vindiciae* in 1614, in which he associated the treatise with texts such as William Barclay's *De regno et regali potestate* (1600), which authorized individual resistance, and argued that the *Vindiciae*'s "infernal doctrine had placed in the hand of that monster Ravaillac the cunning dagger with which he pierced the heart of the invincible Henri IV."[105] For Baricave, the *Vindiciae* moves its readers to regicide.

Members of the Catholic league also privileged the radical interpretation of the *Vindiciae*, recognizing its political potential and wishing to use it for their own ends, namely, resistance to Henri III, who they deemed insufficiently committed to preserving the Catholicism of France, and resistance to Henri IV, who, because he was at heart a Protestant, could not legitimately reign, despite his conversion to Catholicism. Leaguer pamphlets such as *Le dialogue du royaume* (1589) and Jean Boucher's *De justa Henrici Tertii abdicatione* (1589) did not take as much care as the *Vindiciae* to distinguish between the rights and duties of particuliers and their representatives, nor between the various kinds of representatives, from magistrates to extraordinary liberators to foreign princes. As a result, leaguer texts could more easily be read as justifying resistance by private individuals. Indeed, we can understand Jacques Clément's assassination of Henri III as a particularly striking example of this tendency to confuse the *Vindiciae*'s categories and exploit its own ambiguities. Garnett notes that, while "we have no evidence that" Clément, a catholic, "had read the *Vindiciae* himself," he may well have been influenced by leaguer interpretations of the text: "the *predicateurs* who inspired [Clément] to act may well have [read the *Vindiciae*] themselves or absorbed its arguments at second hand, and Boucher, who in the aftermath of the assassination converted his book into a proclamation of Clément's martyrdom, undoubtedly had."[106] Whether Clément had read the *Vindiciae*, his actions aligned with available interpretations of the treatise, which authorized private persons to take up arms against a king they perceived to be heretical and thus tyrannical.

While it is tempting to see this radical interpretation of Huguenot resistance treatises by their Catholic critics (and appropriators) as a deliberate misreading by political and religious rivals, something more complicated is at work. By positioning signs of affection as evidence of a public representative's legitimacy, these treatises leave open the possibility that anyone might legitimately take up arms against the king. Pushed to its logical bounds, the *Vindiciae*'s assertion that love, charity, and piety bind all persons, whether private or public, made it theoretically possible for any private person to become a public representative. As we have seen, the *Vindiciae* and other resistance treatises base the right of resistance to tyranny on both the public representative's perception of injustice and that of the people. The relationship between these two perceptions—the subjective and collective—authorizes resistance to tyranny. Boucher, by casting Clément as a martyr, implied that Clément acted not on his own behalf but for the good of (Catholic) France as a whole.[107]

The theoretical possibility that any private person could claim to be acting as a public representative intensified the performance questions embedded within sixteenth-century resistance theory by multiplying the number of potential representatives whose emotional ties to the people—and thus political legitimacy—would presumably require assessment. Given this theoretical possibility, affective evidence, the means by which true representatives could be distinguished from mere pretenders, becomes all the more crucial.

Performing Representation

During the religious wars, the idea that resistance treatises effectively authorized resistance by private individuals was both seductive and frightening (depending on one's point of view) in part because of the general sense of disappointment with traditional representatives. In *Francogallia* for example, Hotman laments the historical decline of the Estates and *parlements*. Whereas, he claims, once these bodies held assemblies that had an important role in ratifying laws and protecting the common good, they now, Hotman argues, are little more than hotbeds of pettiness and infighting. These assemblies had long ago ceased to perform their roles. What is more, he writes, public offices are increasingly something to be bought, rather than something to train for and attain. "Worthy men call [this practice] traffic in national office, base commerce and public robbery, because office, which ought to be the most sacred of human affairs, has been made merchandise to be bought and sold for cash."[108] For Hotman, the sale of offices contributes to the decline of public representation. Those who buy offices may have the trappings of previous office holders, but they have lost their sacred charge.

The *Vindiciae* similarly expresses disappointment in the current state of public representation, using the theater as a metaphor. The treatise imagines how a reader might scoff at the assertion that those who hold public office would defend the people and the public good against tyranny: "Tu nous proposes ici," the *Vindiciae*'s imagined reader remarks, "des Pairs, des Seigneurs, des Officiers de la Couronne. Au contraire, de ma part, je ne voy plus que des masques et des robes à l'antique, comme s'il faloit se presenter sur un eschafaud: je n'apperçoy pour le present presques aucunes traces de l'ancienne liberté et authorité" (You are telling me about patricians, nobles, and officers of the kingdom. But I, on the contrary, see nothing but spectres and antique costumes, like those in the tragedies. I discern scarcely any surviving trace of ancient liberty and authority).[109] Much like those whom Hotman criticizes for purchasing their offices, the representatives described by the reader are all show and no substance. Like actors on a stage, they wear masks and costumes, but they do not protect the people in the way that the *Vindiciae* describes. These public representatives share only external adornments with their ancient, biblical, and European predecessors.

Although these Huguenot resistance treatises express their disappointment with the current state of public representation, they also maintain that this state may be improved. In these treatises, descriptions of virtuous public representatives in the past serve as examples of what the people might expect from their present and future representation. In other words, the ideal forms of public representation in the past remain latent possibilities for the present and future. *Du droit des magistrats* evokes the Roman senate as an example of the possibility of rejuvenation after decline: "Neron empoisonneur & successeur [de Claudius], usurpa l'Empire d'une violence toute manifeste, mais sa fin nous fournit d'un exemple singulier de l'authorité que le Senat avait encores lors, usant de ses droits, qui avoient longuement dormi" (Nero, however, succeeding to [Claudius], . . . seized the imperial power by undisguised violence. But his death furnishes us with a striking example of the authority which the Senate even then retained. For making use of its right, which had long lain hid as if lulled asleep).[110] Although the Roman senate's authority had lapsed, it had not disappeared. Just as the people's sovereignty persists, despite the fact that they no longer physically elevate the king, so does the capacity of public representatives to defend the people against the sovereign. As Paul-Alexis Mellet has argued, this idea of renewal, or reactivation of "[les] restes résiduels d'un âge d'or" (the residual remainders of a golden age) is central to Huguenot resistance theory.[111] In these treatises, the past is not over and gone but instead serves as an ongoing, palpable resource for the present and future.[112]

Despite the antitheatrical sentiment expressed in *Francogallia* and the *Vindiciae*, tragic drama offered an ideal space from which to explore what reinvigorated or renewed forms of public representation might look and feel like during a time of religious violence and civil war. During the wars and in their aftermath, tragedy staged traditional forms of public representation, such as nobles, magistrates, and members of the Estates and the *parlements*, while also considering potential alternatives, from extraordinary liberators and foreign princes to private individuals. Tragic drama's exploration of the public representative's limits and possibilities is particularly salient given the genre's relationship to the legislative bodies of sixteenth-century France. As Marie Houllemare has explained, theatrical metaphors were frequently used to describe the Paris parlement. Members of the parlement shared with actors the need for oratory skills and often looked to tragedy for rhetorical and narrative models. Indeed, as Jean Balsamo has noted, at least one member of the parlement turned to tragedy as a genre that enabled political deliberation when his parlement became too contentious and dysfunctional.[113]

In addition to these historical resonances between tragedy and the political concerns of sixteenth- and seventeenth-century France, tragedy also serves an ideal site from which to examine the persistent structure of resistance theory given its long tradition as a genre that explores the relationship between individuals and collectives. As Jean-Pierre Vernant and Pierre Vidal-Naquet (among others) have argued, tragedy shows us how our individual actions are shaped by forces that exceed us.[114] Individual tragic figures, such as those I examine in the following chapters, are constitutionally collective, even if it might not always appear to be the case. By examining how tragic drama continually took up and reanimated the conceptual structure of resistance theory during the religious wars and in their long aftermath, I demonstrate how this genre provides us with enduring examples of political subjectivity that is both individual and collective. As we will see, tragedy allowed readers and spectators to see, hear, and feel the emotional and embodied ties that allowed individual subjects to emerge as representatives of the people's collective authority.

Chapter Two

The Mourner

During a discussion of the difference between legitimate resistance and sedition, the *Vindiciae contra tyrannos* compares two examples from ancient Rome: Pompey's opposition to Caesar and Cinna's plot against Augustus. The treatise concludes that the first example constituted legitimate resistance and the second mere sedition. The difference, it turns out, is timing. Pompey's opposition to Caesar took place after the tyrant had seized power, during a time of tumult and unrest, whereas Cinna's plot took place after the people had consented to Augustus's rule. Pompey, along with Cato, Cicero, and several others, "faisoyent devoir de bons patriotes, lors qu'ils prindrent les armes contre Cesar qui abolissoit le gouvernement de l'Estat" (performed the office of good citizens by snatching up weapons against Caesar when he was overturning the commonwealth).[1] The treatise argues that Pompey and his compatriots should be celebrated, even though they ultimately did not succeed in curbing Caesar's tyranny. Cinna, in contrast, "doit estre tenu pour un vray seditieux, qui conspira contre Auguste, apres l'emologation de la loy Royale, par laquelle le peuple consignoit toute sa puissance entre les mains d'Auguste" (But Cinna was clearly seditious, for we read that he conspired against Augustus when the royal law . . . by which the people had conferred all its power on Augustus, had already been passed).[2] Once the people had conferred authority on Augustus, neither Cinna nor any other public representative could take it away. For resistance to be legitimate, a public representative had to respond immediately to the people's outcry.

In this chapter I examine two tragedies that foreground the urgency of resistance: Robert Garnier's *Cornélie*, which was first published in 1574, and Pierre Corneille's *La mort de Pompée*, which was published in 1644 following a successful theatrical run.[3] Both these tragedies depict the political crisis engendered by Caesar's usurpation of power and efforts to resist his tyranny. Whereas the *Vindiciae* lists Cato and Cicero as Pompey's fellow *bons patriotes* who likewise took up arms against Caesar, in

Cornélie and *La mort de Pompée* the task of sustaining resistance falls to Pompey's wife Cornelia. I argue that in these tragedies Cornelia's grief in the wake of Pompey's assassination emerges as a form of opposition to Caesar's tyranny when she joins her grief at the loss of her husband to the laments of the Roman people. *Cornélie* and *La mort de Pompée* situate Cornelia as the kind of public representative who responds to the affective evidence of the people's distress and opposes tyranny on their behalf.

By casting a woman as a public official and mourning as a means of opposition, these tragedies stretch the limits of who counts as a public representative and what counts as resistance. While sixteenth-century resistance treatises often cite Pompey as an ideal public representative, these texts leave unexplored the possibility that his grieving widow might also serve this role. Cornelia's lack of consideration as a public figure can be explained by the treatises' broader position on women: that they are unfit for leadership. When resistance treatises mention women, it is usually to critique them as tyrannical usurpers of power. For example, during a longer discussion about the tyranny of usurpation, the *Vindiciae* condemns "des femmes qui se fourrent au gouvernement des Royaumes que les loix du pays deferent aux masles seulement, & s'en font Reines et maistresses, comme Athalia fit de Juda: Semiramis, d'Assyrie: Agrippine, de l'Empire Romain du temps de son fils Neron: . . . & quelques Brunechildes du Royaume de France" (women who occupy kingdoms, which, by ancestral laws, are accustomed to descend only to males; or who snatch the administration for themselves, as Athaliah did in Judah, Semiramis in Assyria, Agrippina in the Roman empire under her son Nero . . . and several Brunhildas in the Frankish kingdom).[4] These women are out of bounds. They want too much. In the *Vindiciae* as in other resistance treatises, these women are portrayed as too ambitious and willful to govern appropriately. Focused only on their personal desire and particular will to power, they are not suitable as public representatives.

The *Vindiciae*'s rule is that women in power are illegitimate usurpers, but the treatise provides for one exception: the extraordinary liberator. As I discussed in chapter 1, the *Vindiciae* and other resistance treatises allow that in certain circumstances of tyranny and oppression when no formally recognized public official heeds the people's calls for assistance, God may provide the people with an extraordinary liberator who comes to their aid. An extraordinary liberator need not necessarily be a recognized public official but might instead be a private person, or particulier, who takes on a public role through divine command. One of the most frequently cited extraordinary liberators in the resistance treatises is Deborah, the biblical prophetess and judge who led the Israelites to military victory against the Canaanites. As a judge, Deborah occupied a public role usually reserved for men even before leading her people to military victory. Her military triumph served further to underscore her exceptionality. According to the resistance treatises, Deborah's break with gender conventions is not an aberration but is instead a divinely authorized irregularity.[5]

The Cornelia of Garnier's *Cornélie* and Corneille's *La mort de Pompée* fits neither of the roles that sixteenth-century resistance treatises assign to women. She neither usurps power nor claims divine direction. Instead, she becomes a public representative through her affective attachment to Pompey. Cornelia's grief over the loss of her husband joins with the Roman people's grief over the loss of their hero. This combination of personal and collective grief serves as affective evidence of Cornelia's devotion to Rome and connection to its people. By examining how Cornelia's grief affords her political legitimacy, this chapter demonstrates how affect allows a private person to emerge as a public representative. Cornelia's primary role in *Cornélie* and *La mort de Pompée* is that of a widow. She is not a military general like Pompey, nor does she have a recognized public role like Deborah, the biblical judge. She is defined instead by her personal loss, her particular grief. And yet, as we will see, in these plays her personal loss is not just personal. This loss is also the ground on which she stakes a public position.

One of my aims in reading Garnier's *Cornélie* and Corneille's *La mort de Pompée* together is to demonstrate how the category of the public representative continued to be reimagined long after the religious wars. As noted above, *Cornélie* was first published in 1574, during the religious wars and contemporaneous to the Huguenot resistance treatises I examined in chapter 1. In contrast, Corneille's *La mort de Pompée* appeared during the 1640s, after the official end of war.[6] Corneille does not refer to Garnier's *Cornélie* as a source for *La mort de Pompée* and mentions only Lucan and Plutarch in his "Examen."[7] As John E. Matzke points out, however, the two plays include similar depictions of Cornelia and her grief, suggesting that Corneille may have drawn on Garnier's drama while constructing his own.[8] My aim here is not to adjudicate the extent to which *Cornélie* is a source for *La mort de Pompée* but rather to draw out how the resonances between these two plays encourage us to read across divisions of historical context: between the sixteenth century and the seventeenth, war and peace, disorder and order. Cornelia's emergence as a public representative in both plays allows us to consider how the political possibilities of one period remain thinkable within another.

Cornelia's Grief, Rome's Lament

In the dedication of *Cornélie*, addressed to Nicolas d'Angennes, seigneur de Rambouillet, Garnier draws an explicit connection between the genre of tragedy and the condition of civil war in France. Taking Garnier's dedication as a point of departure, I demonstrate how *Cornélie* situates this grieving widow as an ideal public representative. In the dedication Garnier writes that he would gladly leave behind "les cris et les horreurs de mes Tragedies" (the cries and horrors of my tragedies) for other poetic endeavors, which would perhaps better celebrate Rambouillet's grandeur and nobility.[9] Garnier nonetheless offers a tragedy, with all its suffering and horror, because the genre so perfectly matches the situation in France. Tragedy, he writes, is "[un] poeme à mon regret trop propre aux malheurs de nostre siecle" (a poem, to my regret, too well suited to the misfortunes of our time).[10] The dramatist does, however, provide Rambouillet with a measure of consolation: "Cependant, vous verrez les pleurs de Cornélie, qui se va présenter pour son auteur aux yeux de votstre debonnaireté" (You will see, however, the tears of Cornelia, who will stand for her author before the eyes of your goodness).[11] Figuring the grieving Cornelia as a proxy for himself, Garnier asks Rambouillet to witness her (and thus his) predicament: "Et suis bien seur qu'encor que le principal faix et les plus serieux des affaires Polonoises repose aujourd'huy sur vos epaules, comme y tenant le premier lieu en l'absence de sa Majesté, vous ne dedaignerez toutefois d'abaisser la veüe sur elle, pour entendre les plaintes de sa calamité" (And I am sure that, although the principal weight and the most serious Polish affairs fall on your shoulders, as you take the first place in the absence of his Majesty, you will nevertheless deign to cast your eyes on her and hear her cries in her calamity).[12] Garnier expresses confidence that despite Rambouillet's pressing political concerns he will make time to see Cornelia and listen to her tears.

Offering an example of virtue and righteousness in the midst of war, Cornelia stands in contrast to the comportment of the French nobility during the religious wars. In his dedication to Rambouillet, Garnier registers his general disappointment with the current state of the French nobility: "L'ignorante barbarie, qui par l'assiduité des guerres c'est de tout temps emparee de l'esprit des Seigneurs, leur a faict dedaigner les lettres" (The ignorant barbarism, which has for all this time occupied the spirit of the lords, has made them despise letters).[13] Much like the authors of the sixteenth-century resistance treatises discussed in chapter 1, Garnier finds his country's public officials wanting.[14] Phillip John Usher has suggested that Garnier used the dedications of some of his

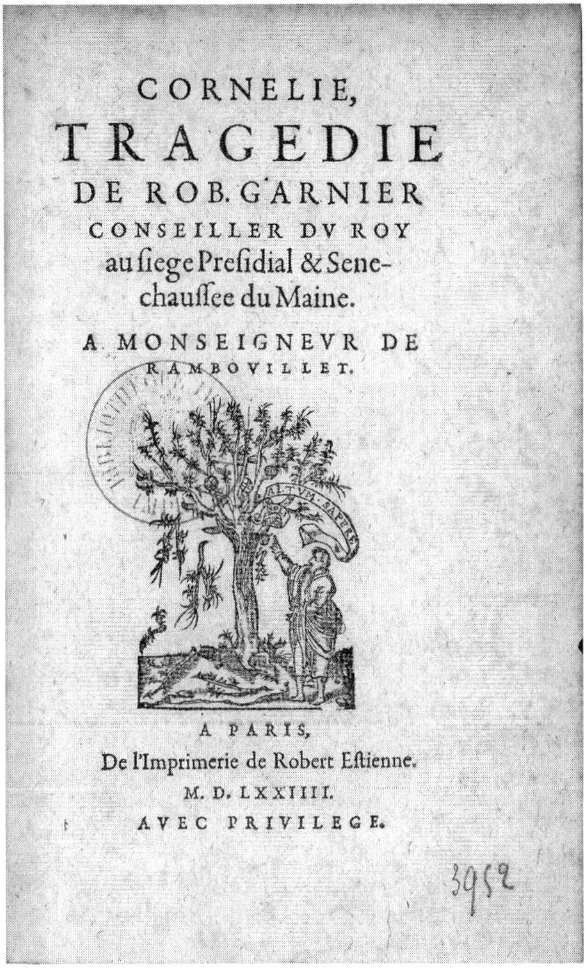
CORNELIE,
TRAGEDIE
DE ROB. GARNIER
CONSEILLER DV ROY
au ſiege Preſidial & Senechauſſee du Maine.
A MONSEIGNEVR DE RAMBOVILLET.
A PARIS,
De l'Imprimerie de Robert Eſtienne.
M. D. LXXIIII.
AVEC PRIVILEGE.

Fig. 1. Title page of Robert Garnier, *Cornélie* (Paris: Robert Estienne, 1574). Bibliothèque nationale de France.

other plays to bring the political concerns of these plays to the attention of the Parlement of Paris.[15] A similar gesture is at work in the dedication of *Cornélie*. Addressing Rambouillet, Garnier states that the seigneur is exceptional. Unlike those nobles whose inclinations have declined during the wars, Rambouillet and members of his family have remained virtuous and kind. The dramatist celebrates Rambouillet's virtue by placing his name "sur le front de Cornélie" (on Cornelia's brow). Garnier refers here to the act of dedication. As was common practice during the sixteenth century, the dedicatee's name appears on the tragedy's frontispiece (fig. 1).

Garnier's dedication calls our attention to the physicality of the printed page, on which the names Cornelia, Garnier, and Rambouillet appear in close proximity to one another. By associating both Rambouillet and Garnier with Cornelia, the dedication suggests that the two men, by honoring Cornelia's example, have maintained their virtue during a time of general decline. The other names that appear on the frontispiece lends this virtuous example the imprimatur of authority. Garnier's title as "conseiller du Roy" in the top half of the frontispiece associates the king's name with Cornelia and Rambouillet as well as with Garnier. The bottom half of the frontispiece reinforces this association with the "Avec Privilege" signaling that Robert Estienne has published Garnier's play with royal approval. These signs of authority help the printed play frame Cornelia's example as one of political virtue rather than anarchic sedition.

Garnier's dedication points us toward the duality inherent in Cornelia's position as an exemplar. On the one hand, her virtue sets her apart from others and makes her a figure of veneration. On the other, her virtue brings her closer to others and makes her a figure of emulation. This interplay of veneration and emulation structures Cornelia's emergence as a public representative within the play itself. In *Cornélie* she stands alone with others. She becomes a public representative through her physical and affective ties to Pompey, as well as to the people of Rome.

Cornélie opens on the city of Rome in crisis. While previously content to share power, Caesar has since conspired against his allies and subjected the Roman people to his tyrannical rule. Potential rivals to Caesar's authority have been either killed or driven out of the city. Beginning in such a state of crisis, much of the tragedy centers on the consequences of Caesar's tyranny for the city's inhabitants. When Caesar makes his first appearance in act 4, he reveals himself to be unaware of this reaction to his rule:

> O superbe Cité, qui vas levant le front:
> Sur toutes les citez de ce grand monde rond:
> Et dont l'honneur gaigné par victoires fameuses
> Espouvante du ciel les voûtes lumineuses!
> O sourcilleuses tours! ô coustaux decorez!
> O palais orgueilleux! ô temples honorez!
> O vous murs que les dieux ont maçonnez eux-mesmes,
> Eux-mesmes étoffez de mille diadêmes,
> Ne ressentez-vous point de plaisir en vos cueurs,
> De voir vostre Cesar le vaincueur des vaincueurs.
> (Garnier, *Cornélie*, 4.1303–12)[16]

O Rome, that with thy pride dost overpeer
The worthiest of cities of the conquered world!
Whose honour, got by famous victories,
Hath filled heav'n's fiery vaults with frightful horror!
O lofty towers! O stately battlements!
O glorious temples! O proud palaces!
And you brave walls, bright heaven's masonry,
Graced with a thousand kingly diadems,
Are ye not stirred with a strange delight,
To see your Caesar's matchless victories?[17]

Caesar's monologue, which begins as an encomium to Rome and ends as a speech of self-praise, is jarring in both tone and content. The public outcry that has dominated the first three acts of the play clearly has not affected Caesar. Portraying himself as a great ruler who seeks to secure Rome's glory, he remains utterly oblivious to his tyrannical reputation.[18]

What Caesar offers in this speech is a misreading of the source of his power. Addressing Rome's dazzling structures, he locates his glory in these structures themselves, the towers and walls, the palaces and temples. These imposing structures, Caesar argues, evince his strength and virtue. Their construction and beauty legitimize his rule. By interpellating this architectural audience, Caesar's speech effectively conflates Rome's structures and its people and turns both Rome's structures and its inhabitants into surfaces that reflect his self-perceived glory. He suggests that the people of Rome find pleasure at the sight of him, the "vaincueur des vaincueurs," who valiantly defends these magnificent structures and serves as the source of magnificence. "Ne ressentez-vous point de plaisir en vos cueurs?" But this question is no question at all. The people's pleasure is assumed. By making this assumption, Caesar fails to recognize the people's affective orientation toward him. As *Cornélie*'s readers and spectators know by this point in the play, the people are not happy with Caesar's rule. Contra his assumption, it is not pleasure but displeasure that they feel in their hearts. In addition to mistaking the people's pain for pleasure, Caesar also fails to recognize the people's affection as the source of his power. Blithely thinking that Rome's imposing architecture cements his rule, he does not register the people's displeasure, the affective evidence of his illegitimacy.

Caesar's failure to perceive the people's displeasure marks him as a tyrant. In Garnier's play, as in sixteenth-century resistance theory, identifying tyranny is crucial because the perception of tyranny allows for the possibility of legitimate resistance. In other words, to identify tyranny, in this case to feel the disconnect between the people's displeasure and Caesar's self-satisfaction, is to make a judgment that opens up inquiry about who can organize resistance. *Cornélie*'s depiction of Caesar provides for readers and spectators an example of how tyranny looks and sounds: boastful, arrogant, and self-centered. By contrasting Caesar's self-conception with Rome's perception of his rule, the play also provides an example of how tyranny feels. A tyrant not only produces displeasure among the people but also fails to recognize this displeasure. He makes the people feel badly and is bad at feeling their pain.

Cornélie foregrounds the people's pain and makes it a locus of political force. Throughout the play, the people of Rome (rather than its structures) emerge as the true source of political power, whose discontent with Caesar's rule renders that rule illegitimate. As the *Vindiciae* notes, Caesar's rival, Pompey, recognizes that power resides with the people: "Rome est, ce dit Pompee, là où est le Senat: & le Senat se trouve là où se trouve la reverence des loix, l'amour de liberté, le desir de conserver la patrie" ("But Rome," said Pompey, "is where the senate is; and the senate is where there is reverence for the laws, love of liberty, and zeal for the preservation of the country").[19] For Pompey, Rome's location is both fixed and flexible. Rome is coextensive with the senate, the site of public representation, but the senate's location may vary, depending on where one finds reverence for law, love of liberty, and desire to protect the country. The *Vindiciae*'s Pompey implies that the senate may be composed of not just those previously recognized as senators but also those who revere the law and love their country. In Garnier's *Cornélie*, whereas the official senate has ceased to function and traditional public representatives such as Pompey have been killed, Pompey's widow Cornelia comes to serve as a public representative who registers the people's displeasure and offers legitimate opposition to Caesar's tyranny.

At the outset of *Cornélie*, it is not Pompey's widow but rather a more traditional public representative—the statesman Cicero—who articulates Rome's pain. Sixteenth-century resistance treatises often cite Cicero to bolster their critiques of tyranny and justifications of legitimate opposition. In Garnier's tragedy Cicero's account of the problem that Caesar's tyranny represents for Rome's inhabitants helps us to understand how a private person such as Cornelia can become a public representative. With his opening monologue Cicero explains that Caesar has violated the innate liberty of Rome's citizens:

> Voyant sous un Tyran nos cœurs abastardis
> Laschement soupirer, voyent nos ames pleines

De vergoigne endurer mille hontes vileines.
Meschante Ambition, des courages plus hauts
Poison enraciné, tu nous trames ces maux!
Tu renverses nos loix, mortelle Convoitise,
Et de nos libres cœurs arraches la franchise.
(Garnier, *Cornélie*, 1.20–26)

Under a tyrant see our bastard hearts
Lie idly sighing, while our shameful souls
Endure a million of base controls.
Poisoned ambition, rooted in high minds,
'Tis thou that train'st us into all these errors:
Thy mortal covetise perverts our laws,
And tears our freedom from our franchised hearts.[20]

Cicero condemns "Meschante Ambition" as the poisonous force that produces tyranny, upends the just laws of Rome, and deprives Romans of their liberty. In so doing, he provides a theory of Roman freedom. Referencing the hearts and souls of Roman citizens, Cicero depicts their liberty as fundamentally interior. The common condition of all Roman citizens (before Caesar's coup) is the freedom that each should be able to enjoy in their heart. Caesar's tyranny, these verses suggest, has thus violated the liberty of each Roman citizen and the Roman people as a whole. Cicero's account of Roman liberty parallels the dual structure of resistance theory. In resistance treatises, as for Garnier's Cicero, liberty is both subjective and collective, something held within each heart and shared by the body politic. In these verses, Cicero combines the subjective and collective by including himself as a citizen whose freedom has been violated through the repetition of the possessive *nos* ("our"): "nos cœurs," "nos ames," "nos loix." Cicero figures himself as someone who feels the collective's pain because he is part of it. Responsive to the affective evidence of this collective pain, Cicero shows himself capable of representing the people against tyranny.

In contrast to Cicero, Cornelia initially stands apart from the collective, distinguishing her pain from that of Rome as a whole. When Cornelia enters in the second act, she does not join Cicero in decrying the general loss of liberty for all Romans. Instead, she focuses on the particularity of her own loss. Cornelia emphasizes her status as Pompey's widow and thus as the widow of one of Caesar's most formidable rivals. Furthermore, she underscores, she is also the widow of Crassus, another Roman general who had once formed a triumvirate along with Caesar and Pompey. Surviving both her husbands and left to experience Caesar's tyranny alone, Cornelia's only wish is to die. Cornelia's laments, which are often directed at the gods, dominate the second act:

> Voulez-vous arroser mes angoisses cruelles,
> Les voulez-vous nourrir de larmes eternelles,
> Mes yeux, et voulez-vous que, faute de tarir
> Vos renaissants pleurs, je ne puisse mourir?
> Faites couler le sang de mes tortices veines
> Par vos tuyaux cavez, deux larmeuses fontaines:
> Et si bien espuisez mon corps de sa liqueur,
> Que l'ame contumace abandonne mon cœur.
> (Garnier, *Cornélie*, 2.223–30)
>
> And will ye needs bedew my dead-grown joys,
> And nourish sorrow with eternal tears,
> O eyes, and will ye ('cause I cannot dry
> Your ceaseless springs), not suffer me to die?
> Then make the blood from forth my branch-like veins,
> Like weeping rivers, trickle by your vaults;
> And sponge my body's heat of moisture so,
> As my displeased soul may shun my heart.[21]

Begging the gods for death, Cornelia demands an emptying out of herself; she asks that the unceasing tears flowing from her eyes ("deux larmeuses fontaines)" be replaced with the blood of her veins ("le sang de mes tortices veines"). Draining her body of its blood, she suggests, will allow her "ame contumace" to leave her heart. What she desires is a mortal body left with neither blood nor soul. Cornelia ties her emotional state (sadness, grief) to a physical response (tears) and insists that this physical response should be taken further (loss of blood). These verses insist on the embodied nature of grief. Cornelia's description of her body indicates its material staying power, its ability to remain. After her body has been drained of tears, moisture, liquid, blood, and soul, it will remain as an empty container, or as a set of empty containers (eyes, veins, branches, fountains). Together, these containers will act as a physical monument to her grief.

For Cornelia, to be alive, to continue to inhabit her body in the wake of her husbands' deaths, represents something of a scandal or a mistake. Surviving Pompey is particularly troubling, since she experienced his assassination as partially her own:

Je l'ay veu, j'y estois, et presque entre mes bras
Il sentit le poignard, et tomba mort à bas.
Lors le sang me gela dans mes errantes veines,
Le poil me herissa comme espics dans les pleines:
Ma voix se cacha morte au gosier, et le poux
En mon froid estomach doubla ses foibles coups.
(Garnier, *Cornélie*, 2.401–6)

I saw him, I was there, and in mine arms
He almost felt the poniard when he fell.
Whereat, my blood stopped in my straggling veins,
Mine hair grew bristled, like a thorny grove;
My voice lay hid half-dead within my throat;
My frightful heart, stunned in my stone-cold breast,
Faintly redoubled every feeble stroke.[22]

Cornelia first describes herself as a witness to the assassination ("Je l'ay veu, j'y estois") but quickly makes clear what a proximate vantage point she held. She is more participant than observer, nearly holding Pompey as he receives the fatal blow. This blow affects not only Pompey's body, Cornelia explains, but also her own, causing a series of physical responses that affect her blood, hair, voice, and stomach. Her desire for death is in part a desire to rectify the incongruous situation of her continued life. She has already died and yet goes on living.[23] Throughout the drama, Cornelia continues to wish for a death that she insists has already taken place.

Cornelia's interminable grief initially sets her apart from the rest of Rome. Her objections to Caesar's rule are distinct from those of the city as a whole. As a result, she speaks not as a public representative but rather as a private person. When Cicero urges her to curb her lamentations by suggesting that—gods willing—Caesar will eventually experience a change of fortune and that the city will again enjoy its natural liberty, Cornelia responds that her interlocutor has missed her true source of sadness:

Les bons Dieux pourront bien remettre en liberté,
Si tost qu'il leur plaira, nostre pauvre Cité:
Mais, las! Ils ne sçauroient, en eussent-ils envie,
Ranimer à Pompee une seconde vie.
(Garnier, *Cornélie*, 2.373–76)

'Tis true, the heav'ns—at least wise if they please—
May give poor Rome her former liberty.
But though they would, I know they cannot give
A second life to Pompey, that is slain.[24]

Acknowledging the plight of the city, Cornelia distinguishes this plight from her very particular loss of Pompey. This distinction rests on the gods' capacities. They may easily alter the common fortune of Rome, "nostre pauvre Cité," but their divine powers do not extend to reviving a fallen individual. Although Cornelia situates herself as part of the city, with her words "nostre pauvre Cité" echoing Cicero's "nos cœurs," "nos ames," and "nos loix," she foregrounds the personal loss that cannot be restored.

Cornelia maintains that her personal loss of Pompey is distinct not only from Rome's collective pain but also from the personal losses suffered by other Romans. Cicero again attempts to quiet her tears, this time by arguing that her loss parallels that of others: "Madame, il ne faut pas vous transporter ainsi, / Vous souffrez de l'angoisse, hé qui n'en souffre aussi? / Le desastre est commun" (2.433–35) (Madam, you must not thus transpose yourself. / We see your sorrow, but who sorrows not? / The grief is common).[25] Cicero points out that nearly everyone has lost a family member to Caesar and suggests that the shared suffering of the entire population should ease Cornelia's pain. Cornelia argues in response that the common experience of grief does not remove the specificity of her anguish: "Moindre n'est mon tourment, ny moindre ma douleur, / Pour voir à tout le monde un semblable malheur" (2.441–42) (If all the world were in the like distress, / My sorrow yet would never seem the less).[26] Cornelia again acknowledges that the whole city suffers, but she maintains the particularity of her grief.

The dialogue between these two characters, the statesman and the widow, echoes gendered fault lines that have long structured debates about the politics of mourning. Nicole Loraux identifies a conflict between public and private forms of mourning in her work on ancient Athens. She explains that official ceremonies of public mourning were largely masculine affairs designed to glorify fallen heroes of war and reinforce fidelity to the Athenian state. In contrast, familial mourning rituals were largely feminine affairs that were conducted most frequently by the mothers of the fallen. Laws attributed to Solon, Loraux notes, began during the early sixth century B.C. to regulate such private, expressions of grief out of concern that they would interfere with the public ceremonies' lessons of heroism and political fidelity.[27]

As Helen Foley has argued, the gendered dynamics of mourning in Greek politics were rehearsed and reimagined on the tragic stage. Greek tragedy often featured female figures whose mourning transgressed the boundaries of what was considered politically permissible. These tragic figures were often much bolder and more brazen than women could be in Athenian society. Foley explains: "the Athenian social system seems to have made a concerted effort to control the public behavior of women, especially in relation to death ritual. Tragedy, however, allows the politics of the past, whether real or imaginary, to reemerge on stage, and to reenact the sort of social scenarios, including tensions between mass and elite, that may well have led to the earlier funerary legislation."[28] As Foley is careful to note, tragedy's tendency to revive political debates did not mean that tragedy had what we might call a feminist bent. Female figures on the tragic stage functioned less as representations of historical Greek women and more as indexes of how expressions of loss and longing could expose ongoing political divisions in ways that are often deeply gendered.[29]

Drawing from Greek tragedy, as well as from Roman tragedy and epic (which I will return to later), Garnier's *Cornélie* presents us with a female mourner who, like her ancient counterparts, refuses to accept limitations on her grief. In Garnier's tragedy, as we have seen, Cicero takes on the role of the statesman whose primary concern is the public good. As a result, he urges Cornelia to subsume her private grief within the public grief of the city. By maintaining that her grief is singular rather than shared, Cornelia refuses to sacrifice her private loss for Rome's. This refusal appears as a kind of feminine excess that threatens the possibility of a shared political project, in this case resistance to Caesar's tyranny. In the context of sixteenth-century France, Cornelia's status as a widow would have made her refusal to channel her grief particularly powerful. As Marie Houllemare has noted, widows enjoyed a special legal status during this period because they were not under the control of either fathers or husbands. Widows were permitted to own property and had more freedoms than maidens or wives. Given this special legal status, widows were often seen as potentially transgressive and placed under suspicion.[30] Tragic drama contributed to the cultural fears about the widow's power. For example, a case heard by the Parlement of Paris in 1577, which involved a widow whose lover had allegedly killed one of her children, was compared to the *Oresteia*.[31] Tragedy rendered widows as mythic, larger than life, whether they remained faithful to their late husbands. Acting as a steadfast widow who does not yield to limits on her grief for Pompey, Cornelia's valence as a tragic figure is multiple. On the one hand, as Garnier maintains in his dedication, she is a paragon of nobility and virtue. On the other hand, echoing mourning women both ancient and modern, of both history and myth, she raises the specter of an uncontrollable feminine grief.

Although Cornelia rejects Cicero's request that she incorporate her personal grief within the collective loss of Rome, this personal grief does emerge as the emotional force that allows for shared resistance. Cornelia eventually joins her particular complaints to those of the Roman people, grounding this juncture in the notion of a shared future. The conception of a future that is free from Caesar's tyranny becomes crucial to the project of sustaining resistance to Caesar in the present. As the play unfolds, Cicero shifts from anticipating a change in Caesar's fortune to actively hoping for a brave citizen to take up arms and assassinate the tyrant. Another character, the senator Cassius, also advances this hope and argues that Caesar's many wrongs justify his assassination:

> C'est trop long temps souffert, c'est par trop enduré,
> L'on deust avoir desjà mille fois conjuré,
> Mille fois prins le fer, mille fois mis en pieces
> Ce Tyran, pour vanger nos publiques detresses.
> (Garnier, *Cornélie*, 4.1233–36)
>
> The wrong is great, and over-long endured:
> We should have practisèd, conspired, conjured
> A thousand ways and weapons to repress,
> Or kill outright this cause of our distress.[32]

Cassius appeals to affective evidence in order to justify taking up arms against Caesar, noting that Rome has suffered too long and endured too much. To resist tyranny is to avenge public distress. Given this affective evidence, for Cassius resistance is not only legitimate but also overdue. A plan to conspire against Caesar would rectify past inaction. Given what Rome has already endured, the people should already have taken up arms against the tyrant a thousand times over: "Mille fois conjuré, mille fois prins le fer, mille fois mis en pieces." The repetition of "mille fois" acts as a kind of incantation in the present that, as a call to future action, brings vividly to mind what Cassius (along with his fellow senators and statesman) should have done in the past.

The choral ode that follows Cassius's verses echoes this turn toward the future. Reiterating the people's displeasure with Caesar, the chorus of Roman women affirms its desire for a public representative to oppose his tyranny. Whoever acts against Caesar, they argue, will win the people's enduring thanks and favor:

Son renom, porté par la gloire
Sur l'aile des siecles futurs,
Franchira les tombeaux obscurs
D'une perdurable memoire.
Les peuples qui viendront aprez
Luy feront des honneurs sacrez,
Et chaque an la jeunesse tendre
Ira le chef de fleurs orné,
Chanter au beau jour retourné
Dessur son heroïque cendre.
(Garnier, *Cornélie*, 4.1251–60)

His glory spread abroad by fame,
On wings of his posterity,
From obscure death shall free his name,
To live in endless memory.
All after-ages shall adore
And honor him with hymns therefore.
Yearly the youth for joy shall bring
The fairest flowers that grow in Rome.
And yearly in the summer sing
O're his heroic kingly tomb.[33]

The chorus states that he who rises up against the tyrant will be celebrated not only by Rome's current inhabitants but also by future generations. His courageous act, they argue, will be remembered as an important event for years to come. Their celebrations will emphasize renewal, including singing youths adorned with flowers. The anticipated hero's physical remains, his ashes, will serve as the focal point of these joyous future celebrations.

The fusion of past and future, or of remains and potentiality, is precisely what eventually unites Cornelia's grief and the people's lament. Earlier in the play, Cornelia is presented with an urn containing Pompey's ashes. At the sight of the urn, the grieving widow reiterates that she should have died with Pompey. Addressing the urn, she laments, "O douce et chere cendre, ô cendre deplorable / Qu'avecques vous ne suis-je! ô femme miserable" (3.855–56) (O sweet, dear, deplorable cinders! / O miserable woman, living dying!).[34] In close physical proximity to Pompey's remains, Cornelia laments that the divide between life and death nonetheless keeps them apart. Given Cornelia's personal grief at the sight of Pompey's ashes, we might expect her to distance herself from a chorus that situates a fallen hero's remains at the center of public ceremonies that celebrate resistance to tyranny. Pompey's remains, however, end up bringing Cornelia and the chorus together. Toward the end of the play, the tenor of Cornelia's grief shifts. While absorbing yet more personal loss (that of her father, Scipio), she joins her grief with that of the people, enlisting the chorus in her renewed laments: "Pleurons Dames pleurons, nous n'avons autres armes / Contre nostre malheur qu'un long torrent de larmes" (Weep, women weep, our only weapon against our misfortune is a long torrent of tears).[35] In these verses "nostre malheur" seems to encompass the women's personal losses as well as Rome's more general loss of freedom. For Cornelia, mourning these losses represents a form of opposition, an idea that the drama reinforces through the rhyme "armes" and "larmes." Although, as we have seen, mourning women are often relegated to the private realms of family and household, these verses suggest how a woman's mourning allows her to emerge as a public representative.

Pompey's urn is a key object in Cornelia's emergence as a public representative. She secures her political legitimacy through her affective connection to Pompey, which is made concrete through her possession of his remains. As Jean-Claude Ternaux has noted, the scene of Cornelia receiving the funerary urn containing Pompey's ashes was inspired by Lucan's epic poem, the *Pharsalia*, or, *De bello civili* (A.D. 61–65), which was one of Garnier's primary sources for *Cornélie*.[36] Lucan's poem recounts how Cornelia witnessed Pompey's assassination in Egypt and how her ship was then sped away to safety against her will. Lucan tells of how Pompey was beheaded so that his head could be presented to Caesar—an episode that, as we will see, Corneille dramatizes in his *La mort de Pompée*—and of how a member of Pompey's entourage subsequently recovered Pompey's body from the sea, stoked a makeshift funeral pyre, and pledged to deliver Pompey's ashes to Cornelia in the future.[37] Lucan does not narrate Cornelia's eventual reception of Pompey's ashes, but does describe how she marks her loss in the meantime. When Cornelia's ship reached safe harbor on the Libyan coast, Lucan explains, "she gathered up the garments and glorious medals" that had belonged to Pompey, as well as "his arms and gold-stamped spoils / that he used to wear, his fine embroidered togas," and placed them all as offerings on a funeral pyre.[38] Cornelia had the remnants of Pompey's wardrobe and the symbols of his honor stand in for the as yet unattainable remains of his body. Lucan goes on to describe how Pompey's followers then "followed [Cornelia's] example" making their own funeral pyres for Pompey and thus creating their own provisional remains.[39] This episode in the *Pharsalia* calls our attention to how remains serve as placeholders, as physical gathering points that stand in for the deceased.

The Cornelia of Garnier's tragedy becomes a public representative when she links her loss to Rome's through her possession of Pompey's ashes. We have already seen how earlier in the drama she rhetorically empties out her own body, figuring it as a container for her loss. This container is provisional, the best Cornelia can hope for until her own death, much as the Cornelia of Lucan's epic must make do with the remains of Pompey's clothes and honors, rather than those of his body. The physical locus of Cornelia's grief in Garnier's tragedy shifts, however, when she receives the urn containing Pompey's ashes. At this point in the play, the gathering point of her grief becomes the urn, an object on which the people of Rome can also center their outpouring of emotion. When presented with the urn, Cornelia continues her grief, but she also begins actively to imagine Caesar's assassination:

> Non, je verray bien tost (Dieu m'en face la grace)
> Son corps souillé de sang estendu dans la place,
> Ouvert de mille coups, et le peuple à l'entour
> Tressaillant d'allegresse en bénire le jour.
> (Garnier, *Cornélie*, 3.903–6)
>
> Else, God tofore, my self may live to see
> His tired corpse lie toiling in his blood,
> Gored with a thousand stabs, and round about,
> The wrongèd people leap for inward joy.[40]

Whereas Cornelia was previously focused only on death, once in possession of the urn, she explicitly articulates Caesar's demise as her dying wish. In her vision of Caesar's end, Cornelia depicts this scene as one of both personal satisfaction and public joy. She imagines that the people will be shaking with joy, their emotional satisfaction made legible on their bodies. By prompting this shift in Cornelia from personal grief alone to personal grief joined with the possibility of public celebration, the urn serves as the object that eventually brings Cornélie and the people of Rome together, acting as enduring evidence of their affective connection.

Cornelia's emergence as a public representative follows a pattern established in sixteenth-century resistance treatises, wherein a public representative's political legitimacy—and thus ability to organize resistance—is secured through evidence of the representative's affective orientation toward the people. This process is double: First, the representatives must register and respond to the people's collective joy or pain. Second, the people must endorse the representative through expressions of joy or approval that he has taken up their cause. Garnier's *Cornélie* presents a similar dynamic, as it alternates between the words of characters and those of the chorus. Cicero and Cassius both show themselves to be responsive to the people's displeasure, whereas Caesar remains oblivious to the people's discontent. The chorus ratifies these political positions by reiterating Cicero's and Cassius's assertions that the people desire resistance to Caesar's tyranny. The chorus similarly affirms Cornelia's role as a public representative by agreeing to participate in her campaign of tears:

> Nous te pleurons, Pompee, à la gloire Romaine,
> Et de la liberté la defense certaine:
> Ta vie estoit la nostre et le tombeau noircy
> Qui t'enveloppe mort, nous enveloppe aussi.
> (Garnier, *Cornélie*, 150)[41]

> We weep for you, Pompey, for Roman glory
> and for the liberty of certain protection
> Your life was ours and the dark tomb
> that envelops you envelops us as well.[42]

Praising Pompey's glory, the chorus echoes the temporal structure of life and death that Cornelia articulates in the second act. The chorus yokes its life to that of Pompey and claims to share his tomb. It thus claims to have already lost its collective life. Its lamentations, however, are ongoing and stretch into the future. The chorus's promise to mourn Pompey, "Nous te pleurons Pompee," becomes a refrain in the drama's last scene. Just as Cornelia previously argued that she had already died with Pompey and could not wait to join him in death, the chorus claims to share his tomb while pledging to commemorate his life through its ongoing, interminable tears.

As a public representative, Cornelia binds her particular loss to Rome's general lament. At previous moments in the drama, such a stance seemed unacceptable. Cornelia maintained that her specific loss could not be subsumed within the city's general plight. But when she calls on the chorus to join her lament, Cornelia does not propose to leave her particular grief behind. Nor does she quite add her voice to that of the chorus. Rather, she suggests that she and the chorus might cry alongside each other to commemorate Pompey as both a husband and a Roman general. These two modes of lamentation, the singular and the plural, converge at the resting place of Pompey's body. Echoing the chorus, we might say that

Pompey's tomb envelops them or wraps them all up together. By focusing on the corporeal connections between Cornelia, Pompey, and the chorus, Garnier's tragedy underscores how the body of one public representative may become a locus of legitimate resistance through which other representatives emerge. The drama establishes Cornelia's legitimacy in part by insisting on her physical and affective ties to Pompey and his remains.

The physical and affective ties that bind together Cornelia, Pompey, and the people in a shared project of mourning enable their sustained resistance to tyranny. At the end of the play, Cornelia articulates how she plans to survive her husband and father in order to eventually add her remains to theirs:

> Mon Pere je vivray, je vivray mon Espoux,
> Pour faire vos tombeaux, et pour pleurer sur vous,
> Languissante, chetive, et de mes pleurs fumeuses
> Baigner plaintivement vos cendres genereuses:
> Puis sans humeur, sans force, emplissant de sanglots
> Les vases bien-heureux qui vous tiendront enclos,
> Je vomiray ma vie, et tombant legere Ombre,
> Des esprits de là bas j'iray croistre le nombre.
> (Garnier, *Cornélie*, 5.1927–34)
>
> No, lovely father, and my dearest husband,
> Cornelia must live–though life she hateth–
> To make your tombs, and mourn upon your hearses:
> Where, languishing, my fumous faithful tears
> May trickling bathe your generous sweet cinders;
> And afterward, both wanting strength and moisture,
> Fulfilling with my latest sighs and gasps
> The happy vessels that enclose your bones,
> I will surrender my surchargèd life,
> And when my soul earth's prison shall forgo,
> Increase the number of the ghosts below.[43]

Projecting her own death into the future, Cornelia outlines a mode of survival based on commemoration. In these, the play's final lines, Cornelia proposes once again to empty herself out. Having already lost her "cœur" (heart) and "âme" (soul) in the moment of Pompey's death, she now proposes to succeed him by releasing all her tears and then eventually rejoining the remains of her body to his. By projecting her own physical death into the future and by dedicating the remainder of her life to Pompey's remains, Cornelia refuses to give herself over to Caesar's tyranny. She instead sustains her opposition to Caesar through her tearful commemoration of Pompey's life and legacy. As we have seen, the tragedy figures tears as weapons through the rhyme "armes" and "larmes." By combining her defiant tears with those of the chorus, she suggests how her opposition might survive her eventual death. *Cornélie* ends on a moment of suspension, with the promise of ongoing resistance.

By foregrounding Cornelia's grief and by situating this grief in relation to a chorus of lamenting Roman women, Garnier's tragedy demonstrates how mourning sustains resistance to tyranny. In sixteenth-century resistance theory, as we have seen, to sustain resistance is to refuse consent. Once a people grant consent to a tyrant, they can no longer legitimately resist his tyranny. In the *Vindiciae*, as we have seen, this difference in timing distinguishes Pompey's honorable resistance from Cinna's sedition. In *Cornélie* the people's laments signal Rome's refusal to consent to Caesar's tyranny, and Cornelia's tears serve as weapons that allow this resistance to persist.

Returning to the figure of the grieving widow, Corneille's *La mort de Pompée* reanimates the political potential of Garnier's tragedy. In Corneille's tragedy as in Garnier's, the grieving widow emerges as a public representative whose subjective sense of justice is coupled with that of the collective. Whereas *Cornélie* appeared during the religious wars, Corneille's *La mort de Pompée* was performed and published during the 1640s, at a time when the wars had been brought to a close and their political concerns thought to have been resolved. By attending to the relationships between these two plays, I offer an example of how the conceptual structure of resistance theory persists in seventeenth-century tragedy.

Pompey's Remains, Cornelia's Glory

In Corneille's *La mort de Pompée*, as in Garnier's *Cornélie*, Pompey himself never appears onstage. The titular character nonetheless drives much of the play's action. Corneille makes note of this paradox in his 1660 "Examen." He writes, "Il y a quelque chose d'extraordinaire dans le titre de ce Poème, qui porte le nom d'un Héros qui n'y parle point; mais il ne laisse pas d'en être en quelque sorte le principal Acteur, puisque sa mort est la cause unique de tout ce qui s'y passe" (There is something extraordinary about the title of this poem, which carries the name of a hero who never speaks in it but who is in a sense the principal actor, because his death is the sole cause of all that happens).[44] The machinations of the staged characters, including Caesar and Cornelia, revolve around this "principal Acteur," as they seek to gain control over Pompey's remains. As in *Cornélie*, in *La mort de Pompée* the hero's remains serve as a locus of resistance to tyranny. Mobilizing her grief, Cornelia attempts to secure her political legitimacy by insisting on not only her possession of Pompey's remains but also her right to shape his legacy.

Whereas *Cornélie* ends on a moment of suspended resistance, Corneille's *La mort de Pompée* ends on a moment of consolidated power. Corneille's drama takes place in Egypt, rather than in Rome, and focuses on the power struggle between Ptolemy and Cleopatra in the wake of their father's death. Both siblings seek Rome's favor. The play opens as Ptolemy consults his advisers about whether to offer Pompey safe harbor or to assassinate him in an attempt to win Caesar's approval. As the play's title suggests, the arguments for assassination win out: Pompey dies. Rather than winning Caesar's approval of Ptolemy as expected, Pompey's assassination provokes Caesar's ire and reinforces the Roman emperor's reverence for Cleopatra. Ptolemy's political machinations are no match for his sister's charms. The play ends with Caesar planning an official funeral for Pompey and endorsing Cleopatra's ascension to the throne, and with Caesar and Cleopatra planning to marry, having vanquished Ptolemy, who has drowned in an attempt to flee the lovers' alliance.

As readers of *La mort de Pompée* have acknowledged, the play's ending is less triumphant than it initially seems. Serge Doubrovsky notes that the future remains uncertain at the drama's close: "Cleopatra is crowned, and Pompey posthumously revered: but the love of Cleopatra and Caesar? Caesar's global conquest? The fate of Rome and Egypt? No prophetic vision . . . appears to guarantee the future that stretches beyond the tragic present. The play ends with everything remaining unresolved."[45] For Doubrovsky, while Caesar does emerge triumphant from the battle to shape Pompey's legacy by staging an official funeral for his former rival, and while Cleopatra and Caesar do outmaneuver Ptolemy, their ability to marry and the political consequences of such a project remain tenuous. The twists and turns of the drama's plot may have come to an end, but their consequences are far from clear.

While I agree with Doubrovsky about the lack of resolution in *La mort de Pompée*, I locate a different source of uncertainty: Cornelia's grief. Doubrovsky focuses on the future of Caesar and Cleopatra. Questioning whether their amorous and political designs will be achieved, Doubrovsky nevertheless assumes Caesar's ability to control Pompey's legacy settled: by arranging Pompey's official funeral, Caesar has successfully turned his rival's death to his advantage. Doubrovsky implies that Caesar's defeat of Pompey and his control over the fallen general's legacy has no real opposition: "Pompey is no more than a decapitated body, ashes in an urn. His widow Cornelia claims to continue the fight, but she does not have the means."[46] The assumption here is that, given her position as a grieving widow, Cornelia's claims to sustain Pompey's resistance are purely rhetorical. She has no means of resistance but only her tears. However, as Garnier's *Cornélie* has shown us, tears can serve as means of resistance—recall the rhyme "larmes" and "armes."[47] *La mort de Pompée* recalls this earlier drama's figuration of mourning as resistance by similarly positioning Cornelia as a public representative whose physical and affective connections to Pompey's remains authorize her to promote ongoing opposition to tyranny. Echoing the singular grief of Garnier's heroine and the shared lament of Rome, the Cornelia of *La mort de Pompée* turns her unforgettable loss into a promise of future vengeance.

By foregrounding Cornelia's responses to indications of tyrannical excess, *La mort de Pompée* situates her grief as a means of resistance to Caesar. Corneille's play figures the heart and soul as private spaces of subjective freedom, echoing Garnier's *Cornélie* as well as sixteenth-century resistance treatises. As I explored in chapter 1, resistance treatises understand liberty of conscience as something governed by divine law and therefore beyond legitimate monarchical control. A king who attempts to regulate his subjects' conscience thus marks himself as a tyrant. In *Cornélie*, as we have seen, several characters, including Cornelia, argue that Caesar holds his subjects captive by enslaving their hearts through his tyranny. Corneille's Caesar also makes Cornelia a more literal captive by keeping her in Egypt following Pompey's assassination. Lamenting her captivity, Corneille's heroine, like Garnier's, regrets that she has lived too long and maintains that she should have died along with Pompey:

> J'ai vu mourir Pompée, et ne l'ai pas suivi,
> Et bien que le moyen m'en ait été ravi,
> Qu'une pitié cruelle à mes douleurs profondes
> M'ait ôté le secours, et du fer, et des ondes,
> Je dois rougir pourtant après un tel malheur
> De n'avoir pu mourir d'un excès de douleur.
> Ma mort était ma gloire, et le Destin m'en prive
> Pour croître mes malheurs, et me voir ta captive.
> (Corneille, *La mort de Pompée*, 3.4.995–1002)[48]

I have seen Pompey die and have not followed him;
And though the means of death were snatched from me—
Though a compassion cruel to my deep grief
Hath taken from me all help of waves or dagger—
Rightly I blush still, after such a disaster,
That I could not die from excess of woe.
Death would mean honor, and Fate robs me of it,
To increase my misery making me thy captive.[49]

The physicality of this speech differs considerably from its counterpart in Garnier's play. Specifically, these verses put more distance between Cornelia's body and Pompey's. Corneille's heroine does not proclaim physically to feel the blows within her own body but instead witnesses his death: "J'ai vu mourir Pompée, et ne l'ai pas suivi." Nor does Corneille's heroine claim to have already died and yet go on living. She instead expresses shame at having watched Pompey die and at having failed to follow him in death: "Je dois rougir pourtant, après un tel malheur / de n'avoir pu mourir d'un excès de douleur." Emotions do not lead to their expected actions in these verses. Overwhelming sadness should have prompted Cornelia to turn her sword against herself or to cast herself into the sea. Having failed to induce her death, Cornelia's sadness turns to shame. The grief that propels Cornelia's resistance in *La mort de Pompée* is occasioned both by the loss of her husband and by the loss of her glory: "Ma mort était ma gloire, et le Destin m'en prive."

In *La mort de Pompée*, Cornelia's efforts to properly commemorate her husband are bound up in her efforts to restore her own glory. While arguing with Caesar, for example, she emphasizes her origins and pedigree:

Je te l'ai déjà dit, César, je suis Romaine,
Et quoique ta captive un cœur comme le mien
De peur de s'oublier ne te demande rien.
Ordonne, et sans vouloir qu'il tremble ou s'humilie,
Souviens-toi seulement que je suis Cornélie.
(Corneille, *La mort de Pompée*, 3.4.1022–26)

I told thee, Caesar, I am a Roman woman;
And though thy prisoner, one with heart like mine
Asks naught of thee lest she forget her duty.
Do thy will; only hope not I shall tremble
Or bow; remember that I am Cornelia.[50]

In these verses, which read as both compliant and defiant, Cornelia recognizes Caesar's authority while also preserving her heart as that which he cannot control. He can give orders, she suggests, and can restrict her physical movements but should refrain from making demands on her heart. The heart emerges in these verses as that which is proper to Cornelia. Importantly, her heart belongs to her primarily as a Roman woman. In Corneille's lexicon, as well as during the seventeenth century more broadly, "cœur" was often used to denote one's courage or bravery. By appealing to her heart in these lines Cornelia emphasizes her civic fortitude. Whereas in sixteenth-century resistance treatises the heart as a locus of freedom ties one's subjective liberty to one's inclusion in a community of believers, in *La mort de Pompée* the heart links Cornelia's personal liberty to her civic belonging to her sense of civic belonging. The "Romaine" and "mien" reinforces this connection, showing us that what is proper to Cornelia is secured through her attachment to Rome. Her liberty is both subjective and collective.[51]

Cornelia proves herself worthy of her Roman liberty by maintaining possession of Pompey's remains. Like the heroine of Garnier's *Cornélie* before her, the heroine of *La mort de Pompée* is presented an urn containing Pompey's ashes. A rare example of a prop appearing in seventeenth-century theater, this urn makes present the absent Pompey. As Corneille notes in the "Examen," Pompey, in his absence, is the force that propels the play's action. To be in possession of Pompey's remains is to gain a measure of this power. Cornelia's continued grasp on the urn signals her effort to honor her husband's glorious legacy and to prevent this legacy from being co-opted by Cleopatra or Caesar. The Egyptian princess and Roman emperor both attempt to manipulate Pompey's legacy to their own ends. For her part, Cleopatra suggests that Cornelia might moderate her calls for vengeance, intimating that the two women have interests and aims in common. But Cornelia will have none of this logic, refusing to settle for a vengeance half-pursued, and responds to Cleopatra, "Comme nos intérêts nos sentiments diffèrent" (5.2.1574) (Our feelings, like our interests, are different).[52] These defiant lines call our attention to the connection between emotion and political legitimacy. Cornelia distinguishes between Cleopatra's affective orientation toward Pompey and her own. Without sharing in Cornelia's grief, Cleopatra cannot legitimately join the widow's cause.

Cornelia's hold on Pompey's ashes also works against Caesar's attempts to control Pompey's legacy. While Pompey still lived, Caesar considered him a rival. After Pompey's death, however, Caesar works to turn Pompey's memory to his advantage. The official funeral that Caesar stages for his former rival coincides with Cleopatra's ascension to the Egyptian throne. Caesar announces this double ceremony in the drama's final lines: "Couronne Cléopâtre, et m'apaise Pompée, / Élève à l'une un Trône àl'autre des Autels, / Et jure à tous les deux des respects immortels" (5.5.1810–12) (Crown the queen and make my peace with Pompey, / Let him have altars, her the throne ascend, / And swear to both a reverence without end).[53] Speaking the drama's final lines, Caesar seems to have the last word on how Pompey will be remembered. Honoring Cleopatra and commemorating Pompey, he frames the glory of both his current ally and his former rival as part of his own strength.

Since Caesar speaks the drama's last lines, Cornelia cannot contradict his assertions the way she contradicted Cleopatra's. But in the penultimate scene, Cornelia delivers a tirade that undermines the apparent finality of Caesar's subsequent declaration. Against Caesar's suggestion that the official funeral will "apaise," or pacify, Pompey's spirit, Cornelia argues that nothing short of vengeance will properly honor her husband or calm his spirit:

> Non pas, César, non pas à Rome encor.
> Il faut que ta défaite et que tes funérailles
> À cette cendre aimée en ouvrent les murailles,
> Et quoiqu'elle la tienne aussi chère que moi,
> Elle n'y doit rentrer qu'en triomphant de toi.
> Je la porte en Afrique, et c'est là que j'espère
> Que les fils de Pompée et Caton et mon père,
> Secondés par l'effort d'un Roi plus généreux,
> Ainsi que la Justice auront le Sort pour eux.
> C'est là que tu verras sur la Terre et sur l'Onde
> Les débris de Pharsale armer un autre Monde,
> Et c'est là que j'irai pour hâter tes malheurs
> Porter de rang en rang ces cendres et mes pleurs.
> (Corneille, *La mort de Pompée*, 5.4.1701–12)
>
> No, no, Caesar; not to Rome; not yet.
> Thy overthrow and thy death are necessary
> To make Rome ready for these belovèd ashes;
> And though she holds them no less dear than I,
> They must return there but in triumph *o'er thee*.
> To Africa I bear them, where I hope
> That Pompey's sons and Cato and my father,
> With the assistance of a nobler king,

Will have on their side Fate as well as justice.
There shalt thou see, on land and on the waves,
Pharsalia's remnant arm a whole new world.
There I will go—to speed thy fall—and show
Throughout their ranks these ashes and my tears.[54]

Forced to bide her time in Egypt, Cornelia makes certain her future resistance. She refuses to accept Caesar's plan. For Cornelia, an official funeral will not properly avenge Pompey's death. This Cornelia, like Garnier's, speaks of her interminable tears, but she departs from her predecessor's example by figuring these tears as a central part of a military campaign. Describing how Pompey's family and followers will rise up to avenge him, she places herself in the middle of the action. She will appear alongside Pompey's most valiant defenders, carrying his ashes "de rang en rang."

As in *Cornélie*, the urn containing Pompey's ashes is the focal point for Cornelia's resistance to Caesar in *La mort de Pompée*. Corneille's rendition of the scene in which Cornelia receives the urn echoes Garnier's. Like her sixteenth-century counterpart, this Cornelia addresses the urn, animating this object. In the following lines she shifts from speaking to Phillipe, the man formerly enslaved by Pompey who had found and cremated Pompey's body, to speaking to the urn itself about the conflicting emotions that seeing it produces within her:

Cette Urne que je tiens contient-elle sa cendre?
Ô vous, à ma douleur objet terrible et tendre,
Éternel entretien de haine et de pitié,
Reste du grand Pompée, écoutez sa moitié.
(Corneille, *La mort de Pompée*, 5.1.1457–59)

This urn I hold contains his ashes?
O thou sweet, dreadful object of my sorrow,
Eternal theme for hatred and for pity,
Remains of the great Pompey, hear his wife![55]

Cornelia holds Pompey's ashes dear, but they are also a source of deep sadness. The urn both repels and compels her, inspiring both hatred and pity or compassion. As Cornelia holds the urn, she acknowledges its particular hold on her. This Cornelia does not, however, promise interminable tears. Instead she pledges to convert her sadness into vengeance, a promise that she reaffirms, as we have seen, in her final speech to Caesar.

Through her promise of vengeance, Cornelia contests Caesar's attempt to impress his own designs on the urn. As Phillipe explains to Cornelia, when he entered the palace with plans to deliver the urn to her he was intercepted by Caesar, who took hold of it and addressed Pompey's ashes:

> Restes d'un Demi dieu, dont à peine je puis
> Égaler le grand nom, tout vainqueur que j'en suis,
> De vos traîtres, dit-il, voyez punir les crimes,
> Attendant des Autels recevez ces victimes.
> (Corneille, *La mort de Pompée*, 5.1.1527–30)
>
> Ye ashes of a demigod,
> Whose great name will be hard for me to equal
> Although I am his conqueror, see punished
> The crime of those who have been treacherous to him.
> Till altars can be reared to him, accept
> These victims.[56]

Phillipe's report of Caesar's speech echoes Cornelia's promise of vengeance to the urn. Caesar promises to rectify the wrong done to Pompey by punishing those responsible and by delivering them to Pompey's alter. In the following lines Phillipe explains to Cornelia that Caesar kissed the urn and asked that it to be given to Cornelia as a gift on his behalf. Through these words and gestures Caesar attempts to divert Cornelia's vengeance by convincing her that their love for Pompey is mutual.

Cornelia's possession of the urn signals her refusal to accept Caesar's overtures. She maintains her hold on the urn from the moment she receives it at the beginning of act 5 until the end of the play. Through this sustained gesture, she pledges to maintain her grasp on Pompey's remains in the future. Cornelia's grip on the urn, coupled with her last speech of defiance, extends beyond the time of the play to interrupt Caesar's ending. Caesar's assurances in the play's final lines that Pompey has been duly honored are thus preemptively contradicted by Cornelia's pronouncements. Cornelia's enduring grasp on Pompey's legacy can be seen through the iconography of this figure. She is often portrayed holding the urn, such as in the portrait of the actress Adrienne Lecouvreur as Cornelia in an eighteenth-century production of *La mort de Pompée* (fig. 2).[57]

In addition to preserving Pompey's memory, Cornelia's hold on her husband's remains also serves as a means of recuperating the honor she lost by surviving him. Corneille's heroine echoes Garnier's by articulating her

Fig. 2. Adrienne Lecouvreur as Cornelia in Corneille's *La mort de Pompée*. Engraving by Pierre-Imbert Drevet after Charles-Antoine Coypel (after 1700). In. Bibliothèque nationale de France.

work of commemoration as a form of resistance. Tears are the weapon of Garnier's Cornelia. Her interminable tears signal her refusal to consent to Caesar's rule and offer affective evidence of his tyranny. The Cornelia of *La mort de Pompée* channels her tears into an explicit call for vengeance, placing herself at the center of a future scene of armed resistance. By refusing to accept Caesar's claim that Pompey has been duly honored and laid to rest, Cornelia recuperates her honor as both a surviving spouse and a representative of Rome.

By speaking as a Roman and by insisting that Pompey's followers will join her opposition to Caesar, the Cornelia of *La mort de Pompée* suggests that her calls for vengeance exceed her singular interests. Her plan to avenge Pompey is in the service of Rome. In Garnier's play, the heroine ties her personal grief to the laments of Rome by turning to a chorus of Roman women and asking them to join her tears. In *La mort de Pompée*, however, Cornelia has no chorus to address. Instead, by imagining herself at the head of what was once Pompey's army and by drawing strength from her civic virtue, she positions herself as a worthy captain of the people's opposition. Pledging to organize and maintain Rome's resistance as well as her own, Cornelia incorporates the Roman people into the tragedy. She operates as a staged mediator, a representative, of the unseen people's potential. Recognizing this Cornelia as a public representative allows us to see how the voice of the people persisted in seventeenth-century tragedy, even after the chorus had largely disappeared.

The Chorus Remains

The lack of a chorus in *La mort de Pompée* corresponds to a broader historical trend in seventeenth-century tragedy. Although it was common for sixteenth-century French tragedies to include at least one chorus (many, like *Cornélie*, had more than one), these collective bodies appeared much less frequently on the seventeenth-century stage. Indeed, Racine's biblical tragedies, *Esther* (1689) and *Athalie* (1691), which I will discuss in chapter 5, are among the few examples of what we now call neoclassical French tragedy to feature a chorus. What accounts for this change? One possibility is a shift in dramatic theory. In his *De l'art de la tragédie* (1572), which is often considered one of the foundational documents of French tragic theory, Jean de La Taille argues that a chorus is a necessary component of tragedy: "Il fault qu'il y ait un Chœur, c'est à dire, une assemblee d'hommes ou de femmes, qui à la fin de l'acte discourent sur ce qui aura esté dit devant: & et sur tout d'observer ceste maniere de taire & supplier ce que facilement sans exprimer se pourroit entendre avoir esté fait en derriere" (There must be a chorus, meaning a group of men or women, who discuss at the end of the act what has been said before them: and above all, to maintain silence and supply that which can easily be understood to have occurred offstage without being shown).[58] For La Taille, the chorus's task is to observe and be observed. At the end of each act, the chorus comments on what has just been said and done. During each act, the chorus stands as a silent, plaintive, collective witness that makes itself heard without actually speaking. Commenting on one type of staged action—that of the individual characters—the chorus exemplifies another.

Seventeenth-century dramatic theorists acknowledged the chorus's historical importance to tragedy, despite the fact that this staged collective had largely become obsolete. François Hédelin, the abbé d'Aubignac, notes in his *La pratique du théâtre* (1657) that his readers might well be surprised to find that his treatise addresses the role of the chorus at all. "On pourroit s'imaginer, que presentement le discours des Chœurs est absolument inutile dans cette pratique du Theatre, où je n'ay rien promis que de necessaire à la composition de nostre Poëme & à la connoissance de l'Art" (One might imagine that currently a statement on the chorus is completely useless in this treatise on the practice of theater, where I promise nothing except that which is necessary for the composition of our poem and the knowledge of Art).[59] D'Aubignac goes on to explain that a consideration of the chorus is not "absoluement inutile" but rather offers insight into the essence of tragedy as a genre. He writes, "Comme le Chœur fut le principe de l'estre de la Tragédie, il le fut sans doute aussi de ses qualitez plus naturelles; c'est le fondement de toute l'œconomie de ce Poëme, et la lumiere presque de toutes ses regles" (Given that the chorus was the essence of tragedy, it was also certainly one of its most natural qualities; it is the foundation of the entire economy of this poem and sheds light on almost all of its rules).[60] To understand the ancient chorus is to understand not only what tragedy once was—or what it was "originally"—but also what tragedy should continue to be, even if the chorus itself no longer appears.

For d'Aubignac and his contemporaries, the chorus of ancient tragedy helped to foster some of the fundamental precepts of seventeenth-century dramatic theory, namely, the unities of place and time.[61] In ancient tragedy, d'Aubignac explains, the chorus would remain onstage as individual actors came and went. As a result, the chorus made drastic changes of scene implausible: "Il est indubitable que le lieu ne pouvoit pas changer, autrement il eust esté ridicule que des personnes qui ne changeoient point de lieu, qui ne sortoient point de la Scéne, eussent passé d'Asie, en Europe; de France, en Dannemarc; d'Athénes, à Thèbes; de Paris à Reims; sans avoir marché, et sans estre disparus aux yeux des Spectateurs" (It is inarguable that the location cannot change, otherwise it would be ridiculous for these people who do not change location, who do not leave the stage, to go from Asia to Europe, from France to Denmark, from Athens to Thebes, from Paris to Reims, without having walked and without having left the spectators' view).[62] By serving as a physical index of verisimilitude for the audience, the chorus encouraged ancient dramatists to observe a unity of place.

D'Aubignac goes on to assert that a similar dynamic between chorus and audience encouraged the Greeks to observe a unity of time, that is, to limit the amount of time represented onstage. Following Aristotle's *Poetics*, seventeenth-century dramatic theorists tended to fix the ideal length of tragedy somewhere between twelve and twenty-four hours, or "a single daylight period."[63] "Si le Poëte eust renfermé dans sa Tragédie une année entiere, un mois, une semaine," d'Aubignac writes, "comment eust-il pû faire croire aux Spectateurs, que des gens qui n'avoient pas disparu, avoient passé tout ce longtemps, entre le moment de leur entrée au Theatre et celui de leur sortie? par quel artifice, ou par quelle magie pouvoit-il rendre cela vraysemblable, et donner raison de ce qu'on ne les avoit veus ny boire, ny manger, ny dormir?" (If the poet restricts his tragedy to an entire year, a month, or a week, how can he make the spectators believe that these people, who haven't left, have spent all this time, between the moment of their entrance onstage until their exit? By what artifice or what magic could the poet make it believable and reasonable that that they have not been seen eating, or drinking, or sleeping).[64] The physical needs and limitations of the chorus as a group of actors that remains onstage kept the length of tragedy in check. The chorus gave ancient Greek tragedy its shape, helping to define the genre's spatial and temporal boundaries.

If the ancient chorus was so crucial to establishing the unities of place and time in tragedy, as well as to maintaining verisimilitude—all concepts near and dear to seventeenth-century dramatic theory—why do seventeenth-century tragedies so often omit the chorus? John D. Lyons suggests that any admiration dramatic theorists and dramatists may have held for the ancient chorus would likely have been tempered by the social and political structures of seventeenth-century France, particularly as they pertained to the organization of public and private space. In Greek tragedy, Lyons argues, the chorus represented the wider community that could observe, judge, and question the actions of individual characters. "Although many things happened within the palace or the tent of the heroes and out of sight of the chorus and audience," Lyons writes, "the play itself as spectacle was a place common to the tragic heroes and to the chorus." In other words, the space of ancient tragedy was both private and public. Lyons argues that the absence of the chorus in seventeenth-century French tragedy can be understood in part as this period's general concern with maintaining boundaries between the public and the private. Without the chorus, the place of the "play itself as spectacle" becomes "a quasi-private area for the heroes and their intimates." Rather than integrate the wider community or "the people" into the tragic community onstage, seventeenth-century tragedy relegates this collective to the audience. The people as audience are still present as witnesses and observers of the tragic action, but the spatial divide between actors and audience—*la scène et la salle*—severely limits their ability to influence or inform that action.[65]

Christian Biet has also suggested that the theatrical audience became a kind of tragic chorus during the seventeenth century. For Biet this change can be explained by the violence of the religious wars. He argues that the violence of these wars and the political uncertainty they engendered made it impossible to have a unified collective body appear on stage to comment on and judge the political and social cleavages portrayed in tragedy. The religious wars had destroyed the idea that a conflict could be resolved by a collective judgment that would be widely accepted. For Biet the audience as chorus represents the fragmentation of collective judgment as well as the removal of the collective from the public scene.[66]

I find much to admire in Biet's and Lyons's accounts of how changes to the tragic scene paralleled ideological changes that reorganized political life in the wake of the religious wars, but I worry that they overstate the case. By making shifts in political ideology the cause of the chorus's disappearance, these arguments risk making these shifts seem more coherent and thorough than the historical record bears out, while also obscuring how the chorus persisted. Acknowledging the general absence of a chorus in seventeenth-century tragedy, I maintain that the people nonetheless remain present. As Gillian Jondorf has noted, seventeenth-century tragedies without a chorus rely on individual characters to communicate public opinion or sentiment.[67] Jondorf cites Corneille's *Horace* (1640) as a particularly salient example of this practice, noting that in the final act, the elder Horace states, "Rome tout entière a parlé par ma bouche" (All of Rome speaks through my mouth).[68] The elder Horace claims that people speak through him.

Citations of public opinion or sentiment in seventeenth-century tragedies, Jondorf argues, are vestiges of the choruses that populate their sixteenth-century counterparts. The link between chorus and citation is one of many that Jondorf uses to demonstrate how indebted seventeenth-century tragedies are to those of the sixteenth century—a project she offers as a corrective to scholars' long-standing practice of minimizing the poetic merits of sixteenth-century dramas, both in their own right and with respect to the development of neoclassical tragedy.[69] Indeed, where the chorus is concerned, this practice of eschewing the influence of earlier French tragedies begins in the seventeenth century itself, as evidenced in d'Aubignac's *La pratique du théâtre*. D'Aubignac, as we have seen, discusses the chorus of ancient Greek tragedy in detail. He does not, however, acknowledge the tradition of staging choruses in Renaissance France.[70]

Following Jondorf's lead, I read the people invoked by Cornelia in *La mort de Pompée*—the family and followers of Pompey—as the seventeenth-century remains of a chorus. Offstage and unseen, this collective is nonetheless incorporated into the drama. Corneille's "Examen" sets a precedent for recognizing an unseen actor's effect onstage. Although Pompey is never seen alive, he is nonetheless the play's central figure. Further, as we have seen, the possession of Pompey's remains, and thus the ability to control his legacy, exerts great force on stage. Similarly, the people invoked by Cornelia—the remains of the chorus—exert their pressure on the dispute over Pompey's legacy. The family and followers of Pompey, whom Cornelia states will rise up and seek vengeance against Caesar, add a collective dimension to her grief and to her promises of resistance.

In both *Cornélie* and *La mort de Pompée*, Cornelia's grief ultimately binds her to the collective and allows her to emerge as a public representative. In Garnier's play the chorus ratifies Cornelia's legitimacy as a representative of the people by adding their tears to her ongoing project of commemoration. But in *La mort de Pompée*, Cornelia speaks for the people herself. As a result, although she claims that she speaks for the Roman people, how are the people to know that she is more than self-interested or that she will indeed sustain opposition to tyranny? While there is no independent verification of Cornelia's legitimacy from the people themselves, the play nonetheless suggests that she is worthy of the people's approval by portraying her as virtuous and honorable. Through her Roman origins and her grief for Pompey, she stands as figure whose calls for vengeance are noble and just.

Cornelia as *Femme Forte*

In the context of 1640s France, Cornelia's exemplarity ties her not only to the collective of the Roman people but also to the group of female figures known as the femmes fortes, or strong women. As Joan DeJean and others have noted, the appellation *femme forte* was used to celebrate female figures from history. DeJean is careful to point out, however, that only certain kinds of strong women were celebrated as femmes fortes. In other words, the category of the femme forte was highly regulative

Fig. 3. "Porcie." In Pierre Le Moyne, *La gallerie des femmes fortes* (Paris: Antoine de Sommaville, 1647). Engraving by Abraham Bosse after Claude Vignon. Bibliothèque nationale de France.

in its idealization of a particular form of womanhood that did not radically disrupt traditional gender divisions between men and women.[71] The seventeenth-century ideal of the femme forte is most closely associated with gallery books, such as Pierre Le Moyne's *La gallerie des femmes fortes* (1647), which bring together images and textual descriptions of a set of women widely recognized for their virtue and valor. These books make clear that the phenomenon of the femme forte is collective as well as

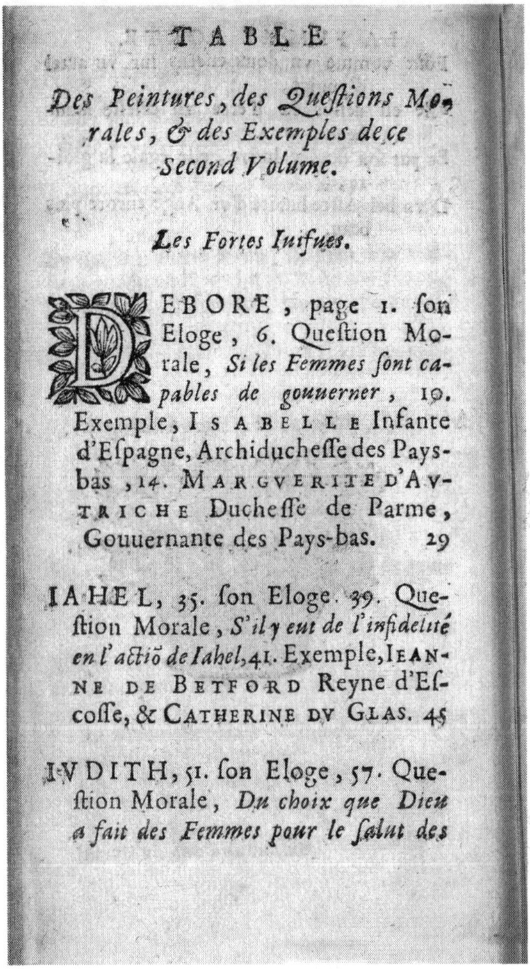

TABLE

Des Peintures, des Queſtions Morales, & des Exemples de ce Second Volume.

Les Fortes Iuifues.

DEBORE, page 1. ſon Eloge, 6. Queſtion Morale, *Si les Femmes ſont capables de gouuerner*, 19. Exemple, ISABELLE Infante d'Eſpagne, Archiducheſſe des Pays-bas, 14. MARGVERITE D'AVTRICHE Ducheſſe de Parme, Gouuernante des Pays-bas. 29

IAHEL, 35. ſon Eloge. 39. Queſtion Morale, *S'il y eut de l'infidelité en l'actiõ de Iahel*, 41. Exemple, IEANNE DE BETFORD Reyne d'Eſcoſſe, & CATHERINE DV GLAS. 45

IVDITH, 51. ſon Eloge, 57. Queſtion Morale, *Du choix que Dieu a fait des Femmes pour le ſalut des*

Fig. 4. "Les fortes Juifves." In Pierre Le Moyne, *La gallerie des femmes fortes* (Paris: Antoine de Sommaville, 1647). Engraving by Abraham Bosse after Claude Vignon. Bibliothèque nationale de France.

individual. Although each image and description foregrounds one woman and depicts her actions as singular in their fortitude or honor, DeJean maintains that the book's structure as a gallery assemble these women into a formidable collective.[72] Portraits of individual women feature prominently in the gallery (see, e.g., fig. 3), but readers must nonetheless identify and navigate these individual portraits using indexical lists that gather femmes fortes together in historical cohorts (see, e.g., fig. 4).

As Timothy J. Reiss has suggested, the Cornelia of *La mort de Pompée* hews closely to the model of the femme forte championed by Le Moyne and others.[73] And yet, Cornelia does not appear as one of the figures in seventeenth-century gallery books. This absence may be explained by Cornelia's relative lack of coverage in the sources used for these books. Boccacio's *De claris mulieribus* (1361–62), for example, discusses Portia, the wife of Brutus who legend has it swallowed hot coals to end her life after Brutus's death, but makes no mention of Cornelia.[74] Cornelia does appear alongside Portia in Christine de Pizan's feminist response to Boccacio and his ilk, *Le livre de la cité des dames* (1405). For Christine, these Roman women together offer cautionary tales of why husbands should listen to their wives.[75]

Beyond the question of sources, I would like to suggest that Portia's presence in these gallery books and Cornelia's absence from them might be explained by the former's relative confinement to the private space of her quarters and the latter's public-facing resistance. We find this distinction in the tragedies by Garnier that focus on these two figures. In *Cornélie*, as we have seen, we find a woman in mourning who refuses either to retreat into private space or to subsume her private mourning into public grief. But the heroine of Garnier's *Porcie* (1568) expresses unease with the uncertainties of political machination and ends her life within her chambers. If Portia represents a steadfast female figure who privately refuses to participate in a new political order, Cornelia refuses to keep her resistance private. As such, she offers a potent example of how private grief can be marshalled for collective political ends.

Chapter Three

The Rebel

Robert Garnier's *Antigone, ou La pieté* (1580) opens with a tender scene between father and daughter. Antigone and Oedipus enter together slowly, with Antigone leading her blind father by the hand. Oedipus thanks his daughter for her support, calling her "mon soustien, mon addresse" (1.2) (my aide, my guide).[1] But ultimately he urges her to let go and leave him to wander alone: "Retire donc ta main qui tendrement me serre" (1.21) (Remove your hand that holds me tenderly).[2] Antigone refuses his request and instead insists that he should return to Thebes and put an end to the conflict between her brothers, Eteocles and Polynices. The series of events that have led father and daughter to this moment will be familiar to readers who have encountered Sophocles's tragedy or another version of the myth. Once Oedipus realized that he had killed his father and slept with his mother, he blinded himself, renounced his crown, exiled himself from Thebes, and declared that in his absence his sons would take turns as king, with each one ruling for a year at a time. Oedipus's plan overlooked a key characteristic of sovereign power: it is difficult to share. When Eteocles refused to cede the throne after his year as king, Polynices declared war. In the first act of Garnier's play, Antigone attempts to pull her father back to Thebes before this fraternal war destroys the entire city:

> Quand vous n'auriez, mon pere, autre cause de vivre,
> Que pour Thebes defendre et la rendre delivre
> Des combats fraternels, vous ne devez mourir,
> Ains vos jours prolonger pour Thebes secourir:
> Vous pouvez amortir cette guerre enflammee,
> Seul vous avez puissance en l'une et l'autre armee:
> Des mains de vos enfants vous pouvez arracher
> Le fer desja tiré pour s'entredehacher.
> (Garnier, *Antigone, ou La pieté*, 1.325–32)

> Even if, father, you have no other reason to live than to defend Thebes and to deliver it from fratricidal combat, you should not die. Instead, you should extend your life in order to lend Thebes your help. You can calm this fiery war. You alone have power over both armies. From your children's hands you can wrestle the swords that they have drawn to hack each other apart.[3]

Imploring Oedipus to return to Thebes to stop Eteocles and Polynices, Antigone makes clear that the fate of her father and city are profoundly intertwined. Oedipus must extend his life (*vivre*) to deliver (*delivre*) Thebes from civil war. Only Oedipus, Antigone suggests, has the capacity to make her brothers lay down their arms. Only Oedipus can save Thebes from total devastation.

Holding her father with her hand, Antigone literalizes a gesture that the play will repeat over and over as it explores the dynamic between family and city, ruler and ruled. Lamenting her brothers' tight hold on their weapons, Antigone's speech attunes us to the hand as a symbol of power. The hand, after all, holds the scepter, that striking emblem of sovereign authority and control. Antigone's gesture also introduces us to the hand as a symbol of familial devotion. Communicating familial attachment and political power, the forms of touch and reach in Garnier's tragedy are both literally embodied, as in Antigone's opening gesture, and more abstract, as in the powerful impression that Oedipus's return would presumably have over his warring sons. In other words, the tragedy suggests that its characters are swayed not only by each other's physical touch but also by the push and pull of affective influence. Although the Theban people may not hold the scepter or make claims to the throne, the play's emphasis on affective influence allows them to participate in this push and pull as well. Through the interventions of staged choruses, along with invocations of their collective voice, the Theban people impinge on the tragedy's actions and impress their concerns and preferences on the royal characters.

In Garnier's tragedy Antigone emerges from this constellation of physical and affective influence as a representative of the Theban people. Much like Garnier's *Cornélie*, his *Antigone, ou La pieté* draws parallels between ancient scenes of conflict and those that were ravaging sixteenth-century France. In this case, however, Garnier turns to Thebes rather than Rome. As Phillip John Usher has noted, Garnier makes this connection between the (mythic) past and present explicit in his dedicatory letter to "Monseigneur Brisson, conseiller du Roy en son Conseil privé, et President en sa Cour de Parlement" (My Lord Brisson, advisor to the King in his private council, and President in his Parliament Court).[4] Holding these two titles, Brisson serves as both a counselor to the king and as a public representative, charged with maintaining the public good on behalf of the people. As was common in such dedicatory prefaces, Garnier praises Brisson, who Usher explains had "very recently played a key role, in Poitou, in bringing peace and restoring order," and asks Brisson to attend to "des infortunes de ceste pitoyable Antigone" (the misfortunes of the pitiful Antigone), who Garnier argues is "revivant en nostre France" (living in today's France).[5] One imagines that it will be hard for Brisson to ignore Antigone, since Garnier has her reach out of the play to make physical contact with Brisson himself. The dramatist states that the Theban princess "se vient, comme esperdue, jetter entre vos bras" (comes, disheveled, throwing herself into her your arms).[6] In so doing, Antigone, who acts as a support to her "miserable" (pitiful) father, in turn seeks Brisson's support. With this "breaking of boundaries between play and nonplay, between the dramatic and (because of Brisson's real-world position) the parliamentary public sphere," Usher notes, Garnier signals that the concerns raised by his tragedy are worth consideration in parliament, much like more traditional rhetorical forms, such as the *remontrance*.[7] Reaching out to Brisson, a recognized public official, Antigone herself begins to emerge as such a representative.

In this chapter I argue that tragedy is not only one genre among several capable of raising political concerns in the time of civil conflict, but instead enables a specific kind of political work, namely, the binding together of individual and collective concerns through its emphasis on the interactions between bodies, both on stage and off. By attending to the gestural repertoire and poetic structures of Garnier's *Antigone, ou La pieté*, as well as Jean de Rotrou's subsequent *Antigone*, which was published in 1637 and performed in 1639, I demonstrate how Antigone emerges as the kind of public representative called for in sixteenth-century resistance treatises, whose affective relationship with the people authorizes her resistance. In both these tragedies, Antigone makes personal claims that are similar in structure to those of Pompey's widow, Cornelia, whose expressions of grief in Garnier's *Cornélie* and Corneille's *La mort de Pompée* I examined in the previous chapter. Despite this structural similarity, Antigone's claims, however, carry a different political valence. When Cornelia asserts her personal freedom and attachment to her slain husband, the legitimacy of these assertions is not in question. In contrast, when Antigone makes claims of personal freedom and attachment to her brother Polynices they raise suspicion and doubt. Cornelia seems to act appropriately, given her role as Pompey's widow, his surviving "époux noble et digne moitié" (noble spouse and worthy half).[8] Antigone, however, supports her disgraced father, who has committed both incest and parricide, and then opposes Creon on behalf of a brother rather than a husband. Whether her attachments to Oedipus and Polynices justify her claims or whether these attachments instead confirm her family's unseemly legacy is a central question in both *Antigone, ou La pieté* and *Antigone*.

Recognizing Antigone as a public representative in these two plays allows us to see how tragedy sustains the conceptual framework of resistance theory even after the official end of the French religious wars. Whereas Garnier's *Antigone, ou La pieté* was published (and perhaps performed) during the wars and clearly draws parallels between the fraternal conflict in Thebes and the civil conflict in France, by the time Jean de Rotrou's *Antigone* premiered at the Hôtel de Bourgogne in 1637, wars were officially over.[9] However, while Henri IV's Edict of Nantes (1598) had more success than the many preceding edicts of pacification, religious and civil conflicts continued to erupt throughout the following decades. As Mack P. Holt has argued, a more fitting date for the end of the religious wars is 1629, after the crown's defeat of the Protestant stronghold city La Rochelle.[10] Fear of the renewed outbreak of civil war marked French political life longer still. Lasting fears of civil conflict would undoubtedly have affected how audiences at the Hôtel de Bourgogne experienced the scenes of devastation in the divided Thebes of Rotrou's *Antigone*. Warring factions may have put down their arms, but the possibility that they might reach for them again haunted seventeenth-century France.

As I noted in this introduction to this book, the theory of absolute monarchy presented itself as a solution to the lingering problem of civil conflict. The religious wars had destroyed any notion that the French body politic was united as one *corps mystique*, or spiritual body, which meant that, as Reinhart Koselleck observes, "the entire social order became unhinged."[11] Sixteenth-century resistance theory rested in part on the idea that the people's collective power authorized them to support public representatives who would oppose a king's tyranny on behalf of the common good. To make this argument, resistance treatises like the *Vindiciae contra tyrannos* rhetorically presumed a stable emotional community that was in agreement about distinctions between the good and the bad, the pious and the impious. If the continued existence of this "performative commons," to borrow Elizabeth Maddox Dillon's term, was already in doubt when resistance treatises first appeared in the 1570s and 1580s, it had clearly collapsed by the beginning of the seventeenth century.[12] This meant that there was no longer even any pretense to identify a consensus about what constituted tyranny and what constituted legitimate resistance. Instead, according to Koselleck, "high treason and the struggle for the common good became interchangeable concepts depending on the point of view of the ascendant faction."[13] The theory of absolute monarchy addressed this problem by maintaining that what united the French body politic was the king himself and the state apparatus he controlled. As a result it was the king and the logic of raison d'état that had the authority to adjudicate disputes. According to this conception of political power, a potential public representative or a contingency of subjects professing collectively to represent the public good had little theoretical ground on which to stand. How could an individual or collective claim to answer only to an authority higher than the king's if the king was now positioned as the only representative of the highest authority?

Antigone has long been celebrated as a tragic figure who opposes the king in the name of a higher authority, whether it be divine law or natural law, the rights of the individual or the sacred bonds of kingship. By reading Garnier's *Antigone, ou La pieté* and Rotrou's *Antigone* together, and thus by reading across the historical divide created by the putative end of the religious wars, I demonstrate how these tragedies position Antigone as a public representative whose authority is constituted by the people's collective power, which supersedes that of the king. As we will see, in both tragedies the people's affective attachments to Antigone work to assuage concerns about her potentially unseemly attachments to her father and brother Polynices. In other words, the people's love for Antigone serves as affective evidence of her legitimacy. By sustaining the conceptual framework of resistance theory, which vests political authority in both the individual representative and the collective that legitimizes her, Garnier's *Antigone, ou La pieté* and Rotrou's *Antigone* ultimately help us to rethink the limits and possibilities of Antigone's role as a model for contemporary political action.

Antigone's Reach

Through their poetic construction and gestural repertoire, Garnier's *Antigone, ou La pieté* and Rotrou's *Antigone* (1637–39) help us to locate a political potential in this tragic figure that often eludes the grasp of modern and contemporary "Antigone Studies." Garnier's and Rortrou's tragedies draw from many of the same sources, incorporating elements from the various versions by Aeschylus, Euripides, Seneca, Sophocles, and Statius, as well as from sixteenth-century versions of Sophocles's *Antigone*, such as that of Italian dramatist Luigi Alamanni.[14] Rotrou also draws from Garnier's tragedy directly. Working from this plurality of sources, Garnier and Rotrou do not simply mimic the dramatic arc established by Sophocles's more famous *Antigone*. Whereas Sophocles's tragedy opens as Antigone receives the news of Creon's edict, both early modern versions begin at an earlier point in the family's story. As we have seen, Garnier's tragedy opens with Antigone leading Oedipus through the wilderness after his self-blinding and abdication. Rotrou's begins with Jocasta lamenting that Eteocles and Polynices have not managed to share the throne as Oedipus had envisioned. Both tragedies go on to treat Antigone's reactions to the brothers' fatal duel and to conclude with Antigone's defiance of Creon. Garnier and Rotrou thus cover two conflicts in one play, a construction that serves to link Antigone's resistance to the many misfortunes of her family and city.

Linking the two conflicts, Garnier's *Antigone, ou La pieté* and Rotrou's *Antigone* hold together what have come to be understood in Antigone Studies as two sides of this tragic heroine: the dissident and the devoted daughter and sister. As Bonnie Honig has noted, conceptions of Antigone as a tragic figure in modern political theory and philosophy tend to take one of these two sides.[15] Antigone the dissident has long been associated with the emergence of the modern subject of rights during the eighteenth century. She is cited by Louis de Jacourt in his entry "Sujet" for the *Encyclopédie* (1752–71), as an exemplary political subject who asserts the primacy her individual rights—as guaranteed by divine and natural law—over the edicts of a king.[16] Antigone's association with the modern individual has had no small amount of staying power within the French tradition. After surveying the many dramatic and critical inflections of this figure across centuries of French cultural and political history, Simone Fraisse concludes that "For the French in particular, Antigone will always be the daughter of the Revolution."[17] To cast Antigone as the daughter of the Revolution is to situate her as an example par excellence of the liberal political subject. The form of subjecthood she stands for is not just free from monarchical rule but constitutionally autonomous and distinct or discrete from other individuals. This Antigone's legacy extends far beyond the French tradition, contributing to a broader trend that understands Antigone as an autonomous, solitary political dissident. As Honig writes, this trend, which she terms the "legalist," casts Antigone as a "heroic conscientious objector who on political grounds violates an unjust law, challenges a powerful sovereign, and all by herself dares speak truth to power."[18]

In contrast, the portrayal of Antigone as a picture of sisterly devotion is most closely associated with G. W. F. Hegel, whose account of the conflict between family and state in the *Phenomenology of the Spirit* (1807) is often read as a gloss on the conflict between Antigone and Creon. For Hegel, a woman's burial of her male family member constitutes an ethical act that secures his particularity. As a result, the act of burial works against the state, which instead understands him as a replaceable citizen. By burying her kin, the woman thus takes up the family's particular interests against those of the state, or the broader community. Judith Butler notes that Hegel "variably" uses the terms "community," "government," and "state" to name the entity in conflict with the family.[19] Uniting these terms as the "public sphere," Butler reminds us that for Hegel the conflict between this sphere and the family is dialectical. She writes, "The public sphere . . . only acquires its existence through *interfering* with the happiness of the family; thus, it creates for itself 'an internal enemy—womankind in general. Womankind—the everlasting irony [in the life] of the community.'"[20] Exemplifying "Womankind" as "the everlasting irony of the community," the Antigone of Hegel's formulation marks a continual turning away from the common interests of the public sphere in favor of the private interests of the family. As Butler explains, Hegel's Antigone thus remains a "prepolitical subject," forever representing the "internal enemy" of the public sphere.[21]

The differences between Hegel's Antigone and the legalist Antigone point us toward some persistent patterns in modern conceptions of this figure. The legalist framework renders Antigone solitary and political. Hegel's Antigone (and the Womankind she represents) is not solitary but rather appears deeply devoted to the family. As Honig notes, this private attachment, however, makes her into an ethical rather than a political figure. An emphasis on Antigone's attachments tends to occlude the political potential of her speech and actions. Our options seem to be for a political, autonomous Antigone, or for a nonpolitical, attached Antigone. In other words, to separate the ethical from the political Antigone is to suggest that to act politically we must act alone.[22] To make this separation is also to suggest that our attachments to others have no political connotations or consequences.

Butler and Honig have both critiqued this tendency, arguing on the contrary that Antigone's attachments undergird her capacity for political disruption. In *Antigone's Claim*, Butler suggests that Antigone wields the language of sovereignty, acting out a perverse familial legacy in ways that trouble canonical interpretations (including Hegel's), which often position her as an incarnation of a pure, prepolitical kinship. Butler argues that Antigone, far from representing normative, heterosexual kinship positions, instead reveals the fatality inherent in such positions:

"Although not quite a queer heroine, Antigone does emblematize a certain heterosexual fatality that remains to be read."[23] Antigone prompts us to ask, "What in her act is fatal for heterosexuality in its normative sense? And to what other ways of organizing sexuality might a consideration of that fatality give rise?"[24] More recently, in *Antigone, Interrupted*, Honig proposes an agonistic, partisan Antigone, who acts conspiratorially in cooperation with her sister Ismene. Together, Butler's and Honig's work demonstrate how it is not Sophocles's tragedy as such that necessitates a choice between a solitary, political Antigone, and a devoted, ethical Antigone, but rather a persistent set of reading practices and interpretive biases that impose these categories.

And yet, Honig argues that even feminist and queer critics who offer powerful critiques of Hegel's relegation of Antigone to the prepolitical ultimately depoliticize Antigone's attachments by rendering them indices of a universal humanity. Calling this tendency the "Antigone-effect," Honig writes that "a certain pull from action and natality to lamentation and mortality exerts itself on those feminist and queer theorists who turn to Antigone."[25] Whereas Hegel's focus was on what we might call normative familial attachments, these feminist and queer readings position attachments as that which brings us all together as humans. Whatever their potentially nonnormative specificity, these attachments have a universalizing effect. By mourning her brother, Antigone thus becomes the standard-bearer of what Honig terms "mortalist humanism," a humanism grounded not in universal rationalism but rather universal mortality and finitude. Honig maintains that even Butler herself perpetuates this kind of mortalist humanism, thus falling prey to the Antigone-effect. Over the course of Butler's work on Antigone, Honig writes, "we shift from an Antigone who stops the future operations of the paternal law in order to claim its power (as Butler says in *Antigone's Claim*) to one (as in *Precarious Life*) who laments its operations on us. . . . From *Antigone's Claim* to *Precarious Life* and, most recently, *Frames of War*, Butler's earliest Antigone of rival citational sovereignty gives way to the humanist lamenter of the dead."[26] Against this false choice between rival citational sovereignty to humanist lamenter of the dead, Honig offers her account of an agonistic Antigone who conspires with her sister and contests Creon's exclusive claim to power.[27]

I contend that to more fully break the critical impasse that pits the solitary, political Antigone against the attached, lamenting Antigone we need to return this figure to the scene of theater. By this I mean that what has in part allowed us to separate these two kinds of Antigones—and thus to depoliticize and universalize her particular attachments—is a tendency to read her as an abstract figure or model, rather than as an entity enmeshed in the embodied, collective work of theater. Among political theorists, Honig is most attentive to the specificities of theater. She considers questions of staging and movement, often thinking dramaturgically about the possibilities Sophocles's text affords.[28] Honig is also sensitive to genre expectations, suggesting how reading *Antigone* as a melodrama instead of a tragedy opens up previously occluded interpretive possibilities.[29] But *Antigone is* a tragedy. And even in hands as careful as Honig's, when we look to its eponymous heroine as a model of political action, we are in danger of conflating Antigone the character with *Antigone* the tragedy, and thus missing the extent to which the former only exists as an effect of the latter. By reading Garnier's *Antigone, ou La pieté* and Rotrou's *Antigone* as dramatic texts that contain both "poetry and performance," one of my aims is to demonstrate how the structure of these particular, early modern tragedies allows us to reach across the divide that continues to separate Antigone the dissident from Antigone the devoted.[30]

Fraisse notes the appearance of these two Antigones within Garnier's tragedy, a duality that she traces to Sophocles's *Oedipus at Colonus* and *Antigone*, respectively. In *Oedipus at Colonus*, Fraisse writes, "Antigone is the model of a loving and pious daughter, who seeks peace and reconciliation."[31] In *Antigone*, however, the tragic figure is combative: "Without a law to break, without a tyrant to confront, she would no longer be Antigone."[32] In the first case she is loyal daughter, in the second a dissident. Fraisse goes on to suggest that the different portraits of Antigone from within Sophocles's works afford this character "a dual lineage" within French literary and cultural history, arguing that subsequent dramatic interpretations have tended to favor one over the other.Fraisse aligns Garnier's *Antigone, ou La pieté* with the devoted Antigone, noting how Garnier "makes beautiful use" of a touching scene of affection between Antigone and Oedipus that appears in *Oedipus at Colonus*, as well as in *The Phoenician Women* of both Seneca and Euripides.[33] However, Garnier's tragedy also stages the conflict between Antigone and Creon, presenting both the dissident and the devoted Antigone. More than merely presenting both these roles, the play firmly establishes their mutual constitution and eschews the very idea that they might be separated. Rotrou's tragedy performs a similar work, offering an Antigone whose inextricable attachments to family and people shape her objections to sovereign power.

The frontispiece that accompanies early editions of Rotrou's tragedy illustrates this close relationship between Antigone's objections to Creon's edict and the misfortunes of her family and city (fig. 5).[34] Engraved by Claude Vignon and Michel Lasne, the frontispiece depicts Jocasta in the

Fig. 5. Frontispiece of Jean de Rotrou, *Antigone* (Paris: Antoine de Sommaville et Toussaint Quinet, 1640). Engraving by Claude Vignon and Michel Lasne. Bibliothèque nationale de France.

left foreground as she attempts to pull apart her warring sons. The right background shows the final confrontation between Creon and his son Haemon, which takes place over the body of Antigone. These two scenes of parental alarm serve as bookends for the plot, depicting a tragic action that is both at its beginning and near its end. The many outstretched arms in the image create visual tension, pulling the scenes apart even as they remain tied together. It is impossible to see Jocasta's outstretched arm restraining her son in the foreground without also seeing Creon's raised arm imploring his son in the background. The impossibility of viewing the image's foreground without the background seems to suggest a linear passage from one conflict to the other. But it is likewise impossible to see the background without passing through the foreground, a common optic in early modern frontispieces, which suggests a continual repetition and a lack of any final resolution. The image thus refuses a chronological passage from one scene to another, suggesting instead a kind of perpetual suspension that underscores the enmeshment of Antigone's opposition to Creon and the communal crisis that her brothers' conflict engenders. The temporality of this image suggest how we might begin to read Antigone in a way that does not dissociate her affective attachments from her political agency.

Holding these two conflicts in suspense the frontispiece alerts us to the outstretched arm as a key gestural motif. In both tragedies, characters and entities reach toward each other, attempting to exert their influence. No individual or group acts alone, but rather all are pushed and pulled by the physical tug of another's arm, or by the affective sway of another's laments. Within Rotrou's tragedy, Antigone reaches most explicitly toward Polynices. In Garnier's her reach extends first toward Oedipus and then toward Polynices. Her outstretched arms function as corporeal manifestations of her attempts to move her father and brother, both physically and emotionally. These gestures also signal how she is moved by them. In both plays Antigone's reach and grip attach her to her family's troubled legacy. Rather than function only as signs of Antigone's apparent piety and virtue, as I have previously suggested, these gestures also raise questions about the legitimacy of Antigone's claims. In the sections that follow, I demonstrate how Garnier's tragedy raises questions about Antigone's legitimacy through the idiom of piety, whereas Rotrou's focuses primarily on that of nature. I then show how the tragedies mobilize the Theban people as staged choruses or unseen collectives, who ratify Antigone's claims by providing affective evidence of her legitimacy.

Corrupting Piety

In Garnier's *Antigone, ou La pieté*, the heroine exerts a unifying effect on what might otherwise feel like a diffuse or sprawling play.[35] Although the tragedy presents a number of events in the family's history, all these events rotate around Antigone's "pieté."[36] Derived from the Latin concept *pietas*, "la pieté" is a capacious concept that encompasses religious, familial, and patriotic devotion. During the sixteenth century the idea of piety often overlapped with that of pity or compassion.[37] In Garnier's tragedy the charity or compassion that Antigone expresses for her brother Polynices carries a particularly Christian connotation. Piety thus operates as an elastic concept that allows the play to harmonize pagan values with Christian virtues.[38] The elasticity of "la pieté" renders Antigone a "point of convergence" or "affective pole" that pulls together the tragedy's affective registers and the elements of its plot.[39] As we will see, Antigone's piety, however, also pushes her toward other characters in ways that call into question her unifying virtue.

Garnier's tragedy highlights Antigone's pieté in the first act by contrasting her virtues with Oedipus's vices. As we have seen, the act begins as the father-daughter pair enters, with Antigone slowly leading Oedipus by the hand.[40] As Oedipus's first lines indicate, Antigone's filial gesture operates as a sign of her piety; she serves as his dutiful guide: "Toy, qui ton pere aveugle et courbé de vieillesse / Conduis si constamment, mon soustien, mon addresse" (1.1–2) (You who escort with such constancy your father, blind and buckled by old age, my aide, my guide).[41] The lines do not merely offer a portrait of Antigone's piety, they also signal the distinction between father and daughter. Antigone is constant and steady, whereas Oedipus is bent over and blind. Such physical distinctions have a clear moral valence, which the play develops further as the act progresses. Antigone's physical steadfastness operates as the outward sign of her rectitude, just as Oedipus's sloped posture marks not only his age but also the bent nature of his past conduct. Although Oedipus lauds Antigone's fidelity, he also urges her to leave his side and return to Thebes alone. When Antigone refuses and maintains her constant grip, Oedipus explains that he fears a repetition of his incestuous union with Jocasta if Antigone remains:

> penses-tu qu'il me reste
> Encore un parricide, et encore un inceste?
> J'en ay peur, j'en ay peur, ma fille laisse moy:
> Le crime maternel me fait craindre pour toy.
> (Garnier, *Antigone, ou La pieté*, 1.49–52)

> Are you waiting for further parricide? For further incest? How I fear that, how I fear just that. My daughter, leave me. My crime against my mother makes me fear for you.[42]

In addition to communicating Oedipus's fear that either he or his progeny will repeat his past crimes of regicide and incest, these verses also remind us that Antigone herself is a product of incest. She is the remainder, the "reste" of her mother and father's ruinous union. Oedipus's warning indicates that Antigone's grasp on her father, the very gesture that communicates her piety, also signals its possible corruption.

Oedipus's worst fears do not come to pass. Antigone eventually releases his hand and returns to Thebes. The play's language, however, complicates this separation, suggesting a persistent form of influence between them. The continued emphasis on their physical and moral distinction works paradoxically to create a kind of anxiety about the permeability between her purity and his corruption. The more the tragedy contrasts Antigone with Oedipus, the more their qualities attach to one another through rhymes and other resonances. For example, pleading with Antigone to leave in yet another instance, Oedipus says:

> Pourquoy me serres-tu de ta virgeale main
> Ma dextre parricide, et mon bras inhumain,
> Taché du mesme sang qui me donna naissance?
> Mechante, abominable et pestifere engence!
> (Garnier, *Antigone, ou La pieté*, 1.99–103)
>
> Why do you hold on, with your virgin's hand, to my parricidal hand? To my inhuman arm, stained by the same blood that gave birth to me? What wicked, abominable, and pestiferous breeding![43]

The verses clearly identify a difference between Antigone's hand and Oedipus's arm, labeling hers "virgeale" and his "inhumain." The rhyme between "main" and "inhumain," however, complicates this distinction, associating Antigone's hand with the less desirable characteristics of Oedipus's arm. Worried about this corrupting association, Oedipus points out that his "bras inhumain" is, like the rest of his body, stained with his father's cursed blood. He begs Antigone to release his arm for fear of contamination. And yet, is not Antigone born of the same blood? Does she not also carry this incestuous legacy? Oedipus himself raises these questions, wondering, "Se peut-il faire helas! qu'un lict incestueux / Ait peu jamais produire un enfant si vertueux" (1.87–88) (Is it possible that, alas, an incestuous bed could have produced such a virtuous child?).[44] Like the rhyme of "main" and "inhumain," the pair of "vertueux" and "incestueux" communicates a certain anxiety about the distinction between father and daughter. Oedipus argues that his cursed blood continues to course through him, working out its effects. Suggesting how his influence may extend beyond the release of her grip, the tragedy implies that his legacy contaminates her virtue.

Much of the disagreement between father and daughter takes up precisely the question of persistent influence. When Oedipus is not urging Antigone to let go and leave, he is deploring his cursed fate and rehearsing his crimes. Whereas Oedipus maintains that these crimes forever mark him, Antigone holds up the possibility of redemption: "Vostre malheur est grand, mais un cœur genereux / Surmonte tout malheur, et n'est point malheureux" (1.123–24) (Your sorrow is great, but a courageous heart can overcome any sorrow, indeed knows not what sorrow is).[45] Their disagreement turns on whether one's heritage and previous acts can be overcome, as well as on whether one can successfully detach from family and former self. Antigone's verses express the possibility of detachment, locating responsibility and blame in the individual will. A tension exists between her gesture and speech: Antigone extolls the freedom of the individual will even as she refuses to relinquish her grip on Oedipus. With Antigone articulating the possibility of individual redemption, their disagreement maps onto the play's intermingled value systems: the tragic and the Christian. Antigone answers Oedipus's tragic fatalism with Christian hope.

Although this idea of Christian hope would seem to allow Antigone to shake off Oedipus's lingering influence, or to preserve her piety even while grasping his cursed body, the Christian valences of her gesture in fact deepen the anxiety surrounding her legacy and devotion. Garnier's tragedy is contemporaneous to intense theological battles and physical conflicts between Protestants and Catholics. Notably, Antigone's piety has been linked to both sides of the conflict. For Garnier's modern editor Jean-Dominique Beaudin, Antigone clearly articulates a Catholic point of view. Glossing the argument between Antigone and Creon, Beaudin writes, "It would not seem an exaggeration to say that this controversy is an echo of the debate between Catholics and Calvinists: Affirming the role of man's liberty in the choice between good and evil, Antigone cannot resign herself to the idea of an original and definitive condemnation of the individual."[46] Aligning Antigone's Catholicism with Garnier's, Beaudin continues, "As a good Catholic, Garnier would not adhere to the idea that the individual is subject to divine reprobation even before his birth."[47] Gillian Jondorf also remarks on Antigone's insistence on the individual's liberty, aligning this insistence with Protestant positions. Jondorf argues that "in *Antigone* Garnier shows sympathy for the freedom of the individual conscience; in the sixteenth century this would seem an almost Protestant viewpoint, for Antigone follows her own judgment entirely in deciding where her duty lies and what God requires of her."[48] I cite these divergent views not with the aim of adjudicating between them in favor of either a Protestant or a Catholic Antigone, but rather to point out that they share a similar structure: both suggest how expressions of piety attach individual subjects to religious communities.

Jondorf and Beaudin both suggest how Antigone's articulation of her freedom of conscience binds her to a community that is constituted along religious lines. This communally constituted individual liberty is consistent with appeals to freedom of conscience in the Huguenot resistance treatises I examined in chapter 1. These treatises take their cues from Calvin's understanding of conscience whereby each individual feels the weight of God's judgment from within. Freedom of conscience in this context means that the status of the individual's salvation cannot be determined by a monarch's laws or decrees. The individual's soul is thus freed *from* monarchical control and bound to God and, by extension, a community of similarly bound believers. For Garnier's critics Antigone's proclaimed independence is what renders her position either Catholic or Protestant. As we have seen, the tragedy's interplay of language and gesture highlights Antigone's inseparability from her family's legacy, even while insisting on her independent virtue. Similarly, accounts of the possible historical resonances of Antigone's piety tie her to confessional communities, while also emphasizing her claims of subjective freedom. Articulating a kind of freedom through attachment, these claims illustrate a constitutive feature of the religious conflict: the deep connections between assertions of religious freedom and concerns about collective salvation.[49] During this historical moment, Catholics and Protestants regarded each other's claims as threats to the spiritual well-being of the community. Religious violence during the sixteenth century was not quite (or not only) a clash of communities but rather a conflict about the proper constitution of the community. Barbara Diefendorf explains, "Despite their religious differences, Protestants and Catholics held to an ideal of community in which the sacred and the civic were joined. Members of both faiths nevertheless believed that the social body had been dangerously corrupted and could only be restored by purging it of the errors that defiled it."[50] In this context, acts of piety, such as attending a particular service or worshiping with certain objects, took on a dual significance: from one side of the confessional divide a gesture of piety would have operated as a sign of faith and virtue. From the opposing side the same gesture would signal sin and corruption. Piety and corruption were thus transmutable qualities that could shift with changes in perspective.

The ambiguity surrounding piety during the religious wars helps us to understand the troubling duality of Antigone's gesture within Garnier's tragedy. On the one hand, Antigone comes across as a pure and innocent character, who attempts to pull her father toward redemption while expressing faith in the powers of the individual will. On the other hand, Antigone's grip on Oedipus raises questions about his hold on her, suggesting how his legacy may shape her actions. Just as an act of faith during the sixteenth century might have been seen as both pious and corrupt, Antigone's outstretched arm marks her fidelity, but renders its virtue uncertain. The sustained bond between father and daughter thus illustrates how piety and corruption remain intertwined. Rather than stabilize virtue by uniting the tragedy's constituent parts in her expression of filial love and devotion, Antigone's gesture instead disrupts the very idea of a stable or constant virtue.

The dual nature of Antigone's fidelity carries over into her political claims. She justifies her burial of Polynices by appealing to divine law. But how are these appeals themselves adjudicated? Just as pious gestures held dual valences during the religious wars, so did invocations of the divine. Part of what made the individual's freedom of conscience so politically dangerous during this time was that there was no general consensus about God's will and true belief. As a result there was also no consensus about what constituted the common good and who could legitimately defend it. By foregrounding Antigone's outstretched arm and by suggesting that she may transmit her family's troubled legacy, Garnier's play casts doubt over Antigone's subsequent assertions and raises questions about her proclaimed adherence to divine law. Although Rotrou's tragedy seems on one level to resolve the questions raised by Garnier's play, this subsequent *Antigone* ends up deepening the crisis of legitimacy that Antigone's familial bonds engender.

Questioning Nature

Rotrou's *Antigone* appears on the French theatrical scene after the official end of the religious wars. As I have noted, fear of religious and civil conflict continued to loom large during the seventeenth century despite official declarations of the end of war. Rotrou's *Antigone* foregrounds many of the persistent problems raised by the wars, including divergent conceptions of right and wrong, virtue and vice.[51] Whereas an unstable conception of piety haunts Garnier's play, in Rotrou's it is an unstable conception of nature—and of natural law—that is of highest concern. Beginning with the conflict between Eteocles and Polynices, Rotrou's *Antigone* considers how the brothers' competing claims to the throne produce a situation in which authority and law are contestable. Although Oedipus does not appear on stage in this version, his legacy nonetheless impinges on the scene. The play suggests that Oedipus's influence is to blame for the fraternal conflict. The first lines are spoken by Jocasta who has been woken up in the middle of the night by the tumult caused by her son's conflict: "Qu'ils ont bien à propos usé de mon sommeil! / Ils n'ont pas appelé ma voix à leur conseil" (1.1.1–2) (They took advantage of my slumber and did not seek my voice for their counsel).[52] In printed editions of the play these opening lines are accompanied by a stage direction. The text tells us that Jocasta is "DANS UNE CHAMBRE ACHEVANT DE S'HABILLER" (IN HER ROOM, FINISHING GETTING DRESSED).[53] This is a remarkable opening, in part because stage directions are relatively rare in this period, but also because one does not typically depict royals in a state of undress.[54] With this striking decision to place Jocasta's half-clothed body at the center of the action, Rotrou's tragedy signals that the mother's body—the site of familial legacy—is of great importance. What is more, by placing Jocasta's body front and center, the tragedy suggests that this familial legacy carries a political charge, even as the brothers carry out their political negotiations in her absence.

The political charge of Jocasta's maternal body serves as an explanation for the civil war devastating Thebes. Jocasta worries that Polynices and Eteocles may be propelled by a corrupting familial legacy through references to their incestuous origins. In this scene, she decries the preparations for war between her sons and their armies:

> Allons tôt, c'est trop d'ordre, en ce désordre extrême:
> Ce poil mal ordonné, cette confusion,
> Me sera bienséante en cette occasion;
> Nature, confonds-les, c'est ici ton office,
> Tout dépend de toi seule, et rien de l'artifice:
> Viens te montrer, mon sein, qui les as allaités,
> Avancez-vous, mes bras, qui les avez portés:
> Toi, flanc incestueux, dont ils ont pris naissance,
> Viens, s'ils ont du respect, faire voir ta puissance.
> (Rotrou, *Antigone,* 1.1.8–16)
>
> Let us go quickly, there's too much order in this extreme disorder: this disheveled state, this confusion, suit me well on this occasion. Nature, thwart them, this is your charge, everything depends on you alone, and nothing on artifice. Come show yourself, my breast that fed them, reach out, my arms that held them, and you, incestuous flank that birthed them, come, display your power and see if they show respect.

Rejecting all artifice (including, the stage direction would suggest, clothing) and calling on nature to prevent the impending fraternal hostilities, Jocasta's speech arrives at the central paradox of the brothers' situation. Given their filial bond, their conflict appears unnatural and yet perfectly suited to their incestuous nature. Jocasta offers herself as nature's conduit, naming in particular her "sein," flanc," and "bras," all parts of the body with a strong maternal charge, pointing toward the type of life force that flows to her sons. Jocasta thus invokes a natural, maternal influence, but she also acknowledges the incestuous union that produced them puts their relationship to nature into question.[55]

The question of Jocasta—and Oedipus's—corrupting influence comes to reside at the center of Antigone's dispute with Creon. Throughout *Antigone*, Creon reminds the court of Jocasta and Oedipus's originary incest as a way of undermining Polynices's claim to the throne and Antigone's defense of her brother. The siblings are too corrupted, he argues, for their claims to be taken seriously. Antigone explicitly rejects this argument. When Creon blames Oedipus and his cursed sons for the loss of his youngest son Menoeceus (who leaps to his death in an act of self-sacrifice), Antigone objects, arguing that Oedipus has already sufficiently paid for his crimes:

> Œdipe, quoi? tes yeux par tes mains arrachés,
> Tes mânes, part ta mort, de ton corps détachés,
> Ton Sceptre abandonné, tout ton Royaume en armes,
> Tes enfants divisés, nos soupirs et nos larmes
> Ne peuvent faire encor qu'un innocent péché,
> Moins de toi, que du sort ne te soit reproché?
> (Rotrou, *Antigone*, 1.4.133–38)

> What, Oedipus? Your eyes torn out by your own hands, your spirits detached from your body by your death, your sceptre abandoned, the whole kingdom in arms, your children divided, our sighs and our cries: are these not enough to save you from reproach, for an innocent sin, more Fate's than your own?

The idea that Oedipus should be detached from his children's crimes is communicated not only through the overall content of Antigone's lines but also through the series of actions that these lines contain: "arrachés," "détachés," "abandonné," "divisés." Whereas Garnier's heroine held out the possibility of Oedipus's redemption, suggesting that he might separate himself from his past crimes, Rotrou's focuses on how Oedipus has already paid for his sins and should not be held accountable for those of his children.

Eteocles and Polynices's questionable relationship to nature underscores the tragedy's broader concern with plural conceptions of natural law. As Christian Biet observes, the word "nature" occurs many times throughout the tragedy, often with variable meaning: "Employed variably, this word refers to the natural law that prohibits murder, as well as to the ancestral law that puts a royal heir in position to reign, to maternal love, to the devotion that a sister owes her brother, and to the nature of power."[56] For Biet, Antigone's devotion to her brother Polynices and her consequent objection to Creon constitute a regrounding of divine and natural law that resolves this situation of instability. Antigone, like her brothers, is born from an incestuous union. Her virtuous opposition, however, represents a kind of expiation of her family's acts. Her defense of her brother and martyr-like self-sacrifice allow her to secure the principles of nature and duty. Although Antigone does claim to speak and act in accordance with natural law, as Biet notes, her relationship to nature, like that of her brothers, nonetheless retains much of its questionable inheritance. Antigone rejects Oedipus's influence, but the tragedy presents her attachment to Polynices in ways that exceed and trouble the natural. By elaborating the particularity of this attachment, Rotrou's tragedy puts forward an Antigone whose claims are more unsettling than has previously been acknowledged.

For Haemon—who has the unenviable position of being Creon's son and Antigone's fiancé—the special bond shared between Antigone and Polynices affords Polynices a measure of protection on the battlefield. Haemon confesses to Antigone that he has refrained from killing Polynices, out of affection and deference for her despite the fact that her brother poses a threat to Thebes:

> Son corps semble à dessein s'offrir à mon épée:
> Mais loin d'oser sur lui tenter aucun effort,
> J'ai paré mille coups qui lui portaient la mort.
> L'amitié qui vous joint autant que la naissance,
> M'a fait contre nous même embrasser sa défense:
> Il conserve en sa vie un bien qui vous est dû,
> Bien mieux que sa valeur vous l'avez défendu,
> Vous étiez son bouclier au milieu des alarmes,
> Et vous l'avez sauvé, seule, absente, et sans armes.
> (Rotrou, *Antigone*, 1.4.196–204)

> His body seemed fated to offer itself to my sword. But rather than dare to exert myself against him I instead fended off a million blows that would have killed him. The affection that has joined the two of you [Antigone and Polynices] since birth, caused me to act against us [the Theban army]. The good he retains with his life belongs to you. It was not his valor that defended him but you. You were his shield in the middle of so many attacks and you alone saved him, you who were absent and without arms.

Haemon cedes to Antigone's wishes despite his military duty. Although Antigone is not physically present on the battlefield, this speech incorporates her into the scene of war, figuring her as the "bouclier" (shield) that protects Polynices from harm. Notably, Haemon identifies "l'amitié" as much as "naissance" as the force that connects brother and sister. When Antigone responds to Haemon, she confirms this particular attachment, labeling it an "étroite amitié" (1.4.210) that exceeds any ordinary mutual concern between siblings, and also admitting that the attachment is far stronger than the sense of sisterly duty she feels toward Eteocles. The play characterizes their attachment as more than, or beyond, the natural.[57]

If Antigone's "amitié" is capable of restraining Haemon's sword, might it possibly restrain Polynices's as well? The tragedy positions her "amitié" as holding the power to move Polynices away from his menacing designs. When her brother instead proves unmovable, Antigone laments, "Cette tendre amitié, reçoit donc un refus, / Elle a perdu son droit, et ne vous touche plus" (2.2.401–2) (This tender affection meets a refusal, it has lost its right and no longer moves you). The lines elaborate a connection between "amitié" and "droit," with each word positioned just before the caesura. Arguing that her affection for Polynices should afford her some influence over his actions, Antigone articulates a personal form of right, which she alone possesses. In addition to presenting conflicts between divine, natural, and human law, Rotrou's *Antigone* also explores the reach of this decidedly personal right, a right that is shaped by personal affection in excess of familial devotion.

The tragedy later reiterates Antigone's close connection to Polynices, emphasizing the particularity of her expressed right to influence his actions and to mourn his death. After the brothers have killed each other, after Creon has refused Polynices burial, and after Antigone has set out to bury him anyway, she hears someone else approaching the body and calls out, "Ce soir est tout à moi, seule j'ai droit ici" (2.7.964) (This evening is all mine, I alone have a right to be here). The intrusive fellow mourner turns out to be Argia, Polynices's wife.[58] Antigone then yields and the two women bury him together, but their dialogue further establishes the attachment between brother and sister, as Argia states, "Je paraissais sa sœur, et vous sembliez sa femme" (2.7.1002) (I seemed like his sister and you seemed like his wife). The rhetorical repositioning confirms that what compels Antigone's speech and actions is a surfeit of affection rather than mere sisterly devotion. During the confrontation with Creon, this affection becomes the strongest justification of Antigone's disobedience. After arguing with Creon about the religious and juridical reasons for her rebellion, citing Polynices's claim to the throne and the gods' imperative to honor his death, Antigone finally rests her case on the special bond between them. She states: "Après tout, je l'aimais, et mon affection / Entreprendrait encor cette sainte action" (4.3.1259–60) (After all, I love him and my affection would undertake this holy action again). With the rhyme of "affection" and "action" adding emphasis to Antigone's final justification, she refuses to engage further with Creon's proposed categories of obedient subject and enemy of the state.

Rotrou's tragedy figures this particular affection as the primary motor of Antigone's speech and actions. Antigone does use the language of divine and natural law, but, as we have seen, her relationship to nature remains deeply implicated in her family's questionable legacy. She defends her natural right to bury her brother. But the tragedy also insists that the bond between brother and sister exceeds the natural. Antigone's defense of her right to bury her brother rests primarily on this extranatural attachment. The tender reach between Antigone and Polynices trespasses Creon's law and disrupts his order. Defending this attachment above all, Antigone makes the case for a deeply personal right.

Chastening Creon through this personal right and her particular virtue, Antigone does not resolve the conflict about natural law that is posed at the outset of the play. Nor does she reestablish a shared sense of the common good. Instead, she grounds her opposition in the extranatural bond that she shares with Polynices. As a result, Rotrou's play continues the crisis of legitimacy that Garnier's raises. In Garnier's tragedy Antigone's physical pull on Oedipus engenders fear about his corrupting influence over her. In Rotrou's tragedy Antigone's affective bond with Polynices pushes her to speak and act in defiance of Creon's order. In both cases, Antigone loudly proclaims that her actions are justified, but by focusing on these particular attachments and their destabilizing qualities, the tragedies introduce doubt about whether her claims will help or hurt the public good. Antigone, both tragedies suggest, cannot ratify her own claims. The plays ultimately do propose, however, that despite her troubling connections, Antigone's burial of Polynices is warranted by both natural and divine law. The tragedies legitimize this gesture through the approval of the Theban people who offer affective evidence of Antigone's virtue. As we will see, in both Garnier and Rotrou, the Theban people are figured as a vocal community with strong affective and political preferences. The tragedies authorize the Theban people's preferences and allow them to influence the action. As a result, *Antigone, ou La piéte* and *Antigone* underscore how this collective entity justifies and bolsters Antigone's resistance.

Authorizing the People

Garnier's *Antigone, ou La pieté* initially presents the Theban people as a population that suffers as Eteocles and Polynices fight over the throne. In the play's opening scene, Antigone refers to the people's misfortune as she attempts to pull Oedipus toward Thebes. But throughout the play, the unfortunate people come to exceed their initial roles as passive sufferers by wielding a kind of political potential through the expression of their affective preferences. In Rotrou's tragedy the people take on a similar role, joining their objections to those of Antigone. In both tragedies these postures of passive suffering and active complaint are mediated by characters and choruses, since the people do not appear on stage directly. Examining how the choruses in Garnier's tragedy operate helps us to understand the people's mediated role. The choruses mirror the people's active and passive positions on stage and cite the people's collective voice. Rotrou's play does not feature any choruses, but staged characters in both tragedies cite the people's voice, giving additional expression to the objections and desires of the unseen population. Through these practices of mediation and citation, the plays incorporate the unseen people into the scene.

Garnier's *Antigone, ou La pieté* features three choruses, which represent different segments of the larger Theban people and tend toward different roles in the tragedy. The *Chœur de Thebains* most closely resembles a Greek chorus by commenting on the action at the end of each act and in between some scenes. The *Chœur de filles* and the *Chœur de Vieillards* represent more specific demographics, corresponding in age and gender to Antigone and Creon, respectively.[59] The *Chœur de filles* often acts like a collective confidante, comforting and reassuring Antigone. The *Chœur de Vieillards* acts as a voice of reason that encourages Creon to moderate the rigidity of his opinions and decisions.[60] Standing for different segments of the Theban people, the choruses indicate how the actions of the royal family extend beyond the palace and affect the city's inhabitants. Garnier's multiplication of choruses, which was common in sixteenth-century tragedy, also alerts us to the metonymic nature of these collectives. Each chorus speaks for the people but does so partially. The existence of more than one chorus suggests that we ought to be wary of those who claim to speak for everyone, even as we take these claims seriously.

The *Chœur de Thebains* consistently articulates a dynamic in which the royal family acts and the people of Thebes must endure their actions, lamenting in particular the widespread destruction caused by the brothers' conflict. For example, in act 2, the *Chœur de Thebains* exclaims:

> Que l'ardente ambition
> Nous cause d'affliction!
> Qu'elle nous file d'esclandre!
> Si l'alme paix ne descend
> Sur nous peuple perissant,
> Nous verrons Thebes en cendre.
> (Garnier, *Antigone, ou La pieté*, 2.596–601)
>
> Burning ambition causes / Us so much suffering! / How much misfortune it brings us! / If nurturing peace does not descend / Upon our dying people, / We will see Thebes reduced to ashes.[61]

These verses reinforce the dynamic between family and people, with the chorus repeating the pronoun "nous" as a grammatical object three times in quick succession. The "nous" of the chorus, which in this case encompasses the people of Thebes, only appears as a grammatical subject in the last line, when it observes the city's destruction. The lament suggests that the chorus, and by extension the people, can act only as witnesses to their collective misfortunes.

Elsewhere, the *Chœur de Thebains* chronicles these misfortunes, recounting precisely how the brothers' inability to resolve their dispute will affect the people:

> L'un le retient à son pouvoir,
> L'autre s'efforce de l'avoir:
> Ce pendant le peuple en endure,
> C'est luy qui porte tout le faix.
> Car encor qu'il n'en puisse mais,
> Il leur sert tousjours de pasture.

Mais dedans la campagne bruit,
Nostre beau terroir est destruit:
Le vigneron quitte la vigne,
Le courbe laboureur ses bœus,
Le berger ses pastis herbeus,
Et le morne pescheur sa ligne.
(Garnier, *Antigone, ou La pieté*, 2.972–83)

One brother keeps the scepter, / The other struggles to seize it. / Meanwhile, the citizens suffer on— /It is they who carry the burden. / Even though they are powerless, / They always become war's fodder.

But inland, the countryside rumbles, / Our fine land is destroyed. / The wine-grower abandons his vines, / The stooped-over farmer his cattle, / The shepherd his grassy fields, / And the sad fisherman his rod.[62]

This choral lamentation produces an alternation between the general suffering of the people and the specific situations of one group or another. The formulation "le peuple en endure" indicates that fraternal conflict implicates the entire population, while those like "Le vigneron quitte la vigne" and "Le berger ses pastis herbeus" depict the conflict's more localized effects. Through the oscillation between the general and the specific, the universal and the particular, the tragedy makes the plight of the Theban people vivid and palpable. Inspiring sympathy and pathos, the people exist as passive sufferers who remain at the mercy of the royal family's machinations.

But this is not the Theban people's only role. Garnier's play also figures the people as a collective that speaks out, actively voicing opinions and objections. Whereas the *Chœur de Thebains* describes the extent of the people's misfortune, the *Chœur de filles* articulates the reach of its raised voice. When Antigone addresses the citizenry of Thebes in act 4, as she prepares to enter the tomb-like cave where she will spend her final days, she asks for witnesses to her plight: "Voyez, ô Citoyens qui Thebes habitez, / Le supreme combat de mes adversitez!" (4.2158–59) (Look, citizens, you who live in Thebes, at the final battle in all my afflictions!).[63] In response, the *Chœur de filles* assures her that the people of Thebes will not only witness her unjust punishment but will sing her praises in the future: "Comme à une Deesse, et de mille cantiques / Le peuple honorera vos ombres Plutoniques" (4.2176–77) (We will celebrate you as we would a goddess, and with a thousand hymns the citizens will honor your Plutonic shades).[64] Although not explicitly articulated in political terms, the people's approval of Antigone, as promised by the chorus, carries a political charge by contradicting Creon's disapproval and punishment of her acts.

By promising the people's support and praise, the *Chœur de filles* ties the people's affection to its political potential. The drama cultivates this tie through numerous citations of the people's voice and speculations about their capacities. As the following examples show, it is not only the choruses that invoke the people's power but also the members of the royal family themselves. Indeed, concern about the people's affection and approval enters directly into discussions between Jocasta and her sons, as well as between Creon and his son. In act 2 Jocasta appeals to Polynices's heart, urging him to have pity on the unfortunate inhabitants of his home (whose suffering she describes in great detail). When this tactic has no effect, she turns toward an argument about the necessity to heed public opinion. She shifts her efforts away from Polynices's capacity for pity toward the people's affective preferences. Jocasta suggests to Polynices that Eteocles remains on the throne out of deference to the people, stating, "Il est plus agréable / Aux citoyens que vous" (2.914–15) (He is better liked by the citizens than you).[65] To this citation of public preference, Polynices responds with an expression of his own menacing fortitude: "Et moy plus redoubtable" (2.916) (And I am more feared).[66] The rhyme of "agréable" and "redoubtable" arrives at the center of the clemency-rigor debate, a common debate in sixteenth-century political thought that centers on the ideal measure of the people's affection for their sovereign. On the one hand, a sovereign too loved risks losing his authority. On the other hand, a sovereign too feared might become a tyrant.[67] Polynices, who wishes only to be "et craint et obeï" (2.925) (feared and obeyed) eschews any effort to find a way between these two extremes.[68] Although Polynices dismisses the people's opinion, the play highlights its centrality. Through this debate between mother and son, former queen and would-be sovereign, the play suggests how the people's affective preferences may influence sovereign decision.

A parallel discussion in Rotrou's drama further underscores the people's capacity to hold sway over the sovereign through the exercise of their affection.[69] In this version, the clemency-rigor debate takes place over several scenes, as Jocasta pleads with her sons in succession.[70] Eteocles justifies his refusal to cede the throne to Polynices by citing the people's wishes:

> Sur le désir des miens, mon trône se soutient,
> Je lui cédais l'Etat, mais l'Etat me retient:
> J'étais prêt à quitter le Sceptre qu'on lui nie,
> Le peuple aime mon règne, et craint sa tyrannie:

> Je le possède aussi, moins que je ne le sers,
> Les honneurs qu'il me rend, sont d'honorables fers.
> (Rotrou, *Antigone*, 1.3.81–87)

> I maintain my throne out of my people's desire. I ceded him [Polynices] the state, but the state retains me. I was ready to renounce the sceptre that they deny him. The people love my reign and fear his tyranny. I possess the people less than I serve them. They shackle me with the honors they bestow upon me.

Eteocles figures the love of "le peuple" as a desirable form of restraint, one that keeps him in power and holds his rule in place. For Polynices, however, this rationale is unacceptable, not only because it denies him his birthright but also because it gives the people too much power. Rotrou's Polynices thus shares with the Polynices of Garnier's play a distain for the people's love. When Jocasta reaffirms the people's affection for Eteocles and fear of Polynices, the latter responds:

> Et moi, moins populaire,
> Je tiens indifférent, d'être craint, ou de plaire,
> Qui règne, aimé des siens, en est moins absolu:
> Cet amour rompt souvent ce qu'il a résolu:
> Plus est permis aux Rois, à qui plus on s'oppose,
> Une lâche douceur aux mépris les expose;
> Le peuple, trop aisé, les lie en les aimant,
> Il faut, pour être aimé, régner trop mollement.
> (Rotrou, *Antigone*, 2.4.613–20)

> And me less popular—I remain indifferent to whether I cause fear or pleasure. He who reigns and is loved by his people reigns less absolutely. The people's love often breaks his resolution. The more kings are opposed the more they are permitted, a cowardly sweetness exposes them to disdain. The people, when they are too at ease, restrain their kings by loving them. To be loved, one must rule too softly.

The first line of this speech most succinctly communicates how Polynices is unwilling to accept limits on his rule. "Et moi, moins populaire" not only informs us that the people prefer Eteocles but also suggests the self-centered quality of Polynices's prospective reign through the repetition of "moi, moi[ns]." Beyond marking Polynices as a tyrant, the brothers' dispute describes the potential force of the people. Language from these passages, such as "l'amour rompt" (from Polynices) and "l'état retient" (from Eteocles), figures the people's exercise of its affection through movements of reach and suspension, hold and release.

Although the people stand at a considerable remove from power, and although they do not appear directly on stage, the repeated invocations of their collective voice by characters and choruses endow them with a kind of affective grip on the tragedy's action. In both tragedies, this grip rivals Creon's ability to control the people's perceptions of Antigone's dissent. Garnier's Creon justifies his punishment of Antigone by complaining of her excesses, calling her "une audacieuse" (an audacious woman), "une fille arrogante" (an arrogant girl), as well as "un sujet contumaux" (a rebellious subject), and "contrariant" (contrarian) (4.1984–88; my translation). By labeling Antigone exceptional and aberrant, Creon attempts to distinguish her from the rest of Thebes's inhabitants. But Haemon's response to his father signals that Antigone in fact enjoys the people's support:

> Ceste Vierge exerçant un pitoyable faict
> A contre son vouloir à vos edits forfaict.
> Chacun en a pitié, toute la cité pleure,
> Qu'une Royale fille innocentement meure.
> (Garnier, *Antigone, ou La pieté*, 4.1994–97)
>
> This Virgin, when she committed a crime that deserves our pity, went against your edicts only against her will. Everyone pities her, the whole city bemoans that a royal daughter, innocent, dies.[71]

In these lines, which themselves transform individuals into a collective: "Chacun en a pitié, toute la cité pleure," Haemon objects to his father that Antigone's burial of her brother engenders the people's pity and prompts the expression of its collective voice. Haemon's subsequent verses reiterate the people's support for Antigone, recounting the "rumeur du peuple" (4.2011) (the people's rumors) to his father who remains incredulous about the mounting public outcry (my translation). When Creon again casts Antigone as excessively proud and deserving of punishment, Haemon interjects, "Ce ne sera l'advis de la cité Thebaine" (4.2033) (The City of Thebes will not agree).[72] The play fills this scene between royal son and father with the people's reported discontent by citing their cries, rumors, and opinions.

In Rotrou's tragedy, Antigone herself first cites the people's voice to Creon, although in this case it is the promise of their eventual audible support rather than a citation of their voice that contradicts the king. In what reads as a dare to Creon when he delays ordering her execution, Antigone says:

> Peut-être le temps vous ôterait l'envie,
> Ou l'assurance au moins de nous ôter la vie,
> Le murmure du peuple irait jusques à vous,
> Et pourrait désarmer votre injuste courroux:
> Car, enfin, si la peur ne lui fermait la bouche,
> Vous sauriez à quel point le procédé le touche;
> Mais d'abord un tyran, fait tout ce qui lui plaît,
> On souffre avec respect, on voit, mais on se tait.
> (Rotrou, *Antigone*, 4.3.1229–36)

> Maybe time will rob you of the desire, or at least of the assurance in your decision to rob us of life. The people's grumbling will reach you, and might disarm your unjust fury, because, in the end, if fear does not shut their mouths, you will know how much this matter affects them. But of course a tyrant does whatever he wishes. One must suffer with respect, one sees, but must keep quiet.

If Creon does not act swiftly, Antigone warns, the people will lose their fear of the tyrant and loosen their tongues. What is striking here is how the play figures the "murmure du peuple" as a restraint that will "désarmer" Creon. The rhyme of "bouche" and "touche" reinforces the link between the people's imagined speech and the figurative extent of Creon's power. Antigone's warning also underscores the multivalent possibilities of the word "touche," which in these lines refers, of course, to the people's sympathy for Antigone's plight, but also recalls the reach of the outstretched arm, which is so prevalent in the play's gestural vocabulary. Rotrou's tragedy thus situates the people's affective reach within the push and pull of influence that occurs among staged characters.

This unseen collective intervenes in the conflict between sovereign and subject by attaching to Antigone and working to restrain Creon. The people's intervention disrupts Creon's portrayal of Antigone as excessive and out-of-bounds. In Rotrou's tragedy, just as in Garnier's, Haemon responds to Creon's assertion that Antigone is his only rebellious subject by citing the voice of the people: "Seul, je vous dirai donc, que le commun murmure / Accuse votre arrêt d'offenser la nature" (4.6.1385–86) (I alone will tell you therefore that the common complaint judges your edict an offense against nature). In addition to contradicting his father's perceived control over the people of Thebes, Haemon's verses demonstrate how the play yokes together individual and collective complaint. Speaking alone, Haemon voices the people's shared discontent. This interplay of the "Seul" and the "commun" suggests how both tragedies authorize the people's claims as well as Antigone's. Indeed, it is the people's solidarity with Antigone, rather than Antigone herself, that seems to establish a shared perception of virtue. Antigone's attachments to her father and brother function as signs of her virtue even as they raise questions about her legacy. As we have seen, these attachments do not assuage anxieties about competing claims and relative laws, but rather augment such anxieties by making it impossible to untangle piety and corruption, nature and excess. By raising their voices in support of Antigone, however, the people ratify her speech and actions. The people secure Antigone's virtue, rather than Antigone who secures virtue for the city.

A tension remains, however, between the people's support for Antigone's speech and actions and the particularity of her claims. In Garnier's tragedy, Antigone's care for Oedipus and her burial of Polynices are both cast as solitary gestures. For example, in act 1 Antigone distinguishes herself from her brothers and from their efforts to possess the throne. While they fight over this birthright, Antigone claims only Oedipus himself: "Mon seul pere je veux, il sera mon partage, / Je ne retiens que luy, c'est mon seul heritage. / Nul ne l'aura de moy" (1.61–63) (My father alone do I want, he is my share, I hold on only to him, he is my only inheritance).[73] These verses delineate Antigone's legacy and articulate a certain possessiveness, reinforcing the particular ties between father and daughter. A similar form of possession characterizes her burial of Polynices. Antigone insists on the solitary nature of this act when Ismene claims to have participated, attempting to share and soften the blame, but Antigone rebuffs this offer of solidarity. Such a rejection also takes place in Rotrou's tragedy, as Antigone refuses to share the blame with either Ismene or Argia (who, as we have seen, does assist with the burial). Although Antigone counters Creon's framing of her as the "seule rebelle" in Thebes by promising that the people will speak out in her favor, her own verses lend some support to this framing by insisting on her particularity through the repetition of the word "seule." Creon's accusation, "Et toi seule, entre tous, n'as pu voir sans te plaindre" (4.3.1237) (And you alone out of everyone were not capable of seeing without complaining), serves as a variation on the theme established in verses spoken by Antigone herself. What Creon misses is that these claims receive broad support while still remaining personal and particular.

The tension between the particularity of Antigone's attachments and the broad support they engender is further underscored by an ambiguous moment at the opening of Rotrou's third act, when Haemon enters to find Antigone in mourning. Act 2 ends with the brothers' duel imminent and as act 3 begins Antigone seems to learn of the duel's fatal consequences by reading the signs on Haemon's face. His lines suggest that he assumed the noise of the people had alerted her to the news: "Madame, je croyais que la commune plainte / Vous eût déjà livré cette sensible atteinte, / Et fût cause du deuil que je rencontre ici (3.1.687–89) (Madame, I thought that the collective moan had already put you in this evident distress, and was the cause of the mourning that I encounter you in here). Antigone does not confirm whether she has heard "la commune plainte," instead asking "Ætéocle est donc mort?" (3.1.690) (So Eteocles is dead?). The ambiguity of this moment broadcasts the measure of dissonance in Antigone's relationship to the people. The tragedy situates the people's support as affective evidence of Antigone's legitimacy, but it raises doubts about whether she hears their cries. This moment of ambiguity underscores that it is the people who ratify Antigone's questionable virtue. Although it is unclear whether she hears them, they clearly hear her—and they promote her particular attachments.

In the versions of *Antigone* by Garnier and Rotrou, Antigone's articulation of her individual perception of right and wrong is inextricably bound up with her familial ties, especially those to her father and brother. Because of these affective bonds, her subjective assertions that she acts on behalf of divine and natural law do not reground these laws in the wake of civil conflict. Instead of securing her piety and virtue, Antigone's attachments call these qualities into question. But the Theban people assuage doubts about Antigone's claims. The people ratify the actions toward which her questionable attachments have pushed her. The Theban people allow Antigone to function as a public representative by offering affective evidence of their approval. These early modern Antigones establish ties between heroine, family, and people through a complex network of physical and affective influences. From Antigone's grasp of Oedipus's arm to the mediated reach of the people's voice, the staged characters and unseen people remain profoundly entangled. Such entanglements further suggest how one entity cannot be separated from the other. Within the tragedies, action is coimplicated to the extent that it becomes difficult to distinguish one pull from another. Does Antigone pull Oedipus back toward Thebes? Or does his legacy pull her toward him?

The muddling of forces and the confusion of influences that takes place in Garnier's *Antigone, ou La pieté* and Rotrou's *Antigone* allow these tragedies to intervene into ongoing considerations of Antigone's place within political theory and philosophy. Jonathan Strauss has suggested that Sophocles's *Antigone* fabricates the notion of a living individual and thus serves as a hinge between Greek and modern conceptions of individuality.[74] As Strauss points out, individuality emerges in Sophocles's *Antigone* through its absence, as Antigone laments both the loss of her brother and the marital happiness that she gives up by burying him.[75] Extending Strauss's argument, I maintain that the notion of individuality that Sophocles's tragedy fabricates is thus inextricable from familial and affective bonds. This notion of individuality is far from the autonomous and self-possessed individual of modern rights. Garnier's and Rotrou's tragedies bridge the gulf between these two notions. The early modern Antigone is in full possession of her liberty of conscience, which she proclaims loudly and boldly. But this liberty of conscience achieves its disruptive force through the interventions of her family and the Theban people. Appearing at a historical moment when the modern individual was beginning to emerge, these tragedies offer an alternative subject of rights: the public representative as imagined in sixteenth-century resistance theory whose political authority is mediated through collective attachment.

It would be a mistake to consign the early modern Antigone—with her collectively constituted political subjectivity—to the past. I am interested instead in tracing how we might add this Antigone's gestures to our contemporary political repertoire. Sara Ahmed's *Willful Subjects* begins with a scene from the Brothers Grimm in which an arm refuses to retract its reach. In the story "The Willful Child," a young girl "who would not do as her mother wished" eventually fell ill and died.[76] Unexpectedly, the child remained willful after death: "When she had been lowered into her grave, and the earth was spread over her, all at once her arm came out again, and stretched upwards, and when they had put it in and spread fresh earth over it, it was all to no purpose, for the arm always came out again."[77] The arm finally yielded once the mother struck it with a rod. For Ahmed, this story illustrates a paradox of willfulness. One becomes willful when one has too much will, or when one does not want what the powers that be demand one should want: "Note that willfulness is also that which persists even after death," it is "displaced onto an arm, from a body onto a body part."[78] As Ahmed suggests, Antigone is a paradigmatic willful subject.[79] Her will moves errantly, even queerly, commingling with other wills through forms of physical and affective touch.

Garnier's *Antigone, ou La pieté* and Rotrou's *Antigone*, with their emphasis on how Antigone's physical and affective reach exists as part of a broader push and pull of her family and city, help us to see how the extension of Antigone's arm, her reach, is an expression of willful attachment. This gesture shows us how the notions of will and attachment are linked. To be attached to others is not a renunciation of the will, or of subjectivity or individuality for that matter. Instead, to be attached to others is to be willful, to have a surfeit of will, and thus to exceed the bounds of what our current rights framework will allow.

Chapter Four

The Hero

Pierre Corneille's *Le Cid* (1636) ends with a royal injunction to wait. The king assures his valiant hero Rodrigue that eventually all will be well:

> Espère en ton courage, espère en ma promesse,
> Et possédant déjà le cœur de ta maîtresse,
> Pour vaincre un point d'honneur qui combat contre toi
> Laisse faire le temps, ta vaillance, et ton Roi.
> (*Le Cid*, 5.7.1863–66)[1]
>
> Hope in your courage, in my promise. Hope
> Already your belovéd's heart is yours.
> And, if her sense of honour still resists,
> Leave it to time, your valiance and your king.[2]

Rodrigue already possesses the heart of his beloved Chimène. All he needs is time. Consoling the hero, the king also makes a claim of royal power. With the final line "Laisse faire le temps, ta vaillance, et ton Roi", the king aligns the three forces that will win over the hero's beloved: time, the hero's valor, and the king himself. The hero's valor serves as a mark of royal grandeur and the king's command guarantees that the hero's illustrious past will win over his love in the future. The end of *Le Cid* suggests that the monarch has the power to order past, present, and future into one, seamless whole. Time itself becomes an instrument of royal authority.

Corneille's readers have long understood the relationship between Rodrigue and his king in *Le Cid* as paradigmatic of the relationship between heroes and kings in Corneille's tragic work more broadly. Corneille's heroes are renowned for their physical fortitude and their strength of will.[3] As a result they often find themselves in a delicate political situation. On the one hand, Corneille's heroes valiantly offer service to their kings. On the other, in so doing, these heroes often risk threatening their kings' authority. Their physical prowess and independent spirit threaten the monarch's rule. Several of Corneille's most famous tragedies foreground this political tension, staging the king's efforts to harness and contain the hero's power. In *Le Cid*, Rodrigue transforms from a transgressive noble who flouts the king's authority to a national hero who helps bolster the monarch's strength. In *Horace* (1640) and *Cinna* (1641), the heroes are chastened by their respective kings for their transgressions, but they are also praised and protected as indispensable arms of state power. In these tragedies the king successfully incorporates the hero's grandeur and makes it part of the royal arsenal.

The heroes and kings that populate Corneille's tragedies represent two competing political orders in seventeenth-century France: the aristocracy and the monarchy. Corneille's heroes operate as dramatic analogues of the aristocratic order that once shared power with the monarchy but largely lost its political force during the seventeenth century.[4] Much like the king in *Le Cid* channels the hero's strength by asserting his royal power, during the seventeenth century the monarchy gradually curbed the nobility's independence by incorporating its valor into the structures of the state. As the theory of absolutist monarchy came to dominate French political life, it limited the ability of nobles to articulate and defend a conception of the just or the good that differed from the monarchy's own.[5] In other words, the theory of absolutism limited the ability of nobles effectively to serve as public representatives who could legitimately oppose the king on behalf of the public good. Taken together, Corneille's tragedies can be read as a celebration of the aristocratic ethos that motivated the nobility's role as public representatives, coupled with the recognition of a changed political landscape that ultimately lead to the nobility's decline.

In this chapter I demonstrate how two of Corneille's tragedies challenge the nobility's political obsolescence by sustaining the conceptual framework of sixteenth-century resistance theory, which binds together individual liberty and popular sovereignty. *Nicomède* (1651) and *Suréna* (1674) both position their eponymous heroes as public representatives who speak and act on the people's behalf, and whose authority to contest monarchical power is collectively constituted. As we will see, Nicomède and Suréna's ability to serve as public representatives is based not only by their noble position but also by their affective orientation to other staged characters as well as to the unseen people. In these plays emotional responses to the hero serve as affective evidence of the hero's political legitimacy. While in chapters 2 and 3 I examined how tragedies maintain the ties that bind individual and collective opposition across the historical divide that often separates sixteenth- and seventeenth-century

France—or, the period of religious conflicts and the period when these conflicts were supposedly put to rest—in this chapter (and the one that follows) I bring into relief how resistance theory's political force endures during the period of absolutism itself.

Nicomède and *Suréna* both stage the Cornelian tension between hero and king. They differ, however, in their outcomes. In *Nicomède* the hero triumphs: he ends up schooling the king on how to govern. In *Suréna* the hero dies: three arrows sent by an agent of the king strike Suréna down in a public square. The dramatic arcs of both tragedies elicit comparisons to their respective historical moments. *Nicomède* premiered at the Hôtel de Bourgogne in 1651, during a revolutionary period known as the Fronde (1648–53). During the Fronde, factions of the nobility challenged the way the Regent Anne of Austria and her trusted counselor the Cardinal Mazarin exercised royal authority in the name of King Louis XIV, then a minor.[6] Members of *la noblesse d'épée* (nobility of the sword) and *la noblesse de robe* (nobility of the robe) did not challenge the young king's legitimacy directly, but instead saw themselves as defenders of the king's authority against those who threatened to corrupt it.

During the Fronde, ideas about political power and legitimacy found in sixteenth-century resistance treatises—and in sixteenth-century political thought more broadly—enjoyed a moment of resurgence. Throughout the rebellion nobles of the robe and sword asserted their historic role as public representatives, as individual subjects whose public office and attention to the people's decisions and desires allowed them to defend the public good and actively oppose the exercise of royal power. Judges and princes often cited their concern for the people's welfare and the public good as they attempted to harness public opinion in Paris, as well as in other French cities. The *frondeurs* (as they were known) had some success at key moments, such as when they capitalized on the popular uprising known as the Day of the Barricades (1648) when the people of Paris effectively took over the city in fear and protest of the way the regent and Cardinal Mazarin wielded royal power. Ultimately, however, the Fronde has come to be understood as a failed revolution, a last gasp of aristocratic strength before the eventual triumph of absolutism. Historians have noted that Louis XIV's experience of the Fronde during his minority informed his subsequent enactment of absolutist practices and polices once his majority was declared and he stepped fully into the role of king.

The historical Fronde may have ended unsuccessfully, but *Nicomède* offers the tantalizing possibility of a different outcome. As Paul Bénichou argues, Corneille's tragedy imagines a more successful rebellion: "*Nicomède* paints a picture of an imaginary Fronde, a Fronde that would have ended in victory and in the elevation of the princes. The real Fronde carried with it such hopes at certain moments, but in general it had to be more modest."[7] Reading Corneille's tragedy—this "imaginary Fronde"—casts Nicomède as a hero who exceeds the limitations of the moment, as a rebellious prince who refuses to cede his strength to the state. The tragedy provides a space where the aristocratic order persists, rather than yielding to monarchical power.

Whereas *Nicomède* has been often read as a vision of noble persistence, *Suréna* seems to announce the nobility's ultimate defeat. In *Suréna*, which premiered in 1674 at the Hôtel de Bourgogne during the period of Louis XIV's personal reign (and published the following year), the hero neither emerges triumphant nor cedes his power to the king. Instead, he dies. Given that *Suréna* was Corneille's last tragedy, the king's arrows do not merely strike down Suréna; they also mark the end of the Cornelian hero as such. As Serge Doubrovsky writes, "For the first time in Corneille's theater, in dying, the hero does not rise: he *falls* . . . The death of Suréna is also the Death of the Hero."[8] *Suréna* has come to represent the final stage of the historical process by which the monarchical order eclipses the aristocratic.[9] In Corneille's last tragedy the hero's death announces the nobility's fall and the monarchy's triumph.

Although *Suréna* does capture this sense of noble decline, the play also indicates that something of the nobility's political power endures. I demonstrate how this endurance comes into view by reading *Surèna* and *Nicomède* alongside one another. Despite their different historical moments and their divergent denouements, these tragedies together elaborate a form of heroism that challenges our understanding of the Cornelian hero as a tragic type, as well as of the relationship between Corneille's tragedy and the changing landscape of seventeenth-century political thought.

My goal is thus not to recuperate a narrow sense of aristocratic strength or virtue as vested in individual characters, but instead to demonstrate how the strength and virtue that often seems to coalesce around an—often privileged—individual character is itself a collective project. Reading Nicomède and Suréna as the kind of public representatives imagined by sixteenth-century resistance theory allows us to see how alternatives to absolutism endure beyond the historical defeat of the nobility and beyond the Cornelian hero's death on the tragic stage.

The Myth of the Cornelian Hero

The Cornelian hero occupies a prominent place in French literary history, as well as in the French cultural imaginary more broadly. As John Lyons has noted, the Cornelian hero has achieved the status of myth, a myth that Lyons has called "a curse that hangs over Corneille's theater."[10] The weight of this "cursed" myth has long tipped the interpretive scales away from other concerns and questions. Looming so large, the myth of the Cornelian hero and the forms of political action that accompany it have obscured other forms of political action. Attending to the characteristics of this myth, rather than simply dispensing with it, allows us to bring its limitations more fully into view.[11] More particularly, examining the forms of political action that the myth of the Cornelian hero extols helps us better understand the forms of political action it excludes.

At its core, the myth of the Cornelian hero is a myth of individual prowess in both body and mind. This myth begins during the seventeenth century. In his *Caractères* (1688), for example, the moralist Jean de La Bruyère contrasts Corneille's perceived idealism with Racine's realism:

> Corneille nous assujettit à ses caractères et à ses idées, Racine se conforme aux nôtres ; celui-là peint les hommes comme ils devraient être, celui-ci les peint tels qu'ils sont. Il y a plus dans le premier de ce que l'on admire, et de ce que l'on doit même imiter; il y a plus dans le second de ce que l'on reconnaît dans les autres, ou de ce que l'on éprouve dans soi-même. L'un élève, étonne, maîtrise, instruit; l'autre plaît, remue, touche, pénètre.[12]

> Corneille subjects us to his Characters and Ideas; Racine's are more comfortable to our own: the one paints Men as they ought to be; the other describes 'em as they are. There is in the first more of what we admire, and ought to imitate; and in the second more of what we discover in others, and approve in ourselves. Corneille elevates, surprises, triumphs, and instructs; Racine pleases, affects, moves, and penetrates.[13]

Whereas Racine provides a stirring account of the human condition, Corneille offers an admirable ideal of human potential. Whereas Racine models his characters on fallible humans, Corneille's characters are models of what humans should be. La Bruyère did not originate these distinctions between the two dramatists' work, but his particular formulation has resonated for centuries. In *Le mythe du héros, ou Le désir d'être dieu* (1970), Phillipe Sellier adds a variation to La Bruyère's theme, arguing that "the Cornelian hero is not simply a man, since he is a hero. This hero is neither man as he is, nor man as he should be, it is *man as he dreams himself to be* in his moments of exaltation."[14] From the seventeenth to the twentieth century, the Cornelian hero incarnates that which mere men can only dream of being.

The Cornelian heroic ideal encompasses both physical and mental strength. Returning to *Le Cid*, we find that Rodrigue, the celebrated hero of Corneille's famous play, turns on a conflict of love and duty. Rodrigue finds himself torn between his love for Chimène and his duty to avenge his father, whom Chimène's father has insulted. Rodrigue chooses familial obligation, a decision that illustrates his extraordinary ability to master his passion in favor of his duty. The hero's display of personal strength and self-mastery underscores the importance of the self, the "moi" within Corneille's dramaturgy. For Rodrigue to refuse to avenge his father would be to sully his own honor, which would make him unworthy of Chimène's love. In other words, the dictates of familial and personal glory leave him no choice. Not only Rodrigue's duty but also his own nobility and pride are at stake.[15] The heroic ideal thus includes a fidelity to one's glory and ambition, as well as physical strength and the ability to order one's passions.

The myth of the Cornelian hero centers on the individual, so much so that it has obscured how many of Corneille's heroes operate as public representatives, whose power derives from affective connections to others. This myth emphasizes the hero's personal fortitude and independence without fully recognizing that the hero's individual strengths are the same strengths that ensure his social status. In other words, the hero's attributes as an exemplary individual also make him a worthy representative of the aristocratic order and thus a potential representative of the public good. Understanding the heroes of *Nicomède* and *Suréna* as public representatives in the tradition of sixteenth-century resistance theory, I provide a corrective to the myth of the singular powerful Cornelian hero and emphasize instead how the hero's power instead depends on the speech and actions of others.

The Self-Governed Hero

Nicomède's status as a paradigmatic Cornelian hero derives in large part from his much-celebrated openness. The eldest son of Prusias, the king of Bithynia, Nicomède speaks his mind to all, even his father. Nicomède also goes where he pleases. When the drama opens, he has just returned to Bithynia after a long military campaign abroad. As a leader of one of his father's armies, Nicomède should be subject to his father's command. Instead of waiting for an order from his father to return home, Nicomède instead returns of his own accord to warn his father of a plot by his stepmother, Arisnoé. In an attempt to have her own son, Attale, inherit Prusias's throne, Arisnoé sends two henchmen to assassinate Nicomède. But the henchmen betray Arisnoé's confidence, and Nicomède discovers the plot. The hero's ability to outwit his adversaries alerts us to one of the drama's key political lessons: openness is preferable to secrecy.

In addition to this family drama, a complicated diplomatic plot is also at work in *Nicomède*. King Prusias attempts to strike a balance between retaining some independence from Rome and benefitting from Rome's prowess. When Nicomède returns to his father's court, he finds that a Roman ambassador, Flaminius, also seeks an audience with Prusias to deliver Rome's demand that the king name Nicomède's brother Attale his successor instead of Nicomède. Given that Attale was raised in Rome, the Romans argue that his reign would be more advantageous to them than Nicomède's. The play revolves around the king's difficulty in navigating his competing obligations and choosing between his two sons. Part of what makes Prusias's decision so difficult is that his own authority depends on Nicomède's strength; Nicomède, not Prusias, fights battles and wins wars. For Prusias to jettison Nicomède in favor of Attale would be for the king to jeopardize his own rule.

Nicomède sets up a striking contrast between monarchical weakness and heroic strength. In comparison to Nicomède's self-assurance and confidence, the king's hesitancy and indecision make him seem ineffective and easily manipulated. Although Prusias laments that he must balance competing obligations and concerns to maintain his power, Nicomède argues that sovereignty derives from the self alone. By recognizing the self as the only source of authority, Nicomède articulates one of the drama's paradoxes: he speaks as a sovereign without possessing the throne. As Hélène Merlin-Kajman remarks, "Nicomède, an exemplary hero, a hero in whom all the ideality of the kingdom is concentrated, *is not the king*."[16] Indeed, Nicomède shows himself to be a better sovereign than the king. When he first appears before his father, Nicomède offers the king a lesson about the true sources of sovereign power. King Prusias admits that he is torn between his fatherly love for Nicomède and his marital obligation to Arisnoé. In political terms Prusias is caught between naming Nicomède his successor as planned (and as suggested by the laws of primogeniture) and elevating Attale instead to appease both Arisnoé and Rome. Prusias speaks first during this encounter between father and son:

> J'ai tendresse pour toi, j'ai passion pour elle,
> Et je ne veux pas voir cette haine éternelle,
> Ni que des sentiments, que j'aime à voir durer,

Ne règnent dans mon cœur que pour le déchirer.
J'y veux mettre d'accord l'Amour, et la Nature,
Être père, et mari dans cette conjoncture . . .

NICOMÈDE
Seigneur, voulez-vous bien vous en fier à moi?
Ne soyez l'un, ni l'autre.

PRUSIAS
Et que dois-je être?

NICOMÈDE
Roi.

(*Nicomède*, 4.3.1311–18)

PRUSIAS
Passion for her, Affection pleads for thee,
I would not have this Hate eternal be.
Yet though I prize them, cannot in my brest
Cherish these thoughts onely to break my rest.
I would make Love, and Nature, of accord,
Father, and Husband be, and in a word—

NICOMÈDE
If I may with you and any credit win,
Be neither one, nor t'other.

PRUSIAS
What then?

NICOMÈDE
King.[17]

Prusias describes the two pulls on his heart, suggesting that the conflict between his eldest son and his second wife is at an impasse. As both continue to reign in his heart, the king cannot rule effectively. Nicomède proposes a solution to this problem, suggesting that his father should renounce the roles of "père" and "mari" to be, simply, "Roi." The form of Nicomède's response echoes its content. In the text the single syllable "Roi" definitively ends their shared alexandrine. Furthermore, we can easily imagine how this syllable might ring out on stage, momentarily arresting the action. Standing alone, "Roi" efficiently reinforces Nicomède's insistence that the king should detach himself from paternal and marital entanglements.

Nicomède extolls the virtues of self-governance on more than one occasion. Earlier in the drama, the hero provides a similar admonishment to Attale. In a further complication of the plot, the half-brothers are competing not only for their father's throne but also for same woman's heart. They both love Laodice, the queen of Armenia, who has been placed by her father under the protection of King Prusias's court. When Nicomède prompts Attale to justify his claims to Laodice's heart, Attale cites his parentage as well as his Roman education and continued ties to Rome. Nicomède chastises his younger brother for staking his claims on such external sources. In contrast to Attale, Nicomède justifies his right to occupy Laodice's heart through his own strength alone:

> Prince, faites-moi voir un plus digne rival.
> Si vous aviez dessein d'attaquer cette place,
> Ne vous départez point d'une si noble audace:
> Mais comme à son secours je n'amène que moi,
> Ne la menacez plus de Rome, ni du Roi:
> Je la défendrai seul, attaquez-la de même,
> Avec tous les respects qu'on doit au Diadème.
> Je veux bien mettre à part, avec le nom d'aîné,
> Le rang de votre maître où je suis destiné,
> Et vous verrons ainsi qui fait mieux un brave homme,
> Des leçons d'Annibal, ou de celles de Rome.
> (*Nicomède*,1.5.266–76)

> Yourself Prince, a deserving Rival show.
> And if you dare design to assault me here,
> Still in your looks a noble boldness wear.
> But as I to her Aid am singly come,
> Threaten me not with the King's Power, or Rome's
> As I defend, do you attempt alone,
> I'll set by all pretenses to the Crown.
> Try it thus Prince and we shall soon see then
> If Rome, or Hannibal breeds braver Men.[18]

Laodice's heart is rendered as a physical place in these verses. In particular, her heart becomes a battlefield where the brothers duel, an idea that is underscored by the repetition of "attaquer," as well as by words like "rival," "menacez," and "secours." Through the defense of this metaphorical place, Nicomède rejects his royal parentage and scoffs at Rome's power. Nicomède might easily have taken a different tack and turned Attale's arguments against him. As the older son, Nicomède might have boasted of a stronger tie to the crown and of a right of primogeniture, or *droit de naissance*. Instead, he explicitly proposes to set aside, or "mettre à part," his birthright and rank, arguing that each brother should be judged merely on his ability to act as a "brave homme." On this point, Nicomède highlights a difference in their respective training and ideals. Whereas Attale was raised and educated in Rome, Nicomède remained at home and became an admirer of those who resisted Roman rule. By underscoring Attale's fidelity to Rome, Nicomède marks a distinction between his freedom and Attale's servitude. Attale is content to receive orders from a foreign power and to derive authority from his father. In contrast, as one of the rhymes in the above passage suggests, the only "Roi" or authority that Nicomède recognizes is the "moi." Repeating the rhyme "moi" and "Roi" and reiterating his rejection of the *droit de naissance*, Nicomède insists that sovereignty emanates from the self rather than from the throne. This insistence has contributed to a historical interpretation of the drama as a paean to the aristocratic ethos that the absolutist state threatens with its consolidation.

When Nicomède does eventually recognize his father's rule, he does so in a way that seems to preserve his self-reliance. The recognition of his father's sovereignty occurs only after numerous plot twists and reversals of fortune. Despite Nicomède's recommendations, Prusias decides to name Attale as his heir. This decision, however, presents a problem. The Bithynian people have more affection for Nicomède than for Prusias, their king. Fearing that Nicomède will rally the people and thus mount a challenge to his father's rule, Prusias has Nicomède imprisoned. Although Nicomède cannot rally the people from prison, his imprisonment nonetheless rallies the people. Their uprising causes confusion in the palace, during which Attale sneaks away, dons a disguise, and releases Nicomède. The hero then appeases the people by appearing before them from a palace balcony. Having calmed the people, Nicomède rejoins the other members of the royal family. Shocked to see his eldest son out from behind bars, Prusias says, "Quoi? me viens-tu braver jusque dans mon Palais, / Rebelle?" (5.9.1781–82) (What! comest thou to defy me in my palace, Rebel?).[19] In response, Nicomède assures the king, "Je viens en bon Sujet vous rendre le repos" (5.9.1785) (I come as a good subject, to restore / That peace).[20] Recasting himself from "Rebelle" to "bon sujet," Nicomède recognizes his father's rule. As Merlin-Kajman has noted, this scene, however, is not one of submission. Rather than submit to his father, Nicomède bestows his approval.[21] The son and subject deigns to accept the rule of his father and monarch. For Nicomède, even acts of obedience carry signs of self-reliance.

The Generous Hero

Readers of *Nicomède* have identified the play's self-reliant hero as exemplary of Cartesian *générosité*. As we will see, although this quality at first glance seems to shore up Nicomède's individual strength, upon closer examination the hero's générosité marks his openness to the people's affection.[22] In *Les passions de l'âme* (1649), Descartes describes générosité as the quality expressed by subjects who recognize their capacity to direct their own volition:

> Ainsi je croy que la vraye Generosité, qui fait qu'un homme s'estime au plus haut point qu'il se peut legitimement estimer, consiste seulement, partie en ce qu'il connoist qu'il n'y a rien qui vertiablement luy appartiene, que cette libre disposition de ces volontez, ny pourquoy il doive estre loué ou blasmé, sinon pource qu'il en use bien ou mal; & partie en ce qu'il sent en soy mesme une ferme & constante resolution d'en bien user, c'est à dire de ne manquer jamais de volonté, pour entreprendre & executer toutes les choses qu'il jugera estre les meilleurs. Ce qui est suivre parfaitement la vertu.[23]

> And thus I think that true nobility of soul, in virtue of which a man esteems himself as highly as he may legitimately do, consist in two things and two things only: first, he recognizes that there is nothing that legitimately belongs to him, save this freedom to direct his acts of will, and that there is no reason why he should be praised or blamed except for his good or bad use of it; secondly, he feels in himself a firm and constant resolution to make good use of it, that is, never to lack the willpower to undertake and execute whatever he judges to be best. And this is what it means to follow virtue perfectly.[24]

For Descartes, générosité differs considerably from our modern sense of the word. To label someone as generous today is to remark on her tendency to share what she owns, offering, for example, money, food, or shelter to those in need. In other words, the modern *généreux* is someone who freely gives up her worldly possessions. In contrast, Descartes's généreux has no such possessions to give. His only holding is his own will, which cannot be transferred.

Descartes situates générosité as the culmination of the ethical system outlined in *Les passions de l'âme* and identifies this quality as particularly virtuous on two counts. First, by understanding volition to be his only true possession, the généreux values independence and does not unreflexively let the passions sway him. In other words, he monitors and manages the passions' effect on his body and mind. Second, the généreux routinely eschews self-interests and works in the service of others. Descartes explains:

> Ceux qui sont Genereux . . . n'estiment rien de plus grand que de faire du bien aux autres hommes, et de mespriser son propre interest pour ce sujet, ils sont tousjours parfaitement courtois, affables et officieux envers un chacun. Et avec cela ils sont entierement maistres de leurs Passions: particulierement des Desirs, de la jalousie, et de l'Envie, à cause qu'il n'y a aucune chose dont l'acquisition ne depende pas d'eux, qu'ils pensent valoir assez pour meriter d'estre beaucoup souhaitée; et de la Haine envers les hommes, à cause qu'ils les estiment tous; et de la Peur, à cause que la confiance qu' ils ont en leur vertu, les assure; et en fin de la Colère, à cause que, n'estimant que fort peu toutes les choses qui dependent d'autruy, jamais ils ne donnent tant d'avantage à leurs ennemis, que de reconnoistre qu'ils en sont offencez.[25]

> Those who are noble in this way . . . because they value nothing more highly than doing good to other human beings, for the sake of which they regard their own interests as unimportant, they are always perfectly curious, affable, and helpful towards one and all. Moreover, they are entirely in control of their passions: especially of desires, jealousy, and envy, since there is nothing the acquisition of which is not in their control that they think of sufficient value to warrant being greatly desired; and of hatred, since they esteem all human beings; and of terror, because they are fortified by confidence in their own virtue; and, finally, of anger, since, valuing, as they do, very little whatever is in the control of others, they never give their enemies the satisfaction of acknowledging that they are put out by such things.[26]

In Descartes's formulation, the généreux's independence does not lead him to avoid interactions with others. He does not retreat into himself, alone with his autonomy. He does not allow himself to be overwhelmed with passions like "la Haine," "la Peur," and "la Colère." Instead, the généreux's ability to control his reactions to the passions allows him freely to respond to others' needs. *La générosité* thus constitutes a felicitous combination of self-mastery and magnanimity of spirit. Notably, the généreux's mastery over his passions places him in direct opposition to the tyrant of sixteenth-century resistance theory—and sixteenth-century political thought more broadly. The tyrant is so taken with his own passions and preoccupations, that he neglects the public good. Descartes's treatise, though it does not profess political aims, nonetheless lays the groundwork for us to see the généreux as a self-possessed and thus appropriately attentive political leader.

Nicomède inhabits the ideal of générosité so thoroughly that he inspires others to follow his lead. R. Darren Gobert notes that the hero's exemplary virtue propels the tragedy's action: "*Nicomède*'s dramatic arc involves not a change in its steadfastly generous hero but a transformation of those around him, especially Attale and Prusias, who eventually find themselves situated between [Nicomède] and [Arisnoé], or between 'generosity' and 'hatred.'"[27] By instructing his father and half-brother on how to be a better sovereign and a more self-sufficient son, respectively, Nicomède teaches them in the ways of générosité.

In addition to demonstrating how the generous, self-possessed hero serves as a model for others, the play also emphasizes how Nicomède's status as a généreux is constituted and sustained by those around him. The actions of staged characters, the off-staged people, and the drama's audience all contribute to the hero's self-construction. In other words, although Nicomède appears to be self-contained, this appearance is partially elaborated by the play's other actors. On one level, this form of concerted action can be understood as part of the machinations of the drama's plot. Nicomède's self-assured acquiescence to his father's rule requires the participation of others. The unruly people, Laodice, and Attale, all make his release from prison possible. However, the concerted construction of the hero takes place on another level as well. The drama situates Nicomède as an object to be admired. Staged characters and the off-staged people secure Nicomède's heroism through their admiration. In *Les passions de l'âme*, Descartes maintains that admiration is the first of all passions. Within his ethical system, one must pass through admiration to understand and inhabit generosity. Keeping Descartes's order in mind, we must pass through the dynamics of admiration in *Nicomède* to nuance our understanding of its hero's generosity and autonomy.

In his 1660 "Examen," Corneille foregrounds the importance of admiration. The dramatist suggests that members of the audience were struck by Nicomède's self-mastery and magnanimity. For Corneille, Nicomède's striking virtue engenders a model of the tragic hero that departs from Aristotle's prescriptions:

> Ce héros de ma façon sort un peu des règles de la tragédie, en ce qu'il ne cherche point à faire pitié par l'excès de ses infortunes; mais le succès a montré que la fermeté des grands cœurs, qui n'excite que de l'admiration dans l'âme du spectateur, est quelquefois aussi agréable, que la compassion que notre art nous ordonne d'y produire par la représentation de leurs malheurs. Il en fait naître toutefois quelqu'une, mais elle ne va pas jusques à tirer des larmes. Son effet se borne à mettre les auditeurs dans les intérêts de ce prince, et à leur faire former des souhaits pour ses prospérités.[28]

> This hero of mine departs a bit from the conventions of tragedy in that he does not seek to inspire pity through the excess of his misfortunes; but the success [of the play] has shown that the fortitude of brave hearts, which inspires only admiration in the soul of the spectator, is sometimes as agreeable as the compassion that our art requires that we produce through the representation of misfortune. [Admiration] does give rise to a kind of compassion, but not the sort that goes so far as to prompt tears. Its effects are limited to aligning the audience with the prince's interests, and making them to wish for his good fortune.[29]

Whereas Aristotle argues in the *Poetics* that tragic heroes should be neither too exemplary nor too detestable so that they might inspire pity through their moral mediocrity, Corneille insists that an uncommon virtue can also affect spectators. This exemplary virtue may not move them to tears, but it will move them nonetheless. It is admiration, however, rather than pity, that a figure like Nicomède inspires. During the seventeenth century, admiration primarily denoted wonder or surprise rather than esteem or respect. As we will see, however, these two meanings are linked in *Nicomède*. Corneille suggests that a combination of wonder and esteem calibrates the spectators' sensibility, engaging them in Nicomède's interests and investing them in his success.[30]

Corneille further elaborates on the power of admiration in a critique of Aristotelian catharsis:

> Dans l'admiration qu'on a pour sa vertu [la vertu de Nicomède], je trouve une manière de purger les passions, dont n'a point parlé

> Aristote, et qui est peut-être plus sûre que celle qu'il prescrit à la tragédie par le moyen de la pitié et de la crainte. L'amour qu'elle nous donne pour cette vertu que nous admirons, nous imprime de la haine pour le vice contraire. La grandeur de courage de Nicomède nous laisse une aversion de la pusillanimité.[31]
>
> In the admiration that one has for Nicomède's virtue, I find a way to purge the passions that Aristotle did not discuss, a way that may be more reliable than the kind of purgation he prescribes which relies on pity and fear. Our admiration for Nicomède's virtue inspires a love that impresses us with hatred for virtue's opposite. The grandeur of Nicomède's bravery leaves us with an aversion to spineless weakness.

By presenting Nicomède's example, the drama inspires virtue and purges vice. Admiration thus serves as a conduit, transmitting grandeur and generosity beyond the stage. The process of transmitting such virtues as these is corporeal, which Corneille emphasizes through the verb "imprimer." In this context Nicomède's example is not only metaphorically impressive; it also leaves a physical mark. Admiration of the hero's strength would thus seem to reinforce the importance of Nicomède's self-mastery. His independence and control become the impressive standards that the drama holds up for all to see and revere. But the dynamics of admiration also reminds us that this self-sufficient portrait of Nicomède is more complicated than initially meets the eye. The primacy placed on admiration points toward Nicomède's dependence on others. To secure its hero's admirable autonomy, the drama requires broad recognition and participation.

In Corneille's "Examen," admiration for Nicomède pushes spectators toward virtue and away from vice. For Descartes, admiration does not itself contain a specific moral content but instead acts as a conduit. Admiration is the primary of all the passions, Descartes explains, and to feel admiration is to feel wonder or surprise:

> Lors que la premiere rencontre de quelque objet nous surprent, et que nous le jugeons estre nouveau, ou fort different de ce que nous connoissions auparavant, ou bien de ce que nous supposions qu'il devoit estre, cela fait que nous l'admirons et en sommes estonnez. Et pour ce que cela peut arriver avant que nous connoissions aucunement si cet objet nous est convenable, ou s'il ne l'est pas, il me semble que l'Admiration est la premiere de toutes les passions. Et elle n'a point de contraire, à cause que, si l'objet qui se presente

> n'a rien en soy qui nous surprene, nous n'en sommes aucunement émeus, et nous le considerons sans passion.[32]
>
> When our first encounter with some object takes us by surprise, and we judge it to be new, or very different from what we have previously experienced or from what we expected it to be, this causes us to wonder at it and be astonished. And because this can happen before we have any knowledge of whether the thing is beneficial to us or not, it seems to me that wonderment is the first passion of all. And it has no contrary, because, if the object that presents itself has nothing in itself to surprise us, we are not moved by it in any way and we consider it without any passion.[33]

Admiration describes the relationship between subject and object. For a subject to feel admiration, the subject must experience wonder or surprise when encountering a given object. For Descartes, to feel admiration is thus not necessarily to confer approval or respect, as our current usage implies. In contrast, Cartesian admiration is prereflective. As Christian Biet has underlined, the moment of encounter arrests the subject and may lead either to stupor and bewilderment or to rational contemplation. Morally neutral, admiration is also morally risky. Thus, the reaction to admiration, and not admiration itself, may lead to the recognition of virtue.[34]

From Heroic Subject to Object of Admiration

By positioning Nicomède as an object of admiration, the tragedy presents its apparently self sufficient hero as beholden to others' consideration. Members of the royal family and Bithynian people alike express wonder at Nicomède's strength and interpret this strength as a sign of his virtue. Reflecting on Nicomède's singular glory, the drama's other characters thus suggest how the hero should be received. The co-construction of Nicomède as a virtuous hero begins with the plays's first lines. Laodice speaks these lines, which describe the pleasure she feels at the sight of Nicomède and boast of the obvious influence she exerts over his heart:

> Après tant de haut faits, il m'est bien doux, Seigneur,
> De voir encor mes yeux régner sur votre cœur,
> De voir, sous les lauriers qui vous couvrent la tête
> Un si grand conquérant être encor ma conquête.
> (*Nicomède*,1.1.1–4)

After such mighty deeds, sir, it is sweet
To see that I still reign within thy bosom,—
To see that though his brow is crowned with laurels,
I still hold captive this great conqueror's heart.[35]

Laodice's lines accompany the audience's first encounter with Nicomède. Her enumeration of his honors, framed by her delight at her own influence, mediates the audience's moment of admiration, encouraging a passage from wonder to reflection. Providing a description of his military prowess, she also offers a glimpse of his inner virtue. In addition to being worthy of her attention and love, he submits to her "conquête." As her opening speech continues, she details his many points of honor and suggests that it is his virtue that has stoked Rome's fears and provoked Arisnoé's jealousy. Throughout the scene Laodice encourages Nicomède to be wary of his rivals, but she notes that Nicomède possesses something they do not: the people's approval. "Le Peuple ici vous aime, et hait ces cœurs infâmes" (1.1.115) (The people love you and hate [your rivals'] repugnant hearts).[36] Laodice thus establishes that Nicomède is worthy of the people's love as well as her own, and she posits both romantic and political affection as sources of his strength and as evidence of his political legitimacy.

King Prusias confirms the affective nature of Nicomède's strength in the second act, although the king speaks of his son's strength out of fear rather than love. Nicomède's decision to leave his military post without orders from his father is seen as a particularly audacious move. It is a direct affront to the king's power: "Revenir sans mon ordre, et se montrer ici?" (2.1.365) (Returns without my orders, and comes here?).[37] The king then describes the disruption caused by Nicomède's imminent arrival, placing particular emphasis on the visual:

Il n'est plus mon Sujet qu'autant qu'il le veut être,
Et qui me fait régner en effet est mon maître.
Pour paraître à mes yeux, son mérite est trop grand:
On n'aime point à voir ceux à qui on doit tant,
Tout ce qu'il a fait parle au moment qu'il m'approche,
Et sa seule présence est un secret reproche:
Elle me dit toujours qu'il m'a fait trois fois Roi,
Que je tiens plus de lui, qu'il ne tiendra de moi.
(*Nicomède*,2.1.415–22)

He is now my subject
Only so much as he may wish to be;

And he by whom I reign is in reality
My master. Thus to have appeared before me,
His merit is too great. One does not love
To look on those to whom one owes too much.
All that he did finds voice when he approaches me,
And his mere presence secretly reproaches me.
Ever it tells me that he has thrice over
Made me a king; that I hold more through him
Than he will hold through me.[38]

Whereas elsewhere in the drama, Nicomède's rhyme of "Roi" and "moi" communicates his strength, Prusias's rhyme signals his relative weakness. When Nicomède returns, the king will have to confront the discrepancy in their power. Nicomède's sheer appearance, his "seule présence," makes plain what Prusias would prefer not to see. Without even saying a word, the prince will call Prusias's authority into question and, through his "secret reproche," will make an open secret of the king's borrowed strength. Prusias's concerns instruct the spectators on how to view Nicomède. The king's complaints about his son's prowess build on Laodice's praise to further construct the tragedy's portrait of a hero.

Nicomède's strength and virtue are further confirmed by the Bithynian people, who are never seen on stage, but whose preferences are reported by staged characters. As the palace intrigue unfolds, news of their dissatisfaction with the king and their affection for Nicomède reaches the royal family. Although the queen initially dismisses the uprising, characterizing it as mere "tumulte" (tumult) and "bruit" (noise), and insisting that the king has nothing to fear, the "noise" from the street eventually grows louder and more threatening.[39] In the 1660 edition of Corneille's plays, the frontispiece to *Nicomède* depicts an attempt by the king to end the people's revolt and to restore order (fig. 6). Prusias appears on the balcony in the upper-right background, with the bodies of the people looming in the foreground: the raised arms of the people mirror that of the king.[40] His outstretched arm is met with theirs, a parallel that communicates their refusal to cede to his authority. In French political thought, the outstretched arms of the people operate as a signal of their ability to confer authority on the king. It is a gesture of popular sovereignty. As I discussed in chapter 1, in François Hotman's *Francogallia* (1573) the ancient practice of electing the sovereign included the physical raising of arms. The people literally elevated the king by placing him on a shield and hoisting him above their heads with their arms. For Hotman, this ancient practice of lifting up the king indicates that the people's authority preceded and

Fig. 6. Frontispiece of Pierre Corneille, *Nicomède* (Rouen, 1660). Bibliothèque nationale de France.

exceeded the king's. While the people no longer literally elevate the king in Hotman's time, he argues that their superior power endures, even as the monarchy has become hereditary rather than explicitly elective. With its outstretched arms, the frontispiece to *Nicomède* and the play's description of the people's refusal to yield recalls this ancient gesture of popular sovereignty and remakes it as part of a seventeenth-century repertoire.

Through their speech and actions the people assert their rejection of the king and their preference for Nicomède. As the revolt continues, the people repeatedly demand Nicomède's release. The king considers how he might perversely meet their demands by executing Nicomède and then gruesomely displaying his son's severed head:

> Allons, allons le rendre,
> Ce précieux objet d'une amitié si tendre.
> Obéissons, Madame, à ce Peuple sans foi,
> Qui las de m'obéir en veut faire son Roi,
> Et du haut d'un balcon, pour calmer la tempête,
> Sur ses nouveaux Sujets faisons voler sa tête.
> (*Nicomède*, 5.5.1583–88)
>
> We shall, we shall restore to them this precious
> Object of so affectionate a love.
> Madam, let us obey our faithless people,
> Who weary of obeying me and wish
> To choose their king themselves; and from the height
> Here of a balcony, to calm this tempest,
> Let us throw down his head to his new subjects.[41]

Planning to make a spectacular demonstration of his own force, the king proposes to give the people what they want: a view of Nicomède. Although the king does not have a chance to put this plan into action, his verses reinforce how the drama situates Nicomède as an object to behold. Frustrated with the people's stated affection for his son, Prusias labels Nicomède a "précieux objet." Nicomède's body is thus not only a source of his own strength but also a site of political contestation. In the drama's final act, the very possibility of heroic opposition is articulated through the people's demands. The people require a leader and they have deemed Nicomède worthy. Their approval provides affective evidence of his political legitimacy.

The people confirm their affection for Nicomède when, released from prison, he appears before them to quiet the crowd by making a display of his reversal of fortune. The scene he subsequently reports to the rest of the royal family marks a stark contrast with Prusias's earlier appearance, as depicted by the 1660 frontispiece. "Tout est calme, Seigneur," Nicomède reports to his father, "un moment de ma vue / A soudain apaisé la Populace émue" (5.9.1779–80) (All is calm, sire. The people instantly / Have been appeased by the mere sight of me).[42] Although the people refused to calm itself when the king appeared on the very same balcony, they immediately come to rest with just one look at their hero. Christian Biet argues that this second (reported) balcony scene constitutes a moment of Cartesian admiration. The people are struck with wonder and surprise at the sudden appearance of Nicomède. This moment of admiration, however, does not end with morally neutral wonder, but instead immediately transforms into a positive evaluation of Nicomède's authority. Put another way, the people make a value judgment about Nicomède that is also a political decision. In a move that parallels Nicomède's approval of his father's authority at the denouement, the people confer their approval on Nicomède. As Laodice's line from the drama's first scene makes clear, Nicomède has long held the people's esteem. Their revolt against Prusias and subsequent recognition of Nicomède more fully brings into view how central their ongoing support is to the maintenance of his heroic status.

In contrast to the people, Attale does not begin the drama in support of Nicomède. Instead, as we have seen, the two half-brothers are political and romantic rivals. The drama initially portrays Attale as dependent on his father, mother, and Rome. He shares their preferences, and their decisions are his decisions. In the final scene, however, Attale is revealed to be Nicomède's liberator. When Prusias asks Nicomède how he has escaped, Nicomède explains that a masked man released him and states that this masked man asked for Nicomède's diamond ring as payment or "gage" (5.9.1820). As Nicomède recounts the strange conditions of his liberation, Attale produces the ring and confesses to being this mysterious man. Nicomède then expresses his thanks, referring to the ring as an identifying mark:

> Ah, laissez-moi toujours à cette digne marque
> Reconnaître en mon sang un vrai sang de monarque.
> Ce n'est plus des Romains l'esclave ambitieux,
> C'est le libérateur d'un sang si précieux:
> Mon frère, avec mes fers vous en brisez bien d'autres,
> Ceux du Roi, de la Reine, et les siens, et les vôtres.
> (*Nicomède*, 5.9.1823–28)

> Ah, let me always by this worthy proof
> Know that true kingly blood flows in thy veins!
> This is no more the ambitious slave of Rome;
> This is the liberator of his kindred.
> Brother, thou breakest other chains than mine:
> The King's, the Queen's, Laodice's, and thine.[43]

In this scene the exchange of the diamond signals the brothers' mutual recognition. As the rhyme of "digne marque" and "sang de monarque" suggests, the diamond ring, a valuable object, functions as the outward sign of Nicomède's inner worth and virtue. By returning the ring, Attale demonstrates that he has recognized Nicomède's "sang si précieux." In turn, Nicomède recognizes Attale as more than a pawn in his mother's quest for power. The structure of these verses further underscores the recognition that occurs between the two brothers. When Nicomède says, "laissez-moi toujours à cette digne marque / Reconnaître en mon sang un vrai sang de monarque," he might refer to himself or to Attale. Exchanged between them, the diamond becomes a symbol of their shared pedigree. As we know, however, for Nicomède, pedigree alone does not make the man. By taking action, and specifically by taking action that contradicts the stated wishes of the king, the queen, and Rome, Attale proves himself worthy of Nicomède's respect.

In this final scene Nicomède reiterates the importance of self-sovereignty and independent action. The hero offers one more lesson in générosité. What accompanies Nicomède's lesson, however, is the diamond ring, a prop that makes concrete the drama's figuration of Nicomède as an object to behold. The ring, as an outward sign of Nicomède's inner virtue, parallels how the hero circulates on stage as "un objet précieux." Laodice, Prusias, Attale, and the people all hold up Nicomède as a virtuous hero. If, as Corneille writes in his "Examen," Nicomède provokes the audience's admiration, it is the nonheroic characters and the off-staged people who suggest that the audience's wonder should lead to esteem. If Nicomède appears as a self-possessed généreux, it is in part due to the speech and actions of those that surround him. However boldly Nicomède may eschew his ties to others, *Nicomède* suggests that these ties persist. Attending to this persistence allows us to recast Nicomède's characteristic openness. Instead of functioning merely as an indication of his self-sovereignty, Nicomède's openness also serves as a sign of the affective ties that bind the hero to other staged characters and the unseen people.

Suréna: From Private Liberty to Public Menace

Standing in contrast to Nicomède, Suréna, the hero of Corneille's final tragedy, champions a form of self-enclosure. Whereas Nicomède boldly proclaims the self as the source of his strength, Suréna attempts to hide this strength away. Given this distinction, it would seem that this final Cornelian hero severs the ties between himself and those that surround him. What we find, however, is that the play maintains these ties, albeit in more subtle and less spectacular ways.

Corneille's *Suréna* is set in an absolutist milieu in which the king admits no rival to his authority. And yet, the play's structure allows Suréna to become a public representative whose personal liberty serves as a locus of legitimate opposition to monarchical power. In *Suréna*, romantic love rather than love of God binds together private liberty and the public good. The hero argues that his liberty of conscience allows him to love whomever he wishes, regardless of the monarch's designs. Suréna's king wants the hero to marry his daughter. Suréna, however, loves Eurydice, the daughter of the king's rival. Throughout the drama Suréna and Eurydice maintain their right not only to choose the objects of their affection but also to keep these objects a secret. However, the lovers' passion quickly becomes an open secret, that is, it is known to all without having been explicitly disclosed. Through this open secret the drama subtly undermines absolutist divisions between the private and the public, thus reanimating the right of resistance. Suréna claims only his right to private passion, to interior freedom. But when the hero's private passion becomes public knowledge, it destabilizes the king's authority. Because the hero's love is made public unwittingly, he remains a model absolutist subject even as he becomes a public representative and thus a figure of communal opposition. The right to love freely opens up the possibility of collective dissent.

Suréna's lovers present themselves as model absolutist subjects, claiming that their private passion remains entirely separate from their public roles and duties. Suréna and Eurydice both assert their right to harbor their secret love for each other. In the opening lines Eurydice asks her lady-in-waiting to stop detailing the elaborate preparations for the treaty between her father, the king of Armenia, and Suréna's monarch, Orode, the king of Parthia. Included in the treaty is the stipulation that Eurydice will marry Orode's son. For Eurydice, who loves Suréna and not the prince, the treaty is a source of pain rather than a cause for joyous celebration:

> Ne me parle plus tant de joie, et d'hyménée,
> Tu ne sais pas les maux où je suis condamnée,
> Ormène, c'est ici que doit s'exécuter
> Ce Traité qu'à deux Rois il a plu d'arrêter,
> Et l'on a préféré cette suberbe ville,
> Ces murs de Séleucie, aux murs d'Hécatompyle:
> La Reine et la Princesse en quittent le séjour,
> Pour rendre en ces beaux lieux tout son lustre à la Cour;
> Le Roi les mande exprès, le Prince n'attend qu'elles,
> Et jamais ces climats n'ont vu pompes si belles.
> Mais que servent pour moi tous ces préparatifs,

Si mon cœur est esclave, et tous ces vœux captifs;
Si de tous ces efforts de publique allégresse
Il se fait des sujets de trouble, et de tristesse?
J'aime ailleurs.
(*Suréna*, 1.1.1–15)

Speak not to me of happiness and marriage!
Thou knowest not to what I am condemned,
Ormene. It is here the terms of that
Treaty which two kings chose to make must needs
Be carried out—for which the preference
Is given to this proud city, this Selucia,
O'er Hecatompyle. The Queen and also
The Princess have left there to give the Court
Its brightest luster in this lovely place.
The King expressly summoned them; the Prince
Waits for them only; and these climes have never
Seen such great pomp. But of what good to me
Are all their preparations, if my heart
Hath been enthralled and is not free to hope,—
If it in all these shows of public joy
Finds cause for perturbation and for sadness?
I love elsewhere.[44]

Acknowledging the spectacular celebration that her wedding will occasion, Eurydice establishes the drama's geographical setting and creates a distinction between the public festivities and her private sentiment, or between the space of the court ("Cour") and the space of her heart ("cœur"). At first she situates her heart within the confines of the political order, held captive or "enthralled" by the king's treaty. But she then emphasizes that her love resides elsewhere, beyond the bounds of the king's court. The claim to love elsewhere, while it upholds the absolutist division between the public and private, also reads as a subtle challenge to the king's authority. These opening lines recount how the king has the power to organize space and to compel movement. The king determines in which city the marriage will be held. The king also decides who will be included in the marriage ceremony and what role they will play. By delimiting her heart as a space of private freedom, Eurydice's opening lines suggest that the king's jurisdiction has limits. Although she must physically be present at court, her private preferences are sheltered from public view and thus not subject to the king's control.

With these opening lines Corneille's final drama takes up a question posed by his earlier work, namely, whether feelings and attachments associated with an old political order might survive the transition into a new configuration of power.[45] *Le Cid*, for example, also features a heroine whose king compels her to marry. Unlike Eurydice, however, *Le Cid*'s heroine, Chimène, is ordered to marry someone she loves. The king commands Chimène to marry her beloved Rodrigue, even though Rodrigue has killed her father. The king authorizes Chimène's love in a way that shores up his own power against the feudal order that her late father represents. As we saw at the beginning of this chapter, *Le Cid* ends with the king's assurances to the hero that the marriage will indeed take place, despite Chimène's filial reservations:

> Espère en ton courage, espère en ma promesse,
> Et possédant déjà le cœur de ta maîtresse,
> Pour vaincre un point d'honneur qui combat contre toi,
> Laisse faire le temps, ta vaillance, et ton Roi.
> (*Suréna*, 5.7.1863–66)
>
> Hope in your courage, in my promise. Hope
> Already your belovéd's heart is yours.
> And, if her sense of honour still resists,
> Leave it to time, your valiance and your king.[46]

The rhymes "promesse" and "maîtresse" (promise and mistress) and "toi" and "Roi" (you and King) evoke a chain of attachment that begins and ends with the king.[47] In *Le Cid* romantic passion comes to serve royal interest.

The opening lines of *Suréna* make clear that in this play romantic passion and royal interest remain opposed. Eurydice's love for Suréna cannot be aligned with the king's desires. The king wants her to marry the prince, but she loves elsewhere. Eurydice's love for Suréna cannot be incorporated into the new political order. The king in *Le Cid* makes use of Chimène's love both Rodrigue and her father, bending these romantic and familial attachments to fit his consolidation of royal power. Much like Chimène's, Eurydice's love for Suréna precedes the king's consolidation of power. However, there is no room for flexibility in this case. The only way for Eurydice's love for Suréna to endure is in the secret, private space of her heart. As we will see, however, the insistence on the heart's privacy itself becomes a political problem.

The idea that the heart is a protected locus of private sentiment begins explicitly to take on political connotations in act 2, as Eurydice marshals the language of rights when responding to the prince's suggestion that the treaty between their fathers requires that she openly declare her love for him: "S'il a pu l'une à l'autre engager nos personnes, / Au seul don de la main son droit est limité, / Et mon cœur avec vous n'a point fait de traité" (2.2.502–4) (If it has bound us to each other, solely / To the hand's gift its power was limited, / And never hath my heart made any pact / With thee).[48] The princess maps the split between the public and private onto her own body, separating her hand's duty from her heart's desire. Suréna echoes the idea that the heart is a space of private freedom later in the drama, complaining that the king acts as a "tyran de mon cœur" (5.7.1520) (tyrant of my heart), because he abuses his authority by making demands on his subjects' hearts. By claiming to possess unique authority over their hearts, the lovers delimit the king's power.

Suréna raises the question of whether subjects can maintain their private liberty while faithfully serving their king. For example, when the king suggests Suréna's refusal to marry his daughter signals the hero's disloyalty, Suréna insists that the liberty of his heart in no way compromises his loyalty to the monarch:

> Je lui dois en sujet tout mon sang, tout mon bien,
> Mais si je lui dois tout, mon cœur ne lui doit rien,
> Et n'en reçoit de lois que comme autant d'outrages,
> Comme autant d'attentats sur de plus doux hommages.
> (*Suréna*, 5.2.1523–26)
>
> I owe him, as his subject, all my blood,
> All my possessions; yet though I owe him all
> This, my heart oweth him naught, and it receiveth
> His orders only as indignities,
> Only as crimes against my fonder homage.[49]

Distinguishing his heart from his blood, Suréna enumerates what he gives to the sovereign and what he keeps to himself. The hero's objections seem to create a physiological paradox: one cannot separate one's blood from one's heart and hope to survive, as the heart pumps the blood through the body.[50] In this passage "cœur" (heart) does not refer to a physical organ but instead delimits an immaterial space of subjective freedom. Suréna splits his body and his heart. He serves the king through his body, but his heart remains separate and apart. As a subject he owes the king all his blood and all his possessions: "tout mon sang, tout mon bien." Although Suréna owes every physical thing to the king, his heart is not a thing.

The heart is in a category all its own. It is not something that the king can possess, but is instead a locus of independent action. As the passage makes clear, the heart acts distinctly from how Suréna's body acts as the king's subject.

Suréna's insistence on the separation between his heart and his body recalls a trope of sixteenth-century resistance theory, which positions the heart, mind, and soul as interior spaces that the monarch cannot legitimately touch. The *Vindiciae contra tyrannos*, for example, explains how these interior spaces are subject only to divine authority:

> L'homme est composé de corps & d'ame. Dieu a formé le corps & inspiré l'âme en iceluy. Luy seul donc pouvoit s'attribuer & approprier le corps et l'ame de l'homme. Si de sa grace il a permis aux Rois d'user des corps & biens de leurs sujets, à la charge aussi de conserver iceux sujets: certainement les Rois doyvent penser que l'usage leur en est tellement permis, qu'il leur est cependant defendu d'en abuser.[51]

> Man is made up of body and soul: God formed the body and also infused the soul. Therefore He alone could use both of them with absolute right. But if He freely granted to kings that they might use the bodies and goods of their subjects only for the subjects' preservation, they ought clearly to remember that the use was conceded, not the abuse.[52]

The *Vindiciae* goes on to explain how God and the king extract different and distinct forms of tribute from man. "Le Roy prend cense ou tribut du corps & des choses acquises ou maintenues par le service & travail du corps. Dieu principalement exige son droit de l'ame, laquelle besongne par le corps" (The king takes tribute or dues from the body and from those things which are acquired or cultivated by the agency of the body).[53] Tributes of the soul include "les prieres, sacremens, predications de la pure doctrine . . . ce qu'on appelle service divin tant privé que public" (sacrifices, congregations, and divine worship both private and public), while tributes of the body include "les fruicts de la terre, les contributions de deniers, les autres charges reelles & personnelles" (renders in kind, money payments, and other dues both real and personal).[54] Because these two forms of tribute remain distinct, the treatise argues, "l'un ne nuist pas l'autre" (neither impedes the other).[55] God and the king enjoy entirely different purviews. Subjects can meet their obligations to the king and other temporal authorities without neglecting their duties to

God. Suréna makes a similar claim when distinguishing his heart from his blood. The hero's blood belongs to his body, which belongs to the king, but the king cannot claim possession of the hero's heart. But in *Suréna* the heart shelters romantic passion rather than religious devotion. The heart names the ties that bind man to woman rather than the human to the divine. *Suréna* refashions the right of resistance in the idiom of romantic love. As we will see, this romantic refashioning does not depoliticize the freedom of conscience associated with sixteenth-century resistance theory but instead works to expand this freedom's political reach.

Revealing Private Love

Although *Suréna*'s lovers articulate a strict separation between the private space of their hearts and the public space of the king's court, their love nevertheless impinges on this public space, accruing a kind of political power. The hidden passion that binds the two lovers together quickly becomes common knowledge through two forms of disclosure: the wordless vows exchanged between the lovers and their refusal explicitly to confess their love at court. Examining these two forms of disclosure helps us to understand how the lovers' private passion moves into the public sphere while still respecting absolutist requirement that subjects' inner freedom must not interfere with their external obedience.

The drama outlines the first form of disclosure—the silent vows exchanged between Suréna and Eurydice—through the latter's dialogue with her lady-in-waiting. Eurydice explains that she became lovestruck when she first encountered Suréna as an ambassador to her father's court:

> L'amour s'en mêla même, et tout son entretien
> Sembla m'offrir son cœur, et demander le mien.
> Il l'obtint, et mes yeux que charmait sa présence
> Soudain avec les siens en firent confidence;
> Ces muets truchements surent lui révéler
> Ce que je me forçais à lui dissimuler,
> Et les mêmes regards qui m'expliquaient sa flamme
> S'instruisaient dans les miens du secret de mon âme.
> Ses vœux y rencontraient d'aussi tendres désirs,
> Un accord imprévu confondait nos soupirs,
> Et d'un mot échappé la douceur hasardée
> Trouvait l'âme en tous deux toute persuadée.
> (*Suréna*, 1.1.47–58)

> Love, too, had part herein, and all his converse
> Appeared to offer me *his* heart and ask mine.
> He won it; and mine eyes, which he held spellbound,
> Met his with sudden, mutual understanding.
> These mute interpreters revealed unto him
> What I had forced myself to hide from him;
> And the same glance which told me of his love
> Read in my look the secret of my soul.
> I matched his longings with desires as tender;
> An unforeseen accord mingled our sighs;
> And sweet love, staked upon a word let fall,
> Found in each breast a heart completely yielded.[56]

Eurydice confesses her inability to hide her passion from Suréna. She also indicates that his experience paralleled hers. At first sight, they exchanged wordless vows, offered each other their hearts, and divulged the secrets of their souls. The language of this passage emphasizes sight over speech. The lovers communicate through glances: "mes yeux que charmait sa presence / Soudain avec les siens en firent confidence" (mine eyes, which he held spellbound, / Met his with sudden, mutual understanding). The lovers' eyes function as perfect windows into each other's heart. The eyes are "muets truchements" (mute interpreters), through which the true contents of the heart are immediately revealed. In each other's presence, the lovers can hold nothing back, even if they wished to do so, as underscored by the rhymes "presence" and "confidence" (presence and confidence) and "révéler and dissimuler" (reveal and dissimulate). Between Eurydice and Suréna, love is never hidden, but always disclosed. The lovers possess between them what Marc Fumaroli has called "a perfect transparency."[57]

What are the political implications of the perfect transparency that the lovers enjoy? For many of Corneille's readers, the lovers' commitment to preserving this shared space of secret love underscores the drama's profound separation of love and politics. Indeed, as we have seen, the lovers merely wish to be left alone, left free to harbor their love within the secret places of their hearts. They have little interest in worldly affairs and in the machinations of the court.[58] But the very moments when the lovers claim to remove themselves from politics demonstrate how any presumed separation between love and politics is untenable. As Eurydice's lines about the lovers' first meeting indicate, love has a part in politics. Suréna speaks politically in his capacity as ambassador, but as Eurydice's lines tell us, "L'amour s'en mêla même" (Love, too, had part herein). Love intervenes, even when it must be left aside.

The lovers' passion cannot help but get mixed up in matters of the state in large part due to the very public positions that they hold in the king's court: Suréna as an ambassador and Eurydice as the intended wife of the king's son, an object of exchange between the king and her father. The drama repeatedly figures Suréna and Eurydice's love as an obstacle to the king's designs. The king's son Orode, for example, admonishes Eurydice for her reticence and secrecy: "Qui connaît un obstacle au bonheur de l'État, / Tant qu'il le tient caché, commet un attentat" (5.3.1175–76) (One who knoweth / An obstacle to the welfare of the realm / Commits a felony when he conceals it).[59] Following this logic, Suréna and Eurydice's love cannot be divorced from the realm of politics. By creating obstacles that stand in the king's way, they threaten the state's welfare.

Suréna and Eurydice's passion, however, is political in more than this negative sense—as an obstacle to the king's designs. Their love also becomes an alternative form of politics, one that binds private liberty to public protest. As the drama unfolds it becomes clear that the lovers' true crime is not their private love as such, but rather the way that knowledge of their love reverberates through the court. If Suréna and Eurydice disclose their love to each other without saying a word, the lovers' refusal to speak publicly about their love allows the knowledge of their mutual affection to travel far beyond their private confidence. Everyone at court, including the king, is privy to their secret. A conversation between Eurydice and her lady-in-waiting reveals how the lovers' silence functions as a form of disclosure. Eurydice asks her lady-in-waiting to reveal who informed the king of her love for Suréna. The lady-in-waiting responds that Eurydice and Suréna have alerted the king themselves:

> Vous et lui, c'est son crime et le vôtre.
> Il refuse Mandane, et n'en veut aucune autre,
> On sait que vous aimez, on ignore l'amant,
> Madame, tout cela parle trop clairement.
> (*Suréna*, 4.2.1069–72)
>
> Thou and he; the crime is his
> And thine alike. He hath refused Mandane
> And doth not wish to wed anyone else.
> 'Tis known thou lovest; none knows who is thy lover,
> Madame; all these things tell too plain a story.[60]

By insisting so much on their privacy, Eurydice and Suréna inadvertently make their love public. As this passage suggests, silence speaks all too clearly: "tout cela parle trop clairement" (all these things tell too plain a story). Their refusal to disclose the objects of their affection does not produce ignorance or confusion, as one might expect, but instead a form of tacit knowledge. The king and the rest of the court gain knowledge of the lovers' affection, even though it is never explicitly declared or confessed.

In *Suréna* love acts independently of Suréna and Eurydice, a phenomenon that allows the hero to preserve his political legitimacy. We find love in action through both forms of disclosure: the wordless vows exchanged between the lovers and their refusal to confess their love at court. During the initial encounter between Suréna and Eurydice, love silently interrupts Suréna's diplomatic mission, intermingling itself with affairs of state. Throughout the drama, love speaks its own secret. Love broadcasts itself even as those who love refuse to speak its name. As the king's son reminds Suréna:

> L'amour dans sa prudence est toujours indiscret,
> À force de se taire il trahit son secret,
> Le soin de le cacher découvre ce qu'il cache,
> Et son silence dit tout ce qu'il craint qu'on sache.
> (*Suréna*, 4.4.1275–78)
>
> Love is always
> Indiscreet through its very cautiousness.
> In keeping silent it betrays its secret,
> Its care, in hiding that, shows what it hides.[61]

The rhymes "indiscret" and "secret" (indiscrete and secret) and "cache" and "sache" (hide and know) underscore love's inability to contain itself. Love cannot help but trespass on the boundary between the private spaces of the lovers' hearts and the public spaces of the king's court. As a result, Eurydice and Suréna remain model subjects of absolutism; they uphold the absolutist separation between the private and the public. Love undermines this separation and impinges on public life.

The Death of the Hero

The exposure of Suréna and Eurydice's love upsets the balance of power between the hero and the king, engendering a political crisis. If the contents of the hero's heart are common knowledge, then the hero's subjective independence from the sovereign is all too clear. Throughout the drama

Suréna maintains that it is his military prowess—rather than his love—that threatens the king. "Mon crime véritable est d'avoir aujourd'hui / Plus de nom que mon Roi, plus de vertu que lui" (5.2.1511–12). (My real crime is that I have more renown / Today and greater qualities than he).[62] According to Suréna, the king is clearly concerned with a discrepancy in their respective reputations. Although the king is officially the sovereign, everyone knows that Suréna's military strength has kept the kingdom safe. The sovereign is known to depend on the noble subject, a situation that makes the king's rule precarious. In the following scene Suréna repeats that his true crime is his glory rather than his love—"Mon vrai crime est ma gloire, et non pas mon amour" (5.3.1651) (My true crime is my glory, not my love)[63]—insisting that his public standing rather than his private sentiment has sparked the king's ire. In so doing, Suréna's echoes Nicomède's claim that his public glory threatens a jealous king. As we know, however, in this tragedy love cannot be separated from political concerns. Private sentiments do not stay hidden within each subject's heart. Instead, they are made public, available for all to see. By exposing the contents of Suréna's heart, the drama presents him as a subject with his own will and desires rather than as a mere instrument of monarchical authority. Shoring up the hero's personal strength, private love operates as a source of public glory, a glory that makes the hero into the king's rival.

The staging of Suréna's death reinforces the political charge of the hero's love and points us toward how, even in death, he holds open the possibility of legitimate resistance. As I have noted, the hero's death is not depicted on stage but is instead recounted by Eurydice's lady-in-waiting:

> À peine du Palais il sortait dans la rue,
> Qu'une flèche a parti d'une main inconnue,
> Deux autres l'ont suivie, et j'ai vu ce vainqueur,
> Comme si toutes trois l'avaient atteint au cœur,
> Dans un ruisseau de sang tomber mort sur la place.
> (*Suréna*, 5.5.1713–17)
>
> Scarce had he left the palace, and reached the street,
> When from an unknown hand an arrow sped.
> Two others followed it, and I saw this conqueror,
> As if all three of them had struck his heart,
> Fall, in a pool of blood, dead on the spot.[64]

Suréna is struck down in an act that trades in both secrecy and spectacle. The arrows are surreptitiously launched by "une main inconnue" (an unknown hand). The archer remains unseen. The archer's surreptitious act, however, creates a scene. The arrows strike Suréna just as he leaves the palace and enters the public square. Suréna falls for all to see. A public pedagogy is at work in this moment: Suréna's death is an occasion for the display of monarchical power. The lady-in-waiting continues, "Et je pense avoir même entendu quelque voix / Nous crier qu'on apprît à dédaigner les Rois" (5.5.1719–20) (And I e'en thought I heard some voice cry out / To us that one is taught thus to flout monarchs).[65] Those who see—and hear of—the hero's fall are instructed not to follow his example.

The combination of spectacle and secrecy that attends Suréna's death raises questions about Suréna's political legitimacy. If the king wishes to make an example of this hero, why obscure the arrows' origins? The optics of Suréna's death suggest that although the hero has committed no real crime he must be killed anyway. As we have seen, Suréna merely defends his interior liberty, his freedom to love Eurydice in private. But once it becomes public knowledge, Suréna's love exposes his subjective independence from the king, calling into question the king's authority. The right to private love becomes a public menace to the king, as evidenced by the three arrows' ostensible target, that is, the hero's heart: "Comme si toutes trois l'avaient atteint au cœur" (As if all three of them had struck his heart). Since the hero has openly committed no wrong, the scene of his death must be shrouded in mystery. Suréna's death looks neither quite like an execution, through which the king might publicly make the hero's death into a show of royal force, nor quite like an assassination, through which the king might secretly dispense with a rival. In *Suréna* the hidden spectacle of the hero's fall permits the monarch to make an example of him without too closely associating himself with the death of a seemingly virtuous subject.

Communally Constituted Heroism

In sixteenth-century resistance theory the people's collective authority authorizes public representative's speech and actions. *Suréna* similarly suggests that the collective legitimizes the hero's political force. Just as Suréna's private liberty extends beyond the interior space of his heart, so his political power stretches beyond his limits as an individual subject. The hero's love reveals his subjective independence from the king, and this love, by its very nature, is shared. It is the love shared between Suréna and Eurydice that transgresses the boundary between private and public space. Through the drama's dynamics of secrecy and revelation, their shared love circumscribes the king's authority.

Made public through shared love, Suréna's interior freedom does not die with him, but instead becomes a collective good that others may draw on in his wake. The tragedy ends with a dialogue between Eurydice and the hero's sister, Palmis. Hearing the news of Suréna's fall, Eurydice immediately wishes to join her lover in death, stating "Généreux Suréna, reçois toute mon âme" (5.5.1734) (Noble [Suréna], receive all my soul!).[66] For her part, the sister calls for the cessation of mourning and promises vengeance: "Suspendez ces douleurs qui pressent de mourir, / Grand Dieux, et dans les maux où vous m'avez plongée / Ne souffrez point ma mort que je ne sois vengée" (5.5.1736–38) (Lighten, great gods, this weight of mortal grief; / And in the woe in which my heart is plunged, / Let me not die until I am avenged).[67] The women who survive Suréna extend his legacy. Their dialogue reiterates the connection between the hero's love and glory, with Eurydice insisting that their passion lives on and with Palmis maintaining that his honor endures. Together, women insist on the public glory of Suréna's private passion.

Through these forms of feminine endurance, *Suréna* reworks a gendered dynamic common to many of Corneille's tragedies. As Katherine Ibbett has noted, in dramas such as *Horace* (1640) men take action off stage while women stand by, marking time for their return. Rather than simply repeating familiar tropes of heroic masculine activity and of feminine passivity, Corneille's scenes of waiting women help to complicate our understanding of heroic action as such. "Although [the women] cannot act," Ibbett writes, "they possess an importance that suggests that heroic action can be understood only in relation to a wider community. In the bodies of these bystanders, *Horace* marks the remainder, signifying a gravely political endurance that nuances our understanding of heroic action."[68] Standing as a remainder, Corneille's women point a way forward from the hero's loss.[69] In *Suréna* the women boldly press forward in the hero's wake, Eurydice with her pledges of everlasting love and Palmis with her vow to avenge her brother's death. Their dialogue offers the possibility of continued action, though Suréna himself can no longer act. Eurydice's and Palmis's pledges also call attention to how feminine love and devotion underpin Suréna's heroism well before the hero's death. Throughout the drama Eurydice's love and Palmis's devotion extend beyond the private sphere, serving to embolden the hero and broaden his opposition.

A wider community of the king's subjects also helps to constitute Suréna's heroism: the people of Parthia. This population remains a kind of spectral presence in the drama; it is never seen but often quoted. Suréna warns the king, for example, that the people have been grumbling about the treaty between Parthia and Armenia. Suréna suggests that Eurydice's mysterious affection for someone other than the prince might solve a political problem for the king, given that the Parthian people seem to be irritated by the impending marriage. The hero suggests that the people's grumbling may diminish if the wedding does not take place after all. Dismissing this idea, the king chides Suréna for his impertinence: "Est-ce au Peuple, est-ce à vous, Suréna, de me dire, / Pour lui donner des Rois, quel sang je dois élire" (3.3.938–39) (Is it for the people, it is for thee, [Suréna], / To tell me from whose blood to give them kings?).[70] During this exchange, it is Suréna, rather than the king, who attends to the people's opinions and sentiments. The king resembles a tyrant who is indifferent to the people. Suréna resembles a public representative who, without renouncing his own interests, speaks and acts on behalf of the public good.

Suréna's audience also shapes the hero's political force. Readers and spectators are privy to the lovers' secret from the very first scene, when Eurydice declares her love for Suréna to Ormène. In the first acts of the drama, this knowledge creates dramatic irony: the audience knows more than the king and his son, who must guess the objects of Eurydice's and Suréna's affection. But as soon as the royal father and son gain this knowledge, the sense of dramatic irony falls away. Staged characters, unseen collectives, and the tragedy's audience all share the same information. By allowing members of the audience to share in the open secret from the beginning, the drama makes them privileged confidents. The audience comes to function as a collective, off-staged coconspirator.

The political consequences of the audience's knowledge are ambiguous. On the one hand, by making the audience complicit in the open secret, the drama positions them as part of the community for whom Suréna's death is designed to serve as an example. We thus might read the play as a cautionary tableau for audiences living under absolutism. Although absolutist subjects were nominally granted liberty of conscience, this liberty was not to infringe on politics, as Suréna's inevitably does.[71] On the other hand, through its disclosure of the hero's private love, the tragedy makes its audience complicit in a configuration of politics that undoes the absolutist division of public and private life. *Suréna* makes the hero's secret love into a political resource available to those who experience his fall. In so doing, Corneille's final tragedy points us toward theater's particular political potential, as a genre in which interior deliberations and sentiments are placed on display. In theater, that which is private is not hidden away but is instead offered to the public for examination and reflection, a dynamic that makes possible Suréna's communally constituted heroism.

Suréna brings into relief a sense of political ambiguity not usually associated with the historical moment during which it premiered. Corneille's final drama seems on the one hand to mark the triumph of absolutism with the hero's fatal fall. On the other hand, the drama also suggests how absolutist divisions between the private and the public could be subtly undermined, even as they were respected. *Suréna* demonstrates how ties between subjective rights and the collective authority persist, even when these ties are denied.

By sustaining ties that bind the individual and collective dimensions of the right of resistance throughout the seventeenth century, *Suréna* and *Nicomède* help us to recognize how collective forces continue to shape individual rights and responsibilities in our contemporary moment. Our current conception of individual rights is that of liberal political philosophy, which finds its roots in the eighteenth century. Self-possessed and autonomous, the individual of liberal political philosophy enjoys a kind of negative liberty: his or her right to life and property is limited only by the laws of the nation, which ensure the liberty of all.[72] As Mitchell Greenberg and Hélène Merlin-Kajman have noted, Corneille's heroes present us with models of noble individuals who appears to prefigure modern autonomy with their claims of self-sovereignty.[73] With Nicomède's insistence on his apparent authority and Suréna's insistence on his interior freedom, these heroes stand (and fall) as precursors to the rights-bearing individual at the center of modern, liberal political philosophy.

As I noted in the introduction, while this concept of the rights-bearing individual was explicitly developed in opposition to absolutism, it nonetheless followed a path laid out by absolutism in its concept of the individual as a discrete and autonomous entity.[74] Although the individual subject of sixteenth-century political thought had a profoundly communitarian constitution, in following the path laid out by absolutism, the modern rights paradigm lost sight of how the political power of the individual depends on social relationships and attachments. In dismantling the conceptual framework of the right of resistance, absolutism set the stage for the emergence of the modern, individualist model of rights. Casting the Cornelian hero as the kind of public representative that appears in early modern resistance theory, as opposed to a precursor to the modern subject of rights, brings into view an alternative model subjectivity that privileges individual liberty without denying attachment. In other words, *Suréna* demonstrates how individual rights are always also rights of relation.

CHAPTER FIVE

The Savior

Racine's *Esther* (1689) tells the story of the biblical queen whose Jewish identity is hidden from her husband, King Ahasuerus of Persia. Esther's origins remain a secret until the King announces his intentions to execute all the Jews in his kingdom. In an attempt to dissuade the king from carrying out this plan, Esther appears before him and reveals her Jewishness: "J'ose vous implorer et pour ma propre vie, / Et pour les tristes jours d'un Peuple infortuné / Qu'à périr avec moi vous avez condamné" (3.4.1029–31) (I dare to beg you, both from my own life / And for the sad days of a wretched people, / Whom you yourself condemned to die with me).[1] Esther's revelation that her own fate is tied to that of the Jewish people has its intended effect. Realizing that a massacre of the Jews would cost him his own wife, the king nullifies his order.

Esther's revelation and the king's response not only save lives but also transform the moral and political valences associated with being a Jew. But this transformation does not happen immediately. The king's first reaction to Esther's revelation is incredulity, the result of the incongruity he perceives between her apparent character and that of the Jews as a people:

> Vous la fille d'un Juif? Hé quoi! Tout ce que j'aime,
> Cette Esther, l'innocence, et la sagesse même,
> Que je croyais du Ciel les plus chères amours,
> Dans cette source impure aurait puisé ses jours?
> (*Esther*, 3.4.1036–39)

> What, the daughter of a Jew? You? All I love,
> My Esther, soul of innocence and wisdom,
> Whom I believed the dearest love from heaven,
> Could draw her life from such an impure source?[2]

To descend from a Jewish father, the king states, is to come from an impure source, a source that contrasts sharply with Esther's presumed innocence. The king's solution to this incongruity is not to reevaluate Esther, and thus condemn her to death with the rest of her people, but instead to reevaluate the Jewish people as a whole. He resolves the dissonance between her innocence and her impure lineage by removing this impurity through royal decree. The king proclaims the Jews to be a people deserving the same honor and respect as the Persians themselves. Esther's apparent innocence refashions the status of an entire people.

Eve Kosofsky Sedgwick has argued that Esther's "coming out" as a Jew captures something of the fantasies surrounding the act of coming out as gay or lesbian in the twentieth century. Reading Racine's tragedy (via Proust), Sedgwick states that the "revelation of identity in the space of intimate love effortlessly overturns an entire public systematics of the natural and the unnatural, the pure and the impure."[3] Sedgwick emphasizes how much Esther's success seductively dramatizes the possibility that a personal coming out might engender the reversal of social stigma on a grand scale. By vulnerably exposing her true self to power, Esther prompts a transformation in the social structure that power enforces. Despite the differences between the Jewish and the sexual closet, Sedgwick explains that she "lingers" with Racine's *Esther* precisely because of its affective force.[4] The king's love for Esther extends beyond their marriage to encompass all the Jews. *Esther*'s promise is that a well-loved individual's coming out disrupts the status quo, creating a better future for his or her once imperiled community.

In this chapter I linger some more with Racine's *Esther* and its relationship to questions of political survival by reading *Esther* and Racine's other biblical tragedy *Athalie* as plays that ask us to reconsider the affective charge associated with scenes of revelation in which a virtuous figure has a salvific effect on an entire community. As many queer theorists including Sedgwick have noted, these scenes of revelation, while highly seductive, ultimately lack a transformative political force. The flows of feeling in these scenes—whether from the king to Esther to all the Jews, or from an unenlightened parent to a queer child to "the queer community" more broadly—serve to reinforce normative social structures and a liberal model of politics. In other words, these scenes help to expand our notion of what a rights-bearing individual might look like, who a rights-bearing individual might love, or how a rights-bearing individual might pray, but they but they do not necessarily allow us to question the structural constitution of the rights-bearing individual itself.

Rather than turn away from scenes of revelation altogether, I argue instead that we must widen our view to situate these scenes within a broader play of affective relationships between individual subjects and the collectives to which they belong. Racine's biblical tragedies feature a virtuous subject who acts as a savior to her or his people. In *Esther*, as we have seen, the queen's unveiling of her Jewishness saves the Jews from extermination in Persia. In *Athalie* the discovery that Athaliah's grandson Joash still lives reignites Jewish hopes that they will survive her apostasy and tyranny. But the effects of the disclosure of both Esther's and Joash's identity are not unidirectional. These savior figures do not merely affect, but are also affected by, their familial and communal attachments. The public disclosure of the saviors' once hidden identity, while extending virtue to Esther's and Joash's attachments, threaten at the same time to corrupt these saviors themselves. Reading *Esther* and *Athalie* in light of the multidirectional flows of feeling that transmit vice as well as virtue helps us to imagine political futures that do not simply repeat the structures of liberalism, which govern our present.

To bring into relief the affective dynamics between savior and saved in *Esther* and *Athalie*, I consider the historical moment in which these plays were initially performed. Commissioned from Racine by Louis XIV's second wife, Françoise d'Aubigné, Marquise de Maintenon, *Esther* and *Athalie* were first performed in 1689 and 1691, respectively, by students at Saint-Cyr, Madame de Maintenon's school for girls from impoverished noble families. The tragedies premiered at Saint-Cyr in the wake of Louis XIV's Revocation of the Edict of Nantes (1685), an act that rekindled memories of the previous century's religious wars, legitimized hostilities against Protestants—thousands were killed, forced to convert to Catholicism, or driven into exile—and also renewed questions about political legitimacy, representation, and the possibility of resistance. Katherine Ibbett has demonstrated that this historical moment was one in which the Protestants and Catholics used emotional rhetoric to draw and redraw the contested boundaries of the Christian community.[5]

In addition to considering *Esther* and *Athalie*'s present, I also draw from the plays' future and past. As we will see, the post-Revocation moment reanimated ideas from sixteenth-century resistance theory, while also calling these ideas into question. In chapter 1 I examined how resistance treatises such as the *Vindiciae contra tyrannos* argued that all Christians were united in the body of Christ and were thus united as an emotional community with shared notions of virtue and vice. The legitimacy of political leaders or divinely inspired public representatives could thus be determined by evidence of their affective orientation to the people.

Rhetorically claiming the unity of Christendom during the religious wars allowed the treatises to ignore how fractured this emotional community had already become. As a result, they appear to take the stability of shared virtue for granted. In the pages that follow, I demonstrate how the performance history and poetic structures of Racine's biblical tragedies amplify the political ambiguity that—despite the unifying rhetoric—is already inherent in sixteenth-century resistance treaties by raising questions about the extent to which affective evidence of a public representative's virtue or vice is enough to determine that representative's political legitimacy.

Performing *Esther*, Corrupting Innocence

We have more information about the performance history of *Esther* than most seventeenth-century plays. The first performances of Racine's tragedy took place during the winter of 1689 at La maison royale de Saint-Louis, a boarding school for girls located in the village of Saint-Cyr, located about four kilometers west of Versailles. Run by Madame de Maintenon, the school at Saint-Cyr received students from noble families whose fortunes had dwindled, and the school functioned in particular as a place of education and refuge for the daughters of military officers who had died or who had lost a great deal of money in service to the king. An official genealogist verified prospective students' noble birth to ensure that they came from worthy families.[6] Once admitted, most of the girls entered the school between the ages of seven and twelve and remained until their twentieth birthday, at which point they either married or entered convents. Madame de Maintenon devised an educational program specifically befitting these young charges. She writes in her memoires that, given their fathers' service, the girls at Saint-Cyr should be raised "dans les principes d'une véritable et solide piété, et reçoivent toutes les instructions qui peuvent convenir à leur naissance et à leur sexe" (according to the principles of a true and stalwart piety, and should receive all the instruction that would befit their birth and sex).[7]

Esther arrived at Saint-Cyr when Madame de Maintenon commissioned Racine to write a piece for the girls to perform that would further their pious education. Relating Madame de Maintenon's wishes in the tragedy's preface, Racine explains that he was to create "sur quelque sujet de piété et de morale une espèce de Poème, où le chant fût mêlé avec le récit; le tout lié par une action qui rendît la chose plus vive et moins capable d'ennuyer" (on some pious and edifying theme, a sort of poem where song might be mingled with speech, the whole to be bound together by a plot to make the work more alive and less likely to bore).[8] Correspondingly, Racine's version of the biblical story of Queen Esther includes choral odes so that the pupils at Saint-Cyr would have plenty of opportunities to sing as well as to recite verse.

Conceived as a means of instructing and pleasing Madame de Maintenon's students, the initial staging of *Esther* benefited from relatively high production values. Jean-Baptiste Moreau, *maître de musique de la chambre du roi*, composed the music. The girls wore beautiful costumes, and lavish sets created by Jean Berain adorned the room off their dormitories that served as a theater.[9] The entire endeavor enjoyed the support and attention of Louis XIV, who immediately praised the production after attending the first performance on January 26, 1689. Other illustrious attendees at this initial performance and those that followed included a select group of nobles as well as prominent political and literary figures, such as King James II of England and Marie de Rabutin-Chantal, Marquise de Sévigné. Invitations to performances quickly became highly sought after within the upper echelons of French society.[10]

Esther initially seemed to call for a straightforward expression of piety, with little of the moral complexity of Racine's earlier work. This tendency to "sacralize" the play, as Richard Scholar has noted, persisted well into the twentieth century, with Racine's mention of Madame de Maintenon's explicitly pious commission in his preface operating as an interpretive last word.[11] On one level, the play itself demands this interpretation, especially in light of its prologue, a monologue during which a personified Piety addresses the audience, lauds Louis XIV, and endorses the virtuous curriculum at Saint-Cyr:

> Du séjour bienheureux de la Divinité,
> Je descends dans ce lieu par la Grâce habité.
> L'Innocence s'y plaît ma compagne éternelle,
> Et n'a point sous les cieux d'asile plus fidèle.
> (*Esther*, 1–4)
>
> From blest abodes where the Divinity resides
> I come down to this house where Grace abides:
> Here finds sweet Innocence, my sister twin,
> No safer place on earth to wander in.[12]

Piety frames the drama by casting Saint-Cyr as a fitting location to stage the story of Esther. She deems the school worthy of her presence, as well as that of her companion, Innocence. The play begins with the blessings of these two sanctified visitors, which link *Esther* to Madame de Maintenon's school and its students. The girls at Saint-Cyr are cast as worthy performers of Esther's story in light of the necessary virtue required of them as Madame de Maintenon's charges. In turn, performing the play provides them with the suitable pedagogical activity of emulating Esther's exemplary character.

The logic of virtuous association that binds together *Esther* and its performers in Racine's text also appears in accounts of the play's performance. Those who attended performances such as Madame de Sévigné consistently praised the girls for their expressions of innocence and their ability to move the audience.[13] These accounts of *Esther*'s performance, however, also evince a persistent anxiety about the need to protect the girls' virtue and ward off their corruption. The performances continually exceeded Madame de Maintenon's pedagogical intentions, leading the queen to attempt a series of corrective measures, to little avail. The queen's commission of *Esther* from Racine was reportedly itself a corrective, as her pupils had responded too passionately to profane dramas such as Racine's *Andromaque*.[14] Once performances of *Esther* were underway, a lead actress performed so well that she threatened the production's innocent simplicity. The performances as a whole were so successful that they reportedly seduced men and inspired clerical condemnation. And the girls themselves were collectively so taken with performing that they not only missed its pedagogical value but also jeopardized the educational project of Saint-Cyr as a whole. This series of correctives suggests a need to reign in an activity with a powerful potential. The drama's capacity for instruction was vast, and yet it repeatedly exceeded its initial intentions.

Although the "*Esther* debacle" is well known, I revisit this episode of early modern performance history because it so powerfully demonstrates the affective complexity inherent in the presentation of virtue. After seeing a performance of *Esther*, for example, Madame de Sévigné writes to her daughter, Madame de Grignan, on February 28, 1689, "Tout y est simple, tout y est innocent, tout y est sublime et touchant. Cette fidélité de l'histoire sainte donne du respect; tous les chants convenables aux paroles, qui sont tirées des Psaumes ou de la Sagesse, et mis dans le sujet, sont d'une beauté qu'on ne soutient pas sans larmes" (Everything about [the production] is simple, everything is innocent, everything is sublime and moving. This fidelity to biblical history inspires respect. All the songs fitting the words are derived from Psalms or the Book of Wisdom and are arranged with such beauty that one cannot listen without crying).[15] For Sévigné, tears function as the inevitable reaction to such a spectacle. It is impossible not to be moved by the innocence and simplicity with which the girls deliver this biblical story. In this case, the production's need to move its audience remains in balance with its insistence on the innocence of its performers and the sanctity of its subject matter. To maintain this innocent quality, the production must be "touchant," but not overly so. In both letters Sévigné appeals to simplicity as the quality that will ensure that innocence is not performed so powerfully as to corrupt it.

Maintaining the right balance of innocence and pathos while performing *Esther* proved a difficult task. Before seeing the drama, Sévigné writes several times of her desire to do so, chronicling the artistic and social buzz that surrounded it. These earlier letters serve as an archive of the drama's reception as an expression of piety and as a pedagogical exercise. Sévigné's letters also indicate how theatrical prowess threatened the expression of virtue. In one of the letters that predate her viewing of the drama, Sévigné tells of a casting change that speaks to the ways in which the drama's various social and institutional functions sometimes strained against each other.[16] On February 11, 1689, she writes to her daughter, "On continuera à représenter *Esther*. Mme de Caylus, qui en était la Champmeslé, ne joue plus. Elle faisait trop bien, elle était trop touchante. On ne veut que la simplicité toute pure de ces petits âmes innocentes" (The performances of *Esther* will continue. Madame de Caylus, who was the play's Champmeslé, is no longer in the role. She was too good at it, her performance too moving. One wants from now on only the purest simplicity of these young, innocent souls).[17] Comparing Madame de Caylus (who happened to be Madame de Maintenon's niece) with Marie Champmeslé, one of the more renowned interpreters of Racine's profane drama, Sévigné suggests that the young woman possessed a theatrical talent that had begun to work against the drama's expression of innocence. The ability of these amateur actresses to affect the audience was "trop touchante" and had disrupted the delicate balance required of the production.

Concern about the play's emotional force also arose from the order of women running Saint-Cyr, the *dames de Saint-Louis*, as well as from Madame de Maintenon herself. Madame de Pérou, who served as the group's annalist, recounts for example that, after the first few performances, the dames de Saint-Louis mostly abstained from attending, finding their time better served in prayer or other devotional activities. Her accounting of the dames' preferences should not, however, be interpreted as a wholesale rejection of the girls' theatrical activities. While certain clerics raised objections about the entire endeavor, citing the undesirability of theatrical performance in general, as well as invoking the particular risks of presenting young female bodies that possess the power to move their audience, Madame de Pérou instead characterizes performances of *Esther* as an innocent pleasure.[18] Indeed, she argues that the performances are innocent enough that the dames de Saint-Louis who did continue to attend "étoient bien plus occupées de [la présence de Dieu], que tout ce qui s'offroit à leurs yeux" (were much more occupied with God's presence than with all that was presented before their eyes).[19] According to Pérou, the spectacle remained innocent precisely because its powers of distraction could be avoided or resisted.

The production ultimately fell prey to its own charms. The girls' ability to move their audience proved too strong a threat to their innocence and virtue. The performances had become a major distraction if not to the dames' devotion, then to the girls' instruction, not only because these performances demanded considerable time and energy but also because girls' attraction to performing and the attention the play afforded them began to affect their comportment. The dames de Saint-Louis complained that the girls "devinrent fières, dédaigneuses, hautaines, peu dociles" (became proud, disdainful, haughty, and intractable).[20] For her part, Madame de Maintenon had trouble disciplining them and coaxing them to do their lessons. Intended as a tool to serve the school's pedagogical aims, *Esther* became an obstacle to attaining them. As a result, Madame de Maintenon reduced the frequency of their performances and more tightly limited their audience before eventually ending the performances all together.

The scandal of *Esther*'s first performances tells us something about the performance of virtue more generally. Virtue, like the innocence of Madame de Maintenon's schoolgirls, is difficult to maintain when put on display. The girls' apparent innocence was what so powerfully moved their audiences. But by exposing the girls' innocence to public view, the play also exposed this innocence to the social dynamics of the court, to the condemnation of clerics, and to the romantic and sexual desires of men. The girls' apparent innocence, as a sign of their virtue, offered affective proof of their ability to piously represent *Esther*. The making apparent, or revelation of this innocence, however, threatened to destroy it.[21]

Esther's performance history also suggests something counterintuitive about the temporality of innocence's corruption. We tend to think about efforts to stem corruption or contagion as aimed at stopping something that has started, as attempts to contain a menace that threatens the future. The measures taken at Saint-Cyr to contain the frivolity and idleness engendered by theatrical performances seem to operate according to this timeline, with the past, present, and future existing in linear succession. While contagion may spread in succession, however, the fears that accompany it possess a different temporality. The menace presented by infectious performances of *Esther* might be thought of as simultaneously originary and of the future. Efforts to contain this menace work as prophylactics as well as correctives. These measures attempt to address that which is to come, as well as that which has occurred, binding together future and past in the concerns of the present. The repeated assertions of the girls' innocence, coupled with the often expressed need to protect their virtue, suggest that the threat of contamination is a threat of the future, a future that has already begun.

What does the twisted temporality of *Esther*'s performance history mean for our understanding of the play's configuration of a better and brighter future for marginalized communities like that of the Jews in Ahasuerus's kingdom or, for that matter, for queer communities in the twentieth and twenty-first century? In *Esther* the heroine emerges as a public representative whose virtue will secure her people's future. Before Esther reveals her Jewishness to the king, the threat of impending violence to the Jewish people constitutes a threat to the very possibility of future persistence. "Quel carnage de toute parts!" (1.5.316) (What slaughter all around!)[22] sings a member of the chorus of young Israelite girls who act as Esther's handmaidens:

> On égorge à la fois les enfants, les vieillards;
> Et la sœur, et le frère;
> Et la fille, et la mère;
> Le fils dans les bras de son père.
> Que de corps entassés! Que de membres épars,
> Privés de sépulture!
> (*Esther*, 1.5.317–22)

> Old men and babes are murdered found,
> Sister and brother,
> Daughter and mother,
> The son in the arms of his father!
> What battered corpses, limbs scattered and bound,
> With no one to bury.[23]

The young Israelite sings of future violence in the present tense, as if the destruction of her people imposes a rhetorical limit. In these lines, the total destruction of a family—"la sœur," "le frère," "la fille," "la mère," "le fils," "son père"—stands in metonymically for the destruction of the Jews as such. The scattering of limbs, which literally figures the dissolution of the body, also represents the dissolution of a community, obliterating any possible future. The reversal of fortune that Esther's revelation precipitates not only saves the day, but the days to come as well. By *Esther*'s end, the once imperiled Jews have been saved. Previously considered the part of kingdom that had to be destroyed, the Jews are transformed into the most favored of all Ahasuerus's subjects.[24] The impossibility of survival gives way to the assurance of future persistence.

For Lucien Goldmann, *Esther*'s reversal of fortune is so complete that the play cannot be called tragic. Unlike Racine's earlier plays, Goldmann argues, *Esther* and *Athalie* do not offer us a glimpse into the tragic worldview of Jansenist theology. Rather than displaying the extent to which God has renounced the world, as Racine's profane tragedies had done so well, *Esther* and *Athalie* are examples of sacred drama, of "*God present and apparent*".[25] By the time *Esther* concludes, God's will has been done in the world itself. It is true that within the drama God's presence secures the Jews future. As Richard Scholar has noted, however, there is more to the story. Objecting to the long-standing "sacralization" of Racine's *Esther*, Scholar notes that the biblical story of Esther contains two different explanations for the king's favorable reaction to Esther's revelation. The Greek version cites divine intervention and suggests that Esther's faith and the prayers of Esther and her people made this divine intervention possible. In contrast, the Hebrew version emphasizes a cycle of vengeance and retribution, interpreting the transformation of the Jews' social status as but another revolution of this cycle. Racine's *Esther*, Scholar observes, incorporates elements from both the Greek and the Hebrew version. In so doing, the play presents conflicting notions of grace and providence. Whereas in the Greek account all will is God's will, the Hebrew account makes room for human will, and thus for political machination. *Esther*'s political dimensions, Scholar argues, cannot be decoupled from its presentation of piety and innocence since many of the tragedy's plot points appear to be both miraculous and mortally calculated. The play suggests, for example, that the king's fortunate selection of Esther as his bride from scores of other candidates could be the work of her uncle Mardochée, or that of God himself. Viewed in this light, Esther's exceptionality is man-made as well as divine. It is both political and pure.[26]

Accounts of *Esther*'s first performances parallel the text's combination of divine providence and human politics. As we have seen, these accounts evince the inevitable comingling of the innocent and worldly, the pure and corrupt. Presented by even the most virtuous of performers in Madame de Maintenon's young charges, this specially commisioned play "sur quelque sujet de piété et de morale" (on some pious and edifying theme), engenders all sorts of unexpected vice. As we have seen,

Madame de Maintenon, the dames de Saint-Louis, and members of the audience such as Madame de Sévigné all praise the productions for its innocence and virtue while attempting to ward off the unintended effects of the production's already present future. They simply cannot protect their Edenic stage and its inhabitants from the arrival of sin. In this way, the performance history of *Esther* suggests that the play carries more of a Jansenist charge than Goldmann admits. The schoolgirls are doomed from the beginning to corrupt and be corrupted.

With its combination of virtue and vice, the performance history of *Esther* points us toward a vision of the future that is much less clear than that heralded by the play's sacralization. Rather than operating only as the bright time of salvation, the future also functions as the dark time of corruption. By offering a more ambiguous future, *Esther* shows us how a community might undergo a change in perceived status from corrupt to innocent without being fully incorporated into existing regimes of power, as the liberal model that Sedgwick points to in her comparison of the queer and Jewish closets would demand. By turning to Racine's second biblical tragedy, *Athalie*, I demonstrate how this more ambiguous vision of the future offers a less politically rigid mode of communal persistence than a straightforward exchange of vice and virtue would allow.

Athalie: The Virtues of Resistance

A few years after the scandal that plagued the performances of *Esther*, Madame de Maintenon commissioned another biblical drama from Racine. Conceived as a corrective to the excesses of *Esther*, the production of *Athalie* boasted no elaborate sets or costumes. Instead, the girls recited Racine's lines and sang to Moreau's music wearing their typical school uniforms during the first performance in 1691 and the few performances that followed.[27] Although Louis XIV and several dignitaries attended these recitations, and rumors circulated that *Athalie* was just as beautiful and well constructed as *Esther*, Racine's second biblical tragedy was not the social phenomenon its predecessor had been. Given *Athalie*'s scaled-back production values, concerns about the morality of the girl's performance and the corruption of their innocence did not circulate the way they had during performances of *Esther*. Instead, parallel concerns about the corruption of virtue reside within Racine's dramatic text. Centering on the need to protect an innocent child, who, like Esther is positioned as the savior of his people, *Athalie* stages an anxiety about the relationship between the need to display affective evidence of a would-be savior's virtue and the fear that to display affective evidence is to risk its corruption.

By raising concerns about the exposure of affective evidence, Racine's *Athalie* complicates the version of the biblical story that appears in a key sixteenth-century resistance treatise, the *Vindiciae*. As I noted in chapter 1, the *Vindiciae* frequently turns to biblical examples to build its case for legitimate resistance to tyranny. The treatise references Athaliah during a discussion about the possible virtues of political conspiracy. The *Vindiciae* states that the queen Athaliah was clearly a tyrant. She came to power by illegitimately seizing the throne from her male descendants and then ruled illegitimately as a woman: "La Loy n'appeloit pas les femmes au gouvernement du royaume de Juda" (the law of the Judaic kingdom did not call women to the sceptre).[28] She turned away from the Jewish God and embraced the prophets of Baal, welcoming their idolatrous practices of worship in her realm, and she committed "une unfinité de maux" (innumerable crimes).[29] Arguably the most striking manifestation of her tyranny was her order to have all her descendants killed. The *Vindiciae* states: "La Roine Athalia[h], apres la mort de son fils Ochozias Roy de Juda, donna ordre de faire mourir toute la race royale" (After the death of her son Ahaziah, king of Judah, Queen Athaliah endeavored to extirpate almost the whole royal line).[30] With her descendants destroyed, Athaliah continued her rule without fear of a rival claim to the throne. Yet one of her descendants survived the massacre. Her grandson Joash was rescued by his aunt, Jehoshabeath, and raised secretly within the confines of the Jewish temple by Jehoshabeath and her husband Jehoiada, the temple's high priest. Joash's survival allowed the high priest to hope that Athaliah's tyranny might one day be overthrown. For the *Vindiciae*, Athaliah's tyranny justified legitimate resistance.

The *Vindiciae* identifies Jehoiada, the high priest, as a public representative who could oppose tyranny on the people's behalf. "[Il] n'estoit point un homme privé & particulier, ains souverain Sacrificateur, à qui lors apartenoit la conoissance des causes civiles" ([He] was not a private individual, but the high priest to whom cognisance even of civil matters then pertained).[31] Given his status as a public representative, the high priest of the Jewish temple did not have to bide his time in hopes that Athaliah's rule would come to an end. Instead, the high priest actively cultivated resistance to the queen's tyranny. "Le Souverain Sacrificateur [Jehoiada], mari de [Jehoshabeath], ayant fait secrettement une ligue et une conjuration avec les principaux du royaume, fait sacrer et couronner Roy . . . [Joash], agé de sept ans. Il ne se contente pas seulement de chasser la Roine mere du trone Royal, mais aussi la fait mettre à mort, et racle incontinent l'idolatrie de Baal" (Jehoiada the high priest and husband of Jehoshabeath, after secretly devising a plan with the princes of Israel and having duly established a league arranged the anointing and coronation of the seven-year-old Joash. Not only did he cast down the mother from her throne, but killed her and without delay destroyed the idolatry of Baal).[32] The high priest organized a conspiracy against Athaliah from within her government, had her killed, installed her young descendant on the throne, and banished the worship of Baal from the kingdom.[33]

Whereas the *Vindiciae* portrays the plot against Athaliah as a clear example of legitimate resistance, Racine's *Athalie* complicates this picture. As I discussed in chapter 1, the treatise states that "une conjuration est bonne ou mauvaise, selon que la fin où elle vise est bonne ou mauvaise, et selon aussi que sont affectionnez ceux qui la font" (a league is good or bad, as its purpose is good or bad [and according also to how those who undertake it are loved]).[34] In other words, conspiracies are good if they serve good ends and are undertaken by good people, and bad if they serve bad ends and bad people. This formulation presumes that the distinction between good and bad can easily be drawn. In the *Vindiciae* this distinction could not be more apparent. Athaliah rules as a tyrant, and the high priest serves goodness and justice. But in Racine's tragedy the difference between good and bad does not hold. Instead, the tragedy figures virtue and vice, innocence and corruption, as both changeable and mutually reinforcing. In so doing, *Athalie* puts pressure on the ability to distinguish between kingship and tyranny, as well as between legitimate resistance and sedition.

The Irony of Innocence

In *Athalie* the confusion about virtue and vice centers on Joash, the young child who improbably survived the queen's massacre of her descendants. This play opens seven years into Athaliah's rein, seven years since she turned away from the Jewish temple and welcomed the prophets of Baal into the kingdom of Judah. In the first lines, Abner, an officer of Athaliah's court who has nonetheless retained ties with the temple, laments that the queen's pagan idolatry has also led many of her subjects astray. *Athalie* takes place during Shavuot, the holiday commemorating the Hebrew God's communication of the law to Moses on Mount Sinai.[35] The setting brings the people's rejection of the temple into particularly sharp relief. Speaking to the temple's high priest, Abner notes that, whereas the holiday used to be celebrated with elaborate decorations, lavish offerings, and an impatient crowd who would throng at the temple gates, this is no longer the case: "L'audace d'une Femme arrêtant ce concours / En des jours ténébreux a changé ces beaux jours" (1.1.13–15) (A woman's hardihood has halted that, / And turned to funeral days those festive days).[36] Abner marks a clear shift from good to bad, with the advent of Athaliah's rule signaling the end of good times and the beginning of the bad.

At the outset of the play, there appears to be no alternative to Athaliah's rule, and no possibility of reversing the shift in moral ambiance that her coming to power has engendered, since she has killed all her descendants as an act of vengeance—and as a means of assuring that her rule will continue unopposed. Although the tragedy seems to announce a crisis of succession, the dramatic interest quickly moves away from a question of how to proceed given Joash's apparent death to a concern about how to communicate the news that he still lives. For Jehoshabeath the high priest's wife, there is more risk than reward in openly recognizing Joash. When the high priest announces that the moment for revelation approaches, she responds:

> Doutez-vous qu'Athalie, au premier bruit semé
> Qu'un fils d'Ochosias est ici renfermé,
> De ses fiers Étrangers assemblant les cohortes,
> N'environne le Temple et n'en brise les portes?
> (*Athalie*, 1.2.217–20)

> You well know, on the slightest rumour spread,
> That Ahaziah's son is guarded here,
> Bold Athaliah will surround the Temple
> With her fierce, foreign troops and force the doors.[37]

In these lines "semé" belongs most clearly to the register of spreading the word, of broadcasting news. And yet we might also note this word's more corporeal connotations, for the verb *semer* pertains not only to the dissemination of information but also to the sowing of seed, a register associated with reproduction and regeneration.[38] As Jehoshabeath's worries suggest, the drama closely intertwines these two registers, tying the suspense about the news that Joash lives with the suspense about what kind of seed he has inherited. On the one hand, Joash's survival reestablishes the prophetic link between the House of David and Christ. If Joash had not lived, this link would have foundered, throwing the veracity of prophecy into question. The prophetic connotations of Joash's lineage cast him as virtuous and good. On the other hand, as many readers of Racine have pointed out, Joash's status as Athaliah's grandchild affords him a legitimate claim to the throne, but this birthright also inspires worry that he might take after his grandmother and similarly turn against the temple.[39] Revealing Joash's identity is necessary to overthrow Athaliah, but it risks exposing him to the less virtuous elements of his family line.

Much like the revelation of Jewishness in *Esther* parallels scenes of coming out as queer, the anxiety about intergenerational influence in *Athalie* bears striking resemblance to anxiety about the influence queer individuals or communities might have on children, those whose apparent innocence and purity promise a better and brighter future. According to what Lee Edelman has identified as the ideology of "reproductive futurism," the figure of the Child stands as the bearer of the social good, and the figure of the Queer as its nemesis.[40] The Queer figure threatens to corrupt the Child figure, whose innocence and purity society must strive vigilantly to protect. Since the Child represents the guarantor of society's future, the Queer menaces this future, representing all that would thwart its realization.[41] *Athalie* both exemplifies and complicates Edelman's equation. On the one hand, Racine's play stages a conflict between a Queer figure—Athaliah—who threatens to corrupt the innocence and purity of a Child Joash—whose protection will ensure a triumphant repetition of the future in the past, which in this case is the fulfillment of divine prophecy and the recuperation of the line of descendants between King David and Christ. On the other hand, Joash's relationship to Athaliah nuances our understanding of the Child's relationship to the Queer and gestures toward a politics of futurity not included in Edelman's formulation.

Although Athaliah kills her grandchildren, it is not only, and perhaps not even principally, this murderous act that makes her a Queer figure, but rather the power that the act affords her, a power characterized as excessive and horrific. Displaying a form of excess desire, namely, a political ambition untethered to prophecy that is deemed out-of-bounds and unseemly, she defies a theological and political logic that demands she cede power to those who would destroy her. A mark of Athaliah's excess is the play's frequent use of adjectives such as "superbe," which in this context means proud, haughty, or arrogant, to describe her. Although her excess constitutes a rejection of a divinely prophesied vision of the future, it does not represent a rejection of the future as such. Athaliah is not a nihilist, but a survivor. Indeed, to her list of excesses we might add the risk that she will live on into the future, beyond her more appropriate ends. Juliette Cherbuliez notes that Athaliah's ongoing existence represents a particular kind of survival or "overlife." Athaliah, Cherbuliez writes, "has not just lived longer than maybe she should have, or longer than others; she has lived in relative excess to others' mortal suffering: Her life has required the excess of their pain and death."[42] Athaliah's untimely survival contributes to her apparent monstrosity.[43]

But Athaliah does not survive forever. Her life does not exceed the time of the play, since her assassination brings the drama to an end and allows Joash's coronation and restoration of the future as prophesied. Thus, whereas she can be read as a Queer figure acting in opposition to reproductive futurism's pull, the play's denouement suggests an ultimate triumph of this inevitable pull. And yet to read the play in this way is to ignore how it presents her relationship to Joash, the child whose innocence the temple must protect, and on whose survival providence depends. As we have seen, Joash functions as a Messiah-like figure who will console his people because his innocence and birth will allow him to triumph over Athaliah. Although these two qualities, his "innocence" and his "naissance," are often lauded together, their link is far from straightforward, for Joash's birth is precisely that which both legitimizes him as a savior and ties him to Athaliah's corrupting lineage.

Whatever duality Joash may possess, his remarkable receptivity to the laws of God bodes well for his role as a savoir. As part of his temple education he must copy these laws by hand, a task that he completes dutifully.[44] Athaliah herself marvels at Joash's remarkable piety. Drawn to the temple after having a dream in which an unknown child kills her, Athaliah encounters Joash, although she does not know he is Joash. (Nor, for that matter, does he. At this point in the drama, Joash is still unaware of his parentage.) When Athaliah asks him how he passes the time, he responds with a list of pious chores and prayers. Athaliah's reaction to this profession of piety suggests that her threat to the temple's future stems from her attempt not only to kill her offspring but also to influence the temple's surviving savior: she invites Joash to come live in her palace, assuring him that he may continue to pray to his God.[45] Although Joash refuses Athaliah's invitation, the incident makes visible the bond between them. Cherbuliez argues that Athaliah acts as an ideal spectator to Joash; her sensitivity toward him communicates to the audience that he is deserving of pity and compassion.[46] That Athaliah should be so taken with Joash also suggests that there is something within him other than his apparent piety, something that would mark his affiliation with Athaliah rather than his difference from her. Indeed, as Cherbuliez is careful to point out, when Athaliah encounters Joash, she experiences horror along with pity and compassion: "[Athaliah] does what an ideal audience should do, and in so doing, she shows us how to experience the messianic Joas[h] and the prophetic horrors that contextualize his emergence from the temple."[47] Given its inherent ambiguity, the affective connection between Athaliah and Joash threatens his role as legitimate savior, or public representative of his people.

As Racine acknowledges in his preface, Joash will eventually turn away from the temple and murder the high priest's son Zechariah, with whom he has been raised as a brother. The young savior's connection to Athaliah's horror is thus already inscribed within biblical prophecy. Indeed, Racine mentions the biblical recognition of this eventuality to assuage potential concerns about false prophecy on stage, noting that "les Prophètes joignent d'ordinaire les consolations aux menaces" (the prophets usually added consolations to their threats).[48] But Joash's murderous act takes place after the time of Racine's tragedy and after the death of Athaliah. The high priest speaks the drama's last words, which explain Athaliah's downfall as comeuppance for her transgressions and reassert the temple's power over Joash, its ideal student:

> Par cette fin terrible, et due à ses forfaits,
> Apprenez, Roi des Juifs, et n'oubliez jamais,
> Que les Rois dans le Ciel ont un Juge sévère,
> L'Innocence un Vengeur, et l'Orphelin un Père.
> (*Athalie*, 5.7.1813–16)
>
> To this disastrous end, due to her crime,
> King of the Jews, pay heed: remember, rather,
> That kings in Heaven have a Judge sublime,
> Avenger of the oppressed, of orphans Father.[49]

If these final lines make it possible to read the tragedy as a reassertion of religious authority, they also suggest a different reading, one that accounts for the anxiety surrounding Joash's proclaimed innocence. Beginning at the end, we might read the high priest's command to Joash, "n'oubliez jamais," as a sign of this anxiety, for the need to make such a command expresses a concern that it will not be followed.

The high priest's command contradicts his own prophetic knowledge. He has already foretold that Joash will prove to be both a savior and a menace to his people, relating a vision of a priest—Zechariah—slain in the temple. And he will later speak to Joash directly of a dangerous future, emphasizing the role that political necessity will have on the eventual corruption of the child's innocence:

De l'absolu pouvoir vous ignorez l'ivresse,
Et des lâches Flatteurs la voix enchanteresse.
Bientôt ils vous diront, que les plus saintes Lois,
Maîtresses du vil peuple, obéissent aux Rois;
Qu'un Roi n'a d'autre frein que sa volonté même;
Qu'il doit immoler tout à sa grandeur suprême;
Qu'aux larmes, au travail le Peuple est condamné,
Et d'un sceptre de fer veut être gouverné;
Que s'il n'est opprimé, tôt ou tard il opprime.
Ainsi de piège en piège, et d'abîme en abîme,
Corrompant de vos mœurs l'aimable pureté,
Ils vous feront enfin haïr la Vérité,
Vous peindront la vertu sous une affreuse image.
Hélas! ils ont des Rois égaré le plus sage.
(*Athalie*, 4.3.1388–1402)

You do not know the wine of absolute power,
Nor the seductive voice of flatterers.
They will soon tell you that the holiest laws
Bind subjects, but must bend before their kings;
The only brake a king has is his will;
And to his greatness must all immolate.
His people are condemned to tears and toil,
And want a rod of iron ruling them;
That if they're not oppressed, they will oppress.
And thus from trap to trap, from chasm to chasm,
Corrupting the pure sweetness of your soul,
They'll end by making you detest the truth
And painting virtue in a hideous guise.
Alas! They led astray our wisest king.[50]

Absolute power does not come out well in these verses. Instead, this form of rule is characterized by excess and drunkenness, as well as a susceptibility to flattery. In other words, the king with absolute power is a tyrant. The language of Racine's tragedy echoes those of political pamphlets that objected to Louis XIV's Revocation of the Edict of Nantes. Texts like *Les soupirs de la France esclave qui aspire après la liberté* chastise the king for acting as if he is above the law.[51] Like the resistance treatises from the previous century, these texts maintain that the king must serve the people, rather than the other way around.

In the high priest's prophecy, the pressures of politics divorced from virtue—as presented by imagined flatterers who may captivate Joash's attention—threaten to contaminate Joash and turn him away from his role as savior. Joash is thus caught between two notions of fidelity. On the one hand, his role as spiritual savior demands that he continue faithfully to uphold divine precepts. On the other, his position as the kingdom's heir renders him responsible for mortal governance. Indeed, what the drama presents as the inevitable possibility that Joash will be corrupted by political contingency further connects him to Athaliah, whose permissive politics and will to temporal power brought about her betrayal of the temple. Thus, Athaliah's excess of political will and lack of spiritual fidelity represent forms of dangerous inheritance to her grandson.

The high priest's prophecy is a particularly powerful (and often cited) example of the anxieties surrounding Joash's future. But the drama forecasts the corruption of the child's purity well in advance of this prophesy. In act 1 Jehoshabeath worries that Joash's lineage has tainted him irreparably, casting doubt on the innocence of his birth. She wonders: "Qui sait si cet Enfant par leur crime entraîné / Avec eux en naissant ne fut pas condamné?" (1.2.237–38) (Perhaps this child, entangled by their sins, / Has also been condemned with them, from birth).[52] From beginning to end, the drama foreshadows Joash's turning away from the temple, even as it heralds him as the innocent child whose birthright will allow for a successful challenge to Athaliah's rule. Joash's duality stands as one set of what Ralph Albanese identifies as the drama's "ironic polarities."[53] It would be tempting to narrativize these polarities, with Joash's innocence characterizing the play's present, and his corruption polluting its future. But to do so would be to miss how thoroughly the drama entangles these two "poles."

Joash loses his innocence in a future that occurs beyond the time of the episode that the play performs, but concern about this loss permeates the drama's present. The "ironic polarities" that characterize Joash thus occur simultaneously, interrupting each other. This mutual interruption occurs throughout the drama, but one of its most striking forms can be found in the choral odes that conclude the first two acts. These odes seem to be songs of praise and piety. And yet they resonate with Joash's corruption, even while proclaiming his innocence:

> Ô bienheureux mille fois
> L'Enfant que le Seigneur aime,
> Qui de bonne heure entend sa voix,
> Et que ce Dieu daigne instruire lui-même!
> Loin du monde élevé, de tous les dons des Cieux

Il est orné dès sa naissance,
Et du Méchant l'abord contagieux
N'altère point son innocence.
(*Athalie*, 2.9.768–75)

O thousand times blessed is he,
The child the Lord loves and ordains,
Who hears His voice from infancy,
Whom God Himself to chasten deigns!
Brought up far from the world, he is endowed
From birth with Heaven's munificence;
No tainting contact with the proud
May mar his innocence.[54]

In this passage, which the chorus repeats several times, the rhymes "innocence" and "naissance" and "cieux" and contagieux" produce an irony that undercuts the portrait of Joash it seems to present. His innocence mingles with the ambiguity of his birthright. These oppositions afford the odes an ironic potential, a potential that locates anxieties about Joash's future in the present and interrupts the play's seemingly triumphant denouement, its narrative end.

The end of *Athalie* suggests that good has triumphed over evil and that virtue has overcome vice. The high priest, who is positioned as the Hebrew God's earthly emissary, successfully lures Athaliah into a trap. She rushes into the temple looking for Joash, of whose true identity she has finally been made aware. At the high priest's command, a legion of Levite soldiers spring out to overtake her in a spectacular coup de théâtre that reinforces the sense of divine triumph. But the end of Athaliah's last speech disrupts the finality of this divine triumph. Echoing Jehoiada's own concerns about Joash, Athaliah says:

Qu'indocile à ton joug, fatigué de ta Loi,
Fidèle du sang d'Achab, qu'il a reçu de moi,
Conforme à son Aïeul, à son Père semblable,
On verra de David l'héritier détestable
Abolir tes honneurs, profaner ton Autel,
Et venger Athalie, Achab, et Jézabel.
(*Athalie*, 5.6.1785–90)

That chafing at Thy yoke, Thy tiresome law,
Staunch to the blood of Ahab I bestow,

> In the ways of his sire and grandsire versed,
> Men shall behold Thy David's heir accursed
> Attack Thy worship, all Thy prophets slaughter,
> Avenging Ahab, Jezebel, me, their daughter.[55]

Athaliah's speech reinforces the anxiety surrounding Joash's character. She warns that the boy's turn from God will take place in the future, but she insists that the cause of this future vengeance has already been transmitted to him through blood.[56] Athaliah's threat of Joash's transgression thus stretches into the future, even as it finds its force in the past. More menacing still is the simultaneity with which Athaliah articulates Joash's duality. Her speech contrasts Joash as a descendant of David, with Joash as a descendant of Athaliah, Achab, and Jezebel. She contaminates all the markers of a pious Joash under the influence of the high priest/God ("ton joug," "ta Loi," "David," "tes honneurs," "ton Autel"), foretelling another Joash who both will come into being and already exists. Finally, the three rhymes "Loi" and "moi," "son père semblable" and "l'hériter detestable," and "Autel" and Jézabel" economically telegraph the double legacy that Joash carries at any given moment.

Athaliah's final speech functions remarkably like the choral odes, although her perception of Joash is diametrically opposed to that of the chorus. What the singing chorus of young girls and the vengefully threatening queen have in common is their communication of the irony surrounding Joash's character, an irony that saturates the entire drama. Joash is both completely innocent and already corrupted. And the simultaneity of this contradiction disrupts the drama's triumphant end. For Paul de Man, irony's power to interrupt narrative as a rhetorical trope resides in its continual turning away from apparent meaning. He writes that "any theory of irony is the undoing, the necessary undoing, of any theory of narrative, when irony is precisely what makes it impossible ever to achieve a theory of narrative that would be consistent."[57] Racine's play performs this ironic disruption of its own narrative through its characterization of Joash and his relationship to Athaliah. Returning to Edelman's critique of reproductive futurism—which draws from de Man's work on irony—we might see the play as both affirming this ideology and disrupting it. Whereas for Edelman the dialectic of reproductive futurism functions as a totalizing system pitting the figure of the innocent Child against the figure of the corrupt Queer, Racine's tragedy stages an innocent child who is never just innocent, largely because the futurity of his crime impinges on his purity in the present.[58]

The futurity of Joash's crime makes up an important part of Athaliah's legacy, suggesting that queerness disrupts the future by contaminating what is understood as the Child's purity. This suggestion of an ironic queer futurity that disrupts the narrative of reproductive futurism offers a possibility not explored by Edelman, who argues that, because futurism positions the Queer negatively as that which acts against the Child (and thus against the future), the Queer should embrace this negativity to maximize its force as an ironic disruption of politics as such. We might remember that for Edelman rejecting the future necessitates a rejection of politics, because for him all politics is futurist. And yet, Athaliah's audacity and her superb ambition, her acceptance of religious plurality, and her corrupting influence over Joash, all figure a form of politics that does not endorse the repetition of the past in the future, but rather exposes the anxieties and uncertainties inherent in this drive to repeat.

Through Joash's duality—part of the ambiguous legacy that he inherits from Athaliah—Racine's drama stages a queering of the future rather than a queer rejection of the future. The inevitability of the future's pull produces irony in the tragedy. The politics of futurity that makes Joash a not-so-innocent object of contestation stages a continual turning away, whether from a contagious birthright or from a pious education. What we cannot forget is that Joash's irony is double because, despite his betrayal of the temple, his coronation ultimately *does* link the house of David to Christ. As we have seen, when addressing Joash's murder of Zechariah in his preface, Racine acknowledges that "les Prophètes joignent d'ordinaire les consolations aux menaces" (the prophets usually added consolations to their threats).[59] For Racine, the child's double irony fits an understanding of the future as revealed by providential history. Both Racine and Edelman work within temporal systems in which the future constitutes a continual repetition of the past. But whereas Edelman locates the moment of possible resistance in an ironic rejection of the future's terms, Racine's tragedy suggests that disruption resides precisely in the future's ironic duality, and in the anxiety it produces in the past and present. Much like Phaedra, another of Racine's tragic characters, Joash is "ni tout a fait coupable, ni tout a fait innocent(e)" (neither altogether guilty nor altogether innocent).[60] Both a traitor and a savior, Joash figures a future in which virtue and vice are forever intertwined.

The Virtuous Is Political

The *Vindiciae* figures Athaliah as a vicious tyrant and the high priest as a virtuous public representative capable of resisting her tyranny. In this treatise, Joash, the child elevated to the throne who makes possible the high priest's opposition to Athaliah, serves as an object of goodness and virtue. While the *Vindiciae* draws stark distinctions between the good and the bad, the tyrannical and the just, Racine's tragedy makes such distinctions more difficult to draw. The ironic futurity at work in *Athalie* means that Joash represents the possibility of goodness and virtue, as well as the possibility of badness and vice. One cannot remove the child from either Athaliah's influence or that of the temple. What is more, Racine's tragedy also makes it more difficult to characterize Athaliah and the high priest themselves. Although they seem initially to embody the opposite forces that exert their push and pull on Joash, these two figures of authority also contain dualities. The high priest portrays his motives as wholly spiritual, but he cannot avoid making political calculation in his attempt to crown Joash and save the temple. Similarly, Athaliah appears as a monstrous figure who is wholly evil and destructive, but she also shows herself to be sensitive to Joash's desire to worship his god, and thus a figure of tolerance.[61] If we take a narrativized version of this biblical story with a clear beginning, middle, and end, such as that of the *Vindiciae*, virtue clearly triumphs over vice. In contrast, the tragic version of the story, which disrupts its own narrative and comingles the past, present, and future, raises troubling questions about the location of virtue and the clarity of its triumph. In so doing, Racine's tragedy suggests that distinctions between virtue and vice are not universal or fixed but are instead matters of perspective or position.

In chapter 3 I examined the case of Antigone, a figure whose familial and romantic ties raised questions about her virtue and thus her political legitimacy. In Garnier's *Antigone, ou La pieté* and Rotrou's *Antigone*, the Theban people ultimately secure her virtue and ratify her actions. In these tragedies the people's expressions of support for Antigone operate as affective evidence of her righteousness and legitimacy. The popular endorsement of Antigone through the means of affective evidence parallels the public support of representatives in sixteenth-century resistance treatises, such as the *Vindiciae*. However, there are places in the *Vindiciae* where affective evidence of the people's support is absent. When recounting the story of Athaliah, the treatise lets slip that the people did not openly express support for the high priest's opposition. Instead of suggesting that this absence of support rendered the high priest's resistance questionable, the *Vindiciae* blames this absence on Athaliah's tyranny. "Peut-estre que le peuple murmuroit lors entre les dents, et n'osoit à cause du danger dire ce qu'il retenoit en sa pensee" (Perhaps the people muttered then; for to say outright what weighed on its mind was unsafe).[62] It is possible that the people did object to Athaliah's rule, but given the conditions of her tyrannical regime, their objections were imperceptible.

Racine's tragedy does not take the people's affective evidence for granted, but instead heightens the uncertainty about the people's orientation to Athaliah on the one hand and to the temple on the other. Indeed, throughout the tragedy the high priest must manage concerns about the people's apparent acceptance of Athaliah's rule and of the prophets of Baal. For the high priest, the need to win back the people's affection for the temple drives his need to carefully orchestrate the revelation that Joash lives. Without the hope of a legitimate rival to Athaliah, the temple cannot sustain the people's support. In this case, affective evidence is not the precondition of resistance but functions instead as its desirable result.

To regain the people's affection and approval, the high priest must reveal that Joash still lives. If the people can be assured that the prophecy linking the House of David to the Messiah has not been broken, then they are more likely to support the temple and turn against Athaliah. A member of chorus sings, for example:

> Pendant que du Dieu d'Athalie
> Chacun court encenser l'autel,
> Un Enfant courageux publie
> Que Dieu lui seul est éternel
> Et parle comme un autre Élie
> Devant cette autre Jézabel.
> (*Athalie*, 2.9.756–61)

> While Athaliah's god each seeks
> At first clang of Baal's temple bell,
> A child proclaims from his brave peaks
> That God alone is eternal,
> And like another Elijah speaks
> Before this other Jezebel.[63]

The chorus ties the people's spiritual virtue or vice to the promised arrival of this "Enfant courageux." The play repeatedly states that this child's survival must be revealed, or publicized, for the child to publish ("publie") the virtues of the one, true God, who will triumph over this tyrant like he has triumphed over so many others. However necessary, the revelation of this child's continued existence carries certain risks. By publicizing Joash's existence to win the people over, the high priest must also reveal him to Athaliah. As we have seen, Athaliah herself is drawn toward Joash, raising the possibility that he might one day be drawn toward her. To reveal Joash's apparent virtue is to expose him to apparent vice.

Through these questions of secrecy and revelation, Racine's *Athalie* repeats the fraught dynamics of *Esther*'s performance. In both cases, virtue and innocence can only remain pure and untouched if they remain hidden. Once virtue and its companion innocence are revealed, they are inevitably corrupted. The girls at Saint-Cyr could not successfully perform their innocence and at the same time preserve it. Similarly, the high priest could not reveal Joash's virtue and keep him hidden from the forces that would corrupt it. Racine's biblical tragedies suggest that to broadcast virtue and innocence is to expose them to the world of politics, as well as to subject them to questions of conflict and division. Staging this sense of virtue's political instability, *Esther* and *Athalie* capture the contingencies inherent in affective evidence. Given these contingencies, the actions or recognition of a public representative cannot be praised as salvific. Instead of the fantasies of salvation and liberation that Sedgwick critiques, whereby a single, virtuous individual manages to change the fate of an entire community, *Esther* and *Athalie* suggest how communities might act through individuals to challenge the assumptions that determine who is virtuous and who is not.

Conclusion

The Subject of Rights

In *The Old Regime and the French Revolution*, Alexis de Tocqueville remarks on the desire of the French revolutionaries to break with their monarchical past:

> Les Français ont fait en 1789 le plus grand effort auquel se soit jamais livré aucun peuple, afin de couper pour ainsi dire en deux leur destinée, et de séparer par un abîme ce qu'ils avaient été jusque-là de ce qu'ils voulaient être désormais. Dans ce but, ils ont pris toutes sortes de précautions pour ne rien emporter du passé dans leur condition nouvelle; ils se sont imposé toutes sortes de contraintes pour se façonner autrement que leurs pères; ils n'ont rien oublié enfin pour se rendre méconnaissables.[1]

> The French made, in 1789, the greatest effort that has ever been made by any people to sever their history into two parts, so to speak, and to tear open a gulf between their past and their future. In this design, they took the greatest care to leave every trace of their past condition behind them; they imposed all kinds of restraints upon themselves in order to be different from their ancestry; they omitted nothing which could disguise them.[2]

What is central for Tocqueville here is the question of effort. The Revolution does not simply spring into being as a rupture, a break, or a cut in time. Instead, the French *worked* to create the rupture. The revolutionaries made an effort, indeed, "le plus grand effort auquel se soit jamais livré aucun peuple," to sever their history into two parts and tear open a gulf between their past and their future. And yet, Tocqueville suggests that—despite this great effort—the French had not fully succeeded in breaking with their past:

> J'avais toujours pensé qu'ils avaient beaucoup moins réussi dans cette singulière entreprise qu'on ne l'avait cru au dehors et qu'ils ne l'avaient cru d'abord eux-mêmes. J'étais convaincu qu'à leur insu ils avaient retenu de l'ancien régime la plupart des sentiments, des habitudes, des idées même à l'aide desquelles ils avaient conduit la Révolution qui le détruisit, et que, sans le vouloir, ils s'étaient servi de ses débris pour construire l'édifice de la société nouvelle.[3]

> I have always fancied that they were less successful in this enterprise than has been generally believed abroad, or even supposed at home. I have always suspected that they unconsciously retained most of the sentiments, habits, and ideas which the old regime had taught them, and by whose aide they achieved the Revolution; and that, without intending it, they used its ruins as materials for the construction of their new Society.[4]

The revolutionaries cannot escape the old regime. They carry forward the sentiments and structures of the past from wish they wish to break. Tocqueville goes on to argue that the old regime society in many ways helped to bring about the Revolution. Although the centralization of state bureaucracy and the weakening of the aristocracy had allowed the monarchy to consolidate its power during the seventeenth century, these processes also contributed to the social and political cleavages that eventually weakened monarchical power during the eighteenth.

Crucially for Tocqueville, the old regime not only made the Revolution possible but also shaped what kind of Revolution it would be. When the revolutionaries overthrew the monarchy, for example, they did not do away with its centralization of power. They traded the king's absolute power for that of the state.[5] The Revolution similarly followed a path laid out by the old regime in its conception of the individual. The monarchy increased its power in part through the curbing of ancient alliances and privileges. The Revolution continued this work, leveling the remaining distinctions between individuals by declaring that all men were equal.[6]

While I do not share Tocqueville's apparent nostalgia for the aristocracy or differentially distributed political privileges, his articulation of continuity and change nonetheless allows us to understand the relationship between the limits and possibilities of political subjectivity under the old regime and the political subjectivity that emerged during the Revolution. Recognizing the close ties between these two forms of subjectivity—that of the old regime, or "absolutist," on the one hand and the modern, or "liberal," on the other—helps explain some of the constituent problems with our contemporary notions of rights and subjecthood.

As political theorists such as Hannah Arendt and Jacques Rancière have observed, the liberal, individualist model of rights associated with the French Revolution presents a number of problems. One problem is that it makes individual rights contingent on membership in a nation and dependent on state protection.[7] As a result, this model has been decidedly more successful in protecting the rights of individuals who are both men *and* citizens. Individuals who are not citizens, who as a result lack state protection have more often than not found their putative rights as members of "mankind" impossible to enforce. As Arendt famously pointed out, the rights of man, or "human rights," as opposed to the rights of the citizen, are merely "the rights of those who have no rights."[8]

Another problem with the liberal, individualist model of rights, which is closely related to this model's dependence on citizenship and state protection, is its failure to take into account how social and ethical attachments affect a given individual's ability to exercise their rights. In other words, the liberal individual often appears conceptually unattached to others, even though his or her political power depends on a set of relationships, from familial bonds to religious affiliations to romantic ties. Feminist and critical race scholars (among others) have called attention to how the liberal model's failure to recognize attachment has perpetuated the political discrepancies between differently marked individuals, despite their formal equality under the law.[9] As has often been noted, the unmarked, or "universal" subject of liberalism usually corresponds to an individual who is white, male, and middle class (at least). By eliding the particularities of this individual subject under the sign of the universal, the liberal model of rights neglects how individuals with other particularities are differently positioned within systems of power and differently attached to others.

Throughout this book I have argued that the preabsolutist conception of rights offers an alternative to the liberal model of individual rights. The right of resistance as articulated in sixteenth-century resistance theory, and as elaborated within French tragic drama, presents us with political ideas that are at once strange and familiar. Subjective liberty and popular sovereignty are both component parts of the liberal system. And yet, the rich and varied links between these ideas, the forms of affiliation and attachment that bind individuals to each other and that shape their political power, seem to have been forgotten or left behind. This book has been an attempt to recuperate those forms of affiliation and attachment, and to show how they persist even when officially or formally denied. At the heart of this recuperative project is the concept of "affective evidence," or the idea that affect serves as an index of the political legitimacy that a collective confers on a public representative. Affective evidence operates as an organizing principal of sixteenth-century resistance treatises, effectively allowing any subject who enjoys collective approval to emerge as a public representative. And, as we have seen, tragic drama exploits the potential of affective evidence by imagining how popular approval might coalesce around unorthodox public representatives.

What if we took the early modern public representative as our model of political subjectivity instead of the liberal subject of rights? Although the liberal subject is formally isolated, and unattached, the public representative's power derives from his or her responsiveness to collective joy or pain. The public representative is thus constitutionally relational. Tragic drama sustained the conceptual framework of the right of resistance, thus allowing for the category of the public representative to be continually rethought, even while this category contracted sharply during the seventeenth century and was officially limited to the king himself. I would like to suggest that the patterns and practices of tragic drama also allow us to recognize and amplify the work of the public representative in contemporary political life.

To take but one example, I vividly recall watching the live coverage of Wendy Davis's filibuster on the floor of the Texas Senate in 2013. Aimed to prevent the passage of Senate Bill 5, which would have banned abortions in Texas after twenty weeks of pregnancy, in addition to imposing other restrictions on women's access to abortion, Davis's filibuster lasted over eleven hours. Although the filibuster prevented the bill from being passed that night, it passed soon after and was signed into law by then Governor Rick Perry. Despite the eventual legislative defeat, the media coverage of the filibuster made Davis a national name and buoyed her political career. She was widely praised for her fortitude and poise. The hot pink trainers that she wore during the filibuster became a particularly recognizable symbol of her protest.

Davis is remembered as a powerful political actor. What is less remembered, however, are her interactions with crowds of (mostly) women during the filibuster. To hold the senate floor, Davis had to speak continuously on the topic of Bill 5. She filled part of this time by reading statements that women had sent to her office. These statements were often emotional accounts of how access to abortion had saved their lives. They were filled with fears about the consequences of the bill's passage. By reading these statements, Davis multiplied the voices in the room, bringing those which are often off-stage and unseen into the glare of the senate spectacle. The affective relationship between Davis and a wider collective of women was further solidified when a few minutes before midnight Lieutenant Governor David Dewhurst ruled that Davis's filibuster was over because she had violated senate rules for a third and final permissible time. The lieutenant governor then began the process of voting on Bill 5. The vote was interrupted and delayed, however, by other members of the senate, such as Leticia R. Van de Putte, as well as by the cheers and protests of the crowd in the gallery. The collective voices of this wider community delayed the vote until after midnight, rendering it invalid.[10] To think of Davis as a public official is to acknowledge the affective interplay between her and this wider community, as well as the political force of the community's contributions. To read this scene through the lens of tragedy, and of theater more broadly, is to keep this collective force in the frame.

Tragedy also helps us appreciate the extent to which invocations of the collective, the community, or the people are necessarily partial and contested. As I explored in chapter 1, sixteenth-century resistance treatises such as the *Vindiciae contra tyrannos* appeal to notions of popular sovereignty to justify active opposition to a tyrannical monarch. These treatises maintain that the people as a whole, corporate body had the power to accept or reject the king's authority. These rhetorical invocations of a unified people were, however, at odds with the historical state of the body politic in sixteenth-century France, as members of Catholic and Protestant factions disagreed vehemently and violently about the proper constitution of the people and about whose actions legitimately served the public good. Whereas sixteenth-century resistance treatises elide these political fractures to put forward a performatively unified people and body politic, tragic drama exposes division and disagreement. As I have detailed throughout this book, in tragic drama, the people appear only through the speech and actions of staged characters and choruses. Structurally, then, tragedy asks us to confront the extent to which "the people" as a collective entity is shaped and reshaped by those who seek the imprimatur of its authority. In other words, claims to represent *the* people are really claims to represent *a* people. These claims offer a particular version of what the people ought to be.

The lessons of tragic drama feel particularly salient as I conclude this book in the midst of the COVID-19 pandemic and in the immediate aftermath of the January 6 attack on the US Capitol. Even as I continue to find resonance between early modern resistance theory and the contemporary political moment, I am well aware—and often painfully so—that resistance theory is also available to those with whom I disagree, and whose views I often find abhorrent. Since at least 2012, members of the Christian Right have turned explicitly to early modern resistance theory to find justification for their opposition to the federal and/or state government. Matthew J. Trewhella, a pastor based in Wisconsin, for example, draws extensively from Theodore de Bèze's *Du droit des magistrats* in his self-published book *The Doctrine of the Lesser Magistrates: A Proper Resistance to Tyranny and a Repudiation of Unlimited Obedience to Civil Government.*[11] The public representatives championed by Trewhella include Kim Davis, a county clerk in Rowan County, Kentucky, who refused to carry out a federal court order to issue marriage licenses to same-sex couples, and Dallas Heard, an Oregon state senator who removed his face mask while speaking during a legislative session to protest a state mandate.[12] To be clear, by referencing right-wing uses of early modern resistance theory, and by contrasting them with my own, I do not wish to suggest any kind of straightforward parallel between the early modern period and the present. To do so would be overly simplistic. What I do hope to underscore, however, is that the conceptual structure of resistance theory, with its conjunction of individual and collective authority, remains available in our contemporary moment. The collective dimension of our disagreements is too often elided by a political discourse that emphasizes individual rights and freedoms. Early modern resistance theory, especially as it appears in tragic drama—reminds us that what is at stake is not just who the individual is and what the individual can do, but rather who "we" are and what we ought to do as a people.

NOTES

Introduction

1. For more on the political and historical context surrounding the union and its significance for the royal family, see Denis Crouzet, *La nuit de la Saint Barthélemy: Un rêve perdu de la Renaissance* (Paris: Fayard, 1994).

2. Historical estimates of the number of those killed during the massacre vary. Mack P. Holt suggests that two thousand were killed in Paris and three thousand in the provinces; see Holt, *The French Wars of Religion, 1562–1629*, 2nd ed. (Cambridge: Cambridge University Press, 2005), 76–98. Donald R. Kelley explains that the earliest figures given in the wake of the massacre were much larger, ranging from fifty thousand to three hundred thousand; see Kelley, "Martyrs, Myths, and the Massacre: The Background of St. Bartholomew," *American Historical Review* 77, no. 5 (1972): 1339. See also Denis Crouzet, *Les guerriers de dieu: La violence aux temps de troubles de religion* (Paris: Champ Vallon, 2006); Arlette Jouanna, *La Saint-Barthélemy: Les mystères d'un crime d'état (24 août 1572)* (Paris: Gallimard, 2007); and Robert Kingdon, *Myths about the Saint Bartholomew's Day Massacres, 1572–1576* (Cambridge, MA: Harvard University Press, 1988).

3. Holt, *French Wars of Religion, 1562–1629*, 76–98.

4. I borrow the term "epistemic murk" from Michael Taussig, *Shamanism, Colonialism, and the Wild Man: A Study in Terror and Healing* (Chicago: University of Chicago Press, 1987).

5. Crouzet discusses how the union was advertised as a gesture of affection that would help to repair the political and social rifts of the religious wars. Crouzet, *La nuit de la Saint Barthélemy*, 183–263.

6. The right of resistance does not originate in the sixteenth century, but instead has biblical, ancient, and medieval precedents. See, e.g., Quentin Skinner, *The Foundations of Modern Political Thought: Vol. 2 The Age of Reformation* (Cambridge: Cambridge University Press, 1978), 302–59; Daniel Lee, *Popular Sovereignty in Early Modern Constitutional Thought* (Oxford: Oxford University Press, 2016); and Kathleen Parrow, "From Defense to Resistance: The Justification of Resistance during the French Wars of Religion," *Transactions of the American Philosophical Society* 83, no. 6 (1993): 1–79.

7. For example, in *Les six livres de la république* (Paris, 1580), a foundational text in the development of absolutist doctrine, Jean Bodin argues that during the religious conflicts the category of tyranny had been misused to the point of being meaningless. Providing standard descriptions of the theoretical differences between kings and tyrants, he writes that "le roi se conforme aux lois de nature, et le tyran les foule aux pieds. L'un entretient la piété, la justice, et la foi; l'autre n'a ny Dieu, ny foi, ny loi" (289) [Quoted in Ellen McClure, *Sunspots and the Sun King: Sovereignty and Mediation in Seventeenth-Century France* (Urbana:

University of Illinois Press, 2006), 35]. Bodin goes on to explain, however, that because perceptions of piety, fidelity, justice, and natural law varied widely during the conflicts, the distinction between a king and a tyrant was impossible to maintain. If expressing piety and upholding natural law was what distinguished the king from the tyrant, and if there was no stable definition of either piety or natural law, then any king could be a tyrant and any tyrant, a king. Ellen McClure discusses at length the importance of Bodin's treatise to the subsequent theories of absolutism. McClure, *Sunspots and the Sun King*, 27–35).

8. See Skinner, *Foundations of Modern Political Thought*, 2:189–359; Paul-Alexis Mellet, *Les traités monarchomaques: Confusion des temps, résistance armée et monarchie parfaite (1560–1600)* (Geneva: Librairie Droz, 2007); and Arlette Jouanna, *Le devoir de révolte: La noblesse française et la gestation de l'état moderne, 1559–1661* (Paris: Fayard, 1989).

9. See, for example, *Dialogue du royaume* (1589) and Jean Boucher, *De justa Henrici Tertii abdicatione* (1589). I will discuss Catholic resistance theory in more detail in chap. 1.

10. These treatises have historically been referred to as the work of "monarchomaques" (in French) or "monarchomachs" (in Latin), meaning "those who oppose the king." On the origins and limitations of this term, see Mellet, *Les traités monarchomaques*, 15–20.

11. Skinner discusses these ideas throughout *Foundations of Modern Political Thought*, vol. 2. See also Dale Van Kley, *The Religious Origins of the French Revolution: From Calvin to the Civil Constitution, 1560–1791* (New Haven, CT: Yale University Press, 1996); and John Witte Jr., *The Reformation of Rights: Law, Religion, and Human Rights in Early Modern Calvinism* (Cambridge: Cambridge University Press, 2007).

12. On the concept of popular sovereignty during this period more broadly, see Arlette Jouanna, *Le pouvoir absolu: Naissance de l'imaginaire politique de la royauté* (Paris: Gallimard, 2013); Donald R. Kelley, *The Beginning of Ideology: Consciousness and Society in the French Reformation* (Cambridge: Cambridge University Press, 1981); and Lee, *Popular Sovereignty in Early Modern Constitutional Thought*.

13. Théodore de Bèze, *Du droit des magistrats sur leurs subjets: traitte tres necessaire en ce temps pour advertir de leur devoir, tant les magistrats que les subjets publié par ceux de Magdebourg l'an M.D.L., maintenant reveu, augmenté de plusieurs raisons, exemples* (1575), 39; and Theodore Beza, *The Right of Magistrates Concerning the Rights of Rulers Over Their Subjects and the Duty Of Subjects Towards Their Rulers, A brief and clear treatise particularly indispensable to either class in these troubled times*, ed. Patrick S. Poole and trans. Henry-Louis Gonin (Cape Town: H.A.U.M., 1956), 13, http://www.yorku.ca/comninel/courses/3020pdf/Beza.pdf. All translations of *Du droit des magistrats* are from this 1956 edition.

14. Jouanna, *Le devoir de révolte*.

15. William Reddy, *The Navigation of Feeling: A Framework for the History of Emotions* (Cambridge: Cambridge University Press, 2001); and Barbara Rosenwein, *Generations of Feeling: A History of Emotions, 600–1700* (Cambridge: Cambridge University Press, 2016).

16. Sara Ahmed, *The Cultural Politics of Emotion* (New York: Routledge, 2004) and *Willful Subjects* (Durham, NC: Duke, 2014); Lauren Berlant, *The Female Complaint: The Unfinished Business of Sentimentality in American Culture* (Durham, NC: Duke University Press, 2008); Teresa Brennan, *The Transmission of Affect* (Ithaca, NY: Cornell University Press, 2004); Ann Cvetkovich, *Depression: A Public Feeling* (Durham, NC: Duke University Press, 2012); and Rei Terada, *Feeling in Theory: Emotion after the "Death of the Subject"* (Cambridge, MA: Harvard University Press, 2001).

17. "Affection," *Dictionnaire de l'Académie française* (1694), University of Chicago: ARTFL Dictionnaires d'autrefois, https://artflsrv03.uchicago.edu/philologic4/publicdicos/navigate/3/232/. My translation.

18. Jean Baricave, *De la defense de la monarchie françoise* [. . .] (Toulouse, 1614). Quoted in George Garnett, introduction to the *Vindiciae, Contra Tyrannos: or, Concerning the Legitimate Power of a Prince over the People, and of the People over a Prince*, by Stephanus Junius Brutus, the Celt, ed. and trans. George Garnett (Cambridge: Cambridge University Press, 1994), xx (hereafter cited as *Vindiciae*, trans. Garnett).

19. For an excellent account of the liberal subject's emergence during the early modern period with a particular emphasis on the English context, see Victoria Kahn, *Wayward Contracts: The Crisis of Political Obligation in England, 1640–1674* (Princeton, NJ: Princeton University Press, 2004).

20. Barbara B. Diefendorf, "Rites of Repair: Restoring Community in the French Religious Wars," in *Ritual Violence: Natalie Zemon Davis and Early Modern France*, ed. Graeme Murdock, Penny Roberts, and Andrew Spicer, Past & Present Supplement new series 7 (Oxford: Oxford University Press, 2012), 34; and Hélène Merlin-Kajman, *Public et littérature en France au XVIIe siècle*, 2nd ed. (Paris: Les Belles Lettres, 2004), 14–87.

21. Henri IV, *Édict du Roy et déclaration sur les précédens édicts de pacification. Publié à Paris, en Parlement, le 25 febvrier, 1599* (Paris, 1599), sec. 1, http://gallica.bnf.fr/ark:/12148/bpt6k317003w. My translation.

22. For an account of how the Edict of Nantes reshaped aspects of public life and of how religious difference was addressed in French courts in the aftermath of the religious wars, see Diane C. Margolf, *Religion and Royal Justice in Early Modern France: The Paris Chambre de l'Edit, 1598–1665* (Kirksville, MO: Truman State University Press, 2003).

23. Reinhart Koselleck, *Critique and Crisis: Enlightenment and the Pathogenesis of Modern Society* (Cambridge, MA: MIT Press, 1988), 15–22. See also Michel de Waele, *Réconcilier les français: La fin des troubles de religion (1589–1598)* (Paris: Hermann, 2015).

24. On these shifts in French political thought, see Arlette Jouanna, *Le prince absolu: Apogée et déclin de l'imaginaire monarchique* (Paris: Gallimard, 2014), and *Le pouvoir absolu*. See also Koselleck, *Critique and Crisis*, 15–22.

25. For a more detailed account of this split between the public and the private, see Koselleck, *Critique and Crisis*; and Hélène Merlin-Kajman, *L'absolutisme dans les lettres et la théorie des deux corps: Passions et politique* (Paris: Honoré Champion, 2000).

26. Jouanna, *Le prince absolu*, 25.

27. Jouanna, *Le prince absolu*, 140–62.

28. Nannerl O. Keohane, *Philosophy and the State in France: The Renaissance to the Enlightenment* (Princeton, NJ: Princeton University Press, 1980), 20. On the history of protest and civil unrest in seventeenth-century France, see William Beik, *Urban Protest in Seventeenth-Century France: The Culture of Retribution* (Cambridge: Cambridge University Press, 1997). There is also a vast literature on the midcentury uprisings known as the *Fronde*: see, for example, Christian Jouhaud, *Mazarinades: La Fronde des mots* (Paris: Aubier, 1985); and Orest Ranum, *The Fronde: A French Revolution, 1648–1652* (New York: W. W. Norton, 1993).

29. A famous, and much critiqued, example of such a study is Norbert Elias, *The Civilizing Process: Sociogenic and Psychogenic Investigations*, rev. ed. (Malden, MA: Blackwell, 2000).

30. William Beik, *Absolutism and Society in Seventeenth-Century France: State Power and Provincial Aristocracy in Languedoc* (Cambridge: Cambridge University Press, 1985); and Sharon Kettering, *Patronage in Sixteenth- and Seventeenth-Century France* (Aldershot, UK: Ashgate, 2002).

31. Sarah Hanley, *The Lit de Justice of the Kings of France: Constitutional Ideology, Ritual, and Discourse* (Princeton, NJ: Princeton University Press, 1983); and Jouanna, *Le pouvoir absolu*.

32. Juliette Cherbuliez, *The Place of Exile: Leisure Literature and the Limits of Absolutism* (Lewisburg, PA: Bucknell University Press, 2005).

33. Claire Goldstein, *Vaux and Versailles: The Appropriations, Erasures, and Accidents that Made Modern France* (Philadelphia: University of Pennsylvania Press, 2008).

34. Goldstein provides an excellent account of how Louis XIV's spectacles at Versailles were designed to overwhelm the king's subjects in ways that prevented them from personal or subjective engagement in the workings of power. See, e.g., her reading of Madeleine de Scudéry's *La Promenade de Versailles* (1669) in Goldstein, *Vaux and Versailles*, 147–53.

35. Katherine Ibbett, *Compassion's Edge: Fellow Feeling and Its Limits in Early Modern France* (Philadelphia: University of Pennsylvania Press, 2017), 27, 159–95.

36. Chloé Hogg, *Absolutist Attachments: Emotion, Media, and Absolutism in Seventeenth-Century France* (Evanston, IL: Northwestern University Press, 2019).

37. See Timothy Murray, "Richelieu's Theater: The Mirror of a Prince," *Renaissance Drama* 8 (1977): 275–97; and Déborah Blocker, *Instituer un "art": Politiques du théâtre dans la France du premier XVIIe siècle* (Paris: Honoré Champion, 2009).

38. Jean-Marie Apostolidès, *Le roi-machine: Spectacle et politique au temps de Louis XIV* (Paris: Les Éditions de Minuit, 1981).

39. Alessandro Fontana, "Du droit de résistance au devoir d'insurrection," in *Le droit de résistance: XIIe–XXe siècle*, ed. Jean-Claude Zancarini (Lyon: ENS Éditions, 2000), 15–33.

40. McClure, *Sunspots and the Sun King*.

41. Hélène Bilis, *Passing Judgment: The Politics and Poetics of Sovereignty in French Tragedy from Hardy to Racine* (Toronto: University of Toronto Press, 2016), x.

42. Katherine Ibbett, *The Style of the State in French Theater, 1630–1660: Neoclassicism and Government* (Farnham, UK: Ashgate, 2009).

43. For critical accounts of this narrative's origins and limitations, see John D. Lyons, *Kingdom of Disorder: The Theory of Tragedy in Classical France* (West Lafayette, IN: Purdue University Press, 1999); Christian Jouhaud, *Sauver le Grand-Siècle: Présence et transmission du passé* (Paris: Seuil, 2007); and Hélène Merlin-Kajman, "Un siècle classico-baroque?" *Dix-septième siècle* 223, no. 2 (2004): 163–72. On how this narrative elides tragedy's constitutive violence, see Juliette Cherbuliez, *In the Wake of Medea: Neoclassical Theater and the Arts of Destruction* (New York: Fordham University Press, 2020), 8–22.

44. See Madeleine Lazard, *Le théâtre en France au XVIe siècle* (Paris: Presses Universitaires de France, 1980), 93–97.

45. See Andrea Frisch, *Forgetting Differences: Tragedy, Historiography, and the French Wars of Religion* (Edinburgh: Edinburgh University Press, 2015), 104–40.

46. Jean de La Taille, "De l'art de la tragédie," in *Saul le furieux* (Paris, 1572), 2r. My translation.

47. See Gillian Jondorf, *French Renaissance Tragedy: The Dramatic Word* (Cambridge: Cambridge University Press, 1990).

48. See, for example, René Rapin, *Les réflexions sur la poétique d'Aristote et sur les ouvrages des poètes anciens et modernes* (Paris, 1674), 61.

49. Christian Biet, introduction to *Théâtre de la cruauté et récits sanglants en France (XVIe–XVIIe siècle)*, ed. Christian Biet (Paris: Laffont, 2006), v–xlvii.

50. See Richard Goodkin, "Neoclassical Dramatic Theory in Seventeenth-Century France," in *A Companion to Tragedy*, ed. Rebecca Bushnell (Oxford: Wiley-Blackwell, 2009), 373–92.

51. Frisch, *Forgetting Differences*, 1–25.

52. Frisch, *Forgetting Differences*, 172–74.

53. Michel de Certeau, *The Writing of History*, trans. Tom Conley (New York: Columbia University Press, 1992), 4. Emphasis in original.

54. Certeau, *Writing of History*, 4.

55. W. B. Worthen, *Drama: Between Poetry and Performance* (Chichester, UK: Wiley-Blackwell, 2010), 1–34.

56. Diana Taylor, *The Archive and the Repertoire: Performing Cultural Memory in the Americas* (Durham, NC: Duke University Press, 2003).

57. See, for example, Joy Palacios, *Ceremonial Splendor: Performing Priesthood In Early Modern France* (Philadelphia: University of Pennsylvania Press, forthcoming).

58. See Rebecca Schneider, *Performing Remains: Art and War in Times of Theatrical Reenactment* (New York: Routledge, 2011); and W. B. Worthen, *Drama: Between Poetry and Performance*. On the relative ephemerality of the archive itself, see Adair Routhwaite, *Asking the Audience: Participatory Art in 1980s New York* (Minneapolis: University of Minnesota Press, 2017).

59. Stephen K. White describes this challenge in *The Ethos of a Late-Modern Citizen* (Cambridge, MA: Harvard University Press, 2009).

Chapter 1

1. *Vindiciae contra tyrannos: Traduction française de 1581*, ed. Arlette Jouanna, Jean Perrin, Marguerite Soulié, André Tournon, and Henri Weber

(Geneva: Librairie Droz, 1979), 5. All citations are from this edition unless otherwise noted. All translations are from George Garnett's critical edition, *Vindiciae*, Garnett trans, 8.

2. *Vindiciae contra tyrannos*, 5; *Vindiciae*, Garnett trans., 8.

3. As Garnett point out, some modern readers of the *Vindiciae* have questioned the extent to which the treatise makes good on this promise of a refutation of Machiavelli. References to Machiavelli and his ideas are scant throughout the treatise itself. Garnett objects to this critique, however, noting that the *Vindiciae* refutes Machiavellianism in part by refusing to engage on its terms. See *Vindiciae*, Garnett trans., xx–xxii. During the sixteenth century, the *Vindiciae* and Bèze's *Du droit des magistrats* were bound and published with *The Prince* to highlight the differences in the political philosophies of these texts. See A. A. van Schelven, "Beza's De Iure Magistratuum in Subditos," *Archiv für Reformationsgeschichte* 45 (1954): 62–83.

4. See, for example, Mark Greengrass, *Governing Passions: Peace and Reform in the French Kingdom, 1576–1585* (Oxford: Oxford University Press, 2007); Gisèle Mathieu-Castellani, *La rhétorique des passions* (Paris: Presses Universitaires de France, 2000); and Lucie Desjardins, *Le corps parlant: Savoirs et representations des passions au XII*[e] *sicècle* (Laval: Presses Universitaires de Laval, 2001).

5. On the largely negative reception of Machiavelli during the sixteenth century in France, see Edmond M. Beame, "The Use and Abuse of Machiavelli: The Sixteenth-Century French Adaptation," *Journal of the History of Ideas* 43, no. 1 (1982): 33–54; and Donald R. Kelley, "Murd'rous Machiavel in France: A Post Mortem," *Political Science Quarterly* 85, no. 4 (1970): 545–59.

6. Skinner, for example, references the form of subjective liberty articulated in Protestant resistance theory as a precursor to the individual rights of man; Skinner, *Foundations of Modern Political Thought*, 302–59. In contrast, Lee focuses on Protestant resistance theory's place in genealogies of popular sovereignty; Lee, *Popular Sovereignty in Early Modern Constitutional Thought*.

7. Hotman and Bèze did, however, write directly about the conflicts elsewhere. See, for example, Hotman, *Epistre envoyé au Tigre de la France* (1560); and Bèze, Histoire ecclesiastique des Eglises reformes au Royaume de France (1580).

8. On the relationship between the notions of spiritual and political community, see Hélène Merlin-Kajman, *Public et littérature en France au XII*[e] *siècle*, 59–87.

9. Rosenwein, *Generations of Feeling*, 3.

10. Elizabeth Maddox Dillon discusses the formation of "performative commons" in the context of early modern England and the Atlantic world in *New World Drama: The Performative Commons in the Atlantic World, 1649–1849* (Durham, NC: Duke University Press, 2014). See especially the introduction, "The Performative Commons and the Aesthetic Atlantic," 1–30.

11. Crouzet, *La nuit de la Saint-Barthélemy*, 183–263.

12. Merlin-Kajman *Public et littérature en France au XVII*[e] *siècle*, 59–87.

13. Crouzet, *La nuit de la Saint-Barthélemy*, 461–530.

14. *Vindiciae contra tyrannos*, 129. My translation.

15. Mellet, *Les traités monarchomaques*, 187–214.

16. François Hotman, *La gaule francoise*, ed. Christiane Frémont (Paris: Fayard, 1991), 94. Unless otherwise noted all citations in French are to this edition.

17. François Hotman, *Francogallia*, ed. Ralph E. Giesey, trans. J. H. M. Salmon (Cambridge: Cambridge University Press, 1972), 295. All translations are from this edition, hereafter cited as Salmon trans., unless otherwise noted.

18. *Vindiciae contra tyrannos*, 129.

19. Robert Estienne, "Charitas," in *Dictionarium latinogallicum* (1552), University of Chicago: ARTFL Dictionnaires d'autrefois. http://artflsrv02.uchicago.edu/philologic4/latinogallicum/. My translation.

20. For how a detailed account of how "charitas" was a complicated, contested concept during the religious wars and in their aftermath, see Ibbett, *Compassion's Edge*, 98–133.

21. Hotman, *La gaule francoise*, 94.

22. Bèze, *Du droit des magistrats*, 12; Beza, *Right of Magistrates*, 5.

23. Bèze, *Du droit des magistrats*, 6; Beza, *Right of Magistrates*, 2.

24. Bèze, *Du droit des magistrats*, 12; Beza, *Right of Magistrates*, 5.

25. Bèze, *Du droit des magistrats*, 12; Beza, *Right of Magistrates*, 5

26. *Vindiciae contra tyrannos*, 25; *Vindiciae*, Garnett trans. 21.

27. *Vindiciae contra tyrannos*, 25; *Vindiciae*, Garnett trans., 21. Garnett translates "alliance" as "covenant" from the Latin *foedus*.

28. *Vindiciae contra tyrannos*, 27–28; *Vindiciae*, Garnett trans., 23. Garnett's translation reads "agreement" and "sealed," respectively.

29. *Vindiciae contra tyrannos*, 21; *Vindiciae*, Garnett trans., 18.

30. Estienne, "Cognatio," in *Dictionarium latinogallicum* (1552), University of Chicago: ARTFL Dictionnaires d'autrefois. http://artflsrv02.uchicago.edu/philologic4/latinogallicum/. My translation.

31. Jean Nicot, "Alliance," in *Thresor de la language francoyse tant ancienne que moderne* (1606), University of Chicago: ARTFL Dictionnaires d'autrefois, https://artflsrv03.uchicago.edu/philologic4/publicdicos/navigate/1/642/. My translation.

32. Bèze, *Du droit des magistrats*, 67; Beza, *Right of Magistrates*, 22–23.

33. Hotman, *La gaule francoise*, 92. My translation.

34. For example, the *Vindiciae* echoes Acts 4:19 and Acts 5:29 by asking rhetorically why Christians would have endured so much suffering to follow God's law when it conflicts with a king's if God's law were not the highest authority. "Autrement pourqouy les Apostres auroyent-ils respondu qu'il faut obeir plustot à Dieu qu'aux hommes?" (Why otherwise the opinion of the apostles, that God should be obeyed rather than men?). *Vindiciae contra tyrannos*, 15; *Vindiciae*, Garnett trans., 14.

35. Hotman, *La gaule francoise*, 55; Hotman, *Francogallia*, Salmon trans., 205.

36. Hotman, *La gaule francoise*, 61.

37. Hotman, *Francogallia*, Salmon trans., 217.

38. On the question of the historical accuracy of these ceremonies, see Richard A. Jackson, "Elective Kingship and Consensus Populi in Sixteenth-Century France," *Journal of Modern History* 44, no. 2 (1972): 155–71; and Richard A. Jackson, *Vive le Roi! A History of the French Coronation from Charles V to Charles X* (Chapel Hill: University of North Carolina Press, 1984), 115–30.

39. Hotman, *La gaule francoise*, 67; Hotman, *Francogallia*, Salmon trans., 233.

40. Hotman, *La gaule francoise*, 66–67; Hotman, *Francogallia*, Salmon trans., 231. Translating from the Latin "iudicio" and "studio," Giesey and Salmon

render this dyad "decision and desire." I have used "consent and will" to be more faithful to the valences of the French text.

41. Jean Nicot, "Volonté," in *Tresor de la langue francoyse tant ancienne que moderne* (1606), University of Chicago: ARTFL Dictionnaires d'autrefois, https://artflsrv03.uchicago.edu/philologic4/publicdicos/navigate/2/9018/.

42. Michel de Montaigne, *Les essais*, III.5, edited by P. Villey and V.-L. Saulnier; online edition by P. Desan. University of Chicago: ARTFL, https://artflsrv03.uchicago.edu/philologic4/montessaisvilley/navigate/1/5/6/?byte=2661323.; *The Complete Essays of Montaigne*. Translated by Donald Frame. (Stanford, CA: Stanford University Press, 1965), 649.

43. *Vindiciae contra tyrannos*, 96; *Vindiciae*, Garnett trans., 68. Garnett's translation reads in full, "born entirely by the same lot as other men, and that they are elevated from the ground to their position by the votes and, as it were, on the shoulders of the people."

44. *Vindiciae contra tyrannos*, 189.

45. *Vindiciae*, Garnett trans., 134–35.

46. Richard A. Jackson notes that the *Vindiciae* repeats the formulas used in the official coronation ceremonies as described in Th*éodore* Godefroy *and Denys* Godefroy, *Le cérémonial français* (Paris, 1649). Jackson, *Vive le Roi!*, 119.

47. Hotman, *La gaule francoise*, 94.

48. *Vindiciae contra tyrannos*, 128–30; *Vindiciae*, Garnett trans. 92–93.

49. Bèze, *Du droit des magistrats*, 60; Beza, *Rights of Magistrates*, 20. The reference to Elizabeth I as an ideal monarch is on one level not surprising given the affinities between Protestant communities across national borders. On another level, the reference is striking in that for the most part Huguenot resistance treatises express contempt for the idea of female rulership, offering examples of how excessive female ambition leads to tyranny. I will address this issue in more detail in chapters 2 and 5 when I discuss Cornelia, the wife of Roman general Pompey, and the biblical queen Athaliah, respectively.

50. Bèze, *Du droit des magistrats*, 60–61.

51. Beza, *Rights of Magistrates*, 20–21.

52. Domna Stanton, "The Ideal of 'Repos' in Seventeenth-Century French Literature," *L'Ésprit Créateur* 15, no. 1/2 (1975): 75–104.

53. *Vindiciae contra tyrannos*, 61–62; *Vindiciae*, Garnett trans., 45–46.

54. *Vindiciae contra tyrannos*, 62; *Vindiciae*, Garnett trans., 46.

55. Hotman, *La gaule francoise*, 93; Salmon trans., 291, 293.

56. *Vindiciae contra tyrannos*, 219. My emphasis.

57. *Vindiciae*, Garnett trans., 156. My emphasis.

58. Bèze, *Du droit des magistrats*, 97; Beza, *Rights of Magistrates*, 33.

59. Bèze writes, for example, "Quand aux personnes du tout privees, si elles ont consenti expressement, et volontairement à la domination d'un injuste usurpateur, comme le Peuple Romain accepta volontairement Auguste et ses successeurs: ou si le legitime Magistrat deviant Tyran manifeste . . . il n'est licite à aucun particulier d'opposer force à la force du Tyran de son authorité privee: ains il faut ou qu'il se retire ailleurs, ou qu'aiant recours à Dieu il souffre le jong, sans toutefois . . . se faire minister de la Tyrannie contre quelqu'un, ou rien obmettre de ce qu'il doit à Dieu, et à son prochain." Bèze, *Du droit des magistrats*, 27–28. This idea of private, quiet submission derives from Calvin. See John Witte Jr.,

The Reformation of Rights: Law, Religion, and Human Rights in Early Modern Calvinism (Cambridge: Cambridge University Press, 2007), 1–80.

60. The *Vindiciae* states, for example, "[et] le Roy et les sujets sont d'une mesme masse, en telle sorte que le peuple a eslevé en ce degré les Rois, afin qu'ils tinssent de luy et possedassent comme par emprunt toute leur authorité et puissance" (*Vindiciae contra tyrannos*, 107).

61. *Vindiciae contra tyrannos*, 127; *Vindiciae*, Garnett trans., 91.

62. *Vindiciae contra tyrannos*, 65; *Vindiciae*, Garnett trans, 49. Garnett translates this last clause as "and according to whether it is formed by those whose business it is to do so or not."

63. *Vindiciae contra tyrannos*, 246; *Vindiciae*, Garnett trans., 174.

64. *Vindiciae contra tyrannos*, 86; *Vindiciae*, Garnett trans., 62. For his part, Bèze very briefly mentions the possibility of extraordinary liberators but does not pursue this possibility. "je dy que sans extraordinare vocation de Dieu à laquelle je ne touche point, il n'est licite à aucun particulier d'opposer force à force du Tyran de son authorité privee." Bèze, *Du droit des magistrates*, 27.

65. *Vindiciae contra tyrannos*, 86; *Vindiciae*, Garnett trans., 62.

66. *Vindiciae contra tyrannos*, 68–69, 85–86; *Vindiciae*, Garnett trans., 51–52, 61–62.

67. *Vindiciae contra tyrannos*, 86; *Vindiciae*, Garnett trans., 62.

68. *Vindiciae contra tyrannos*, 86–87; *Vindiciae*, Garnett trans., 62.

69. *Vindiciae contra tyrannos*, 87; *Vindiciae*, Garnett trans., 62.

70. *Vindiciae contra tyrannos*, 87; *Vindiciae*, Garnett trans., 63.

71. *Vindiciae contra tyrannos*, 245; *Vindiciae*, Garnett trans., 174.

72. *Vindiciae contra tyrannos*, 251; *Vindiciae*, Garnett trans., 178.

73. *Vindiciae contra tyrannos*, 251–52; *Vindiciae*, Garnett trans., 178.

74. The use of the Turks as an external enemy as well as the structure of the rhetorical questions (to which the answers are presumed obvious) portray a unity among Christians (which is in question at this historical moment), even as it points to divisions among Catholics and Protestants through the idea of Christian tyranny (linked in this period to heresy) and liberty of conscience. For more on the role of "the Turk" in early modern French thought, see Marcus Keller, "The Turk of Early Modern France," *L'Esprit Créateur* 53, no. 4 (2013): 1–8; and Clarence D. Rouillard, *The Turk in French History, Thought, and Literature (1520–1660)* (Paris: Boivin, 1941).

75. *Vindiciae contra tyrannos*, 264; *Vindiciae*, Garnett trans., 185.

76. *Vindiciae contra tyrannos*, 241; *Vindiciae*, Garnett trans., 141–42.

77. *Vindiciae contra tyrannos*, 263; *Vindiciae*, Garnett trans., 184.

78. *Vindiciae contra tyrannos*, 263; *Vindiciae*, Garnett trans., 184.

79. *Vindiciae contra tyrannos*, 243; *Vindiciae*, Garnett trans., 173.

80. *Vindiciae, contra tyrannos*, Edinburg (1579), 216, electronic facsimile, Universitätsbibliothek Basel, http://dx.doi.org/10.3931/e-rara-17.

81. See Charlton T. Lewis and Charles Short, "Scientia" and "Conscientia," *A Latin Dictionary* (Oxford: Clarendon Press, 1879).

82. Estienne, "Conscientia," *Dictionarium latinogallicum* (1552), University of Chicago: ARTFL Dictionnaires d'autrefois, http://artflsrv02.uchicago.edu/philologic4/latinogallicum/. My translation.

83. Nicot, "Conscience," *Thresor de la language francoyse tant ancienne que modern* (1606), University of Chicago: ARTFL Dictionnaires d'autrefois, https://artflsrv03.uchicago.edu/philologic4/publicdicos/navigate/1/3894/. My translation.

84. See Witte, *Reformation of Rights*, esp. 81–142.

85. John Calvin, *Institutes of the Christian Religion* [1559], ed. John T. McNeill, trans. Ford Lewis Battles (Philadelphia: Westminster Press, 1960), III.4, 119.

86. Witte, *Reformation of Rights*, 45–56.

87. A large amount of scholarship is devoted to Calvin's conception of the conscience and to the role of the conscience during the Reformation more broadly. In addition to Witte, *Reformation of Rights*, see, e.g., David Bosco, "Conscience as Court and Worm: Calvin and the Three Elements of Conscience," *Journal of Religious Ethics* 14, no.2 (1986): 333–55; Denis McEnnerney, "Philosophy and Politics of Résistance in Early Modern France," *Historical Reflections / Réflexions Historiques* 35, no.1 (2009): 59–71; and Darren Walhof, "The Accusations of Conscience and the Christian Polity in John Calvin's Political Thought," *History of Political Thought* 24, no.3 (2003): 397–414.

88. Walhof, "Accusations of Conscience," 401.

89. Walhof, "Accusations of Conscience," 400–401.

90. *Vindiciae contra tyrannos*, 244; *Vindiciae*, Garnett trans., 174.

91. *Vindiciae contra tyrannos*, 244; *Vindiciae*, Garnett trans., 174.

92. *Vindiciae contra tyrannos*, 264; *Vindiciae*, Garnett trans., 185.

93. *Vindiciae contra tyrannos*, 259; *Vindiciae*, Garnett trans., 182.

94. Palacios, *Ceremonial Splendor: Performing Priesthood in Early Modern France*.

95. *Vindiciae, contra tyrannos*, Edinburg [1579], 231. My thanks to Nicholas Gressens for his assistance parsing the Latin edition of the *Vindiciae*.

96. *Vindiciae*, Garnett trans., 182.

97. See, for example, *Vindiciae contra tyrannos*, 9–12; *Vindiciae*, Garnett trans., 10-12.

98. Calvin, *Institutes of the Christian Religion*, III.19, 332.

99. As Garnett notes, the *Vindiciae* argues that the people enter into two different, though related contracts, spiritual contract with God and a temporal contract with the king. *Vindiciae*, Garnett trans., lv–lxxvi.

100. The treatise uses Cicero and notes that even the pagans can teach Christians this lesson. *Vindiciae*, Garnett trans., lii–liii.

101. *Vindiciae contra tyrannos*, 257; *Vindiciae*, Garnett trans., 181.

102. *Vindiciae contra tyrannos*, 257; *Vindiciae*, Garnett trans., 181.

103. *Vindiciae*, Garnett trans., lii–iiii.

104. *Vindiciae*, Garnett trans., liii.

105. Baricave, *De la defense de la monarchie françoise*. Quoted in Garnett, introduction, xx.

106. Garnett, introduction, liv.

107. For a detailed account of Catholic resistance theory, see Frederic J. Baumgartner, *Radical Reactionaries: The Political Thought of the French Catholic League* (Geneva: Droz, 1976).

108. Hotman, *Francogallia*, Salmon trans., 519. This passage does not appear in the 1574 French edition of the treatise, from which I have been quoting. It does appear in the 1577 French edition and subsequent French editions.

109. *Vindiciae contra tyrannos*, 124; *Vindiciae*, Garnett trans., 89.

110. Bèze, *Du droit des magistrats*, 49; Beza, *Right of Magistrates*, 16.

111. Mellet, *Les traités monarchomaques*, 362. My translation.

112. Mellet, *Les traités monarchomaques*, 362.

113. Jean Balsamo, "Rhétorique et politique dans *Les Gordiens et les Maximins (1589)* d'Antoine Favre," *Seizième Siècle* 6 (2010): 39–49. Of the many connections between tragedy and political representation in sixteenth-century France, two biographical points are of particular note to my study. First, Théodore de Bèze, author of the resistance treatise *Du droit des magistrats*, was also a tragedian. His *Abraham sacrifiant* (1550) has a foundational status in literary history as one of the first vernacular tragedies in the French tradition. Second, Robert Garnier, the well-known sixteenth-century dramatist whose tragedy I discuss in detail in chapters 2 and 3, was an *avocat* in the Parlement of Paris as well as a magistrate in *présidal* of Le Mans. Marie-Madeleine Mouflard has provided the most detailed account of Garnier's life and work to date: *Robert Garnier, 1545–1590*, vol. 1, *La vie* (La Ferté-Bernard: Bellanger, 1961); *Robert Garnier, 1545–1590*, vol. 2, *L'œuvre* (La Roche-sur-Yon: Imprimerie Centrale de la Ouest, 1963); and *Robert Garnier, 1545–1590*, vol. 3, *Les sources* (La Roche-sur-Yon: Imprimerie Centrale de la Ouest, 1964). See also Marc Fumaroli, *L'âge de l'éloquence: Rhétorique et "res literaria" de la Renaissance au seuil de l'époque classique* (Geneva: Droz, 1980); and Joseph R. Roach, *The Player's Passion: Studies in the Science of Acting* (1993; reprint, Ann Arbor: University of Michigan Press, 2011.

114. Jean-Pierre Vernant and Pierre Vidal-Naquet, *Myth and Tragedy in Ancient Greece*, trans. Janet Lloyd (New York: Zone Books, 1990), 49–84.

Chapter Two

1. *Vindiciae contra tyrannos*, 213; *Vindiciae*, Garnett trans., 152.

2. *Vindiciae contra tyrannos*, 214; *Vindiciae*, Garnett trans., 153.

3. See Pierre-François Godard de Beauchamps, *Recherches sur les théâtres de France depuis l'année onze cent soixante-un jusques à présent* (Paris, 1735), II.148.

4. *Vindiciae contra tyrannos*, 198; *Vindiciae*, Garnett trans., 142. Garnett notes that the reference to Brunhilda would likely have been interpreted as an "implicit attack on Catherine de Medici," a comparison that was commonplace during the 1570s (142–43n507).

5. *Vindiciae contra tyrannos*, 68-69; *Vindiciae*, Garnett trans., 51–52.

6. As Holt has persuasively argued, the the wars effectively continued until 1629. Holt, *French Wars of Religion*.

7. Pierre Corneille, "Examen," *La mort de Pompée*, in *Œuvres complètes*, vol. 1, ed. Georges Couton (Paris: Gallimard, 1980), 1074–78.

8. John E. Matzke, "The Sources of Corneille's Tragedy *La mort de Pompée*," *Modern Language Notes* 15, no. 5 (May 1990): 142–52.

9. Robert Garnier, *Cornélie: Tragédie*, ed. Jean-Claude Ternaux (Paris: Honoré Champion, 2002), 27. All translations of Garnier's dedication are my own.

10. Garnier, *Cornélie*, 27.

11. Garnier, *Cornélie*, 27.

12. Garnier, *Cornélie*, 27.

13. Garnier, *Cornélie*, 26.

14. Garnier's disappointment with the nobles of his time echoes the complaints voiced by resistance treatises such as the *Francogallia* and the *Vindiciae*, both of which lament how current public representatives do not live up to their past glory and full potential. (I discuss the tone of disappointment in these treatises at more length in chap. 1.)

15. Phillip John Usher, "Courtroom Drama during the Wars of Religion: Robert Garnier and the Paris *Parlement*," in *French Renaissance and Baroque Drama: Text, Performance, Theory*, ed. Michael Meere (Newark: University of Delaware Press, 2015), 139–52.

16. Unless otherwise noted, text references are to the act and line numbers of Jean-Claude Ternaux's critical edition of *Cornélie*, which uses the 1585 edition of Garnier's collected works as its base text. I sometimes refer to variants from the 1574 edition, which Ternaux includes as an appendix.

17. Thomas Kyd, trans., *Cornelia*, 1594, in *Robert Garnier in Elizabethan England: Mary Sidney Herbert's* Antonius *and Thomas Kyd's* Cornelia, ed. Marie-Alice Belle and Line Cottegnies (London: Modern Humanities Research Association, 2017), 4.2.1–10. Unless otherwise noted, all translations of Garnier's *Cornélie* are from this edition of Kyd's translation, for which Kyd most likely used Garnier's 1585 edition.

18. In Renaissance tragedies, it is common for tyrants to appear in the middle of the play rather than in the first act, which means that their tyrannical reputation has been established before their entrance. Rebecca W. Bushnell discusses this practice in Bushnell, *Tragedies of Tyrants: Political Thought and Theater in the English Renaissance* (Ithaca, NY: Cornell University Press, 1990).

19. *Vindiciae contra tyrannos*, 215; *Vindiciae*, Garnett trans., 153.

20. *Cornelia*, Kyd trans., 1.1.21–27.

21. *Cornelia*, Kyd trans., 2.1–8.

22. *Cornelia*, Kyd trans., 2.184–90.

23. Emily Wilson examines the concept of "living too long" as a common trope in ancient and early modern literature. Wilson, *Mocked with Death: Tragic Overliving from Sophocles to Milton* (Baltimore, MD: Johns Hopkins University Press, 2004).

24. *Cornelia*, Kyd trans., 2.158–61.

25. *Cornelia*, Kyd trans., 2.214–16.

26. *Cornelia*, Kyd trans., 2.222–23.

27. Nicole Loraux, *Mothers in Mourning: With the Essay "Of Amnesty and Its Opposite,"* trans. Corinne Pache (Ithaca, NY: Cornell University Press, 1998), 21–28.

28. Helen P. Foley, *Female Acts in Greek Tragedy* (Princeton, NJ: Princeton University Press, 2001), 54–55.

29. Foley, *Female Acts*, 21–55.

30. Marie Houllemare, *Politiques de la parole: Le parlement de Paris au XVI siècle* (Geneva: Droz, 2011), 475.

31. See Houllemare, *Politiques de la parole*, 475.

32. *Cornelia*, Kyd trans., 4.1.182–85.

33. *Cornelia*, Kyd trans., 4.1.204–9.

34. *Cornelia*, Kyd trans., 3.3.26–27.

35. Variant A, in Garnier, *Cornélie*, 150. My translation. Garnier's modern editor, Jean-Claude Ternaux, does not include this passage in his "édition de base" of 1585. The passage appears in what Ternaux designates Variant A, which appeared in 1574. For more details on the editions and variations, see Garnier, *Cornélie*, 139–51.

36. Garnier, *Cornélie*, 20, 86–87.

37. Lucan, *Civil War*, trans. Matthew Fox (New York: Penguin Classics, 2012), 8.688–1076.

38. Lucan, *Civil War*, 9.212–16.

39. Lucan, *Civil War*, 9.217–25.

40. *Cornelia*, Kyd trans., 3.3.69–72.

41. Variant A, in Garnier, *Cornélie*, 150.

42. My translation.

43. *Cornelia*, Kyd trans., 5.455–65.

44. Corneille, "Examen," *La mort de Pompée* 1076. My translation.

45. Serge Doubrovsky, *Corneille et la dialectique du héros* (Paris: Gallimard, 1963), 281. My translation.

46. Doubrovsky, *Corneille*, 278. My translation. Doubrovsky reads Caesar's actions in the final scene as a gesture of magnanimity toward a formal rival. For Doubrovsky, Caesar is thus similar to Augustus, the Roman emperor of Corneille's *Cinna*, who generously forgives those who have conspired against him: "César, vainqueur, veut donc asseoir sa domination absolue sur la magnanimité et reproduire, en quelque sorte, le geste salvateur d'Auguste dans *Cinna*" (Doubrovsky, *Corneille*, 278). See also Richard Goodkin, *Birth Marks: The Tragedy of Primogeniture in Pierre Corneille, Thomas Corneille, and Jean Racine* (Philadelphia: University of Pennsylvania Press, 2000), 78–96. Goodkin reads this final scene as marking a passage from one era to another, with Pompey figuring the old order of "inherited debts and benefits" and Caesar figuring "the forces of the present," which include political ambition and calculation.

47. Variant A, in Garnier, *Cornélie*, 150.

48. All text references to *La mort de Pompée* are to the act, scene, and line numbers in Corneille, *Œuvres complètes*.

49. Pierre Corneille, *The Death of Pompey*, in *The Moot Plays of Pierre Corneille*, trans. Lacy Lockert (Nashville: Vanderbilt University Press, 1959), 36.

50. Corneille, Death of Pompey, Lockert trans., 37.

51. On the relationship between Roman and Christian virtue in Corneille's play, see A. Donald Sellstrom, "*La mort de Pompée*: Roman History and Tasso's Theory of Christian Epic," *PMLA* 97, no. 5 (October 1982): 830–43.

52. Corneille, Death of Pompey, Lockert trans., 52.

53. Corneille, Death of Pompey, Lockert trans., 58.

54. Corneille, Death of Pompey, Lockert trans., 55. Translator's emphasis.

55. Corneille, Death of Pompey, Lockert trans., 49.

56. Corneille, Death of Pompey, Lockert trans., 50.

57. William Howarth, *French Theatre in the Neo-Classical Era: 1550–1789* (Cambridge: Cambridge University Press, 1997), 544.

58. La Taille, "De l'art de la tragédie," 3v–4r. My translation.

59. Abbé d'Aubignac, *La pratique du théâtre* (Paris, 1657), 250. Translations of d'Aubignac are my own.

60. D'Aubignac, *La pratique*, 250–51.

61. For a comprehensive account of the role that these unities played in debates about the aesthetics of seventeenth-century tragedy and about this genre's social function, see Lyons, *Kingdom of Disorder*.

62. D'Aubignac, *La pratique*, 269–70.

63. Aristotle, *Poetics*, trans. Gerald Else (Ann Arbor: University of Michigan Press, 1967), 24.

64. D'Aubignac, *La pratique*, 270–71.

65. Lyons, *Kingdom of Disorder*, 145, 145, 145.

66. Christian Biet, "A 'Senecan Theatre of Cruelty: Audience, Citizens, and Chorus in Late-Sixteenth and Early Seventeenth-Century French Drama," *Choruses Ancient and Modern*, eds. Joshua Billings, Felix Budelmann, and Fiona Macintosh (Oxford: Oxford University Press, 2013), 189–202.

67. Jondorf, *French Renaissance Tragedy*, 69.

68. Pierre Corneille, *Horace*, act 5, scene 3, line 1728, quoted in Jondorf, *French Renaissance Tragedy*, 69.

69. Jondorf, *French Renaissance Tragedy*, 69.

70. This may in part be the result of d'Aubignac's distaste for Seneca's tragedy and its use of choruses. See, for example, d'Aubignac, *La pratique*, 253. Although d'Aubignac does not deem Seneca's tragedies worthy of much attention, the Roman's work had been widely studied and adapted by French dramatists of the sixteenth century. See Jondorf, *French Renaissance Tragedy*.

71. Joan DeJean, *Tender Geographies: Women and the Origin of the Novel in France* (New York: Columbia University Press, 1991), 1–42. See also Derval Conroy, *Ruling Women, Vol. 1: Government, Virtue, and the Female Prince in Seventeenth-Century France* (Basingstoke, UK: Palgrave Macmillan, 2016); and Ian Maclean, *Woman Triumphant: Feminism in French Literature, 1610–1652* (Oxford: Clarendon Press, 1977).

72. DeJean, *Tender Geographies*, 41.

73. Timothy J. Reiss, "Corneille and Cornelia: Reason, Violence, and the Cultural Status of the Feminine. Or, How a Dominant Discourse Recuperated and Subverted the Advance of Women," *Renaissance Drama* 18 (1987), 3–41.

74. Giovanni Boccaccio, *On Famous Women*, trans. Guido A. Guarin, 2nd ed. (New York: Ithaca Press, 2011), 181–82.

75. Christine de Pizan, *The Book of the City of Ladies*, trans. Rosalind Brown-Grant (New York: Penguin Books, 1999), 2:126–27.

Chapter Three

1. Robert Garnier, *Antigone, ou La pieté*, ed. Jean-Dominique Beaudin (Paris: Honoré Champion, 1997). All citations from Garnier's drama are from this edition and text citations refer to act and line numbers. Robert Garnier, *The Tragedy of Pious Antigone*, trans. Phillip John Usher (Tempe: Arizona Center for Medieval and Renaissance Studies, 2018), 9. Unless otherwise noted, all translations of *Garnier's Antigone, ou La pieté* are by Philip John Usher.

2. Robert Garnier, *The Tragedy of Pious Antigone*, trans. Phillip John Usher, 10.

3. Garnier, *Tragedy of Pious Antigone*, Usher trans., 22.

4. Usher, "Courtroom Drama," 143. All translations of Garnier's dedication to Brisson are Usher's.

5. Usher, "Courtroom Drama,"144.
6. Usher, "Courtroom Drama," 144.
7. Usher, "Courtroom Drama," 144–45.
8. Corneille, *La mort de Pompée*, 3.4.1027. My translation.
9. It is uncertain whether Garnier's drama was performed during the sixteenth century. Beaudin argues, however, that the composition of the text suggests that Garnier certainly had performance in mind. Beaudin, introduction to Garnier, *Antigone, ou La pieté*, 45–53.
10. Holt, *French Wars of Religion*, 3-4; 178–94.
11. Koselleck, *Critique and Crisis*, 17; On the relationship between the *corps mystique* and the *corps politique*, see Merlin-Kajman, *Public et littérature*, 59–87.
12. Maddox Dillon, *New World Drama*, 1–30.
13. Koselleck, *Critique and Crisis*, 17. As I noted in the introduction, Jean Bodin recognized the problems caused by the existence of different factions with different perceptions of tyranny as early as 1580 in his *Les six livres de la République*.
14. For further discussion of Garnier's sources, see Beaudin, introduction to Garnier, *Antigone ou La pieté*, 7–54. See also Usher's introduction to his English translation of Garnier's *Antigone* in Garnier, *Tragedy of Pious Antigone*, xv–xxxviii. For a longer discussion of Rotrou's sources, see Bénédicte Louvat's introduction to *Antigone*, in Jean Rotrou, *Théâtre choisi*, ed. Marianne Béthery, Bénédicte Louvat, and Pierre Pasquier (Paris: Société des Textes Français Modernes, 2007), 199–249.
15. Bonnie Honig, *Antigone, Interrupted* (Cambridge: Cambridge University Press, 2013), 1–10.
16. Louis de Jaucourt, "Sujet," in Denis Diderot and Jean le Rond d'Alembert, eds., *Encyclopédie, ou Dictionnaire raisonné des sciences, des arts et des métiers, etc.*, in University of Chicago: ARTFL Encyclopédie Project (Autumn 2017), ed. Robert Morrissey and Glenn Roe. In this entry Jaucourt references a biblical verse that was a commonplace in early modern debates about the *droit de résistance*. The verse, from Acts 29:5, in which the Apostle Peter states that it is "better to obey God rather than men," is cited in Huguenot treatises in particular. Although Jaucourt's biographical relationship to Protestantism remains a subject of debate, Jaucourt's writing suggests intellectual ties to some aspects of Protestant. See Daniel Brewer, "Encyclopedic Transfers and the Internationalization of Intellectual Work: Louis de Jaucourt," in *The Internationalization of Intellectual Exchange in a Globalizing Europe, 1636–1780*, ed. Robert Mankin (Lewisburg, PA: Bucknell University Press, 2018), 143–62.
17. Simone Fraisse, *Le mythe d'Antigone* (Paris: Armand Colin, 1974), 167. All translations of Fraisse are my own.
18. Honig, *Antigonie, Interrupted*, 7.
19. Judith Butler, *Antigone's Claim: Kinship between Life and Death* (2000; reprint, New York: Columbia University Press, 2002), 35.
20. Butler, *Antigone's Claim*, 35.
21. Butler, *Antigone's Claim*, 34–35.
22. Honig, *Antigonie, Interrupted*, 7–9.
23. Butler, *Antigone's Claim*, 72.
24. Butler, *Antigone's Claim*, 72.
25. Honig, *Antigonie, Interrupted*, 54.

26. Honig, *Antigonie, Interrupted*, 54.
27. Honig, *Antigonie, Interrupted*, see esp. 85–189.
28. Cherbuliez also makes this point in *In the Wake of Medea*, 42.
29. Honig, *Antigonie, Interrupted*, 67–70.
30. The phrase is from W. B. Worthen, *Drama: Between Poetry and Performance*, 1–34.
31. Fraisse, *Le mythe d'Antigone*, 14.
32. Fraisse, *Le mythe d'Antigone*, 15.
33. Fraisse, *Le mythe d'Antigone*, 15–17. The historical periods during which one side or another of this dual lineage seemed to be in vogue. Fraisse suggests that during the Renaissance and nineteenth century the devoted Antigone reigned. In contrast, during eighteenth and twentieth centuries, the dissident Antigone who speaks out as "la voix du faible contre le puissant" was more in favor.
34. The frontispiece appears in editions from 1639 and 1640 that were published by Antoine de Sommaville and Toussaint Quinet. Louvat, introduction to *Antigone*, in Rotrou, *Théâtre choisi*, 251–54.
35. Usher points out that Garnier's *Antigone, ou La pieté* is the longest of Renaissance tragedies, except for Pierre Matthieu's *Esther*. Usher, introduction to *Tragedy of Pious Antigone*, xv.
36. As Fraisse points out, Garnier's tragedy is "la seule qui présente pour le théâtre l'histoire d'Antigone dans sa continuité." Fraisse, *Le mythe d'Antigone*, 22. Beaudin underscores that the actor playing Antigone would remain on stage during nearly the entire duration of the drama in his introduction to *Antigone, ou La pieté*, 39. Fraisse and Beaudin are in part responding to Émile Faguet's assertion that Garnier's drama lacks unity. Faguet, *La tragédie française au seizième siècle* (Paris: Librairie Universitaire, 1894), 205–6.
37. Fraisse writes, "Piété fraternelle qui se confond avec la pitié, les deux mots qui procèdent du même radical étant au XVIe encore mêlés dans l'usage. En ensevelissant son frère, Antigone se montre 'piteuse' ou 'pitoyable,' c'est-à-dire qu'elle pratique la charité." Fraisse, *Le mythe d'Antigone*, 24.
38. George Steiner, *Antigones* (New York: Oxford University Press, 1985; New Haven, CT: Yale University Press, 1996), 139–40.
39. Beaudin, introduction to *Antigone, ou La pieté*, 40; Fraisse, *Le mythe d'Antigone*, 22.
40. Florence Dobby-Poirson notes that this slow, deliberate pace would have produced maximum emotional effect on the drama's spectators. Dobby-Poirson, *Le pathétique dans le théâtre de Robert Garnier* (Paris: Honoré Champion, 2006), 234.
41. Garnier, *Tragedy of Pious Antigone*, Usher trans., 9.
42. Garnier, *Tragedy of Pious Antigone*, Usher trans., 12.
43. Garnier, *Tragedy of Pious Antigone*, Usher trans., 14.
44. Garnier, *Tragedy of Pious Antigone*, Usher trans., 13.
45. Garnier, *Tragedy of Pious Antigone*, Usher trans., 15.
46. Beaudin, introduction to *Antigone, ou La pieté*, 22. My translation.
47. Beaudin, introduction to *Antigone, ou La pieté*, 22. My translation.
48. Jondorf, *Robert Garnier and the Themes of Political Tragedy*, 104–5.
49. Diefendorf, "Rites of Repair," 35.

50. Diefendorf, "Rites of Repair," 34. For more on the concept of the common good and the stress that this concept underwent during the religious wars, see Merlin-Kajman, *Public et littérature*, 14–87.

51. Christian Biet writes, "Dans cette période qui suit les guerres de religion et qu'on qualifiera plus tard de 'baroque,' on est en droit de considérer qu'aucune des lois de référence ne peut être totalement partagée par tous les citoyens." Biet, "Droit divin, droit naturel, et droit humain dans *Antigone* de Jean Rotrou," *Littératures Classiques* 17 (1992): 66.

52. Rotrou, *Antigone*, in Rotrou, *Théâtre choisi*. All citations of Rotrou are from this edition and refer to act, scene, and lines. All translations of Rotrou are my own.

53. Rotrou, *Antigone*, 261.

54. I thank Juliette Cherbuliez for calling the exceptionality of Jocasta's state of underdress to my attention.

55. Biet underscores this paradox, remarking that in Rotrou's drama, "la loi de la nature se trouve avoir été bafouée par celle qui la défend." Biet, "Droit divin, droit naturel," 77.

56. Biet, "Droit divin, droit naturel," 69–70. My translation.

57. As Steiner observes, Rotrou's use of words like "amitié," "tendre," "respect," "titre d'invincible," "ravie," and "déférence," all of which "belong to the baroque politics of eros," would have rendered Antigone's speech to and about Polynices both "erotic and sisterly" to its seventeenth-century audience. Steiner, *Antigones*, 162.

58. Louvat notes that Rotrou elaborates on Statius's version of this scene in her introduction to *Antigone*, 209–10.

59. Jondorf suggests that these choruses would have entered and exited with their respective characters. Jondor, *French Renaissance Tragedy*, 84.

60. See Dobby-Poirson, *Le pathétique dans le théâtre*, 543.

61. Garnier, *Tragedy of Pious Antigone*, Usher trans., 36.

62. Garnier, *Tragedy of Pious Antigone*, Usher trans., 50–51.

63. Garnier, *Tragedy of Pious Antigone*, Usher trans., 107.

64. Garnier, *Tragedy of Pious Antigone*, Usher trans., 107.

65. Garnier, *Tragedy of Pious Antigone*, Usher trans., 47.

66. Garnier, *Tragedy of Pious Antigone*, Usher trans., 48.

67. For a discussion of this debate within Garnier's theater and political writing more generally, see Jondorf, *Robert Garnier and the Themes of Political Tragedy*, 105–21.

68. Garnier, *Tragedy of Pious Antigone*, Usher trans., 48.

69. Garnier is one of Rotrou's principal sources for this scene. For a breakdown of Rotrou's sources based on act and scene, see Louvat, introduction to *Antigone*, 213.

70. Whereas Eteocles has a speaking role in Rotrou's version, this brother is not figured in Garnier's.

71. Garnier, *Tragedy of Pious Antigone*, Usher trans., 99–100.

72. Garnier, *Tragedy of Pious Antigone*, Usher trans., 101.

73. Garnier, *Tragedy of Pious Antigone*, Usher trans., 12.

74. Jonathan Strauss, *Private Lives, Public Deaths: Antigone and the Invention of Individuality* (New York: Fordham University Press, 2013).

75. See, in particular, Strauss's chapter "Inventing Life" in *Private Lives, Public Deaths*, 85–100.

76. Quoted in Sara Ahmed, *Willful Subjects* (Durham, NC: Duke University Press, 2014), 1.

77. Quoted in Ahmed, *Willful Subjects*, 1.

78. Ahmed, *Willful Subjects*, 1.

79. Ahmed, *Willful Subjects*, 137.

Chapter Four

1. Pierre Corneille, *Le Cid*, in *Œuvres complètes*, vol. 1, ed. Georges Couton (Paris: Gallimard, 1980). Text references are to act, scene, and line numbers.

2. Pierre Corneille, *The Cid / Cinna / The Theatrical Illusion*, trans. John Cairncross (New York: Penguin Books, 1975), 109.

3. On the myth of the Cornelian hero and the interpretive pressure this myth has exerted on scholarship, see John Lyons, "Le mythe du héros cornélien," *Revue d'Histoire Littéraire de la France* 107, no. 2 (2007): 433–48.

4. For a classic articulation of Cornelian heroism as an expression of the aristocratic ethos, see Paul Bénichou, *Morales du grand siècle* (Paris: Gallimard, 1948), 15–148.

5. Jouanna, *Le devoir de révolte.*

6. Ranum, *Fronde.*

7. Bénichou, *Morales du grand siècle*, 91. My translation.

8. Doubrovsky, *Corneille et la dialectique du héros*, 467. My translation, italic in the original.

9. Michel Prigent outlines this process in *Le héros et l'état dans la tragédie de Pierre Corneille* (Paris: Presses Universitaire de France, 1986), 1–30, 421–524.

10. Lyons, "Le mythe du héros cornélian," 433. My translation.

11. Lyons, "Le mythe du héros cornélian."

12. Jean de La Bruyère, *Les caractères, ou Les mœurs de ce siècle*, in *Oeuvres complètes*, ed. Julien Benda (Paris: Gallimard, 1951). University of Chicago: ARTFL-FRANTEXT. https://artflsrv03.uchicago.edu/philologic4/frantext0917/navigate/522/table-of-contents/

13. Jean de La Bruyère. *The Characters, or Manners of the Present Age. The Works of Monsieur de La Bruyere*, 6th ed., vol. 2 (London, 1713), 23–24, https://books.google.com/books?id=2GCQcxD7AUcC.

14. Philippe Sellier, Le mythe du héros (Paris: Bordas, 1990). Quoted in Lyons, "Le mythe du héros cornélien," 434. Sellier's emphais. My translation.

15. Bénichou, *Morales du grand siècle*, 61. Bénichou writes, "un sentiment orgueilleux de supériorité est dans Corneille l'auxiliaire indispensable de la rigueur morale."

16. Hélène Merlin-Kajman, "*Cinna, Rodogune, Nicomède*: Le roi et le moi," *Littératures* 37 (1997): 74. Merlin-Kajman's emphasis. My translation.

17. Pierre Corneille, *Nicomède, a tragi-comedy*, trans. John Dancer (London, 1671), 40; *Nicomède*, in *Œuvres complètes*, vol. 2, ed. Georges Couton (Paris: Gallimard, 1984). Text citations in French refer to act, scene, and line numbers.

18. Corneille, *Nicomède, a tragi-comedy*, 9.

19. Pierre Corneille, *The Chief Plays of Corneille*, trans. Lacy Lockert (Princeton, NJ: Princeton University Press, 1957), 385.

20. Corneille, *Chief Plays of Corneille*, 385.

21. Merlin-Kajman, "*Cinna, Rodogune, Nicomède*," 75–76.

22. V. L. Sauliner summarizes this critical consensus, noting that "Corneille afait vivre le *généreux* de Descartes." Sauliner, *La littérature française du siècle classique* (Paris: Presses Universitaires de France, 1970), 53. Quoted in R. Darren Gobert, *The Mind-Body Stage: Passion and Interaction in the Cartesian Theater* (Stanford, CA: Stanford University Press, 2013), 55.

23. René Descartes, *Les passions de l'âme* (1649), III, 153. Paris: Vrin 1860. University of Chicago: ARTFL-FRANTEXT, https://artflsrv03.uchicago.edu/philologic4/frantext0917/navigate/2158/table-of-contents/.

24. René Descartes, *The Passions of the Soul, and Other Late Philosophical Writings*, trans. Michael Moriarty (Oxford: Oxford World's Classics, 2015), 258.

25. Descartes, *Les passions de l'âme*, III, 156.

26. Descartes, *Passions of the Soul and Other Late Philosophical Writings*, 259.

27. Gobert, *Mind-Body Stage*, 56.

28. Corneille, "Examen," *Nicomède*," in Pierre Corneille, *Œuvres complètes*, vol. 2, ed. Georges Couton (Paris: Gallimard, 1984), 643.

29. Translations of Corneille's "Examen" are my own.

30. Gobert also discusses the relationship between Cartesian generosity and admiration in Nicomède. See Gobert, *Mind-Body Stage*, 53–70.

31. Corneille, "Examen," *Nicomède*," 643.

32. Descartes, *Passions de l'âme*, II, 53.

33. Descartes, *Passions of the Soul and Other Late Philosophical Writings*, 220.

34. See Christian Biet, "Plaisirs et dangers de l'admiration," *Littératures Classiques* 32 (1998): 121–34.

35. Corneille, *Chief Plays of Corneille*, 333.

36. My translation.

37. Corneille, *Chief Plays of Corneille*, 343.

38. Corneille, *Chief Plays of Corneille*, 345.

39. The queen states: "J'ai prévu ce tumulte, et n'en vois rien à craindre, / Comme un moment l'allume, un moment peut l'éteindre, / Et si l'obscurité laisse croître ce bruit, / Le jour dissipera les vapeurs de la nuit" (*Nicomède*, 5.1.1479–82).

40. Gobert also discusses these mirrored gestures in *Mind-Body Stage*, 64–5.

41. Corneille, *Chief Plays of Corneille*, 379.

42. Corneille, *Chief Plays of Corneille*, 384.

43. Corneille, *Chief Plays of Corneille*, 386.

44. Corneille, *Suréna*, in *The Moot Plays of Pierre Corneille*, trans. Lacy Lockert (Nashville: Vanderbilt University Press, 1959), 437.

45. John D. Lyons demonstrates how this form of attachment to a waning political order appears throughout Corneille's tragic drama in *The Tragedy of Origins: Pierre Corneille and Historical Perspective* (Stanford, CA: Stanford University Press, 1996), 1–37.

46. Corneille, *The Cid / Cinna / The Theatrical Illusion*, 109; *Suréna, Général des Parthes*, in *Œuvres complètes*, vol. 3, ed. Georges Couton (Paris: Gallimard, 1987). Text references are to act, scene, and line numbers.

47. The tensions between familial, romantic, and political attachments in Le Cid have been much discussed in Corneille scholarship. See, for example, Mitchell Greenberg, *Corneille and the Ruses of Symmetry* (Cambridge: Cambridge University Press, 1986), 37–65.

48. Corneille, *Suréna*, 451.

49. Corneille, *Suréna*, 480.

50. The theory of blood circulation had been widely accepted by the 1670s, when *Suréna* appeared on stage and in print. William Harvey's pivotal study *De motu cordis* was published some decades before in 1628 and had been much discussed in French medical and philosophical circles, most notably by René Descartes. For an analysis of points of disagreement between Harvey and Descartes, see Marjorie Grene, "The Heart and Blood: Descartes, Plemp, and Harvey," in *Essays on the Philosophy and Science of René Descartes*, ed. Stephen Voss (Oxford: Oxford University Press, 1993), 324–35.

51. *Vindiciae contra tyrannos*, 33–34.

52. *Vindiciae*, Garnett trans., 27.

53. *Vindiciae contra tyrannos*, 34; *Vindiciae*, Garnett trans., 27.

54. *Vindiciae contra tyrannos*, 34; *Vindiciae*, Garnett trans., 27.

55. *Vindiciae contra tyrannos*, 34; *Vindiciae*, Garnett trans., 27.

56. Corneille, *Suréna*, 438. Translator's emphasis.

57. Marc Fumaroli, *Héros et orateurs: Rhétorique et dramaturgie cornéliennes* (Paris: Droz, 1960), 77. My translation.

58. Fumaroli, for example, maintains that the lovers' "transparence parfaite" (perfect transparency) is apolitical and argues that their connection carries spiritual overtones. Fumaroli, *Héros et orateurs*, 77. See also Georges Forestier, "Corneille et la tragédie: Hypothèses sur l'élaboration de Suréna," *Littératures Classiques* 16 (1992): 141–68; and *Essai de génetique théâtrale: Corneille à l'œuvre* (Paris: Klincksieck, 1996), 31–59.

59. Corneille, *Suréna*, 471. Ellen McClure notes that in becoming an "obstacle" to the king's designs, Suréna exposes a problem inherent in the absolutist conceptions of mediation and diplomacy. However powerful the king was, he could not be present in every location where he had political aims. The king thus needed ambassadors in order to carry out his designs. As McClure explains, theories of absolutism held that the sovereign's power "should pass through the state's agents with as few 'obstacles' as possible." Instead of transmitting Orode's power, Suréna, however, blocks this power by refusing to relinquish his love. McClure demonstrates how the ambassador's own "humanity and individuality" interfered with his ability to serve as a transparent agent of the king's authority. McClure, *Sunspots and the Sun King*, 240–49.

60. Corneille, *Suréna*, 468.

61. Corneille, *Suréna*, 473.

62. Corneille, *Suréna*, 480.

63. Corneille, *Suréna*, 484.

64. Corneille, *Suréna*, 486.

65. Corneille, *Suréna*, 486.

66. Corneille, *Suréna*, 486.

67. Corneille, *Suréna*, 486.

68. Katherine Ibbett, "Heroes and History's Remainders: The *Restes* of Pierre Corneille," *Modern Language Quarterly* 69, no. 3 (2008): 352.

69. Ibbett, "Heroes and History's Remainders," 352.

70. Corneille, *Suréna*, 464.

71. As Koselleck notes, subjects under absolutism had to maintain "a clean break between the internal and the external." Koselleck, *Critique and Crisis*, 19.

72. Article 4 of the *Declaration of the Rights of Man and of the Citizen* (1789) states: "Liberty consists in the freedom to do everything which injures no one else; hence the exercise of the natural rights of each man has no limits except those which assure to the other members of the society the enjoyment of the same rights. These limits can only be determined by law." Yale Law School, *The Avalon Project: Documents in Law, History, and Diplomacy*, http://avalon.law.yale.edu/18th_century/rightsof.asp. On the historical development liberal individualism, see, for example, C. B. Macpherson, *The Political Theory of Possessive Individualism: Hobbes to Locke* (Oxford: Oxford University Press, 2011).

73. Merlin-Kajman argues that Suréna articulates a form of self-sovereignty that anticipates the rights-endowed individual of modernity. See Merlin-Kajman, "*Cinna*, *Rodogune*, *Nicomède*," 67–86, and *L'absolutisme dans les lettres*, 1–16. Mitchel Greenberg also points to a kind of emergent modernity in *Suréna* although his focus is on how the psychological strictures of absolutism engender a form of modern subjectivity. He argues that the "Absolute quest for totality" that is displayed within Corneille's dramas represents a form of psychic violence. This violence, he explains, "is the same violence at the origin of modern Law and thus of the modern subject." Greenberg, *Corneille and the Ruses of Symmetry*, 15, 153–65.

74. See also Merlin-Kajman, *L'absolutisme dans les lettres*.

Chapter Five

1. Jean Racine, *Esther*, in *Œuvres complètes*, vol. 1, ed. Georges Forestier (Paris: Gallimard, 1999). Text references are to act, scene, and line numbers. Jean Racine, *The Complete Plays of Jean Racine*, vol. 2. trans. Samuel Solomon (New York: Random House, 1967), 358. All translations of *Racine* are from this edition.

2. Racine, *Complete Plays of Jean Racine*, 359. Translation revised

3. Eve Kosofsky Sedgwick, *Epistemology of the Closet* (Berkeley: University of California Press, 1990), 76.

4. Sedgwick writes in detail about the structural specificities of a Jewish closet and a sexual one. Whereas Jewish identity and sexual orientation share a relatively fluid dynamic of secrecy and openness (compared with racial identities such as blackness, which are primarily coded through skin color), they differ with respect to familial legacy. One inherits Jewishness in a way that one does not inherit sexual orientation. Sedgwick, *Epistemology of the Closet*, 75.

5. Ibbett, *Compassion's Edge*, 159–95.

6. See Achille Taphanel, *Le théâtre de Saint Cyr* (Paris: Baudry, 1876), 3–4.

7. Quoted in Taphanel, *Le théâtre de Saint Cyr*, 4. On the place of Madame de Maintenon's curriculum at Saint Cyr within wider seventeenth-century debates on educating women, see Hélène Jacquemin, *Livres et jeunes filles nobles à Saint-Cyr (1686–1793)* (Paris: Presses de l'Université d'Angers, 2007). Translations of Taphanel are my own.

8. Racine, "Préface," *Esther*, 946; Racine, *Complete Plays of Jean Racine*, 307.

9. For extensive detail on the production and its budget, see Taphanel, *Le théâtre de Saint Cyr*.

10. Julia Prest examines the resonances between the theatrical curriculum at Saint-Cyr and the use of theater in Jesuit schools for boys during this period. Prest, "Boys Will Be Girls: Cross-Casting in School Drama," in *Theatre under Louis XIV: Cross-Casting and the Performance of Gender in Drama* (New York: Palgrave, 2006), 43–75.

11. Richard Scholar, "'Je ne sais quelle grâce': Esther before Assuérus," *French Studies* 63, no. 3 (2002): 317–27. Scholar argues that the "tendency to 'sacralize' *Esther* unites hostile critics who dismiss the play as simplistic, with those who praise its simplicity" (318).

12. Racine, *Complete Plays of Jean Racine*, 313.

13. Taphanel, *Le théâtre de Saint Cyr*, 81–89.

14. The stories of the girls' overenthusiastic response to *Andromaque* may be apocryphal. Taphanel writes about them in *Le théâtre de Saint Cyr* (32–34), citing Madame de Caylus's own memoir, a source that John Campbell calls somewhat into question on this point. Campbell, "The Metamorphoses of Innocence in *Esther*," in *French Seventeenth-Century Literature. Influences and Transformations Series*, ed. J. Southwood and B. Bourque (Bern, Switzerland: Peter Lang, 2009), 57–74.

15. See Marie de Rabutin-Chantal, marquise de Sévigné, *Correspondance*, vol. 3 (Paris: Gallimard, 1978), University of Chicago: ARTFL-FRANTEXT, https://artflsrv03.uchicago.edu/philologic4/frantext0917/navigate/528/table-of-contents/. My translation.

16. Sévigné's letters appear often in accounts of the play's reception. Taphanel, for example, devotes a chapter to "Madame de Sévigné à Saint-Cyr" in *Le théâtre de Saint Cyr*, 91–105.

17. Sévigné, *Correspondance*, vol. 3, 501. My translation.

18. Taphanel, *Le théâtre de Saint Cyr*, 110–11.

19. Quoted in Taphanel, *Le théâtre de Saint Cyr*, 113.

20. Quoted in Taphanel, *Le théâtre de Saint Cyr*, 116.

21. For more on the question of "innocence" in *Esther* and its historical implications, see Campbell, "Metamorphoses of Innocence," 57–74.

22. Racine, *Complete Plays of Jean Racine*, 327.

23. Racine, *Complete Plays of Jean Racine*, 327.

24. This denouement is not without violence. As John Campbell observes, although the king now favors Esther and Jews, he directs his wrath—and the promise of vengeful violence at Aman and his people, the Amalekites. John Campbell, "Racine's Holy Wars," in *War and Peace: Critical Issues in European Societies and Literature 800–1800*, ed. Albrecht Classen and Nadia Margolis (Berlin: De Gruyter, 2011), 541–55.

25. Lucien Goldmann, *Le dieu caché: Étude sur la vision tragique dans les* Pensées *de Pascal et dans le théâtre de Racine* (Paris: Gallimard, 1959), 440. My translation.

26. Scholar, "Je ne sais quelle grâce," 317–27.

27. Taphanel, *Le théâtre de Saint Cyr*, 108.

28. *Vindiciae contra tyrannos*, 65; *Vindiciae*, Garnett trans., 48.

29. *Vindiciae contra tyrannos*, 65; *Vindiciae*, Garnett trans., 48.

30. *Vindiciae contra tyrannos*, 64; *Vindiciae*, Garnett trans., 48.

31. *Vindiciae contra tyrannos*, 65; *Vindiciae*, Garnett trans., 48.

32. *Vindiciae contra tyrannos*, 64; *Vindiciae*, Garnett trans., 48.

33. Athaliah is also mentioned as a tyrant and terrible woman in other sixteenth-century resistance treatises, such as *Discours politiques des diverses puissance establies de Dieu au monde, du gouvernement légitime d'icelles, & du devoir de ceux qui y sont assujettis*, in Simon Goulart, *Memoires de l'estat de France sous Charles neuvieme* (1578), 157. These references are part of a long tradition that figures Athaliah as a negative exemplar. She appears, for example, in Boccacio's *On Famous Women*, 110. Christine de Pizan urges her readers not to limit their impressions of female rule to Athaliah's bad example in *The Book of the City of Ladies*, II.155.

34. *Vindiciae contra tyrannos*, 65; *Vindiciae*, Garnett trans., 49.

35. The Jewish holiday Shavuot corresponds with Pentecost, a Christian liturgical feast day commemorating the "birth" of the Church.

36. Jean Racine, *Athalie* in *Œuvres complètes*, vol. 1, ed. Georges Forestier (Paris: Gallimard, 1999). Text references are to act, scene, and line numbers. Racine, *Complete Plays of Jean Racine*, 381.

37. Racine, *Complete Plays of Jean Racine*, 388

38. This word also has an important agricultural valence, which the drama frequently invokes. For example, in act 1, Abner figures Joash's blood as having the power to rejuvenate the House of David, which Abner describes as a dry tree in need of nourishment. The play also includes many references to fecundity and harvesting, which Ralph Albanese points out in "Sacred Space and Ironic Polarities in *Athalie*," in *Intersections: Actes du 35e congrès annuel de la North American Society for Seventeenth-Century French Literature*, ed. Faith E. Beasley and Kathleen Wine (Tübingen, Germany: Gunter Narr, 2005), 109–20.

39. See Roland Barthes, *Sur Racine* (Paris: Seuil, 1963); and Mitchell Greenberg, *Racine: From Ancient Myth to Tragic Modernity* (Minneapolis: University of Minnesota Press, 2009).

40. Lee Edelman, *No Future: Queer Theory and the Death Drive* (Durham, NC: Duke University Press, 2004). The figure of the Child and of the Queer should not be confused with actual children and queers, but rather these designations operate as categories within the ideology that Edelman elaborates and critiques. Following Edelman's convention, I capitalize Queer and Child when discussing categories within the ideology of reproductive futurism.

41. See, in particular, Edelman's first chapter, "The Future Is Kid Stuff," *No Future*, 1–31.

42. Cherbuliez, *In the Wake of Medea*, 182.

43. Cherbuliez discusses the nuances between "survie" and Emily Wilson's term "overliving." Cherbuliez, *In the Wake of Medea*, 180–85. See also Wilson, *Mocked With Death*.

44. In the drama's preface, Racine defends himself against those who might accuse him of straying from verisimilitude by portraying a young boy of seven or eight who would complete this solemn task so well, noting that this practice was common in Jewish tradition and holding up the young Dauphin of France as an

example of the real possibility of extraordinary piety and studiousness. Racine, *Athalie*, 1011.

45. As Albanese explains, just as the drama opposes Athalie and the high priest, so it contrasts their respective domains. Where the temple is a space of absolute authority and divine truth, the palace is a place of permissiveness and corruption. Albanese, "Sacred Space and Ironic Polarities," 109–11.

46. Cherbuliez, *In the Wake of Medea*, 192.

47. Cherbuliez, *In the Wake of Medea*, 192.

48. Racine, "Préface," *Athalie*, 1013. Racine, *Complete Plays of Jean Racine*, 378.

49. Racine, *Complete Plays of Jean Racine*, 459.

50. Racine, *Complete Plays of Jean Racine*, 440–41.

51. *Les soupirs de la France esclave qui aspire après la liberté* (Amsterdam, 1689). On the political potential of *Les soupirs* and other late seventeenth-century antimonarchical texts, see Kathrina Ann LaPorta, *Performative Polemic: Anti-Absolutist Pamphlets and their Readers in Late Seventeenth-Century France* (Newark, DE: University of Delaware Press, 2021).

52. Racine, *Complete Plays of Jean Racine*, 389.

53. See Albanese, "Sacred Space and Ironic Polarities."

54. Racine, *Complete Plays of Jean Racine*, 413–14.

55. Racine, *Complete Plays of Jean Racine*, 458.

56. For a longer discussion of blood ties in *Athalie*, as well as in Racine's work more broadly, see Barthes, *Sur Racine*.

57. Paul de Man, "The Concept of Irony," in *Aesthetic Ideology*, ed. Andrzej Warminski (Minneapolis: University of Minnesota Press, 1996), 179.

58. The anxiety surrounding Joash's eventual corruption also points towards the idea of original sin (a past fall from present grace), which was important in Jansenist thought. For more on Racine's relationship to Jansenism and the Port-Royal, see Goldmann, *Le dieu caché*, 338–446, as well as Bénichou, *Morales du grand siècle*, 176–209. For a more recent take on original sin in Racine's *Phèdre*, see Simon Critchley, "I Want to Die, I Hate My Life—Phaedra's Malaise," *New Literary History* 35, no. 1 (2004): 17–40.

59. Racine, "Préface," *Athalie*, 1013; Racine, *Complete Plays of Jean Racine*, 378.

60. Racine, "Préface," *Phèdre, 817*; Racine, *Complete Plays of Jean Racine*, 233.

61. Others have also noted Athaliah's divided nature. See, for example, Greenberg, *Racine*, 233; and Derval Conroy, "Gender, Power and Authority in *Alexandre le Grand* and *Athalie*," in *Racine: The Power and the Pleasure*, ed. Edric Caldicott and Derval Conroy (Dublin: University College Dublin Press, 2001), 67–74.

62. *Vindiciae contra tyrannos*, 64; *Vindiciae*, Garnett trans., 48.

63. Racine, *Complete Plays of Jean Racine*, 413.

Conclusion

1. Alexis de Tocqueville, *L'ancien régime et la révolution* (1856), v.

2. Alexis de Tocqueville, *The Old Regime and the Revolution*, trans. John Bonner (New York: Harper and Brothers, 1856), i.

3. Tocqueville, *L'ancien régime et la révolution*, v–vi.

4. Tocqueville, *Old Regime and the Revolution*, i.

5. Tocqueville, *L'ancien régime et la révolution*, 49–63; *Old Regime and the Revolution*, 32–40.

6. Tocqueville, *L'ancien régime et la révolution*, 119–26; *Old Regime and the Revolution*, 77–81.

7. Hannah Arendt, "The Perplexities of the Rights of Man," in *The Origins of Totalitarianism* (New York: Harcourt Brace, 1951), 290–303; and Jacques Rancière, "Who Is the Subject of the Rights of Man," *South Atlantic Quarterly* 103 (2004): 297–310.

8. This formulation of Arendt's argument in "The Perplexities of Human Rights" is Jacques Rancière's: "[Arendt] stated the paradox as follows: the Rights of Man are the rights of those who are only human beings, who have no more property left than the property of being human. Put another way, they are the rights of those who have no rights, the mere derision of right." As Rancière notes, Arendt was not the first to identify this paradox. Edmund Burke, in his *Reflections on the Revolution in France* (1790), argued that what purported to be the rights of man and of the citizen were in truth only the rights of the citizen. Rancière, "Who Is the Subject of the Rights of Man," 298.

9. The scholarship on these questions is immense. See in particular Nancy Fraser, "Rethinking the Public Sphere: A Contribution to the Critique of Actually Existing Democracy," *Social Text* 25, no. 26 (1990): 56–80; Kimberlé Crenshaw, "Demarginalizing the Intersection of Race and Sex: A Black Feminist Critique of Antidiscrimination Doctrine, Feminist Theory, and Antiracist Politics," *University of Chicago Legal Forum* (1989): 139–67; and Peggy Phelan, *Unmarked: The Politics of Performance* (London: Routledge, 2017).

10. For an example of coverage at the time, see Tom Dart, "Wendy Davis's Remarkable Filibuster to Deny Passage of Abortion Bill," *Guardian*, June 26, 2013, https://www.theguardian.com/world/2013/jun/26/texas-senator-wendy-davis-abortion-bill-speech.

11. Matthew J. Trewhella, *The Doctrine of the Lesser Magistrates: A Proper Resistance to Tyranny and a Repudiation of Unlimited Obedience to Civil Government* (North Charleston, SC: CreateSpace Independent Publishing Platform, 2013).

12. See Heather Clark, "Pastor: Kim Davis Has Duty to Continue to Defy Federal Court as 'Lesser Magistrate' to Uphold God's Law," *Christian News*, September 11, 2015, https://christiannews.net/2015/09/11/pastor-says-kim-davis-has-duty-to-continue-to-defy-federal-court-as-lesser-magistrate-to-uphold-gods-law/; and Matthew J. Trewhella, "2-Minute Video of Melee at Oregon State Capitol: THE PEOPLE Rising," *Defy Tyrants* (blog), December 26, 2020, https://defytyrants.com/2-minute-video-of-melee-at-oregon-state-capitol-the-people-rising/.

BIBLIOGRAPHY

Ahmed, Sara. *The Cultural Politics of Emotion*. New York: Routledge, 2004.

———. *Willful Subjects*. Durham, NC: Duke University Press, 2014.

"Affection," *Dictionnaire de l'Académie Française* (1694), University of Chicago: ARTFL Dictionnaires d'autrefois. https://artflsrv03.uchicago.edu/philologic4/publicdicos/navigate/3/232/.

Albanese, Ralph. "Sacred Space and Ironic Polarities in *Athalie*." In *Intersections: Actes du 35e congrès annuel de la North American Society for Seventeenth-Century French Literature*, edited by Faith E. Beasley and Kathleen Wine, 109–20. Tübingen, Germany: Gunter Narr, 2005.

Apostolidès, Jean-Marie. *Le roi-machine: Spectacle et politique au temps de Louis XIV*. Paris: Les Éditions de Minuit, 1981.

Arendt, Hannah. *The Origins of Totalitarianism*. New York: Harcourt Brace, 1951.

Aristotle. *Poetics*. Translated by Gerald Else. Ann Arbor: University of Michigan Press, 1967.

Aubignac, Abbé de [François Hédelin]. *La pratique du théâtre*. Paris, 1657.

Balsamo, Jean. "Rhétorique et politique dans *Les Gordiens et les Maximins (1589)* d'Antoine Favre." *Seizième Siècle* 6 (2010): 39–49.

Baricave, Jean. *De la defense de la monarchie françoise* [. . .]. Toulouse, 1614.

Barthes, Roland. *Sur Racine*. Paris: Éditions du Seuil, 1963.

Baumgartner, Frederic J. *Radical Reactionaries: The Political Thought of the French Catholic League*. Geneva: Droz, 1976.

Beame, Edmond M. "The Use and Abuse of Machiavelli: The Sixteenth-Century French Adaptation." *Journal of the History of Ideas* 43, no. 1 (1982): 33–54.

Beauchamps, Pierre-François Godard de. *Recherches sur les théâtres de France depuis l'année onze cent soixante-un jusques à présent*. Paris, 1735.

Beaudin, Jean-Dominique. Introduction to *Antigone, ou La pieté*, by Robert Garnier. Edited by Jean-Dominique Beaudin, 7–54. Paris: Honoré Champion, 1997–.

Beik, William. *Absolutism and Society in Seventeenth-Century France: State Power and Provincial Aristocracy in Languedoc*. Cambridge: Cambridge University Press, 1985.

———. *Urban Protest in Seventeenth-Century France: The Culture of Retribution*. Cambridge: Cambridge University Press, 1997.

Bénichou, Paul. *Morales du grand siècle*. Paris: Gallimard, 1948.

Berlant, Lauren. *The Female Complaint: The Unfinished Business of Sentimentality in American Culture*. Durham, NC: Duke University Press, 2008.

Beza, Theodore. *The Right of Magistrates Concerning the Rights of Rulers Over Their Subjects and the Duty Of Subjects Towards Their Rulers, A brief and clear treatise particularly indispensable to either class in these troubled times,* edited by Patrick S. Poole. Translated by Henry-Louis Gonin. Cape Town: H.A.U.M., 1956. http://www.yorku.ca comninel/courses/3020pdf/Beza.pdf.

Bèze, Théodore de. *Du droit des magistrats sur leurs subjets: traitté tres necessaire en ce temps pour advertir de leur devoir, tant les magistrats que les subjets publié par ceux de Magdebourg l'an M.D.L., maintenant reveu, augmenté de plusieurs raisons et exemples*. 1575.

———. *Histoire ecclesiastique des eglises reformes au royaume de France*. 1580.

Biet, Christian. "Droit divin, droit naturel, et droit humain dans *Antigone* de Jean Rotrou." *Littératures classiques* 17, no. 1 (1992): 65–83.

———. Introduction to *Théâtre de la cruauté et récits sanglants en France (XVIe–XVIIe siècle)*. Edited by Christian Biet, v–xlvii. Paris: Laffont, 2006.

———. "Plaisirs et dangers de l'admiration." *Littératures classiques* 32 (1998): 121–34.

———. "A 'Senecan Theatre of Cruelty: Audience, Citizens, and Chorus in Late-Sixteenth and Early Seventeenth-Century French Drama." In *Choruses Ancient and Modern*, edited by Joshua Billings, Felix Budelmann, and Fiona Macintosh, 189–202. Oxford: Oxford University Press, 2013.

Bilis, Hélène. *Passing Judgment: The Politics and Poetics of Sovereignty in French Tragedy from Hardy to Racine*. Toronto: University of Toronto Press, 2016.

Blocker, Déborah. *Instituer un "art": Politiques du théâtre dans la France du premier XVIIe siècle*. Paris: Honoré Champion, 2009.

Boccaccio, Giovanni. *On Famous Women*. Translated by Guido A. Guarino. 2nd ed. New York: Ithaca Press, 2011.

Bodin, Jean. *Les six livres de la République*. Paris, 1580.

Bosco, David. "Conscience as Court and Worm: Calvin and the Three Elements of Conscience." *Journal of Religious Ethics* 14, no. 2 (1986): 333–55.

Boucher, Jean. *De justa Henrici tertii abdicatione*. 1589.

Brennan, Teresa. *The Transmission of Affect*. Ithaca, NY: Cornell University Press, 2004.

Brewer, Daniel. "Encyclopedic Transfers and the Internationalization of Intellectual Work: Louis de Jaucourt." In *The Internationalization of Intellectual Exchange in a Globalizing Europe, 1636–1780*, edited by Robert Mankin, 143–62. Lewisburg, PA: Bucknell University Press, 2018.

Bushnell, Rebecca W. *Tragedies of Tyrants: Political Thought and Theater in the English Renaissance*. Ithaca, NY: Cornell University Press, 1990.

Butler, Judith. *Antigone's Claim: Kinship between Life and Death*. 2000; reprint, New York: Columbia University Press, 2003.

Calvin, John. *Institutes of the Christian Religion* [1559]. Edited by John T. McNeill. Translated by Ford Lewis Battles. Philadelphia: Westminster Press, 1960.

Campbell, John. "Racine's Holy Wars." In *War and Peace: Critical Issues in European Societies and Literature, 800–1800*, edited by Albrecht Classen and Nadia Margolis, 541–55. Berlin: De Gruyter, 2011.

———. "The Metamorphoses of Innocence in *Esther*." In *French Seventeenth-Century Literature: Influences and Transformations Series*, edited by J. Southwood and B. Bourque, 57–74. Bern, Switzerland: Peter Lang, 2009.

Certeau, Michel de. *The Writing of History*. Translated by Tom Conley. New York: Columbia University Press, 1992.

Cherbuliez, Juliette. *In the Wake of Medea: Neoclassical Theater and the Arts of Destruction*. New York: Fordham University Press, 2020.

———. *The Place of Exile: Leisure Literature and the Limits of Absolutism*. Lewisburg, PA: Bucknell University Press, 2005.

Clark, Heather. "Pastor: Kim Davis Has Duty to Continue to Defy Federal Court as 'Lesser Magistrate' to Uphold God's Law." *Christian News*, September 11, 2015. https://christiannews.net/2015/09/11/pastor-says-kim-davis-has-duty-to-continue-to-defy-federal-court-as-lesser-magistrate-to-uphold-gods-law/.

Conroy, Derval. "Gender, Power and Authority in *Alexandre le Grand* and *Athalie*." In *Racine: The Power and the Pleasure*, edited by Edric Caldicott and Derval Conroy, 67–74. Dublin: University College Dublin Press, 2001.

———. *Ruling Women, Vol. 1: Government, Virtue, and the Female Prince in Seventeenth-Century France*. Basingstoke, UK: Palgrave Macmillan, 2016.

Corneille, Pierre. *The Chief Plays of Corneille*. Translated by Lacy Lockert. Princeton, NJ: Princeton University Press, 1957.

———. *The Cid / Cinna / The Theatrical Illusion*. Translated by John Cairncross. London: Penguin Classics, 1975.

———. *The Moot Plays of Pierre Corneille*. Translated by Lacy Lockert. Nashville: Vanderbilt University Press, 1959.

———. *Nicomède, a tragi-comedy*. Translated by John Dancer. London, 1671.

———. *Œuvres completes*. Vols. 1–3. Edited by Georges Couton. Paris: Gallimard, 1980, 1984, 1987.

Crenshaw, Kimberlé. "Demarginalizing the Intersection of Race and Sex: A Black Feminist Critique of Antidiscrimination Doctrine, Feminist Theory, and Antiracist Politics." *University of Chicago Legal Forum* (1989): 139–67.

Critchley, Simon. "I Want to Die, I Hate My Life—Phaedra's Malaise." *New Literary History* 35, no. 1 (2004): 17–40.

Crouzet, Denis. *La nuit de la Saint Barthélemy: Un rêve perdu de la Renaissance*. Paris: Fayard, 1994.

———. *Les guerriers de dieu: La violence aux temps de troubles de religion*. Paris: Champ Vallon, 2006.

Cvetkovich, Ann. *Depression: A Public Feeling*. Durham, NC: Duke University Press, 2012.

Dart, Tom. "Wendy Davis's Remarkable Filibuster to Deny Passage of Abortion Bill." *Guardian*, June 26, 2013. https://www.theguardian.com/world/2013/jun/26/texas-senator-wendy-davis-abortion-bill-speech.

de Man, Paul. "The Concept of Irony." In *Aesthetic Ideology*, edited by Andrzej Warminski, 163–184. Minneapolis: University of Minnesota Press, 1996.

DeJean, Joan. *Tender Geographies: Women and the Origin of the Novel in France*. New York: Columbia University Press, 1991.

Descartes, René. *Les passions de l'âme*. 1649. Paris: Vrin, 1860. University of Chicago: ARTFL-FRANTEXT. https://artflsrv03.uchicago.edu/philologic4/frantext0917/navigate/2158/table-of-contents/.

———. *The Passions of the Soul, and Other Late Philosophical Writings*. Translated by Michael Moriarty. Oxford: Oxford World's Classics, 2015.

Desjardins, Lucie. *Le corps parlant: Savoirs et representations des passions au XIIe siècle*. Laval: Presses Universitaires de Laval, 2001.

Dialogue du royaume. Paris: Didier Millot, 1589.

Diefendorf, Barbara B. "Rites of Repair: Restoring Community in the French Religious Wars." In *Ritual Violence: Natalie Zemon Davis and Early Modern France*, edited by Graeme Murdock, Penny Roberts, and Andrew Spicer, 30–51. Past and Present Supplement new series 7. Oxford: Oxford University Press, 2012.

Dillon, Elizabeth Maddox. *New World Drama: The Performative Commons in the Atlantic World*, 1649–1849. Durham, NC: Duke University Press, 2014.

Discours politiques des diverses puissances establies de Dieu au monde, du gouvernement légitime d'icelles, & du devoir de ceux qui y sont assujettis. In Simon Goulart, *Memoires de l'estat de France sous Charles neuvieme*. 2nd ed. Meidelbourg: Henry Wolf, 1578.

Dobby-Poirson, Florence. *Le pathétique dans le théâtre de Robert Garnier*. Paris: Honoré Champion, 2006.

Doubrovsky, Serge. *Corneille et la dialectique du héros*. Paris: Gallimard, 1963.

Edelman, Lee. *No Future: Queer Theory and the Death Drive*. Durham, NC: Duke University Press, 2004.

Elias, Norbert. *The Civilizing Process: Sociogenic and Psychogenic Investigations*. Malden, MA: Blackwell, 2000.

Estienne, Robert. *Dictionarium latinogallicum* (1552). University of Chicago: ARTFL Dictionnaires d'autrefois. http://artflsrv02.uchicago.edu/philologic4/latinogallicum/

Faguet, Émile. *La tragédie française au seizième siècle*. Paris: Librairie Universitaire, 1894.

Foley, Helen P. *Female Acts in Greek Tragedy*. Princeton, NJ: Princeton University Press, 2001.

Fontana, Alessandro. "Du droit de résistance au devoir d'insurrection." In *Le droit de résistance: XIIe–XXe siècle*, edited by Jean-Claude Zancarini, 15–33. Lyon: ENS Éditions (2000).

Forestier, Georges. "Corneille et la tragédie: Hypothèses sur l'élaboration de *Suréna*." *Littératures classiques* 16 (1992): 141–68.

———. *Essai de génetique théâtrale: Corneille à l'œuvre*. Paris: Klincksieck, 1996.

Fraisse, Simone. *Le mythe d'Antigone*. Paris: Armand Colin, 1974.

Fraser, Nancy. "Rethinking the Public Sphere: A Contribution to the Critique of Actually Existing Democracy." *Social Text* 25, no. 26 (1990): 56–80.

Frisch, Andrea. *Forgetting Differences: Tragedy, Historiography, and the French Wars of Religion*. Edinburgh: Edinburgh University Press, 2015.

Fumaroli, Marc. *L'âge de l'éloquence: Rhétorique et "res literaria" de la Renaissance au seuil de l'époque classique*. Geneva: Droz, 1980.

———. *Héros et orateurs: Rhétorique et dramaturgie cornéliennes*. Paris: Droz, 1960.

Garnier, Robert. *Antigone, ou La pieté*. 1580. Edited by Jean-Dominique Beaudin. Paris: Honoré Champion, 1997.

———. *Cornélie: Tragédie*. Edited by Jean-Claude Ternaux. Paris: Honoré Champion, 2002.

———. *The Tragedy of Pious Antigone*. Translated by Phillip John Usher. Tempe: Arizona Center for Medieval and Renaissance Studies, 2018.

Gobert, R. Darren. *The Mind-Body Stage: Passion and Interaction in the Cartesian Theater*. Stanford, CA: Stanford University Press, 2013.

Goldmann, Lucien. *Le dieu caché: Étude sur la vision tragique dans les* Pensées *de Pascal et dans le théâtre de Racine*. Paris: Gallimard, 1959.

Goldstein, Claire. *Vaux and Versailles: The Appropriations, Erasures, and Accidents that Made Modern France*. Philadelphia: University of Pennsylvania Press, 2008.

Goodkin, Richard. *Birth Marks: The Tragedy of Primogeniture in Pierre Corneille, Thomas Corneille, and Jean Racine*. Philadelphia: University of Pennsylvania Press, 2000.

———. "Neoclassical Dramatic Theory in Seventeenth-Century France." *A Companion to Tragedy*, edited by Rebecca Bushnell, 373–92. Oxford: Wiley-Blackwell, 2009.

Greenberg, Mitchell. *Corneille and the Ruses of Symmetry*. Cambridge: Cambridge University Press, 1986.

———. *Racine: From Ancient Myth to Tragic Modernity*. Minneapolis: University of Minnesota Press, 2009.

Greengrass, Mark. *Governing Passions: Peace and Reform in the French Kingdom, 1576–1585*. Oxford: Oxford University Press, 2007.

Grene, Marjorie. "The Heart and Blood: Descartes, Plemp, and Harvey." In *Essays on the Philosophy and Science of René Descartes*, edited by Stephen Voss, 324–35. Oxford: Oxford University Press, 1993.

Hanley, Sarah. *The Lit de Justice of the Kings of France: Constitutional Ideology, Ritual, and Discourse*. Princeton, NJ: Princeton University Press, 1983.

Henri IV. *Édict du Roy et déclaration sur les précédens édicts de pacification. Publié à Paris, en Parlement, le 25 febvrier, 1599*. Paris, 1599. http://gallica.bnf.fr/ark:/12148/bpt6k317003w.

Hogg, Chloé. *Absolutist Attachments: Emotion, Media, and Absolutism in Seventeenth-Century France*. Evanston, IL: Northwestern University Press, 2019.

Holt, Mack P. *The French Wars of Religion, 1562–1629*. 2nd ed. Cambridge: Cambridge University Press, 2005.

Honig, Bonnie. *Antigone, Interrupted*. Cambridge: Cambridge University Press, 2013.

Hotman, François. *Epistre envoyé au Tigre de la France*. 1560.

———. *Francogallia*. 1573.

———. *Francogallia*. Edited by Ralph E. Giesey. Translated by J. H. M. Salmon. Cambridge: Cambridge University Press, 1972.

———. *La gaule francoise* [1574]. Edited by Christiane Frémont. Paris: Fayard, 1991.

Houllemare, Marie. *Politiques de la parole: Le parlement de Paris au XVI siècle*. Geneva: Droz, 2011.

Howarth, William. *French Theatre in the Neo-Classical Era: 1550–1789*. Cambridge: Cambridge University Press, 1997.

Ibbett, Katherine. *Compassion's Edge: Fellow Feeling and Its Limits in Early Modern France*. Philadelphia: University of Pennsylvania Press, 2017.

———. "Heroes and History's Remainders: The *Restes* of Pierre Corneille." *Modern Language Quarterly* 69, no. 3 (2008): 347–65.

———. *The Style of the State in French Theater, 1630–1660: Neoclassicism and Government*. Farnham, UK: Ashgate, 2009.

Jackson, Richard A. "Elective Kingship and Consensus Populi in Sixteenth-Century France." *Journal of Modern History* 44, no. 2 (1972): 155–71.

———. *Vive le Roi! A History of the French Coronation from Charles V to Charles X*. Chapel Hill: University of North Carolina Press, 1984.

Jacquemin, Hélène. *Livres et jeunes filles nobles à Saint-Cyr (1686–1793)*. Paris: Presses de l'Université d'Angers, 2007.

Jondorf, Gillian. *French Renaissance Tragedy: The Dramatic Word*. Cambridge: Cambridge University Press, 1990.

———. *Robert Garnier and the Themes of Political Tragedy in the Sixteenth Century*. Cambridge: Cambridge University Press, 1969.

Jouanna, Arlette. *Le devoir de révolte: La noblesse française et la gestation de l'état moderne, 1559–1661*. Paris: Fayard, 1989.

———. *Le pouvoir absolu: Naissance de l'imaginaire politique de la royauté*. Paris: Gallimard, 2013.

———. *Le prince absolu: Apogée et déclin de l'imaginaire monarchique*. Paris: Gallimard, 2014.

———. *La Saint-Barthélemy: Les mystères d'un crime d'état (24 août 1572)*. Paris: Gallimard, 2007.

Jouhaud, Christian. *Mazarinades: La Fronde des mots*. Paris: Aubier, 1985.

———. *Sauver le Grand-Siècle: Présence et transmission du passé*. Paris: Seuil, 2007.

Kahn, Victoria. *Wayward Contracts: The Crisis of Political Obligation in England, 1640–1674*. Princeton, NJ: Princeton University Press, 2004.

Keller, Marcus. "The Turk of Early Modern France." *L'Esprit Créateur* 53, no. 4 (2013): 1–8.

Kelley, Donald R. *The Beginning of Ideology: Consciousness and Society in the French Reformation*. Cambridge: Cambridge University Press, 1981.

———. "Martyrs, Myths, and the Massacre: The Background of St. Bartholomew." *American Historical Review* 77, no. 5 (1972): 1323–42.

———. "Murd'rous Machiavel in France: A Post Mortem." *Political Science Quarterly* 85, no. 4 (1970): 545–59.

Keohane, Nannerl O. *Philosophy and the State in France: The Renaissance to the Enlightenment*. Princeton, NJ: Princeton University Press, 1980.

Kettering, Sharon. *Patronage in Sixteenth- and Seventeenth-Century France*. Aldershot, UK: Ashgate, 2002.

Kingdon, Robert. *Myths about the Saint Bartholomew's Day Massacres, 1572–1576*. Cambridge, MA: Harvard University Press, 1988.

Koselleck, Reinhart. *Critique and Crisis: Enlightenment and the Pathogenesis of Modern Society*. Cambridge, MA: MIT Press, 1988.

Kyd, Thomas, trans. *Cornelia* [1594]. In *Robert Garnier in Elizabethan England: Mary Sidney Herbert's* Antonius *and Thomas Kyd's* Cornelia. Edited by Marie-Alice Belle and Line Cottegnies, 179–272. London: Modern Humanities Research Association, 2017.

La Bruyère, Jean de. *Les caractères, ou Les mœurs de ce siècle*. In *Oeuvres complètes*. Edited by Julien Benda. Paris: Gallimard, 1951. University of Chicago: ARTFL-FRANTEXT. https://artflsrv03.uchicago.edu/philologic4/frantext0917/navigate/522/table-of-contents/.

———. *The Characters, or Manners of the Present Age: The Works of Monsieur de La Bruyere*. 6th ed. Vol. 2. London, 1713. https://books.google.com/books?id=2GCQcxD7AUcC.

LaPorta, Kathrina Ann. *Performative Polemic: Anti-Absolutist Pamphlets and Their Readers in Late Seventeenth-Century France*. Newark, DE: University of Delaware Press, 2021.

Lazard, Madeleine. *Le théâtre en France au XVIe siècle*. Paris: Presses Universitaires de France, 1980.

Le Moyne, Pierre. *La gallerie des femmes fortes*. Paris: Antoine de Sommaville, 1647.

Lee, Daniel. *Popular Sovereignty in Early Modern Constitutional Thought*. Oxford: Oxford University Press, 2016.

Lewis, Charlton T., and Charles Short. *A Latin Dictionary*. Oxford: Clarendon Press, 1879.

Loraux, Nicole. *Mothers in Mourning: With the Essay "Of Amnesty and Its Opposite."* Translated by Corinne Pache. Ithaca, NY: Cornell University Press, 1998.

Louvat, Bénédicte. Introduction to *Antigone*. In Jean de Rotrou, *Théâtre choisi*, 199–249. Edited by Marianne Béthery, Bénédicte Louvat, and Pierre Pasquier. Paris: Société des Textes Français Modernes, 2007.

Lucan. *Civil War*. Translated by Matthew Fox. New York: Penguin Classics, 2012.

Lyons, John D. *Kingdom of Disorder: The Theory of Tragedy in Classical France*. West Lafayette, IN: Purdue University Press, 1999.

———. "Le mythe du héros cornélien." *Revue d'Histoire Littéraire de la France* 107, no. 2 (2007): 433–48.

———. *The Tragedy of Origins: Pierre Corneille and Historical Perspective*. Stanford, CA: Stanford University Press, 1996.

Machiavelli, Niccolo. *The Prince*. Edited by Quentin Skinner and Russell Price. Translated by Russell Price. Cambridge: Cambridge University Press, 1988.

Maclean, Ian. *Woman Triumphant: Feminism in French Literature, 1610–1652*. Oxford: Clarendon Press, 1977.

Macpherson, C. B. *The Political Theory of Possessive Individualism: Hobbes to Locke*. Oxford: Oxford University Press, 2011.

Margolf, Diane C. *Religion and Royal Justice in Early Modern France: The Paris Chambre de l'Edit, 1598–1665*. Kirksville, MO: Truman State University Press, 2003.

Mathieu-Castellani, Gisèle. *La rhétorique des passions*. Paris: Presses Universitaires de France, 2000.

Matzke, John E. "The Sources of Corneille's Tragedy *La mort de Pompée*." *Modern Language Notes* 15, no. 5 (1990): 42–52.

McClure, Ellen. *Sunspots and the Sun King: Sovereignty and Mediation in Seventeenth-Century France*. Urbana: University of Illinois Press, 2006.

McEnnerney, Denis. "Philosophy and Politics of Résistance in Early Modern France." *Historical Reflections / Réflexions Historiques* 35, no.1 (2009): 59–71.

Mellet, Paul-Alexis. *Les traités monarchomaques: Confusion des temps, résistance armée et monarchie parfaite (1560–1600)*. Geneva: Librairie Droz, 2007.

Merlin-Kajman, Hélène. *L'absolutisme dans les lettres et la théorie des deux corps: Passions et politique*. Paris: Honoré Champion, 2000.

———. "*Cinna, Rodogune, Nicomède*: Le roi et le moi." *Littératures* 37 (1997): 67–86.

———. *Public et littérature en France au XVIIe siècle*. 2nd ed. Paris: Les Belles Lettres, 2004.

———. "Un siècle classico-baroque?" *Dix-septième siècle* 223, no. 2 (2004): 163–172.

Montaigne, Michel de. *Les essais*. Edited by P. Villey and V.-L. Saulnier. Online edition by P. Desan. University of Chicago: ARTFL. https://artflsrv03.uchicago.edu/philologic4/montessaisvilley/navigate/1/5/6/?byte=2661323.

Mouflard, Marie-Madeleine. *Robert Garnier, 1545–1590*, vol. 1, *La vie*. La Ferté-Bernard: Bellanger, 1961.

———. *Robert Garnier, 1545–1590*, vol. 2, *L'œuvre*. La Roche-sur-Yon: Imprimerie Centrale de la Ouest, 1963.

———. *Robert Garnier, 1545–1590*, vol. 3, *Les sources*. La Roche-sur-Yon: Imprimerie Centrale de la Ouest, 1964.

Murray, Timothy. "Richelieu's Theater: The Mirror of a Prince." *Renaissance Drama* 8 (1977): 275–97.

Nicot, Jean. "Alliance." In *Thresor de la language francoyse tant ancienne que moderne* (1606). University of Chicago: ARTFL Dictionnaires d'autrefois. https://artflsrv03.uchicago.edu/philologic4/publicdicos/navigate/1/642/.

———. "Conscience." In *Thresor de la language francoyse tant ancienne que moderne* (1606). University of Chicago: ARTFL Dictionnaires d'autrefois. https://artflsrv03.uchicago.edu/philologic4/publicdicos/navigate/1/3894/

———. "Volonté." In *Thresor de la language francoyse tant ancienne que moderne* (1606). University of Chicago: ARTFL Dictionnaires d'autrefois. https://artflsrv03.uchicago.edu/philologic4/publicdicos/navigate/2/9018/

Palacios, Joy. *Ceremonial Splendor: Performing Priesthood in Early Modern France* Philadelphia: University of Pennsylvania Press, forthcoming.

Parrow, Kathleen. "From Defense to Resistance: The Justification of Resistance during the French Wars of Religion." *Transactions of the American Philosophical Society* 83, no. 6 (1993): 1–79.

Phelan, Peggy. *Unmarked: The Politics of Performance*. London: Routledge, 2017.

Pizan, Christine de. *The Book of the City of Ladies*. Translated by Rosalind Brown-Grant. New York: Penguin Books, 1999.

Prest, Julia. *Theatre under Louis XIV: Cross-Casting and the Performance of Gender in Drama*. New York: Palgrave, 2006.

Prigent, Michel. *Le héros et l'état dans la tragédie de Pierre Corneille*. Paris: Presses Universitaire de France, 1986.

Racine, Jean. *Œuvres complètes*. Vol. 1. Edited by Georges Forestier. Paris: Gallimard, 1999.

———. *The Complete Plays of Jean Racine*. Translated by Samuel Solomon. New York: Random House, 1967.

Rancière, Jacques. "Who Is the Subject of the Rights of Man." *South Atlantic Quarterly* 103 (2004): 297–310.

Ranum, Orest. *The Fronde: A French Revolution, 1648–1652*. New York: W. W. Norton, 1993.

Rapin, René. *Les réflexions sur la poétique d'Aristote et sur les ouvrages des poètes anciens et modernes*. Paris, 1674.

Reddy, William. *The Navigation of Feeling: A Framework for the History of Emotions*. Cambridge: Cambridge University Press, 2001.

Reiss, Timothy J. "Corneille and Cornelia: Reason, Violence, and the Cultural Status of the Feminine. Or, How a Dominant Discourse Recuperated and Subverted the Advance of Women." *Renaissance Drama* 18 (1987): 3–41.

Roach, Joseph R. *The Player's Passion: Studies in the Science of Acting*. 1993; reprint, Ann Arbor: University of Michigan Press, 2011.

Rosenwein, Barbara. *Generations of Feeling: A History of Emotions, 600–1700*. Cambridge: Cambridge University Press, 2016.

Rotrou, Jean de. *Théâtre choisi*. Edited by Marianne Béthery, Bénédicte Louvat, and Pierre Pasquier. Paris: Société des Textes Français Modernes, 2007.

Rouillard, Clarence D. *The Turk in French History, Thought, and Literature (1520–1660)*. Paris: Boivin, 1941.

Routhwaite, Adair. *Asking the Audience: Participatory Art in 1980s New York*. Minneapolis: University of Minnesota Press, 2017.

Sauliner, V. L. *La littérature française du siècle classique*. Paris: Presses Universitaires de France, 1970.

Van Schelven, A. A. "Beza's De Iure Magistratuum in Subditos." *Archiv für Reformationsgeschichte* 45 (1954): 62–83.

Schneider, Rebecca. *Performing Remains: Art and War in Times of Theatrical Reenactment*. New York: Routledge, 2011.

Scholar, Richard. "'Je ne sais quelle grâce': Esther before Assuérus." *French Studies* 63, no.3 (2002): 317–27.

Sedgwick, Eve Kosofsky. *Epistemology of the Closet*. Berkeley: University of California Press, 1990.

Sellstrom, A. Donald. "*La Mort de Pompée*: Roman History and Tasso's Theory of Christian Epic." *PMLA* 97, no. 5 (1982): 830–43.

Sévigné, Marie de Rabutin-Chantal, marquise de. *Correspondance*, vol. 3. Paris: Gallimard, 1978. University of Chicago: ARTFL-FRANTEXT. https://artflsrv03.uchicago.edu/philologic4/frantext0917/navigate/528/table-of-contents/.

Skinner, Quentin. *The Foundations of Modern Political Thought: Vol. 2 The Age of Reformation*. Cambridge: Cambridge University Press, 1978.

Les soupirs de la France esclave qui aspire après la liberté. Amsterdam, 1689.

Stanton, Domna. "The Ideal of 'Repos' in Seventeenth-Century French Literature." *L'Ésprit Créateur* 15, no. 1/2 (1975): 75–104.

Steiner, George. *Antigones* [1984]. New Haven, CT: Yale University Press, 1996.

Strauss, Johnathan. *Private Lives, Public Deaths: Antigone and the Invention of Individuality*. New York: Fordham University Press, 2013.

La Taille, Jean de. "De l'art de la tragédie." In *Saul le furieux*. Paris, 1572.

Taphanel, Achille. *Le théâtre de Saint Cyr*. Paris: Baudry, 1876.

Taussig, Michael. *Shamanism, Colonialism, and the Wild Man: A Study in Terror and Healing*. Chicago: University of Chicago Press, 1987.

Taylor, Diana. *The Archive and the Repertoire: Performing Cultural Memory in the Americas*. Durham, NC: Duke University Press, 2003.

Terada, Rei. *Feeling in Theory: Emotion after the "Death of the Subject."* Cambridge, MA: Harvard University Press, 2001.

Tocqueville, Alexis de. *L'ancien régime et la revolution*. 1856.

———. *The Old Regime and the Revolution*. Translated by John Bonner. New York: Harper and Brothers, 1856.

Trewhella, Matthew J. "2-Minute Video of Melee at Oregon State Capitol: THE PEOPLE Rising." *Defy Tyrants* (blog), December 26, 2020. https://defytyrants.com/2-minute-video-of-melee-at-oregon-state-capitol-the-people-rising/.

———. *The Doctrine of the Lesser Magistrates: A Proper Resistance to Tyranny and a Repudiance of Unlimited Obedience to Civil Government*. North Charleston, SC: CreateSpace Independent Publishing Platform, 2013.

Usher, Phillip John. "Courtroom Drama during the Wars of Religion: Robert Garnier and the Paris *Parlement*." *French Renaissance and Baroque Drama: Text, Performance, Theory*. Edited by Michael Meere. Newark: University of Delaware Press (2015): 139–52.

———. Introduction to *The Tragedy of Pious Antigone*, by Robert Garnier, xv–xxxviii. Translated by Phillip John Usher. Tempe: Arizona Center for Medieval and Renaissance Studies (2018).

Van Kley, Dale. *The Religious Origins of the French Revolution: From Calvin to the Civil Constitution, 1560–1791*. New Haven, CT: Yale University Press, 1996.

Vernant, Jean-Pierre, and Pierre Vidal-Naquet. *Myth and Tragedy in Ancient Greece*. Translated by Janet Lloyd. New York: Zone Books, 1990.

Vindiciae contra tyrannos: Traduction française de 1581. Edited by Arlette Jouanna, Jean Perrin, Marguerite Soulié, André Tournon, and Henri Weber. Geneva: Librairie Droz, 1979.

Vindiciae, Contra Tyrannos: or, Concerning the Legitimate Power of a Prince over the People, and of the People over a Prince, by Stephanus Junius Brutus, the Celt. Edited and translated by George Garnett. Cambridge: Cambridge University Press, 1994.

Vindiciae, contra tyrannos: Sive, de Principis in Populum, Populique in Principem, legitima potestate, Stephano Iunio Bruto Celta, Auctore. Edinburg, 1579. Electronic facsimile. Universitätsbibliothek Basel. http://dx.doi.org/10.3931/e-rara-17.

Waele, Michel de. *Réconcilier les français: La fin des troubles de religion (1589–1598)*. Paris: Hermann, 2015.

Walhof, Darren. "The Accusations of Conscience and the Christian Polity in John Calvin's Political Thought." *History of Political Thought* 24, no. 3 (2003): 397–414.

White, Stephen K. *The Ethos of a Late-Modern Citizen*. Cambridge, MA: Harvard University Press, 2009.

Wilson, Emily. *Mocked with Death: Tragic Overliving from Sophocles to Milton*. Baltimore, MD: Johns Hopkins University Press, 2004.

Witte, John, Jr. *The Reformation of Rights: Law, Religion, and Human Rights in Early Modern Calvinism*. Cambridge: Cambridge University Press, 2007.

Worthen, W. B. *Drama: Between Poetry and Performance*. Chichester, UK: Wiley-Blackwell, 2010.

Yale Law School. "Declaration of the Rights of Man and of the Citizen (1789)." *The Avalon Project: Documents in Law, History, and Diplomacy*. http://avalon.law.yale.edu/18th_century/rightsof.asp.

INDEX

Page numbers in italics refer to figures.

absolutism: alternatives to, 126; and the aristocratic ethos, 132; cautionary tableau for audiences living under, 157; ceremonial practices of, 12; contradictions of, 14; doctrine of, 11–12, 16–17; emotionally charged, 12; and the end of war, 10–11; the limits of, 11–13; and monarchy, 10–12, 28, 124, 145; resistance theory in the period of, 125; the rights-bearing individual in opposition to, 158; separation between the private and the public of, 153; theoretical framework of, 10–11; theories of, 7, 13, 210n59; traditional accounts of, 12; triumph of, 125, 158. *See also* absolutist theory; kings; tyranny

absolutist theory, 4, 7, 10–14, 17, 94–95, 124. *See also* absolutism; divine right

Académie française, 14

admiration (admiration), 135–39; Cartesian, 137–38, 143; dynamics of, 135–37; object of, 138–44; power of, 136–37

Aeschylus, 95; Works: *Oresteia*, 67

affect: in French political life, 13; as an index of political legitimacy, 22–23; the people's attachments of, 95, 115, 120; and political agency, 101; push and pull of the influence of, 92; of sister and brother in tragic drama, 109–11; surfeit of, 111. *See also* affective evidence; affect theory; emotions; mourning; passions; reach

affective evidence, 8–9, 21–54, 57, 183, 188; of Antigone's legitimacy, 120; of Antigone's virtue, 112, 119–*20*; display of, 170; and the legitimacy of princes, 42–49, 52; of the people's approval, 31–33, 36, 44; readings of, 50; and resistance to tyranny, 68, 71–72, 93. *See also* affect; emotions

affect theory, 8. *See also* affect

Ahmed, Sara, 8; *Willful Subjects*, 121

Alamanni, Luigi, 95

Albanese, Ralph, 177

alliance (alliance), 28–29

amitié (attachment), 110

Anabaptists, 27

Antigone (character): early modern, 120–*21*; and heterosexual fatality, 97–98; individual perception of right and wrong of, 120; lament of, 121; reach of, 95–101; rebellion of, 18, 91–122; relationship to the people of, 18, 120

Antigone (Rotrou), 18, 93–96, 99–101, *100*, 106–12, 115–21

Antigone (Sophocles), 91, 95–96, 98–99, 121

Antigone, ou La piété (Garnier), 18, 91–96, 99, 101–8, 111–21, 181

Antigone-effect (Honig), 98–99. *See also* Honig, Bonnie

antitheatrical sentiment, 54. *See also* tragic drama; theater

Arendt, Hannah, 187, 215n8

Aristotle: *Poetics*, 15, 85, 136

Armenia, 131, 145, 156

arm(s): absent and without, 110; inhuman, 103; against the king, 49, 52; laying down, 92, 94; as offerings on a funeral pyre, 70; outstretched, 101, 106, 140; of protest, 17; against the tyrant, 40, 52, 55, 68; weeping and, 74, 76; weeping as, 70; the whole kingdom in, 108. *See also* violence

Athalie/Athaliah (character), 56, 170–82, 213n33

Athalie (Racine), 19, 83, 160–83

Athens, 66

autonomous individual, 19, 96, 158; Antigone as an, 96–97; of liberal political philosophy, 158; of modern rights, 121. *See also* autonomy; individual subject autonomy, 134; generosity and, 135; modern, 158. *See also* autonomous individual

Balsamo, Jean, 54
Barclay, William: *De regno et regali potestate* (1600), 51
Baricave, Jean, 9, 51
Beaudin, Jean-Dominique, 104–5, 205n9, 206n36
Beik, William, 12
Bénichou, Paul, 125
Berain, Jean, 163
Berlant, Lauren, 8
Bèze, Théodore de: *Du droit des magistrats sur leurs subjets* (1575), 5–7, 18, 22–29, 33–38, 45–50, 53, 190, 196n3, 201n113
Bible: Deborah in the, 56–57; King David in the, 28, 33; King Solomon in the, 28; legitimate resistance in the, 29; liberators in the, 41, 56–57; miraculous examples recounted in the, 41. *See also* Deborah
Biet, Christian, 16, 86, 109, 138, 142, 207n51, 207n55
Bilis, Hélène, 14
Boccacio: *De claris mulieribus* (1361–62), 90, 213n33
Boucher, Jean: *De justa Henrici Tertii abdicatione* (1589), 51–52
Brennan, Teresa, 8
burial: natural right of, 111; refusal of, 110; woman's burial of her male family member, 97, 106, 111, 119, 121
Burke, Edmund: *Reflections on the Revolution in France* (1790), 215n8
Butler, Judith: *Antigone's Claim*, 97–98; *Frames of War*, 98; *Precarious Life*, 98

Calvin, John, 6, 46, 105, 200n87; Works: *Institutes*, 46, 48
Calvinists, 45–47; debate between Catholics and, 104
catharsis, 136–37
Catholic League, 9, 51; *Le dialogue du royaume* (1589), 51
Certeau, Michel de, 16–17
Cesar/César/Caesar (character): Cornelia's opposition to, 65–66, 74, 76–83; justification of the assassination of, 68, 71; people's affective orientation toward, 61; Pompey's opposition to, 55, 62–63, 70, 75–76, 78–79, 87; popular discontent with the rule of, 62, 68, 71–72; reverence for Cleopatra of, 75, 79; self-satisfaction of, 62; speech of, 61; tyrannical rule of, 18, 55–56, 60–64, 67–68, 72–74; virtue of, 61
*charitas (*Latin*)*, 27, 197n20
charité (charity), 27–28, 50–51, 102; of good kings, 25; love and, 50, 52
Charles IX, King, 3–4, 25
Cherbuliez, Juliette, 12, 173–74, 207n54
Childeric, King, 30–31
chorus, 68–74, 83–87, 92, 112–15; ancient, 84–85; Greek, 112. *See also* theater
Christianity: affective bonds that unite the community of, 47; the church as one body of, 39–42; kingdoms of, 43, 49; unity of, 24. *See also* Huguenots; Protestants; religion; Roman Catholics
Cicero, 55, 62
Cicero (character), 62–63, 65-68, 72
Cinna, 55, 74
Clément, Jacques, 51–52
Clovis II, King, 31
Clovis III, King, 31–32
cœur (heart), 62–64, 73, 77–78, 104, 123, 138–39, 146–50, 154–55; *conscience* and, 48. *See also* heart
Coligny, Admiral Gaspard de, 3, 25
collective authority, 9–11, 18; and Antigone's resistance, 112; of the people, 54, 112, 117–18; subjective rights and the, 158. *See also* popular sovereignty
conscience (conscience), 45–46; Calvin's understanding of, 46–48; and *cœur* (heart), 48; freedom of, 105–6, 150; liberty of, 9, 11, 13, 46, 76, 121, 145, 157, 199n74; particularity of, 45. See also *conscientia* (Latin); individual subject
conscientia (Latin), 45. See also *conscience* (conscience)
consentement/*consentir* (consent/to consent), 31
consentio (Latin), 31
contrat/*contracter* (affective covenant, affective contract), 28
Corneille, Pierre, 13–14; Works: *Cinna* (1641), 124, 203n46; *Horace* (1640), 86, 124, 156; *La mort de Pompée*

(1644), 18, 56–57, 70, 74–83, *82*, 87, 90, 93; *Le Cid* (1636), 14–15, 18, 123–24, 128, 147, 210n47; *Nicomède* (1651), 19, 124–44, *141*; *Suréna* (1674), 19, 124–28, 144–58
Cornélie/Cornelia (character), 18–19, 56–57, 87, 93; as *femme forte*, 87–90; glory of, 74–83; grief of, 58–74
Cornélie (Garnier), 18, 55–83, *59*, 87, 90, 92–93
corps mystique (spiritual body), 25, 94
corps politique (political body), 25, 95
Creon (character): attacks on Antigone of, 117; confrontation with Haemon of, 100; edict of, 96, 99, 111; exclusive claim to power of, 98; opposition of Antigone to, 94, 96–99, 101, 104, 108–11; the people's approval of Antigone and their contradiction of, 115, 117–19; rigidity of, 112
Crouzet, Denis, 25, 191n5
Cvetkovich, Ann, 8

d'Aubigné, Françoise (Marquise de Maintenon), 161–69, 211n7. *See also* Saint-Cyr
Davis, Kim, 190
Davis, Wendy, 188–89
Day of the Barricades (1648), 125. *See also* Paris
Deborah, 41, 56–57. *See also* Bible
Declaration of the Rights of Man and of the Citizen (1789), 211n72
DeJean, Joan, 87–89
Descartes, René: *Les passions de l'âme* (1649), 133–35, 137–38
Diefendorf, Barbara, 105
Dillon, Elizabeth Maddox, 94, 196n10
divine right, 12, 28. *See also* absolutist theory; kings
Doubrovsky, Serge, 75–76, 126, 203n46
droit de naissance (right of primogeniture), 132
droit de résistance (right of resistance), 4–5, 10, 150, 158, 187–88, 205n16; conceptual structure of the, 13, 19; precedents of the, 191n6. *See also* resistance theory

Edelman, Lee, 173, 179–80
Edict of Nantes, 10–12, 193n22; Revocation of the, 18, 161, 176
Egypt, 75–76
elector(s), 9, 37. *See also* public representative(s)
Elizabeth I, Queen, 34–35, 198n49
embodied/embodiment: adhering to one's conscience and, 46; ancient elections and, 30–32; collective work of theater as, 99; of early modern political subjectivity, 5; the forms of touch and reach in tragedy as literally, 92; practices of, 17; ties of emotion and, 54
emotional community (Rosenwein), 24
emotions: in ancient elections, 32; community of, 27, 39, 45, 94; conflicting, 80; early modern tragedy and the, 20; in the emphasis on harmony and order, 27; expressions of, 32–33, 36, 64, 101; of the good king to his subjects, 27; history of, 8; and the ideas of physical and affective pain, 40; overwhelming, 77; performance of, 49; of the people of Rome, 71–72; and political legitimacy, 78, 124; popular bonds of, 7, 12, 54; popular responses of, 41–42; and shared resistance, 68; sincerity of others', 49; of the term *alliance*, 29. *See also* affect; emotional community (Rosenwein); love; mourning; passions
Encyclopédie (1752–71), 96
Estates general, 37, 52, 54
Esther (character), 159
Esther (Racine), 19, 83, 159–83; performing, 162–69
Estienne, Robert: *Dictionarium latinogallicum* (1552), 27–29, 45
Euripides, 15, 95; Works: *The Phoenician Women*, 99
extraordinary liberator, 40–45, 48–49, 51, 56, 199n64

feminism, 67, 89; and critical race scholarship, 187; and queer theory, 98. *See also* women
femme forte, 87–90. *See also* women
Foley, Helen, 67
Fouquet, Nicolas, 12
Fraisse, Simone, 96, 99, 206n33
France: aristocratic ethos of sixteenth-century, 7; Catholicism of, 9–10, 51–52; Christian, 24; civil war in, 15, 21–22, 25, 58, 94; early modern, 8, 15, 54; Reformation in, 6; seventeenth-century, 85, 94, 124–25, 194n28;

France (*continued*)
sixteenth-century, 67, 92, 124–25, 201n113. *See also* French Revolution; French Wars of Religion (1562–98)
freedom: assertion of personal, 93; of belief, 10; of conscience, 105–6, 150; the heart as the locus of, 78, 148–49; of the individual will, 104; inner, 150, 156; religious, 105; Rome's loss of, 70; subjective, 10, 105; from tyranny, 68; violation of, 63. *See also* liberty
French Revolution, 185–87. *See also* France
French Wars of Religion (1562–98), 4–5, 23, 58, 94–95, 161–62; the category of tyranny in the, 191n7; pious gestures in the, 106. *See also* France
Frisch, Andrea, 16
Fronde, 18, 125–26, 194n28
frondeurs, 125
Fumaroli, Marc, 151, 210n58

Garnett, George, 48, 50–51, 196n3, 200n99, 201n4
Garnier, Robert, 13, 15, 90, 202n14; critics of, 105; *Antigone, ou La pieté* (1580), 18, 91–96, 99, 101–8, 111–21, 181, 205n9*; Cornélie* (1574), 18, 55–83, *59*, 87, 90–93; *Porcie* (1568), 90
gender: break with conventions of, 57; dynamic of, 156; and the politics of mourning, 66–67; traditional divisions of, 87–88. *See also* sexuality
généreux (courageous, noble), 73, 104, 133–35, 144, 156. See also *générosité*
générosité (capacity to direct one's own volition), 133–35, 144. See also *généreux*
Gobert, R. Darren, 135, 209n30
Goldmann, Lucien, 168–69
Goldstein, Claire, 12
Greenberg, Mitchell, 158, 211n73

Hanley, Sarah, 12
Harvey, William: *De motu cordis*, 210n50
Heard, Dallas, 190
heart: and conscience, 48; courageous, 104; interior space of the, 155; liberty as both subjective and collective within each, 63; the loss of Cornelia's, 73; as a metaphorical place where one's inner perception meets God's judgment, 48; and mind as spaces of private liberty, 6, 76–78; miraculous works of God in the, 42; the people's affective orientation toward Caesar in the, 61; privacy of the, 147–49; of Romans, 63, 78; self-examination as consulting one's own, 48; the space of the, 146–49; tyranny enslaving the, 76. See also *cœur* (heart)
Hédelin, François (abbé d'Aubignac): *La pratique du théâtre* (1657), 84–87, 204n70
Hegel, G. W. F.: *Phenomenology of the Spirit* (1807), 96–98
Henri III, King, 5, 9, 51; assassination of, 51
Henri IV, King, 9, 10, 51. See also *Navarre, Henri de*
heresy, 41, 199n74; of kings, 52
hero, 123–58; the ashes of the, 69–70; communally constituted, 155–58; Cornelian, 19, 126–28, 144, 158, 208n3; the death of the, 153–55; generous, 133–38; as a locus of collective resistance, 19; love and glory of the, 156; political charge of the love of the, 154; political legitimacy of the, 153–55; portrait of a, 140; the remains of the, 73–76; the Roman people's grief over the loss of their, 57; self-governed, 128–33; tragic, 86, 140; virtuous, 137–38; of war, 66. *See also* heroine
heroine, 90, 120; queer, 98; tragic, 96–101, 108. *See also* hero
historiography, 11, 14. *See also* history
history: biblical, 164; early modern performance, 164; of emotions, 8; female figures from, 87–90; French cultural, 96, 99; French literary, 13, 99; intellectual, 5; performance, 166–69; providential, 180. *See also* historiography
Hogg, Chloé, 12
Honig, Bonnie, 96–97; *Antigone, Interrupted*, 98–99. *See also* Antigone-effect (Honig)
Hotman, François: *Francogallia/La gaule francoise* (1573/1574), 5–6, 18, 22–33, 36, 44, 48–54, 140–41
Houllemare, Marie, 54, 67
Huguenots, 3–6; resistance treatises of, 5–9, 26–38, 44, 49–63, 71–72, 76,

93–94, 105, 125, 135, 149–50, 155, 162, 181, 188–89, 198n49. *See also* Protestants; resistance theory
humanism, 98
human rights, 187, 215n8. *See also* rights

Ibbett, Katherine, 12, 14, 156
ideology: ideological changes in the wake of the religious wars, 86; political, 11, 86; of "reproductive futurism," 173
incest, 102–3, 107–9. *See also* sexuality
individual subject: and the collective, 45, 161; and the knowledge of God's demands, 46; liberty of conscience of, 11; the particularities of the, 187; the political power of Suréna stretches beyond his limits as an, 155; and religious communities, 105; as representatives of the people's collective authority, 54, 125. *See also* autonomous individual; *conscience* (conscience)
irony, 157, 179–80; of innocence, 171–80; in tragedy, 180

Jacourt, Louis de, 96, 205n16
James II, King, 163
Jansenism, 214n58
Jews, 159–60, 167–68; holiday (Shavuot) of the, 171, 213n35; salvation of the, 161. *See also* religion
Joas/Joash, 161, 170–75, 177–83, 214n58
Jodelle, Étienne, 15
Jondorf, Gillian, 15, 86–87, 104–5
Jouanna, Arlette, 12
justice, 43–44, 47, 51; subjective perception of, 11

Keohane, Nannerl, 11–12
Kettering, Susan, 12
kings, 6, 13; absolute power of, 176, 186; authority of, 10, 13, 35, 125, 146; Christian, 43; decentering of, 12; dynastic succession of, 33; election of, 30; good, 23, 29, 33, 49; popular approval of, 35–36, 46, 48; resistance to, 28–29, 35, 51; and the status of the individual's salvation, 105; and the true sources of sovereign power, 129; tyrannical, 36–39, 42–43, 191n7. *See also* absolutism; divine right; tyranny
Koselleck, Reinhart, 10, 94–95

La Bruyère, Jean de: *Caractères* (1688), 127
Lasne, Michel, 99
La Taille, Jean de: *De l'art de la tragédie* (1572), 15, 83
law: as contestable, 106; divine, 96, 106, 109–12, 120, 197n34; human, 110; natural, 96, 106, 109–12, 120; paternal, 98
Lecouvreur, Adrienne, 81, *82*
Le Moyne, Pierre: *La gallerie des femmes fortes* (1647), 88–90, *88*, *89*
Les soupirs de la France esclave qui aspire après la liberté (pamphlet), 176, 214n51
liberalism, 19; structures of, 161; "universal" subject of, 187. *See also* rights
liberty: in the choice between good and evil, 104; of conscience, 9, 11, 13, 46, 76, 104, 145, 157, 199n74; defence of, 30; general loss of, 63; of the heart, 148; individual, 158; natural inclination toward, 33; negative, 158; private, 145, 152, 155; Roman, 63; subjective, 23, 78, 187, 196n6. *See also* freedom; Protestants
Loraux, Nicole, 66
Louis XIII, King, 13
Louis XIV, King, 12, 14, 125–26, 161, 163, 169, 176, 194n34
love: and alliance, 29, 75; and charity, 50; and fear, 21, 139; of God, 145; mutual, 81; of the people for the king, 29, 116; and politics, 151–54, 157; revealing private, 150–54, 157; romantic, 145; shared, 155–56. *See also* emotions
Lucan: *Pharsalia*/*De bello civili*, 57, 70–71
Luther, Martin, 6
Lyons, John D., 85–86, 126–27, 209n45

Machiavelli, Niccolò, 14, 21–23, 196n3; critique of, 22; politics of, 27
magistrate(s)/*magistrat(s)*, 6, 9, 11, 35–40, 49, 51, 54; *inferieur(e)*, 35, 37–39; the king's status as a, 39; lower, 37–38. *See also* public representative(s)
Man, Paul de, 179
Matzke, John E., 57
McClure, Ellen, 14, 210n59
Medici, Catherine de, 4, 25
Mellet, Paul-Alexis, 25–26, 54

Merlin-Kajman, Hélène, 25, 129, 132–33, 158, 211n73
monarchomaque(s), 192n10
Montaigne, Michel de, 31–32
Moreau, Jean-Baptiste, 163, 169
mourning, 66–90; cessation of, 156; collective, 120; familial rituals of, 66; gendered dynamics of ancient Greek, 67; personal, 67–74; public, 67, 69–73; as resistance, 76; of women, 67–71, 76–77, 90, 110. *See also* affect; emotions; passions
myth: of the Cornelian hero, 126–28; mourning women of, 67–68

nature: law of, 191n7; questioning, 106–12; relationship of tragic characters to, 109
Navarre, Henri de, 3, 5. *See also* Henri IV, King
Nicomède (character), 126–44, 154, 158; view of, 142; virtue of, 137, 140, 144
Nicomède (Corneille), 19, 124–44, *141*, 158
Nicot, Jean: *Thresor de la language francoyse tant ancienne que moderne* (1606), 29, 45
noble(s), 6–11, 40, 53–54, 59; Catholic, 4; French, 125; transgressive, 124. *See also* public representative(s)

Oedipus (character): Antigone's care for, 119; Antigone's physical pull on, 91–112, 120

Palacios, Joy, 47
Paris, 3–4; people of, 4; public opinion in, 125
parlements (assemblies), 52–54; Estates and, 52, 54; Paris, 54, 59, 67
parricide, 102
Parthia, 145, 156–57
particulier(s) (private subjects), 37–42, 50–52, 56
passions, 22, 64–90, 134, 137–38; conflicting, 80; ordering one's, 128, 134–35; overwhelming, 134–35; private, 145; purging the, 137; romantic, 150; theories of the, 18. *See also* affect; emotions; mourning
Persia, 159, 161
personne(s) publique(s) (public representative(s)), 6–7, 9–11, 13, 36; the king as the only legitimate, 17; legitimacy of the, 18. *See also* magistrate(s)/*magistrat(s)*; public representative(s)
piety, 47, 51–52, 191n7; ambiguity surrounding, 105; corrupting, 101–6; expressions of, 105; idiom of, 101; inner liberty and, 48; profession of, 174; and virtue, 101–2. *See also* religion
Pizan, Christine de: *Le livre de la cité des dames* (1405), 90, 213n33
Plutarch, 57
political theory, 4–5, 99; the clemency-rigor debate in sixteenth-century, 115; French, 140; liberal, 19, 158; seventeenth-century, 12, 126; sixteenth-century, 19, 115, 125, 135, 158; theories of the passions in, 18
Pompee/Pompée/Pompey (character), 18, 55–57, 60–83, 87, 93, 198n49
popular sovereignty, 6–7, 23, 32, 35, 187–89; concept of, 192n12; genealogies of, 196n6; gesture of, 140–41. *See also* collective authority
Portia/Porcie (character): in Boccacio's *De claris mulieribus*, 90; in Garnier's *Porcie*, 90; in Le Moyne's *La gallerie des femmes fortes*, *88*, 90; in Pizan's *Le livre de la cité des dames*, 90
Protestants, 6, 10; conversion to Catholicism of, 9, 51; as marginal subjects, 12; toleration of, 10; viewpoint of, 104. *See also* Christianity; Huguenots; liberty
Prusias, King (character), 128–32, 139–42
public authority, 13, 95
public representative(s), 53–54, 62, 71–73, 93–95, 145, 175, 202n14; divinely inspired, 161; political legitimacy of, 162, 188; as speaking and acting on behalf of the public good, 157; the Theban people allow Antigone to function as a, 120; unorthodox, 188; virtuous, 180. *See also* elector(s); magistrate(s)/*magistrat(s)*; noble(s); *personne(s) publique(s)* (public representative(s)); senator(s); subaltern(s)

queer theory, 98, 160, 173–74

Rabutin-Chantal, Marie de (Marquise de Sévigné), 163–65, 169

Racine, Jean, 13–14, 127, 213n44; Works: *Andromaque* (1667), 164; *Athalie* (1691), 19, 83, 159–83; *Esther* (1689), 19, 83, 159–83; *Phèdre* (1677), 14, 18
Rambouillet, Nicolas d'Angennes, seigneur de, 58–60
Rancière, Jacques, 187
reach: of the absolutist monarchy, 12–*13*; affective, 95–106, 111, 118, 121; mediated, 120; of personal right, 110; physical, 92–93, 118, 121; of raised voice, 114; and suspension, 117; touch and, 92; of willful attachment, 122. *See also* affect
Reddy, William, 8
redemption, 104–5, 108
regicide, 9, 102
Reiss, Timothy J., 90
religion: devotion of, 150; official French, 10; and public life, 10; tragedy as a reassertion of the authority of, 175. *See also* Christianity; Jews; piety; religious wars (1562–98); salvation
religious wars (1562–98), 4–5, 10–13, 18, 25, 86, 106; reception of resistance theory both during and after the, 48–49; theories of legitimate resistance during the, 10, 52; tragic drama and the, 16, 104; violence of the, 86. *See also* Huguenots; Protestants; religion; Roman Catholics; violence
remontrance (remonstrance), 93
Renaissance, 22, 29; ideals of the, 25–26
representation: performing, 52–54; tragic royal, 14
reproductive futurism (Edelman), 173, 179–80
resistance theory, 4–10, 16–18, 26, 125, 187–90, 196n6; Catholic, 200n107; of leaguer texts that justify resistance by private individuals, 51; perception of injustice in, 52, 61; political stakes of, 23; sixteenth-century, 23–24, 28, 52, 56–57, 61, 74, 93–94, 158, 161; structure of, 48, 51, 54, 74. See also *droit de résistance*; Huguenots; sedition
Richelieu, Cardinal, 13–14
rights: individual, 19, 96, 158, 187, 190, 196n6; individualist, 95, 121, 158–60, 187, 190, 196n6; language of, 148; liberal subject of, 9, 19, 187–88; modern subject of, 4, 19, 158; subjective, 158; the subject of, 185–90. *See also* human rights; liberalism
Roman Catholics, 3; conversion to, 9, 51; point of view of, 104. *See also* Christianity
Roman senate, 53–54, 62
Rome, 60–63, 66–72, 75–76, 82–83, 86, 92, 129–32, 139, 143–44
Rosenwein, Barbara, 8, 24
Rotrou, Jean de, 13; Works: *Antigone* (1639), 18, 93–96, 99–101, *100*, 106–12, 115–21, 181

Saint-Cyr, 162–66, 183, 211n7, 212n10. *See also* d'Aubigné, Françoise (Marquise de Maintenon)
salvation: collective, 105; communal, 10; threat to spiritual, 25, 105. *See also* religion
Schneider, Rebecca, 17
Scholar, Richard, 163, 168
scientia (knowledge), 45
Sedgwick, Eve Kosofsky, 160, 169, 183, 211n4
sedition, 18, 55. *See also* resistance theory
Sellier, Phillipe: *Le mythe du héros, ou Le désir d'être dieu* (1970), 127
senator(s), 62, 68; state, 190. *See also* public representative(s)
Seneca, 15, 95; tragedies of, 204n70; Works: *The Phoenician Women*, 99
sense perception, 46
sexuality: closet, 160, 169; heterosexual fatality and, 97–98. *See also* gender; incest
Sophocles, 15, 91, 95; Works: *Antigone*, 96, 99, 121; *Oedipus at Colonus*, 99
Statius, 95
Stanton, Domna, 34
St. Bartholomew's Day Massacre, 3–5, 25, 191n2
Strauss, Jonathan, 121
subaltern(s), 37, 39. *See also* public representative(s)
subjectivity: alternative model, 158; in early modern tragedy, 19; political, 19, 186, 188; two forms of, 186
suicide, 108
Suréna (character), 126, 144–58, 210n59
Suréna (Corneille), 19, 124–28, 144–58

Taylor, Diana, 17
Terada, Rei, 8

Ternaux, Jean-Claude, 70
theater: of cruelty, 16; French, 106; practice of, 84; props in seventeenth-century, 78; scene of, 98; stage direction in, 107–8. *See also* antitheatrical sentiment; chorus; tragic drama
Thebes, 94, 102–3, 107, 109, 112–14, 117–20
time: of general decline, 60; as an instrument of royal authority, 123; of religious violence and civil war, 54–55
Tocqueville, Alexis de: *The Old Regime and the French Revolution*, 185–87
tragic drama, 5, 9, 13–20, 54–90, 171; and absolutist power, 13; aesthetics of seventeenth-century, 204n61; biblical, 159–83; conventions of, 136; development of neoclassical, 86–87; French, 14–18, 58; Greek, 15, 67, 84–85; ideal length of, 85; multiplication of choruses in sixteenth-century, 113; as poetry and performance, 17; political work of, 93; and the religious wars, 16, 104; Renaissance, 202n18; Roman, 15, 67; seventeenth century theory of, 83; voice of the people in seventeenth-century, 83–84. *See also* antitheatrical sentiment; theater
Trewhella, Matthew J.: *The Doctrine of the Lesser Magistrates: A Proper Resistance to Tyranny and a Repudiance of Unlimited Obedience to Civil Government*, 190
tyranny, 6, 13; charges of, 10–11; Christian, 43, 199n74; critiques of, 62; distinction between kingship and, 171; of foreign princes, 47; good kings and, 23, 29; the king with absolute power as, 176; and oppression, 56; reputation of, 61; resistance to, 9, 19, 24, 35–43, 49–52, 68–70, 73–76, 80, 87, 94–95, 170–71, 180; of usurpation, 56. *See also* absolutism; kings

Usher, Phillip, 58, 92–93

Van de Putte, Leticia R., 189
verisimilitude, 84–85
Vernant, Jean-Pierre, 54
Versailles, 12
Vidal-Naquet, Pierre, 54
Vignon, Claude, 99
Vindiciae contra tyrannos (1579), 5–9, 18, 21–55, 62, 74, 94, 149, 161, 170–71, 180–81, 189, 196n3, 197n34
violence: internecine, 23; offstage, 16; refraining from, 109; religious, 54, 86, 105; staged, 15–16; widespread, 25. *See also* arm(s); religious wars (1562–98)
virtue: affective evidence of, 48; Christian, 102; independent female, 105, 109; inner, 139; innocence and, 166, 168; in the midst of war, 58, 109–10; nobility and, 67; object of goodness and, 181; piety and, 101–2; of resistance, 169–80; of self-governance, 131; in the Senecan model of tragedy, 15; shared perception of, 119; strength and, 140; theatrical prowess and the expression of, 165–66; as a threat to sovereign power, 19; in a time of general decline, 60; true nobility of soul and, 133; uncommon, 136; and vice, 102, 106, 137, 161, 168–69, 178, 181–82
volonté (will), 31

Walhof, Darren, 46
women: boldness of, 156; in a conflict of family and the state, 97; control of the public behavior of Greek, 67; endurance of, 156; as the extraordinary liberator, 56–57; independent virtue of, 105–12; love and devotion of, 156; mourning of, 67–71, 76–77, 87–90, 110; portraits of individual, 89; Roman, 78, 90; seventeenth-century debates on educating, 211n7; in tragic drama, 18, 67–78, 106–12; as unfit for leadership, 56. *See also* feminism; *femme forte*
Worthen, W. B., 17